MW01199434

THE NIGHT CLUB PART I.

Jiri Kulhanek

BBG Services

The Night Club: Part One
A Novel

Originally published in the Czech Republic by Jules Verne Club Prague.

The views expressed in this work are solely those of the author and do not necessarily reflect the views of the publisher, and the publisher hereby disclaims any responsibility for them.

This is a work of fiction. All of the characters, names, incidents, organizations, and dialogue in this novel are either the products of the author's imagination or are used fictitiously.

ISBN-13: 978-1456311650

ISBN-10: 1456311654

1

"Should we have gourmet today or prepare her just plain with garlic?" the man asked.

He drew a slender knife across a worn whetstone and with a critical eye checked the blade's edge. The woman, holding a large roasting pan, intently followed the direction of his gaze. The knife looked very dangerous.

"I don't know. She's skinny, no fat; it'll be dry ... So it's gonna be either chops with chard stalks and sauce à la hollandaise or something simple ... like stew," the woman replied.

The man continued to sharpen the steel, rhythmically swishing it back and forth. The last insect of the fall flew in through a half-open window. A circular saw screamed in the distance, and so did the theme song of the Golden Prague radio program from the neighbor's house across the yard. The woman put the pan on the table, smoothed a crease in the flowered wax paper, and stretched her back. The aroma of onions and spices filled the kitchen, and the theme song was replaced by music in the rhythm of a fleeing buffalo.

"You and your hollandaise and chard!" The man pronounced the foreign word *ho-lan-daeeeze*. "This will take forever." He sighed and again checked the knife's edge.

"So, stew it is then," said the woman definitively.

"Fine. Let's go and take a peek at her." The man got up, scratched his chin with the dull side of the blade, and quietly murmured, "Stew, aw man, I'll have to peel potatoes again."

○ ◑ ◑ ●

The woman looked around carefully and opened the door to the cellar. Something didn't feel right. She didn't know what, and that didn't feel right either.

"Don't pick your teeth with that thing!" she snapped at the man, who had decided right at that moment to take care of some acute personal hygiene. *What the hell is eating her today?* he thought, but obediently put his hand down anyway.

The dim hallway was illuminated only by a single forty-watt lightbulb. Not even the sounds of Golden Prague or the saw could get through the tightly closed door leading to the kitchen. A white cat was sitting by a white wall. When the people turned their backs to him, he opened his cerulean blue eyes, swished the tip of his tail, and snuck between the man's legs. The woman turned back one last time. There really wasn't anything unsettling around, so she just shrugged her shoulders. The cellar door closed, and the key click-clicked twice in the lock.

○ ◑ ◑ ●

A downward staircase led to another door and then another after that. The last door was unusual because it had a one-and-a-half-foot thick layer of polystyrene glued to it. The little room beyond contained all sorts of unusual things.

The woman turned on the light, and in the yellow glow of the wire-covered bulb, there appeared an old wrought-iron bed. A stained mattress lay on the frame. On the mattress was a ten-year-old girl with matted hair, large eyes, and dried tear trails on her smudged cheeks. She had shackles around her left ankle, which were securely anchored to a brick wall with a chain. The chain was only long enough to reach a toilet without a seat and a rusty faucet sticking out of the wall.

"Stew," said the man.

○ ◑ ◑ ●

The woman closed the last door. The polystyrene screeched hideously. A brown cat was sitting by a brown wall in the shadow of one of the wires covering the bulb. A long, lightly colored scratch ran through the brown plaster, and there above it was a dark stain. Even though the cat's furry body should have covered both of those things, the light scratch actually ran on top of his brown coat and the stain was visible on his chest and half his head all the way to his ear. The woman's gaze fell right on the animal, but she didn't seem to see anything.

The girl curled up into a ball, and the chain rattled. She didn't cry; she knew that *the woman* didn't like it. She didn't cry, but she trembled so much it made the bed creak.

"But I can't remember the last time we had chops with chard stalks." The woman took a rubber apron from a nail on the wall and thoughtfully examined the girl, who was in fact thin but definitely not scrawny.

"We have some lard in the freezer, left over from last time, if we baste her well …" She leaned over the mattress and rubbed the girl's knee. "I hope she isn't too tough. She looks pretty athletic—must be all those *a-e-rooo-bics*."

Meanwhile, the man pushed a tall butcher block from the corner, positioned it carefully right over the drain in the middle of the floor, and propped up one leg with a piece of folded paper.

"So?" He stabbed the knife into the blackened wood, and the sound pulled the woman out of her deep culinary thoughts.

The girl began crying. She may have been little, but she had no doubt about what awaited her. Even if she had doubts, *the woman* told her already, back when they tied her up. *She* was much worse than *he*—much worse.

"So, little one, what do you think?" The woman pinched the girl's leg. "We're having this for lunch today, but you won't enjoy it much—and no whining! Who wants to listen to that?!"

The girl swallowed her next sob.

The dim lightbulb above the door flickered.

"Damn, who is bugging us again?! Especially now!" The man yanked the knife out of the wood and hid it in his coat pocket.

"I'm coming with you." The woman hung her rubber apron back up on the nail.

"It's probably George. He'll want to borrow another rake or something."

"I'm coming with you. I've had a bad feeling all day today. Anyway, we forgot a bucket for the blood."

Just before the polystyrene screeched again, the girl thought that she saw a pair of cerulean blue eyes down by the wall.

○ ◑ ◐ ●

"Hello." A smiling young woman stood behind the door. She was wearing an orange cap and an orange jumpsuit with a "Prague Gas Company" logo on it. "Mr. Vaclavik?"

"What's going on?"

"Just a routine check of your gas appliances." The orange-clad woman had a small instrument over her shoulder with a coiled cable leading from it to something that looked like a microphone.

"Today?!"

"We put notices into everyone's mailbox." The orange one shrugged her shoulders. "It'll be done in fifteen minutes," she said interrupting his question of how long it would take.

"Well, come on in, miss," smiled Mrs. Vaclavik as she smoothed her hair, which was colored and had an old, outgrown perm. "Are you here alone?"

○ ◑ ◐ ●

"Looks like you're getting ready for a slaughter." The orange-clad woman motioned to the roasting pan on the table and the pots on the countertop.

"Maybe even a bigger one than you might expect." Mrs. Vaclavik smiled as she looked out the window. *So alone—and she came in a sedan, a green one. There are millions of those around. She parked behind Turkovic's barn too; nobody goes back there, and you can't even see it from anywhere in town …*

"Would you like some coffee, miss?"

"Sure, I'd like some, but only after I finish, it would screw up my sensor." The woman in orange stuck the microphone behind the stove and intently studied a small display.

"Good?" Mr. Vaclavik looked curiously at the unfamiliar numbers.

"Yes ... You should also have ..." She pulled a crumpled piece of paper out of her pocket and smoothed it out. "... a water heater and a furnace." The paper, even though crumpled, looked official.

"The water heater is in the hallway, and the furnace ... the furnace is in the cellar." Mr. Vaclavik cast a wary eye at the woman, but she didn't even notice his short pause, which wasn't as much of a pause as it was a gulp.

He couldn't help it.

○ ⊃ ◑ ●

When the door closed behind *them*, the girl lifted her head and looked in the direction where she had seen the blue eyes a minute earlier.

A tabby cat brushed past the butcher block and jumped on the bed.

"Here, kitty," the girl whispered and sat up.

"Meow?" said the cat and carefully climbed into her lap. Her small trembling hand ran across his warm coat, and he began to purr. The girl wasn't at all surprised by the cat's presence. Since she had been in that room, she had seen even stranger things. If someone had asked her now, maybe those strange things would seem more normal to her than the normal things did *before*. Maybe she wouldn't even remember those normal things.

The bright purple cat was purring like a motorcycle, and the girl couldn't help but look into his eyes. If she had been able to realize it, she would have noticed that for the first time in fourteen days, she had stopped trembling.

"You have pretty big eyes for a kitty cat," she said. God only knows why she remembered her name was Paulina, Little Paulina. That was what her mom used to call her, back then, before ... Mommy ... who also had large blue eyes, just like ... like ... The girl's eyes closed, and she sank helplessly to the mattress and smiled just a little.

A wave of rainbow colors ran across the purple cat's coat, and suddenly, he turned black.

Those blue eyes, which a moment ago had reminded the girl of her mother, turned yellow and so frightening that if Paulina had seen them—even after the hell she'd been through in the past fourteen days—she would have fainted with horror.

○ ◌ ◑ ●

"Careful, miss, those stairs are pretty steep." Mr. Vaclavik flipped on the switch and kind of snorted. The aroma of apples and the chilly stench of mold wafted from the cellar, along with something else … something rotten.

"Our sewer leaks a little, you know; that's how it is out here in the country." Mrs. Vaclavik stood behind the woman in orange with her hand behind her back. "So what is your name anyway, miss?"

"Christina."

"Christina." The woman smiled. In the hand behind her back she held a meat mallet.

○ ◌ ◑ ●

"You're gonna move that car before it gets dark."

Mr. and Mrs. Vaclavik were leaning over Christina in the orange jumpsuit. It wasn't as easy as they had imagined, but with a little effort, it finally worked.

"Look at all the jars of canned fruit she broke." Mrs. Vaclavik motioned with her mallet, which still had a clump of blonde hair stuck to it.

"Yeah, she knows some kind of karate or something. We have to be careful with her," said Mr. Vaclavik as he rubbed his chin where she had kicked him. What looked like flab on his fifty-year-old frame was in reality muscle. That's why the orange-clad Christina was now lying among chunks of glass, plums, and syrup.

"She even broke the pickle jars! The two-year-old ones too! Dammit!" Mr. Vaclavik scowled at the body. "And you too—you should finally learn to use that thing, woman!"

The body on the floor moaned.

"Two-year-old pickles!"

"Oh well," said Mrs. Vaclavik in a surprisingly conciliatory tone; every acknowledgement of her culinary skills made her happy, and those two-year-old pickles were especially good. She gave another swift whack with the mallet. "First the little one, otherwise, our sty will be too full, and ..."

At the top of the stairs, the door opened. Considering that it was supposed to be locked, you couldn't miss it.

○ ◌ ◑ ●

"I wish you a pleasant afternoon."

The guy looked like a businessman with a hollow, carefully shaved face and an inconspicuous suit. He was wearing a narrow necktie, a long, loose coat, and a black hat that obscured his eyes.

"Take him down, Jerry!" Mrs. Vaclavik pointed the mallet like a gun. Mr. Vaclavik was already running up the stairs.

"What a warm welcome! I know that country folk are nice and hospitable, but I certainly didn't expect this."

Even though the businessman looked like a stick, Jerry came tumbling right back down, shaking the entire staircase. Mrs. Vaclavik suddenly realized why she had had that bad feeling all day.

"Get up, you moron! You gotta get him! He ... he ... for sure isn't here by accident!"

"What true words, ma'am." The businessman descended slowly but quite effortlessly toward them without even noticing the garden hoe that Jerry had armed himself with.

When the glass pieces crunched under the soles of his heavy boots, which didn't seem businessman-like at all, Mrs. Vaclavik saw his eyes under the brim of his hat. They didn't seem businessman-like either. Mrs. Vaclavik's knees gave out, and she pressed her hands with the mallet against her chest. You can tell a lot about a person by their eyes, and Mrs. Vaclavik—even though she had seen much death—realized she had never seen so much of it at once.

○ ◌ ◑ ●

The garden hoe traced a short, whooshing arc. The next sound was an unmistakable sharp smack, the sound things make when they hit a slab of meat. Within that smack, one could also hear the crunching of breaking bones. The latter sound was echoed by the hoe as it bounced off the wall and broke one of the glass fragments into even smaller pieces. Jerry Vaclavik fell to his knees, eyes wide with surprise and a bloody piece of phlegm hanging from his broken jaw.

"Be careful not to kneel on the broken glass; cut-up knees hurt like hell." The businessman picked up a pickle from the ground, wiped it on his sleeve, and carefully took a bite.

"Excellent, really. My compliments, Mrs. Vaclavik ... Can I call you Helena?"

"Ye ... yes."

"With that mallet, you look like ..." The businessman imitated her crossed arms. "... an Egyptian goddess, Mrs. Helena—the goddess of death?"

"Ye ... yes." Mrs. Vaclavik hung her hands by her side. She didn't even realize it, but she was still seeing that quick moment when the businessman casually ducked out of the hoe's way and with one blow of his fist disfigured her Jerry. She assumed it was his fist; the movement was so fast she didn't really see anything else.

"Dread, what are you doing here?! I have it under control." A voice came from the floor.

"Hmmmm!" The businessman put the rest of the pickle in his mouth. "I'm glad to hear that, Christina," he said still crunching. "How is it down there among the plums? Look, there's a pickle right by you. Why don't you hand it to me, please?" Through his crunching, he was trying to conceal a laugh. The young woman got up. On her left cheek was a streak of blood from the wound on her head, and on her right cheek, a smashed ...

"I bet that's a plum in rum on your face. Try it. Mrs. Vaclavik is a true gourmet chef." Dread took a small bow before the ever-more-stunned mistress of the house. "Oh yes, and with that, we are getting to the real reason for our visit—our *culinary* visit."

Between the bouts of pain from his broken jaw, Mr. Vaclavik briefly thought that maybe he had imagined it. There was no way he could have heard a laugh accompany a voice like that.

"Where did you stash her?" There was nothing in Christina's voice that you'd want to listen to for long either.

Regardless, nobody answered. Dread cracked his knuckles. Mrs. Vaclavik noticed that he was wearing black, fingerless gloves—the impression of her husband's teeth still on the right one.

"There! In the sty!" garbled Mr. Vaclavik, but more articulate than his words was his hand that pointed to one of the shelves. Behind them was the first door leading to the secret spaces of the cellar.

"Well, I guess we'll just have to take a look into your sty. To the sty! Christina, can you please bring my briefcase? It's upstairs in the hallway. After you, my friends." He smiled at the Vaclaviks.

○ ◑ ◐ ●

A black cat was sitting on the mattress in front of the sleeping girl, and his eyes were making Jerry sick to his stomach. He would have done anything for a shot of something strong, especially before what he was about to do—what he was about to try. He hadn't forgotten about the knife in his pocket, not even for a second.

"It's number fourteen, right?"

"What?"

"This." Dread picked up the shackled ankle.

"Yeah, wrench number fourteen, yeah." It really was hard to talk with a busted jaw.

When the businessman leaned over the girl again, Jerry whipped the knife out of his pocket. He knew that he couldn't miss the back in front of him.

○ ◑ ◐ ●

What followed seemed like a slide show to Jerry. The back disappeared. His wrist with the knife was seized by a vise in a fingerless glove. The knife disappeared.

"Jerry, Jerry." Dread shook his head. "Nice knife, nice and sharp … You are right-handed, Jerry, correct?"

"Right … right-handed. Why?"

"So you can write, of course." Dread grabbed Jerry's left hand and slammed it on top of the blackened wood of the butcher block.

"I can't even say, 'Which little hand was it?' It doesn't suit the situation," said the man in the hat. The next sound was again a familiar one: the sound of a blade stabbing deep into a piece of wood. Mr. Vaclavik was staring at something unbelievable. He was staring at his own hand with a knife in the middle of it. Just then, his vocal chords added to the series of familiar sounds.

9

"Let me congratulate you on the great soundproofing you have done here … Ah! My briefcase, wonderful. Christina, look for a number fourteen wrench, please."

○ ◑ ◐ ●

After she had freed the girl and carried her away, Christina returned to the sty and carefully closed the door behind her. The word *sty* seemed very appropriate to her—the stench of Mr. Vaclavik's sweat was almost unbearable.

"So." Dread unlocked his patent leather briefcase. "… A little bit of paperwork, and then we can get to the day's main event." He pulled out a standard light-green paper folder. By then, he and Christina had already pulled on thick rubber gloves.

"So," repeated Dread as he opened the folder and pulled out several sheets of paper, "Mrs. Helena Vaclavik, maiden name Cherov, and Mr. Jerry Vaclavik, I find you guilty on multiple counts of kidnapping, murder, and cannibalism. If you have anything to add, please do so at this time."

"We are innocent!" Mrs. Vaclavik spoke for the first time in the gloomy room. She had no idea what was going to happen, but the papers and the official tone of the man gave her hope that maybe this would all end well. Maybe they were the police, very strange, but police anyway.

"Innocent, yes, that's what I thought. We are all innocent to a certain degree. I will not be reading the names of your victims, since you are innocent, but I would like to ask that you write down what you did with their remains." Dread laid a piece of paper with a writing pad and a pen on the butcher block.

"Don't write anything, Jerry! We are innocent! We have rights!" Mrs. Vaclavik's self-confidence grew by the minute. "And you're gonna get it, stabbing my husband through the hand like that!"

"Write, Jerry, please." Dread took a big pair of pliers with blue rubber handles from the briefcase, and a handgun appeared in Christina's hand.

"What's with the pliers?!"

"I usually use them for a manicure."

Jerry looked into the shadow under the brim of the hat and started writing. There was quite a lot, but he had a good memory and he was the one who always buried the leftover bones.

○ ◌ ◑ ●

"Excellent, excellent ... so there were twelve; we only knew about eight of them." Dread returned the writing pad to the block. "I would also like to ask for a date and a signature—full name."

The pen squeaked.

"Now you, ma'am." He handed the paper to Mrs. Vaclavik, who was sitting on the mattress.

"I will not be signing anything ... and I want my lawyer!"

"A lawyer? You watch too much TV, ma'am. We don't have a lawyer ... but how about a professional manicure? You are also right-handed, correct?" The pliers' steel jaws snapped on empty air, and Mrs. Vaclavik signed.

"So that's that." Dread put the paper back into the light-green folder, returned the writing pad to his briefcase, and took out a large plastic case. "Helena Vaclavik, Jerry Vaclavik, in the name of the Night Club, I hereby sentence you to death."

"Without appeal."

○ ◌ ◑ ●

Jerry Vaclavik felt like he was in a dream. The businessman took a heavy nail gun out of the plastic case, nailed two steel rings into the ceiling, and strung a noose made of blue nylon rope through each of them. Then, he carefully measured the distance to the floor and shortened both ropes just a little.

"The execution will be carried out immediately—by hanging." That's what this unbelievable person said after the case with the nail gun had disappeared back in his briefcase.

"But ... but you can't! The Czech Republic does not have the death penalty! We are sick! We need to be institutionalized!"

"Yes, that may be so." Christina tightened Mrs. Vaclavik's noose and checked that it fit her wrinkled neck. A black cat lay on the mattress and swished his tail. Mrs. Vaclavik had had the flesh on her left cheekbone torn off almost to the bone by a set of four scratches that looked like a tiger had made them.

The Vaclaviks were standing on green crates, one on each, and the blue ropes were glistening in the pale light of the wire-covered bulb.

"Unfortunately, the ceiling here is too low, so you will not die traditionally … by a broken neck; rather, you will suffocate. By what I have seen, it is not pleasant. We apologize," said Dread.

"You can't execute us! The Czech Republic doesn't allow the death penalty!"

"Even though you are starting to repeat yourself, Mrs. Helena, you are correct. The only problem is that we are here—Christina, Cat, and me. That means the Czech Republic is far, far away. Now, with us present, the Night Club is here … Whoops!"

This last word wasn't for Mrs. Helena anymore.

Two swift kicks and the green vegetable crates flew against the wall.

○ ☽ ◑ ●

After the typical theatrics of twitching, eye bulging, relaxing sphincters, and wet stains running down pant legs, Dread pulled a butcher's slaughter hammer and two cartridges out of his briefcase. Two deafening shots rang out in the closed room.

"You can never be too sure," he said as he wiped off the bloody hammer and stashed the hot casings in his pocket.

○ ☽ ◑ ●

"It sounds kind of funny, the way we always say, *'Now this is the Night Club! Or in the name of the Night Club, we sentence you to death.'"* Christina picked her syrup-soaked orange cap up off the floor, pulled the gas meter from beneath a pile of potatoes, and wiped a clump of her bloody hair off the meat mallet.

"Funny, maybe, but notice that they never laugh."

○ ☽ ◑ ●

Upstairs in the kitchen, Dread put the light-green folder in the roasting pan on the flowered wax paper. "Hopefully, the police won't miss this."

"How does Cat do it?" Christina walked into the kitchen with the still-sleeping and still-smiling child in her arms. "Making her fall asleep like this?"

"You know Cat."

○ ○ ◑ ●

"Good-bye, Jerry!" Dread yelled through the door. He waited a bit as if waiting for an answer, then closed the door behind him. The Golden Prague theme again screamed across the yard. The neighbors would be able to tell the police that the man in the coat said a nice, loud goodbye to the Vaclaviks—loud and real friendly.

○ ○ ◑ ●

"It is a very honorable thing to be doing, but saving little girls is getting old. I'd go for something more exciting." Christina put the key in the ignition, and the green sedan's engine turned over and started right up. "Saving kids, that will give our *writer* something to type about."

"I think things will start getting interesting tomorrow or the day after that, at the latest. Maybe even too interesting." The girl was sleeping in the back seat when Dread pulled the blanket up to her chin. "Anyway, I hope it doesn't get interesting today … can you drive with that bump on your head?"

"Don't worry."

A dark green cat was lying under the window on the back seat purring loudly.

○ ○ ◑ ●

2

"Really, some retiree knocked Christina out with a meat mallet?"

"Yeah." Clara snickered. "You didn't see her when she came in, but she looked like canned fruit with a bump on her head. She had two pickles in her pocket. Really! I'm not kidding!" Again, she snickered.

I was leaning against Clara in the covered passage next to the Blanik movie theater, my right hand on her tight rear, deep under her miniskirt. It was slowly getting dark outside, and the yellowish tiles behind Clara's back felt cold against my left wrist.

"I bet Dread put those in there." I pretended to nibble on my companion's earlobe and continued with my quiet inquiry.

"That could be. He was making fun of her all afternoon ..." Clara took a loud, deep breath. "Knock it off!"

I had gotten a little carried away and started kneading her rear a little too much, considering that we didn't really like each other. Hell, like each other? At one time, we couldn't stand each other. Well, actually, Clara couldn't stand me.

"Knock it off, you dumbass!"

I ran my pinky finger under the hem of her panties and slowly pulled down.

"We have work to do here. Stop it!"

I smacked my lips by her ear and bit her lobe. "That's why I'm doing this, so we look believable. You don't think I like this, do you?"

"You jerk!"

I stopped my pinky's descent just before it got really intimate.

"What's the matter? Should I keep going?"

"I won't let you get away with this!" Clara leaned back, and her breathing became heavy. The best thing about it was that she couldn't do anything but stand there. We did have real work to do here, and our making out was not without purpose. First, seeing people smooching in the covered passage is quite normal. Second, seeing people being intimate forces most other people to look away and spend very little time near the intertwined couple. Third, if people are kissing, you can't see their faces. It was an impossible task even for the ever-present surveillance cameras on Wenceslas Square.

"How does it look?" My pinky made it back up and again started its descent. Clara's breathing was really heavy now.

"Five minutes." Her left hand was around my neck so she could see her watch. "Only that Japanese chick is still around."

"You know those Asian perverts." I grinned and again smacked my lips by her ear. If she liked it as much as I did, this had to be real torture for her. However, she was trained much too well to tell me to stop it. She knew that I would make her pay.

"Besides the Japanese chick?"

"Otherwise, it looks good. We successfully drove everyone away. *You* drove everyone away."

"You know me, I am Mister Authentic." This time, my pinky stopped—unexpectedly—a little lower than before, and when Clara moved, my fingertip felt soft, curly hairs.

"You don't shave?"

"You …!!! You're gonna get it! You're soooo gonna get it! Wait till we're back at the Club … Watch out! They're coming!"

The afternoon matinee had ended a little early, and the covered passage was filled with the usual pushing and shoving.

"Hey, dude, did you see how Willis bashed his face?!"

"Or that chick, how she almost kicked that Negro's head off?!"

"… or …!"

We knew that our guy would come out only after everyone else had left. We knew that there was no evening show, and that was why he was going to be there. We knew that he went in only after the show had started. We knew he always sat in the back row, and we knew that he would not miss a new Bruce Willis action flick. A routine lifestyle was generally a good thing for most people: routine wake-up time, routine mealtime, routine visits to the movies, routine bowel movements. For normal people, this was certainly true, but for the chief of the Czech branch of the White Brigade, it certainly was not.

The noisy crowd rolled slowly away.

"Here they come," said Clara, and her breath became instantly quiet and calm. "But there is a problem—there are more of them."

"How many?"

"Five … seven, eight, if you include Vorozin."

"What the hell is this?! They should have been bodyguards, not the whole platoon!"

"More like an army." Clara casually slipped her tongue between my lips. It was now that authenticity was the most important.

Even we don't always know everything. Vorozin always travels with two thugs, never seven.

"Three in the front, then the target, and four in the back," said Clara.

"What about innocent bystanders?"

"Just the Japanese girl."

The elastic hem smacked quietly as my pinky left the vicinity of Clara's panties. Along with my other fingers, it wrapped around the butt of a pistol she had ready by her lower back. I could feel that her weapon had also disappeared from the holster beneath my coat.

○ ◠ ◑ ●

"Go to hell!" screamed Clara and pushed me across the entire covered passage. With that, she concentrated the attention of all the bodyguards on me. It was instinct; even with the best training, a person would always notice the fast-moving object rather than the stationary one, even though the stationary one was, at the given moment, much more dangerous.

With one smooth motion, Clara kneeled on her left knee and squeezed the Glock with both hands. The targeting mechanism popped up in front of her right eye.

Time turned to thick honey.

The Russians were still staring at me.

The first two hits busted open the head of the guy on the left. He was dead after the first shot, but you can't beat the certainty of a one-two combination. In the second flash, I could see Vorozin's face striped with streaks of blood. Clara's next double shot wasn't as successful—the Russians weren't going to pretend to be targets on a shooting range. The first bullet missed, but the second hit another guy in the neck, and the air instantly filled with a gurgling howl and a deep red mist.

By then, I was shooting too.

I hit a tall, fat guy with a short, blonde buzz cut in the belly. He was protecting Vorozin with his body.

The one with a hole in his neck fell to his knees, but that did not prevent him from swinging out a short Kalashnikov with a long magazine from beneath his coat.

What in the blazes is this?!

Being face to face with a Kalashnikov made the honey even thicker—especially around my Glock-toting hand. This was supposed to be a fight with bodyguards not the beginning of fucking World War III!

On top of everything, the blonde fatso was wearing a bulletproof vest, and the standard bullets from my handgun were no match. To make things worse, even he had a Kalashnikov.

Crack! Crack! Clara's Glock fired away, and another bodyguard was dead.

The Kalashnikov belonging to the hole-in-the-neck guy thundered with fire.

Crack! My bullet went through his left cheek and broke off his lower jaw. He kept on shooting – and the fatso started too.

The yellowish-brown tiles shattered like gems under the barrage of high-velocity projectiles from the automatic weapons. The jagged shrapnel stripped the skin off one side of Clara's nose. She aimed carefully, and suddenly, the kneeling guy didn't need a neck specialist anymore.

Unfortunately, the remaining five Russians were also packing Kalashnikovs.

"How rude! Most normal people carry pistols, not these things!" I fumed into the turmoil as my slug slashed a deep groove in fatso's left temple and smoke came from his short buzz cut. The second slug cut through the outer side of his orbital socket, and the liberated eyeball rolled out toward me and looked really surprised.

Everything happened so quickly that the broken-off jaw of the deceased hole-in-the-neck guy was still spinning on the floor.

Fatso's knees were slowly giving away, but unfortunately, his cramped-up index finger was still holding the trigger.

○ ○ ◐ ●

The first two bullets hit Clara in the chest. I saw two puffs of dust rise from her clothes as she was thrown back.

Crack!

Another slug jumped from the barrel of my gun.

As she fell back, a third bullet struck her directly above the upper lip, and I saw a piece of skull along with some hair fly off the back of her head.

Crack! Still another slug from my gun and another bodyguard experienced a final nine-millimeter piercing.

The dead fatso finally fell to his knees and stopped shooting.

Unfortunately, the remaining three did not.

○ ○ ◐ ●

It was about time for the reinforcements to get here, I thought to myself. I was alive only thanks to my vest. Its special construction could stop even slugs from a Kalashnikov. Their energy was dissipated and absorbed so you didn't even get knocked out—as long as you're trained.

The question was: *How long would it last?*

○ ○ ◐ ●

Even though I had an extended nineteen-cartridge magazine, nineteen slugs would run out at some point.

Crack! Crack!

Another killer from the White Brigade was down—I was finally getting into my groove.

Click!

○ ○ ◐ ●

I knew I didn't have a chance to change the magazine. I am a little embarrassed to admit it, but as I was taking it in the vest, my slugs were way off target, but on the other hand, they became that much more ferocious.

With that fateful click, the sluggish time returned to a normal pace. "I guess I'll have to practice more." I grinned at the Kalashnikovs. Even though I knew I wouldn't make it, I had to try.

Time turned sluggish again.

○ ◐ ◑ ●

My empty magazine wasn't even halfway to the broken tiles when something totally unexpected happened. The entire time, I knew that the Japanese girl was hiding behind a small protrusion in the wall. Now, from the corner of my eye, I saw a quick movement from over there. Incredibly, she did a cartwheel right from her knees.

The magazine hit the ground.

The next two projectiles hit me in the vest. It hurt.

As the girl rotated, her left hand landed on the tiles and her right on Clara's Glock.

Smack!

A bullet burned the skin on my cheek and chopped off the tip of my left earlobe.

The girl couldn't stop her cartwheel in time, and she hit her side against the wall—while still upside down.

I noticed two fiery snakes hurtling toward me along the wall and the boutique windows; otherwise, it was pretty hard to see anything in the covered passage. Smoke rolled around like fog over a swamp, and dust from the stucco did not help the overall visibility either.

Despite all that, I noticed that Clara's Glock had disappeared.

○ ◐ ◑ ●

At that point, I was able to yank out an extra magazine.

The Japanese girl bounced off the wall and landed on her back—Clara's gun in hand.

It's useless, I thought in the deafening chaos. *That kind of thing only works in the movies.*

The girl, still on her back, put her hands above her head and started shooting.

Lucky for me, it was in the direction of the Russians.

The magazine in my left hand was already halfway to the pistol; however, the snakes of exploding glass were closer.

Then I noticed another unexpected thing: Not only was the girl shooting, she was hitting her target. The bullets lifted Vorozin high in the air, his arms flailing.

He wasn't dead, but it was his rotten luck that he flew right into the path of the last fiery snake. His bulletproof vest was of high quality, but not nearly as good as mine. His chest exploded, exposing the white pieces of his ribs. I figured they would be scraping his lungs off the ceiling for a good long time.

Then, finally, the reinforcements arrived.

○ ○ ◑ ●

A machine gun is a terrible weapon. Only people that have never seen its effects can mistake it for a rifle or even an Uzi. This one was called the Red Baron, and it was an original that came from the famous red triple plane belonging to an even more famous World War I pilot, Baron Manfred von Richthofen.

Vorozin's already bullet-riddled body exploded into bits, and the last remaining bodyguard disappeared in a shower of venomous phosphorescent traces. When he appeared again, he looked more like a pile of mush than a proper corpse.

Even though everything happened really fast, the last round from the Kalashnikov still had time to hit me in the chest. It was very hard to keep standing after something like that.

○ ○ ◑ ●

"I think we're kind of overdoing it," I said. While coughing, I tried to get to all fours and fish the Glock out from the layers of broken tiles.

A tall man in a loose orange getup, lowered the smoking muzzle. "What's going on, Tobias? Why is it taking so long?!"

"What's going on?! There were eight of them, not three! I should be asking you what's going on. Where the hell were you? They killed Clara!"

"I am sorry, but don't be so selfish. You probably couldn't hear it in here, but there were a few of them outside too—not a few, a lot. Poor Clara. Who is this?!" The man in the orange getup pointed with his machine gun at the incredibly dirty Japanese girl.

"I don't know, but she saved my life—unlike you—so please don't point that thing at her, Ripper."

The man lowered his weapon and shook the lonely braid of long hair hanging from the back of his otherwise bald head.

"Tobias, sometimes you are really unfair. We have to go, so decide what to do with her."

"Do you speak English?" I grinned at her. She looked not only messed up but also stunned. Her face was all but invisible beneath the layer of dust.

"Yes, sir." She surprised me by answering in Czech and took a slight bow.

"Will you come with us?"

"Do I have a choice?"

"You can stay here, but unfortunately, you saw our faces, so …"

"I understand. I'll go with you."

"I think you made the right decision. You don't have to believe me, but nothing will happen to you."

"Maybe," said Ripper grimly. "The Russians won't give up so easily, it seems."

A black Mercedes had stopped abruptly in front of the passage.

○ ◑ ◑ ●

It was obvious that parking in a no-parking zone did not pay. Blood was leaking out of the bullet-riddled car.

We ran out onto Wenceslas Square, and I had to admit that Ripper hadn't been slacking off. A second car, flipped on its roof, was burning. A third was parked across the sidewalk with bullet holes in the hood, shredded tires, and windows white with cracks and red with the most precious of liquids. A hand adorned with gold rings and holding a snub-nosed automatic was hanging out of the passenger-side window.

Blood was dripping off of the barrel. Several mutilated corpses were scattered around on the cobblestones—all Russian looking.

"Freeze! Who ... who are you?!"

○ ◑ ◐ ●

A young policeman was staring right down the smoking barrel of the Red Baron when Ripper turned toward him.

He was stunned.

"Hare Krishna, you asshole." A foot with a heavy boot kicked out from beneath the orange robe, and the policeman's cap flew away in a lovely arc. After a hit in the head like that, he wouldn't be able to remember what his mother looked like, let alone us.

○ ◑ ◐ ●

We didn't run anymore; fast movements would draw attention. We concealed our weapons and in a brisk walk turned left. The ever-present police cameras didn't worry us anymore. About the time the movie ended, they seemed to have experienced a mysterious technical malfunction, which would continue until we disappeared from the streets.

One of our entrances was in the basement of a nearby house.

"After you, miss," said Ripper. Meanwhile, I moved some moldy boxes and stuck a key into the ancient soot. Slow, damp bugs crawled out in all directions, and the sewer cover, which must have been a hundred years old and untouched for just as long, opened. The ladder below was rusty but strong. I had checked it myself two days ago— from beneath, of course.

"It kind of stinks down here, but you'll get used to it." I took Clara's Glock from the girl, waited until she and Ripper disappeared, then slipped into the sewer and closed the cover behind me with a move practiced a thousand times over.

○ ◑ ◐ ●

3

"Mommy, there is a bogeyman in my room! But he's a good bogeyman."

"But, honey, bogeymen don't really exist. Go to sleep, please, okay?" The thirty-year-old woman took off her glasses, turned away from the monitor that glowed in the darkened room, and ran her hand through her four-year-old, pajama-wearing son's hair.

"I know there is no such thing, but there is one in my room—I mean two of them. And they're girls."

"So they're not bogeymen, but bogeywomen? How can you tell?" The woman was proud of her boy; she didn't know any other kid with such an imagination.

"They have boobies, Mommy," said the boy with a scientifically serious face.

"Oh, you smarty pants!" laughed the woman and again stroked his hair. "Should I go in there with you and tell them to go away?"

"No, they're the good guys. I just wanted to tell you that they're here. They're wearing these black ha … hats, all the way to here." He motioned down to his chin.

"OK." She touched his nose and told herself not to let him watch so much TV. It caused him to have dreams about things like this. She looked at her watch, seven thirty and so much work left to do …

"C'mon, give your mom a kiss and back to bed with you, all right?" She liked the way he approached everything so seriously and responsibly. No one else gave such a wet, sloppy kiss.

"Good night, Mommy."

"Good night." With a smile, she watched him leave the room. She turned back to the computer only after the door had closed behind him.

The boy walked through the large living room furnished with simple but pricey pieces. Down the hallway he walked past the guest room to his own and carefully closed the door behind him. There—one on the bed and the other one on the floor by the window—two bogeymen were sitting.

The openings in their black masks reveled eye makeup, and their curves indicated that they really were women.

○ ☾ ☽ ●

When the door behind her back opened again, the lady of the house didn't even turn around, she just smiled. Then she said with a furrowed brow, "Kiddo, shouldn't you be sleeping?!" Despite her stern tone, she was willing to leave her work be and lie down with her boy until he fell asleep.

Instead, a hand in a black leather glove closed around her mouth, and a young man's voice said, "Hello there, business lady." In the distorted reflection of the monitor, she could see two faces in black ski masks.

Her glasses fell on the keyboard, and the glove successfully muffled her frightened scream.

○ ☾ ☽ ●

"So, first jewelry, then account passwords, and then other interesting things."

She was lying on her back with one man sitting on her stomach. Her hands were handcuffed to a heavy bookcase. While the other man took off her slippers, the one sitting on her used a switchblade to cut off her stockings. Her mouth was taped up, and only the thought of her son was keeping her from fainting. She realized, however, that she would probably pee herself.

The man standing, the one with the younger-sounding voice, brought over a black bag and took out … she had seen the instrument once before but forgotten its name.

The smell of gasoline filled the room.

"Get acquainted, business lady. This is a blowtorch." The man laughed, kneeled down, and began to feverishly pump the little lever on the instrument. The gasoline smell was a lot stronger now. The man flicked on a lighter, and in a moment, the torch burned with a hissing flame.

"I discovered that people are more likely to speak after they experience a little pain. Few risk it a second time around. Few ever lie to us," said the man with the blowtorch. The one sitting on her stomach pressed her knees against the floor.

The woman remembered who they were. Once in a while, it was all over the papers—pictures of body bags, pale-faced cops, the coroner … People whispered about legs burned to the bone, about gouged-out eyeballs …

She had never believed it, but now she did.

People also whispered that after the burglars got what they wanted, they tortured their victims to death—just for the fun of it.

At that moment, she peed herself.

○ ◐ ◑ ●

The man with the blowtorch wasn't in any hurry. He liked fear; he loved it. First, he lightly passed the flame across the soles of her feet. Everyone thought it was horrible, but they had no idea how horrible it would be after one second, then ten seconds—how the fat beneath the skin started to melt, how it burned, and how it hissed and dripped on the floor … only if it didn't stink so much. The man with the blowtorch felt a pleasant firmness in the front of his pants.

"Hello boys," he heard behind him.

○ ◐ ◑ ●

At first, the man with the blowtorch thought he was looking into a mirror—the same black ski mask, same black clothes. A mirror, however, didn't usually speak in a woman's voice.

And it didn't kick you in the crotch.

○ ◑ ◐ ●

One of the new masked men in the room caught the rotating blowtorch and in one swift move put it out.

The woman on the floor noticed that the masked man had very characteristic curves on his chest. She did not hear his—*her* voice—even though she realized that the mask spoke. All she heard was the all-encompassing roar of the blowtorch, even though it was put out.

Masked woman, masked *woman*, masked …! The words spun around in her head in an ever-increasing manic spiral.

The man, who had been clutching the flame just a minute ago, was now rolling around on the floor as vomit flowed out of every opening in his mask.

"Get off of her," said the other masked one, also in a woman's voice.

"Women!" A switchblade again appeared in the second man's hand.

"I heard somewhere that men who carry around a switchblade have a short one," said the first masked woman. She put the blowtorch on the side table.

"I'll show you what I have!"

The woman lying on the floor saw only two yellow flames—the cat was as black as night, except for his eyes. In one instant, he wasn't there, and in the next, she saw—in absolutely clear detail—his paw with long, bloody claws. In the same detail, she saw the shiny switchblade freeze in midair along with four cut-off fingers.

○ ◑ ◐ ●

"We are sorry, Mrs. Sweet, but we had to catch them in the act. Don't worry about the boy; he's sleeping and doesn't know about any of this." One of the women removed the tape from her mouth and uncuffed her from the bookcase. In the meantime, the other woman, while grumbling, tied up both burglars and put a plastic bag around the hand of the one with the missing fingers.

"Cat, Cat, you may be a big boy, but you still make a mess."

Mrs. Sweet still felt like she was somewhere else. The trim woman picked her up like a child and put her on the sofa.

"See, we have to ask you not to talk about us, with anyone, ever." She sat next to her and took her hand. "We may not be the police, but I can guarantee that you are the last one these two will ever attack. They will never hurt anyone again."

"Wha ... what will you do with th ... them?"

"It's better that you don't know." The woman stroked her cheek and wrapped a blanket around her. Only now did Mrs. Sweet feel the cold wetness of her underwear. "Don't worry; that happens." The woman reached under the blanket. "Lift your butt please!" She pulled everything off her at once. "You'll sleep now, and I don't want you to catch a cold."

It was only then that Mrs. Sweet broke into tears.

"All right, all right." Again, she stroked her face. "When you wake up, you'll feel much better. Cat!"

After that, Mrs. Sweet saw only a large purple cat with beautiful green eyes, like two stars, like ...

"She's asleep."

"Good, I hope she stops stuttering ... We have to clean up around here a little bit."

They searched for the fourth finger for almost ten minutes.

○ ◒ ◖ ●

4

"Oh my god, I stink really bad!"

His orange robe was covered with green slime and used toilet paper up to his waist.

"You do stink." I laughed.

A minute earlier, Ripper had gotten tangled up in his robe and slipped from the sidewalk into the gutter. If the Japanese girl hadn't caught him, he would have looked much, much worse. Had he let go of his machine gun, it wouldn't have even leaked into his boots. However, he would fall in completely if only to protect his weapon. He knew it could mean the difference between life and death.

That was the most important thing. He was also the Night Club, just like me.

I know it sounds funny when said this way, but honestly no one, *no one*, ever laughs.

The dead don't usually laugh.

○ ◔ ◑ ●

We squeezed through the rusty hatch into a descending air shaft. Ripper had to go last because who would want to crawl behind him?

"Me too?" asked the girl when she saw the narrow black opening almost entirely covered in cobwebs. These shafts were constructed so that visually they appeared much narrower than they actually were. They looked absolutely impassable for a normal person.

"Yes," I said and buttoned up the lapel on my coat.

These air shafts were one of the reasons why we had to be slim. They were the only ways down into the old sewer system and even lower into the medieval catacombs and tunnels. In short, the air shafts were the most frequent routes. There were, of course, more comfortable entrances, but they usually weren't around when you needed them.

This shaft was so narrow that I had to walk with my shoulders sideways just to squeeze through. They were narrow so that people didn't get any ideas about crawling in there. Despite that, sometimes we did run into nosy guys down here—nosy guys' skeletons. All it took was three days without food, and the sewer rats would take you down like a pack of wolves. The shafts weren't called descending for nothing; there were considerably fewer ways back up.

I landed in some dry sand, peeled a veil of cobwebs off my head, and wiped off my headlamp so it became really bright, really fast. The whole place shook as a nearby subway train passed.

The Japanese girl landed and rolled perfectly. I grabbed Ripper's machine gun, and then we were all set.

I walked in the front for a while, but as usual, whenever I was down there, I got lost.

"You're a dumbass, Tobias. If I miss Tatyana because of you …! This way." Ripper motioned with his hand. I shrugged my shoulders. He was one of the First Ones. For them, moving around in this chaos of tunnels, crumbling openings, and mouse holes was perfectly normal. It was for me too, but sometimes I just lost my bearings.

○ ◌ ◑ ●

After a half an hour, we reached a door. Ripper wiped his thumb on his sleeve and pressed it against an inconspicuous display next to the door jam. Nothing happened for a while. A careful observer would notice that even in the narrow shaft of light from our headlamps, the surroundings looked awfully sooty. Once in a while, one of those nosy guys crawled all the way down here—sewer rats or no sewer rats. Cleaning up their burnt bodies was no picnic. Protecting the Club was priority number one.

The door opened.

"Hi, John," I said.

The old man nodded. As long as I could remember, I had never heard him say a single word, and I had lived there since I was eight months old. He was holding a flamethrower and looking at the girl—a small blue flame jumped out of the ignition nozzle.

"That's okay, John. Tobias brought her," said Ripper. The flame went off—even if reluctantly—and the old man stepped aside. I knew that he would burn anybody, without question. I knew that if the enemy broke through the door, he would always be there, and I and everyone else would have time to arm themselves and launch a counterstrike. I knew that he would die in that situation, and I knew that he knew that too. John and his sons guarded both entrances to the Night Club. There were four of them, so they could take turns. I had never heard any of them speak. They didn't speak; it was not necessary. Their lives' purpose was clear; they guarded the entrances, just as their forefathers and their forefathers had done for more than seven hundred years.

○ ○ ◐ ●

A long and well-worn spiral staircase (it turned to the right from the time of swordsmen, so that it was easier to defend) was followed by a door, a large doormat for cleaning off shoes, one more door, and after the stench of the underground, a completely different world.

The Japanese girl, who had accepted her fate, now had her eyes wide open with surprise, taking in a soft rug, old paintings, the aroma of tobacco, dark colors, mahogany woodwork on the walls, and a tiled ceiling.

When we walked through the hallway and a beaded curtain, she said something like, *"Oink."*

○ ○ ◐ ●

The Night Club was, in a way, a *night club*—even though strictly private. It had a long bar made of shiny wood, a long dinner table, several round tables, antique chairs, a piano (a grand piano, a true Steinway), more paintings, and a fireplace. On the shelf behind the bar, there weren't bottles and glasses but rather books. Well, there were some bottles and glasses too.

"Kolachek, did you tape Tatyana for me?! This dumbass got lost again."

"Of course I did, Ripper. How could I forget?" The older portly man with a wreath of gray hair around his temples smiled.

I took off my shredded coat (along with most of the dirt) and hung it on the coatrack.

"What in God's name were you doing up there? You were supposed to remove one criminal, and instead, you are turning Prague into Beirut! And where is Clara?!"

"I am glad to see you too, Dread," I said.

"Which one of you guys fell into shit again? Ripper! I should have known!" Christina straightened up behind the bar, her head wrapped up in white gauze. The incident with the meat mallet must have been true.

"I'm gonna go change," said Ripper and handed his machine gun to the man in a greasy leather apron who appeared from the door next to the fireplace as soon as he heard our voices.

"Tobias?"

I handed him mine as well as Clara's Glock. With that, I answered Dread's question.

"So Clara …" Dread paused. "Won't you introduce your new friend, Tobias?"

"Hmmm … miss?" I smiled at the girl. "Can you please introduce yourself?"

"Hanako Long." The girl took a slight bow.

"Nice name," said Dread, and everyone looked at me.

"She saved my life. I think she shoots better than all of us put together."

The Night Club didn't tolerate mistakes. Dying for someone was normal. If you endangered someone, then it was normal to die. I knew that already when I didn't let Ripper shoot her in the passageway.

The silence was getting uncomfortable.

"Christina, please show Hanako her room and make sure she gets some clothes," said Dread. The Night Club didn't have a leader or anything like that, but Dread was the oldest of the First Ones.

Everyone breathed a sigh of relief, especially me. I had never brought anyone into the Club, and come to think of it, as far as I could remember in my lifetime, it had only happened twice.

John's sons, who were discreetly standing in both entrances to the main hall, disappeared.

They knew that I wouldn't run.

Hanako didn't notice anything. The crust of dirt on her face cracked with a smile. She bowed before Dread and left with Christina.

"What do you want to eat?" Thomas, our cook, peeked out of the kitchen.

"Just give me some soup ... Do we have that one with the dumplings? We do? Thanks. Where is the paper?"

"Catch." Dread threw me the morning *Times* and the *Evening Post*.

"Thanks."

I washed my hands and took my seat at the large table. I read the *Post* until Thomas warmed up my food and brought it to me. There was a story about an unknown man who brought Paulina T. to the Motol Hospital. Paulina had been missing for fourteen days and had suffered partial memory loss but was otherwise completely healthy. Anyone who saw this man—there was a picture of a man wearing a hat over his eyes and a three-quarter-length coat—shortly after twelve near the Motol Hospital today was to report immediately to the nearest police station.

There was also a sensational story about a double homicide in an unnamed village just east of Prague.

... The incredible brutality with which this elderly couple was executed leaves many open questions for the police department ...

"The brutality leaves open questions for the police department," I read out loud and shook my head.

"Yeah, even you can write better than that," said Ripper.

"Oh, Mr. I-swim-in-shit speaks." I aimed my spoon at him. "What did you smear all over yourself? Even the sewer smelled better than that!"

"Ha ha ha, are you jealous of my cologne?!"

"What would you like to eat?" Thomas was sometimes really annoying with his sustenance questions.

"Also soup, but lots of it."

Ripper was dressed normally now; even his stick-on ponytail had disappeared. All that remained was a red circle on the back of his head. He had a hard role to play in that getup today—to capture attention in case Clara and I had to get away. His outrageous getup also had its advantages. When people described him, they would say he had an orange robe, a shaved head, and a ponytail down to the middle of his back. They wouldn't remember anything else about him.

"Do you want the one with dumplings, like Tobias, or borsch?" Seriously, he was annoying, but his cooking was excellent.

"Not now, Thomas." Ripper was fighting with the remote control.

"Give me that." I took the remote from him and turned on the recording of his favorite TV show—Come to think of it, it was the only reason we even had a TV and VCR.

"Which one?"

"Dumplings, I don't feel like Russian today ... Tatyana! Quiet!" breathed Ripper erratically. Thomas shrugged his shoulders and left. Everyone knew that it made no sense to try to talk to Ripper at that time. Normal people watched the weather report for the weather; Ripper watched it because of Tatyana Mikova.

"She looks good today, Tobias! Look, look!"

"Yeah, sure."

"This dress is even better than the black one."

"For sure."

"And that slit!"

"Hmmm."

Some clamor came from the hallway.

"Damn it!" Ripper cursed and turned off the video. "There is never any peace and quiet around here! Never any peace and quiet!"

○ ◑ ◐ ●

Two tall women walked through the curtains wearing tight black outfits. Their blonde hair was flat after they had been wearing ski masks for a long time, and the mask pattern was still visible on the tips of their noses.

"Kamile, Babe, hi. What would you like to eat?" inquired Thomas.

"Hi, everyone."

"Hi, girls."

At that moment, I had my mouth full of a hot dumpling so I just waved.

"Do you have them, Kamile?" Dread shut the display on his laptop.

"We have two."

"There were supposed to be three." Dread tapped his jaw, obviously not pleased. "What shape are they in?"

"One probably won't be able to sire any offspring, and the other one got four fingers ripped off by Cat."

"Considering that you two got them, they are doing okay," said Ripper.

"You too, smartass," smirked the younger of the two women. The older one was going on twenty-eight, and she was a piece of work—a tall blonde with long legs and bright eyes. If the older one was a piece of work, then the younger one was the kind of beauty that after a mere glimpse, causes one's mouth to go dry, hands to shake, and knees to weaken. They say that absolute perfection is no longer beautiful, but what do they say when something is more than perfect?

"Do you want soup with dumplings or borsch?"

"With dumplings," they both said at once.

"Did you leave them in the car?" Dread stood up and stretched his back.

"Yes, we're in the fifth garage."

"Come on, Kolachek." Dread slapped the portly man on the shoulder. "Let's go get 'em. I'd like to get this thing done today."

When they walked past me, Kolachek took me by the chin, turned my wounded earlobe toward the light, and adjusted his glasses. "Stop by and see me, Tobias. We'll do something about that ear of yours." The fact that I spilled soup all over myself didn't bother him one bit.

"Kolachek, don't piss me off!"

He shook my head and smiled. His hands had fascinated me ever since I was little—I didn't know anyone else with such big and strong hands. I knew that with one squeeze, he could easily crush my skull.

"You got some dirt on it in the sewers. Careful with that." He let go of me. "And we'll take a peek at those ribs too." With that, he commented on the bullet hole in my shirt.

34

○ ◑ ◐ ●

"I will take a peek at that for him."

"Hardly! Get away from me, Babe! Get!" I poked the younger blonde in the stomach with my finger.

"Oh, you big baby." She leaned over and simulated a slow kick over the table.

"Stick that leg up your butt. Stuff is falling into my soup!" Ripper raised his voice.

○ ◑ ◐ ●

"Ummm!" I remembered something and quickly swallowed. "Dread, I have a little problem."

Dread was straightening his hat. He flashed his eyes at me from beneath the rim.

"Clara will have my fingerprints on her."

"Where?" asked Babe as she took her seat.

"On her ass."

"You pervert!"

"*Whaaat?* It's perfectly normal to grab a girl's ass."

"I'll give you normal—!"

"Enough," said Dread rather quietly. We shut up immediately.

"We would have gone to get Clara anyway, but we'll just have to do it tonight. First, we must interrogate those two, so they'll tell us who the third thug is. We'll have to get that one tonight too. You guys finish your food, and then everyone downstairs. Tobias, you take Hanako. I hope you remember the rules?"

"Yes," I said. Because I brought her in, I was responsible for her.

○ ◑ ◐ ●

"Wait, wait! Tobias, Clara is …?" Babe put her hand on my shoulder.

"There were eight of them instead of three."

"I'm sorry." She leaned toward me and stroked my face. These tender overtures of hers gave me the creeps; even though she looked like a supermodel, she was one of the most dangerous people I knew.

35

○ ○ ◑ ●

Dread and Kolachek left, and Thomas brought out two more bowls of soup.

"You could try to get here all at once," he grumbled. "Who is supposed to warm these up all the time?"

"Thanks." They both smiled at him.

"Who is Hanako, Tobias?" Kamile looked at me across the table.

"The girl saved our sharpshooter's butt, so he took her with him," said Ripper.

I kept my mouth shut.

"Tobias, your pistol." The man in the greasy apron brought me my Glock and several clips.

"You didn't do any shooting, girls?" he asked.

"No, Theodore, strictly manual labor."

The man in the apron left, and I instinctively checked my weapon. I removed and reinserted the clip. This time, it was a standard seventeen rounds. I knew it wasn't necessary to check because Theodore was one of the best weapons experts in the world. The pistol was thoroughly cleaned and had a new barrel and hammer. If the cops caught me, they could never use the gun to tie me to today's massacre in the passageway.

○ ○ ◑ ●

As I took the last gulps of soup, Christina and Hanako returned. Babe quietly whistled, and Kamile, offended, wrinkled her eyebrows.

"I wish you a pleasant evening," said Hanako and bowed.

Even I almost whistled. Before, she was filthy, wore baggy clothes, had a dirt-covered face, and looked like any normal Japanese girl. Now, though, she looked like what you would call an Asian super-beauty. She was pretty tall for a Japanese woman, which I had noticed before, but I didn't notice that she was of mixed heritage. Euro-Asian women were the most beautiful in the world. She had soft cheekbones, large blue-green eyes, a European nose, exquisite white teeth, even more exquisite red lips, straight-cut black hair, and trim hips. She looked to be about twenty-five …

Ripper swallowed out loud.

"This is one mistake that I didn't make today." I put down my spoon.

"What would you like to eat, Hanako?" asked Thomas. For him, there was nothing more important than to put something nutritious into people—it didn't matter who and didn't matter when.

"Thank you for your kindness, and I apologize, but I don't eat."

"Everybody eats!"

"Yes, of course, but I have unfortunately … diet? Is that correct Czech?" She looked at me and smiled, and my hands got really sweaty. When she spoke for a longer period, you could hear a distinct accent in her Czech, and she pronounced her "r" with certain difficulty.

"Diet? What kind? I can cook anything. I'm used to it." Thomas frowned at Kamile who was constantly battling her weight.

"I have a medicinal one. I have to cook for myself from Japanese ingredients. I am very sorry that I cannot accept your hospitality, but I would get an allergic reaction seriously … I mean serious allergic reaction. I could even be dying."

"Oh, *be dying*." Thomas made a sour face.

"Yes." Again, she smiled. Ripper and Babe were looking at her with dreamy eyes, and even Thomas believed that smile.

He left with some grumbling. "Diet, diet, everyone is on a diet! They have to be strong, but no, they're on a diet. They should take an example from Father Kolachek … *diets*!" He disappeared into the kitchen.

"Have a seat, Hanako." Christina pulled up a chair.

There were three phones sitting on the bar—a green one, a blue one, and a black one. The green phone rang. It was Dread.

"Yes, we're going. Right now, yup." I put down the receiver, and Kamile and Babe made quick work of their soup.

Ripper got up, and his knees cracked. "So an interrogation, that will be something." He sighed.

"Hanako, are you coming with us?" I tapped my fingernails on the receiver.

"Of course, Mr. Tobias." Again, she smiled. *So she isn't dumb either.* She understood very well what was going on. She saved my life; I saved hers—that bound us.

"Just Tobias." I also smiled. It occurred to me that it was impossible not to smile at her.

"Careful, so she doesn't get fingerprints on her butt too," whispered Babe.

○ ◑ ◐ ●

On the way down the stairs, I tried to prepare Hanako for what was coming up, but you can't prepare anyone for something like that.

The interrogation room was deep beneath the Club in a space that wasn't accessible from anywhere outside. The medieval surroundings of the arched catacombs, the sooty ceilings, the stench of mildew, and continuous dripping of water put the incoming condemned into the *right frame of mind*, as Babe liked to say. She was the only one who liked going to interrogations—or rather to interrogations of men. I would have considered her to be somewhat of a sadist if I didn't know what had happened to her when she was seven years old.

○ ◑ ◐ ●

All the interrogation rooms stank, and the stench alone was enough to untie the tongues of people who were perceptive.

Hanako scrunched her nose and with a little shock looked at the soaked man, standing there chained to a wall with a blindfold over his eyes.

Father Kolachek and his son were just tightening up the chains around his ankles. While the older Kolachek stood up with great huffing and grimacing (his knees hurt), the younger Kolachek tied the man's pant legs above his ankles. We sat ourselves on the benches by the wall so that we could see well. On a portable counter, Father Kolachek began to unpack a smallish case lined with black velvet.

Dread sat on a lone chair behind a table across from the suspect and read through the papers in a light-green folder. The stone floor was cold, and the teeth of the man by the wall chattered loudly. He stank of vomit. When the younger Kolachek aimed two large lights at him and turned them on, wisps of vapor rose from his clothes.

Father Kolachek took the blindfold off his eyes.

"Mr. Stanley Hlavaty?" Dread put the open folder on the table. The man by the wall squinted into the bright lights.

"Who are you? I need a doctor."

38

"Mr. Stanley Hlavaty?" Dread repeated the question, apparently with the same tone, but there was something in his voice that gave me the chills. Father Kolachek confessed to me once that it gave him chills too.

"Yeah, I am Stanley Hlavaty, cop. So what? I won't tell you anymore until I get a doctor."

Mr. Hlavaty, like most of those who fall into our hands, was mistaken about the nature of the situation. They all thought they were still in the Czech Republic. Dread was sometimes inhumanly patient.

"All we want is the name of your third accomplice who participated in eight of your assaults. We know it's one of your two friends, but we need to be sure."

"Kiss my ass, copper!"

This, I will never understand. Why did these people act like assholes? He was tied to a wall, and still he cursed. They must get it from TV.

"I suggest that you reconsider your answer. Next time, Mr. Kolachek will be doing the asking."

"Screw you!"

Ripper shook his head. Kamile sighed with disappointment. Hanako was looking Asian. Babe moved closer.

○ ◐ ◑ ●

On the wall, to the left and right of the man's head, were two steel holders with flat rings. Young Kolachek took a wide belt from the counter and laced it through the rings so that it rested across Hlavaty's forehead—loosely for now.

"What are you doing, you bastards?!" screamed the man. "I have my rights!"

Interesting, everyone seemed to remember rights when they were by this wall—especially their rights.

Father Kolachek grabbed the man's chin with his left hand and pressed his right cheek to the bricks. The muscles on Mr. Hlavaty's neck stretched like ropes, but he couldn't do anything. With his other hand, the father straightened the belt and pulled it tight. Young Kolachek took the end of the belt and hooked it over a nail that was seemingly uselessly sticking out of the wall.

"Ouch, that hurts!" Protested the man. That was all he could manage because his head was fixed in place so completely all he could do was roll his eyes. Red impressions of the father's fingers were left on the man's pale skin.

"What are you going to do?! I'm warning you—!"

The father opened the man's mouth and inserted a well-used wooden gag. He stepped back, adjusted his glasses, and folded his arms across his chest.

"So, Mr. Hlavaty, here is what's going to happen. You'll experience pain that will last exactly fifteen seconds. Then I will take out the gag and ask you who your third accomplice is. If you do not answer, you will experience the pain again. This time, it will be for one minute. The records of my ancestors state that in the year fourteen hundred twenty-six, one man was able to withstand this form of pain for about, hmmm, today we would say about five minutes. In the last minute, he fainted every ten seconds, and then he died."

Young Kolachek brought the counter with the velvet case to his father.

The father rolled up his sleeves, pulled on a pair of surgical gloves, and poured a small amount of brown liquid on a cotton ball. The smell of iodine filled the room. The man by the wall was sweating, and the stench of his fear overpowered even the stench of his puke. Hanako started to look tense, but she kept her cool.

Father pulled up the man's sleeve and smeared the man's inner elbow and then his left cheek with iodine. From the case, he took a syringe. He removed the sterile packaging, attached a hypodermic needle, and drew a small amount of bluish liquid from a tiny vial. He lifted the syringe in front of his glasses and squeezed out a small number of droplets that glistened like sapphires in the bright lights.

"To avoid the unpleasant interruptions caused by fainting and to prevent untimely death, someone invented this … I won't bother you with chemical jargon. In short, it removes the blocks each organism has … These safety triggers gradually switch off when pain crosses a certain threshold. A secondary effect of this chemical is that it causes your pain receptors to become … well … significantly more sensitive."

Young Kolachek picked up a knife from the table and cut open Hlavaty's black sweater. The man squirmed, and Hanako again said something like, *"Oink!"* and closed her eyes.

Young Kolachek put on a stethoscope and pressed it against the man's chest. He moved it a little to the right and nodded to his father. He squeezed the man's bicep, waited for the vein to enlarge, stuck the needle into it, and depressed the plunger.

Hlavaty immediately began to sweat so profusely that beads dripped from his nose, and his calves began to shake uncontrollably. Young Kolachek shone a small flashlight into his eyes, moved the stethoscope a little higher, and again nodded to his father.

Father Kolachek lifted the scalpel.

Dread looked uninterested as usual.

Ripper closed his eyes.

Kamile's chin stiffened. So did Babe's gaze.

"Hanako, you should look," said Dread. He got up and pulled a long wooden cork out of the wall next to Hlavaty's mouth.

"This is the trigeminal nerve," said the father. He wasn't talking to the suspect, but rather to his son. This was called passing on knowledge through experience.

The scalpel sliced through the skin, brown from the iodine, and the man's body convulsed.

It was barely a quarter-of-an-inch-long incision, but it was pretty deep.

The father inserted small needle-nosed pliers into the wound.

I will admit that I couldn't stand this. Except for Babe, none of us could stand it—Father Kolachek most of all. However, our presence at interrogations increased our endurance and, more important, our determination. The people that we fought against frequently used the same methods, except they enjoyed it.

I didn't know which was worse: when the suspect screamed or when he was gagged. The noises that came from him would give me a month's worth of bad dreams.

Father Kolachek carefully monitored his watch. After fifteen seconds, he pulled the pliers out of the wound.

Young Kolachek lifted Hlavaty's eyelid, again shone the light into his eye, and again nodded.

Dread stuck the cork back into the wall, and the father took out Hlavaty's gag and wiped the saliva off his chin. The gag had brand-new tooth marks in it along with a piece of a molar.

Hanako was sitting as stiff as a board. Her eyes were as big as saucers and her fingers were digging into her knees, but she was really watching the whole time. I believed that those fifteen seconds were just as long for her as they were for Mr. Hlavaty.

○ ◑ ◑ ●

"So, Stanley, now will you tell us who the third one is? I will have to ask you not to lie; it's in your own best interest. We would rather not, but as a last resort, we can prolong the pain—even more excruciating pain—into hours."

"Tony Kolchik, it was Tony!" The man by the wall was crying. "I am soooo sorry. I didn't … I really didn't want to …!"

It was interesting how everyone always ended up being really sorry by this wall. They were sorry for having raped and killed; they were sorry for having burnt women's feet with a blowtorch.

It was honestly interesting.

"So, Mr. Anthony Kolchik? Yes?" asked Dread.

"Yeees!!!" shrieked Hlavaty, because he heard that the Father had again picked up something from the counter, but because his head was turned, he couldn't see what it was.

"Don't worry. I will numb it for you, son. This will sting a little," said the father. He squirted some anesthetic on the man's cheek and taped up the wound with a Band-Aid. "For your own good, I hope you didn't lie to us," he added in a calm voice, and his son hung the stethoscope around his neck.

"I shit my pants," said Hlavaty with surprise.

We untied the man, put the blindfold back over his eyes, and took him away. In the meantime, Kolachek and his son brought in the second man who was very pale, almost blue. The whole time he was in the next cell. The cell into which led the opening that Dread uncorked for those very long fifteen seconds.

"Mr. Daniel Fingerhut?" said Dread and again set aside the light-green folder.

"Yes, sir." The plastic bag around his right hand was full of black, coagulated blood.

"Mr. Fingerhut, we need to know the name of your third accomplice."

Except for those fifteen seconds of unbearable pain, he did not hear anything else that Hlavaty said.

"It's Tony Kolchik. Tony. Yes."

"It is a pleasure working with you, Mr. Fingerhut." Dread smiled. Babe snorted with discontent—she disliked men who tortured women most of all. I was surprised that Hlavaty and Fingerhut survived the trip back to the Night Club.

"So, Kamile and I will pick up Kolchik. Tobias and Babe will get Clara's body. Ulrich should know by now where they took it." Dread closed the folder and left it on the table.

"Hanako, you okay?" I slapped her knee. She had her hands pressed between her thighs and was swallowing hard.

"Yes, Tobias." She smiled, but it looked really fake. I noticed that she slightly wavered as she stood up. Dread observed her carefully. I knew exactly why he wanted her there during the interrogation—it was a stress test. If you knew it was coming, then it wasn't a test. Shooting people, being shot at, and a torture chamber all in one day was a good audition for any future member of the Night Club.

Hanako took two steps and her knees buckled, but Kamile caught her at the last minute. It was admirable that she lasted this long. During my first interrogation, I threw up just from the stench alone.

"A very good choice, indeed. You'll start teaching her tomorrow." Dread patted me on the shoulder.

I'll admit that a pat on the shoulder from Dread made me feel really good.

○ ◐ ◑ ●

Kamile carried Hanako all the way back up to the Club and gently laid her on the sofa next to the bar. Babe was frowning.

"Don't be jealous, Babe," I said and did a half turn to avoid a strike that would have taken my head clean off. "If Kamile lets you, I need someone to shine my boots …" A slender arm wrapped around my neck from behind. Alas, I knew that I was just too slow for these two. Babe stopped her strike and licked her lips.

"Kamile, I think Tobias needs to have his ear looked at."

"Don't even think about it!"

"Don't worry. Remember, I'm a registered nurse." I tried to free myself, but unfortunately, those two were experts at hand-to-hand combat. I was not. So, in a matter of seconds, I was on my back. Babe had been using me as her favorite sparring partner since we were little, and since then, it regularly ended exactly the same way—her kneeling on me and laughing. When we were younger, she'd tickle me, and when she was in a bad mood, she'd spit in my mouth.

"Christina, darling, can you hand me Kolachek's antiseptic? You know, the one that stings a lot."

"Don't you dare!"

"Or what? Or you'll have to change your underwear again, Toby?"

Everybody, of course, laughed. See, one time, she took the tickling a little too far.

I squirmed, but even though I was forty pounds heavier than she was, I couldn't get rid of her. It didn't help either that Kamile was sitting on my legs.

Christina, that coward, brought Kolachek's entire first-aid kit, so I had nothing left to do but suffer. Babe really was a nurse. In the outside world, she worked in the hospital, in the children's ward.

"So …" She neatly taped up my ear with a waterproof Band-Aid. "How about those undies?" She pressed her fist against my chest, and with a graceful move over my head, she stood up.

"Ha, ha," I said. Thomas and his daughter Janie stood in the kitchen doorway. When I raised my eyes towards them, they were completely serious, but I had heard them well enough laughing at me a minute ago.

○ ◗ ◑ ●

I went to my room to take a shower and change, and when I returned, there was a brand-new bulletproof vest on my chair.

Kolachek was sitting at the table, and when he saw the old vest with the cluster of smashed bullets from a Kalashnikov, he frowned. "You didn't tell me they weren't from a handgun. You have to go get an X-ray."

"That's fine. If there had been anything wrong with me, she'd have already finished me off already." I grinned at Babe. "Hanako, how are you?" The pale Japanese girl was sitting at the table, Kamile on one side, Christina on the other. Her mouth was going a mile a minute—typical post-traumatic chatter. I took a new coat from the closet and my gun and ammunition from the table.

"Where are you blondeie?" I looked at Babe who was examining my old shredded vest.

"A few holes in his shirt, and he makes a huge deal out of it, Mr. Sensitive."

"Go already, you two," said Kamile as Hanako smiled at me.

○ ◗ ◑ ●

"I'm driving," I said as we emerged from a hatch in one of our garages. A dark blue, rusty Ford Transit was waiting with a full tank of gas.

"Go ahead and drive."

"Where did Ulrich say she is?" I started the car.

"At the Armed Forces Hospital, and she is supposedly guarded by the police. I guess they remembered that sometimes bodies disappear from there." Babe got in and closed the door while I pushed the remote and the garage door opened up.

○ ◗ ◑ ●

It was just before eleven, so the Prague traffic had thinned out nicely; plus, it wasn't far.

I stopped behind the hospital, put on my hat, and pulled up my lapel. Babe had a nurse's uniform on underneath her coat. It was nicely fitted and maybe even shorter than usual. She used the mirror to pin the little white cap into her pulled-back hair.

I pressed the remote on the key. The locks clicked, and the turn signals flashed. We walked through the shadowy complex where orange lamps fought a losing battle against the autumn fog. The wind howled through the trees. The fallen leaves rustled, and most of the windows were pitch black.

"There it is. Hopefully, Ulrich has had time to disable the cameras." We reached a concrete ramp leading underground.

Babe rang the doorbell. When the cop saw her smile and white cap, he completely dropped his guard. She knocked him out with a swift strike to the temple. Just then, a second cop came around the corner with a cup of coffee in hand. "What the hell ...?!"

"Come here quickly! Your colleague fainted!" Babe ordered firmly. Because the cop was looking more at her legs than anything else, he didn't even notice me. I was also good with the strike to the temple, and I even caught the coffee cup without spilling a drop. It was hot, but alas, sweet.

We each took one of them by the arms and pulled them into a janitor's closet. Our universal keys could handle locks even more complicated than this one.

"Good ... this way." Babe took off in a quick stride following the arrows labeled 'Morgue'.

○ ◑ ◐ ●

Unfortunately for him, an orderly peeked out of a door just when we stepped into the long hallway—there was nowhere to hide, and he was on the opposite side.

"What are you doin'?!" An anesthetic round from my gun smacked into his forehead, and his head banged against the tiles. I wouldn't want to be in his shoes when he wakes up. Babe pulled him back into the nurses' station, checked his pulse, and placed him in a stable position. In the meantime, I pecked at the keyboard.

"Here we are ... an unknown woman, cause of death is a gunshot to the face, arrived at 9:07 ... number 774."

"Ulrich already told me that, you wiseass."

We found Clara's body pretty quickly. It was in the freezer. However, we missed the fact that there were more people here than just two cops and an orderly. There was one more of each kind.

"Stop, you necrophile!" The orderly weighed about three hundred pounds, and lifting corpses had had an obvious effect on his musculature—he looked like a tank.

"You never told me you're into corpses," Babe whispered.

"Now you know everything about me."

The cop aimed his pistol right at us, and from ten yards away, he couldn't miss.

"Mr. Policeman! I am so glad to see you! This pervert was making me do ... well, I can't even say what!"

"Come this way, miss, and be careful not to get in my line of fire!" Babe looked like a little bundle of sad. If she wasn't with the Night Club, she would certainly be in the movies. She stood behind the cop and held on to the orderly's elbow. He puffed up like a pigeon.

"Would you mind if I worked him over a little? I know violence doesn't solve anything, but these weirdoes are coming in here today and every day and nobody does anything about them."

"You mean they really do it with the corpses?!" asked the cop with disgust.

"You have no idea!"

"Fine, I'll do my rounds, but he has to be able to walk ... and not in the face."

Babe was grinning with amusement behind the beefcake's shoulder as she stroked his biceps.

"Come with me, miss." The cop put his arm around her hips paternally and overtly winked at the orderly. "I have to question you." Babe froze for a second but let him take her away. This cop was not going get out of this one with a humane thump on the temple.

It was okay for now. No one was looking Babe in the face, thanks to her mini-uniform, and I had a hat.

The beefcake came up to me and cocked back his fist, which was the size of a sledgehammer.

"Not the face." I whacked him a couple of times in the solar plexus and a third time under the chin. When you pick the right angle, it's more effective than a shot of anesthetic. As the mountain of a man was folding over, I pushed him onto one of the dissecting tables. There was already a dead body on it. I couldn't help myself and arranged him into a rather compromising position.

A short yelp came from behind the door, and a minute later Babe walked in, fixing her dress.

"I hope you didn't hurt him too much," I said.

"Don't worry."

○ ◑ ◐ ●

We moved Clara onto a gurney. "One, two ...!" The icy body clattered. Suddenly, I noticed that Babe's eyes were tearing up.

"Such a beautiful girl shouldn't end up like this," she said as the sheet slid off Clara's face.

"Kolachek will fix that," I said, but even I had an unpleasant lump in my throat. Even though we anticipated death every day, we anticipated our own, not that of our friends. We may have appeared a certain way, and we may have joked about it, but the death of others affected us much more than we ever dared to admit. Babe squeezed my hand for a second; hers was as cold as ice. The cold room was full of dead bodies, stainless steel, light reflections penetrating the milky glass of the door and two flashlight beams. Our fingers unraveled, and the wheels of the gurney squeaked.

○ ◑ ◐ ●

Without interruption, we arrived at the car, loaded up Clara, and got in.

"You know, I really had no idea you were into corpses."

"I've wanted to ask you for a long time, Babe, who wears the pants at your house? I always thought it was Kamile."

"You just stepped over the line, buddy," she informed me in a dangerously cute voice. "Wait till we get back to the Club. Oh my God, how you're gonna get it! You're sooo gonna get it!"

That freaked me out. Clara had said that exact same thing a few hours ago. I still felt her warm skin, smelled her perfume ... but now she was just a chunk of ice and smelled like meat pulled from the freezer. Babe noticed that something was going on and stopped teasing, even though it must have meant a great deal of self-restraint.

○ ◑ ◐ ●

I pressed my thumb against the sensor next to the door. John opened the door, crossed himself, and bowed before the deceased. We carried Clara into our morgue and laid her on a bier. I was glad this was behind us because that was not an easy trip—mostly due to the descent through the sewers and the fact that we had to carry her for several miles without a stretcher. She was freezing against my hands.

I looked around the cold, vaulted room. The dead belonged in our morgue. There were no stainless-steel freezers, no glass cabinets with bone saws and such things. There was just a cross on the wall.

We covered the bier with a sheet befitting a member of the Night Club.

The sheets were on a shelf right next to the morgue entrance. Even if I had been taking out the first one of my life, it was one too many. Everyone felt that way.

○ ◑ ◐ ●

"Don't even bother going upstairs." We met Ripper by the spiral staircase. "Dread wants to finish up those three today."

"My God." Babe covered a yawn with her hand. "This on top of everything." We walked back into the catacombs, but this time, we didn't turn to the morgue. We walked past the interrogation room and past the holding cells. The lightbulbs on the ceiling grew dimmer and farther apart, and Babe stopped complaining about *'when the hell she was going to get to bed'* that day. It took a good fifteen minutes at a brisk pace to get to our destination, and at such a pace, it was hard to walk and complain at the same time. In these hallways, with very strange acoustics, we heard a repetitive swish-slap, swish-slap. The closer we got, the quieter it became.

We arrived at a double wooden door, and when Ripper opened them, the familiar stench of a slaughterhouse hit me in the face—blood, lots of blood. This room, in contrast with the others down here, had a much higher ceiling with ribbed arches. Traditionally, only torches were used for lighting, but it was not the torches that you noticed first. The most imposing and eye-catching thing was a fat, three-foot-tall, black wooden block with iron bands around it.

Three long swords with round tips and straight crossbar guards hung on the wall across from the entrance. Two axes with wide blades hung beneath the swords. All weapons had hilts shiny from frequent use. Three men stood against the wall on the right. They had black blindfolds over their eyes and their hands were tied to rings bolted high up between the bricks. Dread sat at a table on the other side of the block, the light-green folder in front of him. We sat down on a bench next to Kamile and Christina.

In all honesty, the wooden block didn't totally dominate the room; that was done by two men wearing red executioner's hoods. In the flickering light of the torches, the sight of them didn't make me feel good either.

"What about Hanako?" I whispered to Christina.

"Sleeping. Janie is with her, just in case."

"Quiet, please," said Dread. Even from the back, he looked stern. Our presence at executions was another tradition. To be exact, it was a reminder of *memento mori* (remember you too will die), because in this room, even members of the Night Club—those who disappointed—met their end. They always came here voluntarily, without chains. They kept their dignity and received a proper burial with all due honors. That sword in the middle was reserved exclusively for us.

Dread motioned to Kolachek and his son who removed the blindfolds from the eyes of the convicted. All three had had the hair on the back of their heads cut off and their lapels removed.

"Is this some kind of a joke?" said the one I had not seen yet. Based on the hazy look in his eyes, he was drunk. They must have picked him up in a bar somewhere.

"No, Mr. Kolchik, this is no joke," said Dread and stood up. We all stood up. "On multiple counts of robbery, torture, and murder, I hereby sentence you to death, in the name of the Night Club. The execution will be carried out immediately." Dread closed the light-green folder and tapped it with his fingers. I knew that the folder contained the signed confessions of the two that we arrested first. I knew that Dread had asked them politely to transfer all their money, not just stolen stuff, into our accounts. I also knew that those two had cooperated without any problems. Ulrich would transfer Kolchik's money—nobody was going to discuss that with him now.

"Ha, ha, am I supposed to shit myself or what?" said Kolchik and looked around malevolently.

Hlavaty quietly prayed, and tears ran down his face.

Fingerhut fainted at the first sight of the wooden block, so now he just quietly hung in his shackles.

The drunks were always problematic. I changed the anesthetic rounds in my Glock for live ones and put the weapon on my knee.

"No, if I could ask you not to do that, then no, Mr. Kolchik," said Dread. I knew that Kolachek had made all three of them take a piss, and young Kolachek tied up the pant legs of the two who didn't have them tied up yet.

"Mr. Hlavaty first!" Dread exclaimed. "And I want ..."

"I'll be good! I've returned everything! I'll do anything! I'll ... I'll be good ...!" Hlavaty was at a loss for words. Dread waited patiently for him to finish. Even in this room, everyone said the same stuff. During interrogation, they were sorry; here, they promised to be good.

"They're just bluffing, Stan. Don't worry. There is no death penalty in the Czech Republic." Kolchik spit on the floor. The other two, however, already knew they were no longer in the Czech Republic.

"Any last wishes, Mr. Hlavaty?"

"I will do anything, any little thing ... just ... just ..." Hlavaty's voice gave way along with his knees, and Kolachek had to support him on his last walk. When young Kolachek asked him to kneel down and lay his head down facing the wall, he started to squirm like a fish on a hook.

"There is no sense in struggling," said Father Kolachek. Without any obvious effort, he picked him up and shook him. "The only thing you will achieve is that you'll slow us down, and it'll hurt more. It isn't honorable."

"Any last wishes?" repeated Dread. Hlavaty only wept. Everyone always wept in the end.

In the car, Babe told me he was the one with the blowtorch.

○ ◑ ◐ ●

Young Kolachek took down one of the axes and handed it to his father. He, however, shook his head and put his hands behind his back. So, it would be a special moment, young Kolachek's first execution. The youngster looked at Dread with some surprise, but the man motioned enthusiastically back to him. We all knew he wouldn't disappoint. Since he was six years old, he knew this would be his job. Ever since then, I had seen him many times chopping wood for the fireplace and prepping kindling—with an ax or a sword—and always, he had a much more serious look on his face than was appropriate for such mundane housework.

The youngster moved Hlavaty's head a little to the left, leaned very close to him, and whispered something. I knew he was really good at it—that calming, fatherly voice that told the convict not to be afraid and to quietly kneel there, that he would tell him before it came. Surprisingly, all the convicts believed it. They all thought it couldn't be true, that they couldn't be executed, that if they got along with the headsman, it would help them and they would get out of it. Some might have even thought they could move out of the way.

"I am asking for the final time, any last wishes?"

Hlavaty didn't answer; he just waited for the word from young Kolachek.

The ax whistled, and the head popped off. They always had such a betrayed look in their eyes—*We agreed that you would tell me when!*

Father Kolachek approvingly nodded, even though we all noticed that anxiety made the youngster strike a little too hard. The ax was embedded deep in the wood, and the head jumped over the basket. The headsman carried the body away, and the elder Kolachek washed the blood off the wooden block with a bucket of water.

Fingerhut didn't react at all and died quietly and peacefully. The second cut was much better; the ax rested only gently against the block, and that's how it should be.

Kolchik, on the other hand, was causing a big commotion in his drunken state. Father Kolachek had to hold his head. His hood nodded, and the young man was three for three. If Kolchik had moved just a little, the youngster could have easily cut off his father's hands. The last head fell into the basket, and Father Kolachek looked like a butcher.

"They tortured twenty-two people to death, Hlavaty admitted." Dread turned toward us. "All women. Eight or ten just for the fun of it; he couldn't quite remember."

I heard Babe's teeth grinding. When she was in a state like that, not even Kamile dared to try to calm her down.

"Let's go bury them, Tobias?" She had to cough twice before she could utter the words.

○ ◐ ◑ ●

The headsmen carried away the third body and began cleaning up the floor and the tools. Everyone else went back to the Club. Babe and I turned on our flashlights and turned in the opposite direction, where there was no electricity.

I knew why she wanted to do it. She wanted to erase the last earthly remains of these three. She wanted to be there when they disappeared under the dirt. She wanted to be sure—otherwise, she wouldn't be able to sleep.

I am not sure what happened to her back then when she was seven, but I know that Dread told me that it was better that I didn't know. After a short pause, he added that no one should have survived it and he didn't understand how she was able to. I remember when they brought her in that night, a long time ago. I remember that Cat almost died from exhaustion trying to make her sleep and erase her memories—but he couldn't do it. After that, he just lay on the table, couldn't get up, and heartbreakingly meowed. I know it sounds weird—the words *heartbreaking* and *Cat* don't go together—but that's how it happened back then. Kamile's mom was able to get Babe out of it. Without a second thought, she adopted her, just like she had adopted me seven years earlier. For six months, Babe couldn't handle the presence of an adult man and she couldn't leave Kamile's or her mother's side for even a second. She had to be with them all the time, like a baby, and 'Baby' eventually turned into 'Babe'.

On our way, we met two of John's sons. They were dirty and sweaty from the swish-slap of digging graves. When they saw the expression on Babe's face, they stood with their backs pressed against the wall and their eyes lowered until we passed by.

Pretty soon, we were at the cemetery. Our ancestors buried convicts strictly only by the sides of the tunnel. After World War II, when Dread's father, Kamile's grandma, and others hunted members of the SS and other vermin, it became necessary to start burials in the catacombs. The Prague catacombs went on forever, though, so I wasn't worried that we'd ever run out of room.

We reached three fresh graves along with three bloody jute bags, and we turned off our flashlights. Even this kind of work was better done with torches, and John's sons had left us a couple. For the next hour, we worked our asses off without saying a word, and despite the cool air, we were sweaty as hell. The dirt down there was very heavy. When we finished, I brought over three copper plaques, stamped numbers into them, and left them on the graves. Young Kolachek would put them on the wall when there was time.

"May your bones rot away into oblivion, and may your souls never find peace." Babe delivered the parting words.

We cleaned up the shovels and returned to the Club.

○ ◑ ◐ ●

Everyone had gone to bed already, except for Dread who was typing something into his laptop. Janie, with sleepy eyes and in her bathrobe, brought us each a glass of laurel wine. Janie was the nicest person I knew. She worshipped Babe and wanted to be (look like) her. *But in the kitchen, you always have to taste something*, she confessed to me once. Simply put, she was small and plump. Now she smelled of sleep and looked at us with sad eyes, because we were frowning and not talking. In her presence, however, not even Babe could stay mad for too long.

"So, Janie, what's for breakfast?"

"How about ham and eggs?"

"Yuck! Greasy stuff in the morning? Do you want to kill me?!" Babe stretched out her hand and made a smudge on Janie's nose with her dirty finger. Janie started to giggle like crazy. She was small, plump, and simple. Once, when I was younger, I teased her a little more than Babe could handle and then we had that infamous underwear incident.

"I would make it from a totally lean piece of ham on a drop of olive oil with two home-grown eggs, nice and yellow ones … Anyway, Dread said that you have to rest tomorrow, and good food belongs to a good rest." Janie sounded just like her father.

"Don't mind her, Janie." I took a sip of the wine. "She doesn't really care what she eats. I, on the other hand, would love some ham and eggs."

"All right, two orders, please," said Babe, and Janie blushed. She got that from her pop too. Whenever someone wanted whatever he personally recommended, he was in seventh heaven—if it was Babe, ninth heaven.

"What about Hanako?" Again, I took a sip, and the alcohol began to flow pleasantly through my body.

"Sleeping like a log. At first, she was tossing a bit, but not anymore. I took a peek at her just before you got here."

"Good night," said Dread, laptop under his arm.

"Good night, Dread," we answered in triplicate.

Tomorrow, the police will receive information from an anonymous source, including an exact account of the arsonists' case, copies of signed confessions, and above all, the locations of the missing victims' graves—that was the most important. Since their disappearances, their relatives had been living in hell. The certainty of death was better than the uncertainty of life—even though it didn't seem so at first.

In the next few weeks, all relatives will receive packages from an unknown sender containing a significant amount of their loved one's financial losses plus a portion from the murderers' own assets. That was the law of the Night Club.

I finished my wine and went to bed.

○ ◗ ◗ ●

In the morning—after ham and eggs—I was called into Kolachek's treatment room, no ifs, ands, or buts. Kolachek was again the uncle with the glasses and a wreath of gray hair—the monster in the bloody hood was long forgotten. If Hanako had not been accepted into the Club yesterday, he would have been the one to correct my mistake with that middle sword.

He looked at my ear and put on a fresh bandage. He was much gentler than Babe. Then he examined and X-rayed my chest. It was all black and blue, but not even the bullets from the Kalashnikov could damage my ribs through that vest. So he just applied a salve that smelled like camphor (it tickled and felt cold, but the bruises would be gone by the evening) and ordered, "Lots of rest today and early to bed."

○ ◗ ◐ ●

"All better?" Kamile lifted her head from the paper and looked interested.

"Yeah." I held the door open for Christina.

"Of course he's all right; clowns like him are always lucky," said Babe and made a face at me.

"Be quiet!" exclaimed Kamile. "Are you sure you're okay? You look pale." Even though she knew that Kolachek had just examined me with the latest in modern medicine, she got up and put her hand on my forehead.

I have to clarify our relationship because it is rather complicated. When I was nine years and two months old, Kamile's mom didn't come back one day. Since Kamile was three years older than me and Babe, she naturally took over the motherly role. So I went to her for advice when I was growing up. She sat by my bed when I had a fever, and she took care of me when a bullet slipped under my vest and missed my heart by mere thousandths of an inch. I still called her Mom, when we were alone. However, before that, we were raised as siblings for a long time, so she had no problem with joining Babe and beating on me. Her relationship with Babe was even more complicated. When I was first on my own and started to have a life on the outside—I was just finishing my second semester—they called me back to the Club for an unexpected meeting. I remember Dread pulling me aside. I had never seen him so confused in my life.

"See, Tobias, Kamile and Babe came to see me about getting married. When I asked who their grooms were, they said they wanted to marry each other." He inquisitively looked for my reaction.

"What does the Club think?" I asked.

"They're adults … Yet, it's a bit unconventional, but the Club understands."

"Me too," I said back then.

Then there was a wedding. Both girls wore white and smiled blissfully. Janie cried, then they all cried … a wedding like any other. Only Father Kolachek was a little uncomfortable in another one of his inherited roles, but in the end, he said, "Do you, Kamile, take Carolina to be your wife?"

"Yes."

"And do you, Carolina, take Kamile to be your wife?"

"Yes."

Then they exchanged rings, a kiss, and Clara played the wedding march on the piano—like I said, a normal Club wedding. With all that, I wanted to say that their relationship was really complicated—first they were sisters, then mother and daughter, and now wives until death.

When we bring flowers to the grave of Kamile's mom, all three of us go.

○ ○ ◑ ●

I sat in my spot and became immersed in the latest Steven King book, while trying to convince myself that I should probably write something again. Ripper was watching yesterday's forecast for the third time, and he and Kamile devotedly analyzed Tatyana Mikova's finer qualities. Babe took off her shoes on the rug in front of the bar and practiced some sort of slow and elegant, yet extremely difficult kung fu exercises. She could pull herself up by only two fingers so fast that she easily transitioned into a somersault and jumped to the level of the thing she was pulling herself to (it didn't matter if it was a trapeze bar for instance). She certainly didn't have any problems with her balance, and she could long jump ten yards and high jump three. Her physical attributes weren't one in a million, or even one in a billion, but more like one in a trillion. So was her figure. I gulped and continued to read my book. Yet, despite all of her beauty, she was completely untouchable. In her outside work, one of the doctors committed suicide because of her. I grew up next to her—puberty was cruel.

"Good morning." Hanako walked through the beaded curtain.

"Good morning," we all answered, and Ripper even stopped watching Tatyana for a second.

"Many thanks for having my things delivered from the motel." She walked over to me and elegantly bowed. "Good morning, Tobias. What today program will be ... will be on today's program?"

"Why is he always so lucky?" Ripper complained quietly. Her figure was as perfect as Babe's. She was maybe even a little slimmer in the shoulders; it was totally obvious because she was wearing tight work-out clothes.

I gulped.

"Janie-san said you all work out a lot, so ..." She uneasily looked at her outfit.

"Of course we exercise a lot, but even if we didn't, you can walk around here dressed however you'd like. Nobody minds, definitely not," I said quickly.

Even though Babe didn't feel anything romantic toward men, she certainly hated the presence of a woman who could somehow overshadow her. With a graceful triple cartwheel, she landed next to Hanako.

"Kamile, do you know what Tobias said in the car yesterday?"

"What?" Kamile raised her gaze.

At that moment, I put my book aside and started to get up. "Hanako, let's go exercise!"

"What's your hurry? What did he say?"

"Who *wears the pants* at our house?"

"He said that?" Kamile started to smile, but I didn't feel too good about it. Ripper turned off the video and started cheerfully preparing for a show.

Hanako looked around with confusion, and Babe put her finger thoughtfully in front of her mouth.

"So, Tobias, what kind of underwear are you wearing today?" In our younger days, that used to be their most prized trophy. I used to cry so much back then. I knew they could easily do that same thing to me today. Furthermore, I knew that I could handle Kamile, as long as she didn't use any hard strikes, which she would never use against me.

"Hanako, exercise starts now! Block Babe!" I ordered and like a coward retreated over the table.

○ ◗ ◑ ●

Babe's leg still caught me in the ankle while I was in midair, so instead of a squat, I landed in a roll and turned over and up.

Kamile was already in front of me.

I swept her legs.

As she fell back, she kicked me in the shoulder and landed in a handstand. I took a swing.

"Wait." She was looking somewhere behind me, as her hair hung down to the rug. To be honest, I was surprised that Babe wasn't sitting on my back yet. Hanako could only delay her for maybe half a second.

Despite the fact that it could have been a trick, I turned around.

○ ◐ ◑ ●

"Babe-san, I don't want to hurt you. How strong of a strike can I use?"

"So, she doesn't want to hurt me!" Babe crinkled her eyebrows, those eyebrows that the suicidal doctor wrote a poem about in his good-bye letter. "Fine, my little Japanese girl, not in the head and not in the boobs. Whoever gets the other one on her back, wins. Okay?"

"Hai!" answered Hanako and bowed.

Then I saw something that very few people in the history of the planet have ever seen. Bruce Lee would have returned his kimono and sat on the sidelines. I think Babe was walking on the ceiling at certain times, but surprisingly, it didn't do her any good. In just about two minutes, the tornado of arms and legs stopped, and for the first time in her life, Babe was on the bottom.

"Tickle her!" I couldn't help myself.

"Hanako, get up! Quick!" yelled Kamile.

By then, Hanako was already helping Babe to her feet.

"Excellent fight, Babe-san, for a European girl. Are we going to exercise now, Tobias?" She turned to me like nothing had happened.

"Yes, of course," I said, but I was feeling sort of uneasy. Even though she had won, Hanako was in mortal danger, but I, unlike Kamile, didn't even realize it. It was my *tickle her* that could have been deadly. When Babe is pushed into a corner, she can't control herself and she would kill—it didn't matter who. Maybe that was one of the reasons I always let her win.

○ ◐ ◑ ●

"That was very impressive, Hanako," remarked Dread. I didn't even notice when he came in. "Would you all like to sit down, please? Hanako could tell us something about herself and her family."

"Yes, Mister Dread," was followed by the ever-favorite elegant bow.

"Just Dread." He gallantly offered her a chair—the one where nobody wanted to sit because the chandelier shone right in your eyes. We sat around so we could all see her. Thomas and Janie took their strategic positions by the kitchen door, and Christina brought over Ulrich.

Ulrich was about forty and somewhat chubby, but he was always smiling. He was also blind. He had a perfect memory and was probably the fastest guy on a computer keyboard in the world. He had a chip implanted in his left arm that allowed him to make what he called *direct contact* with his beloved computers. That chip and its implantation cost the Club about a million dollars, but who wouldn't spend that kind of money just to see Ulrich happy? The only thing that he truly regretted was not being able to see the *Matrix*. I'd told him the story a thousand times already, but he wanted to hear it over and over and kept asking about the minutest of details and kept correcting me when I messed up. In short, ever since the movie came out, he had shaved his head, wore mirrored clip-ons, and regretted not being black.

Ulrich sat behind Hanako, so we could see him but she couldn't.

"You could start with your parents, your family, where you were born, and why your Czech is so good ... But if you have any problems with your Czech, you can say it in English," Father Kolachek kindly encouraged her.

"Hai. I will speak Czech. My father is American Navy ... a sailor stationed in Japan. His grandfather was Czech, and my name is supposed to be pronounced *Looong*." She elongated the syllable. Ulrich behind her back nodded. "My mother is ... it is not generally known, do not speak of this please, she's a member of a family ... the Ippon-sugi Clan, a traditional secret army of women warriors. Me also. That is why Babe-san didn't have a chance to win." With a soft smile, she bowed to the aforementioned san.

"Ippon-sugi Clan. Personal bodyguards for hire, there is no better training. Are you Straight Branch or the Leaning Cedar lineage?" asked Ulrich.

"Straight Branch." Her shoulders froze as she stopped herself from turning around.

"That means both genetic disorders at once? Allergy and hypothermia?"

"Hai." Her back was straight as a board, but still, she did not turn. Nice.

"Continue, Hanako." Kolachek's smile was still kind.

"I completed the full traditional training of the clan, and when it came time for secular education, I decided to learn the culture of my father's fathers. I learned Czech from him. He was very proud of that."

"So you are in your first year at the Charles University studying the Czech language, literature, and European history?" asked Dread.

"Hai … yes, that is so."

"Good. Now something about us." Dread got up, looked very serious, and didn't know where to start. Obviously, talking about the one thing, which the first law of the Night Club forbade talking about in any other circumstances was probably not easy. So it would sound a little convoluted and a little pathetic—very convoluted and very pathetic.

"The creation of our organization was made possible in the year twelve hundred seventy-four by Premysl Otakar II, a famous Czech king. One of my ancestors, along with an unknown warrior, saved the king's life during an attack, and in return, the king gave them a piece of land in Prague and a royal decree to *fight evil*. Those were tumultuous times, so there was plenty of work to do. Then the enlightened monarch died, and the succeeding ruler maintained power through unfairness and injustice. At that time, our ancestors decided that they didn't want to live in a country like that, but they also decided that they didn't want to leave. That's how the Fellowship was created. As time went on, laws catered more and more to the wealthy, became increasingly more confusing, slippery, and pliable, and for the normal citizen, unexplainable. That's when the Fellowship set a few simple rules and punished those who violated them. That's how it is to this day—we clean up the filth that would otherwise be locked up in hospitals and prisons, and which would eventually be *cured* and released for good behavior. Only the name of the organization has changed because 'Fellowship' is such an archaic term that draws too much attention; that's why it's the Night Club. However, don't be mistaken, Hanako, the Night Club is not this place here." Dread motioned to the floor. "Even though we all like it and it is our home. The Night Club is what is inside of us—our state of mind. It is that, which determines our victory even when we face opponents stronger than us by a hundredfold. It is the words that the bad guys hear just before their death, the words they never laugh at. We are the Night Club."

It was silent for a few moments, and then Hanako stood up, ritually bowed to Dread, and said, "Hai."

"I am glad we understand each other," said Father Kolachek. "It is up to me to tell you that mistakes are not tolerated, and there is only one punishment."

"Hai."

"You must never speak about the Night Club to anyone except a Night Club member or to a convict in a situation that ends with his death. This is the cardinal rule," explained Dread. "That is all. Tobias will explain the rest. Don't be afraid to ask others, any one of us."

Just as everyone had gathered together a moment ago, they began to leave, but no one forgot to stop by Hanako and shake her hand or pat her on the shoulder—not even John's silent sons and Theodore.

After a few minutes, we continued our morning routine and Ripper turned on Tatyana again. Hanako leaned toward me. "Won't there be an initiation?"

"That was yesterday during the interrogation. You passed." Babe grinned at her. "Tobias, can I borrow her for a second in the gym?" She stared right into Hanako's blue-green eyes. "We could put on some gear and go full contact? What do you think, *pretty one?*"

"Glad to, Babe-san, but I have to warn you that you don't stand a chance."

"Grrrr!" growled Babe. As she was leaving, she turned and said, "Whoever sticks their nose in there will lose it."

So we just listened behind the door to the dull sounds of their blows, the slapping of light feet as they landed, shouts, and the noise of the air being knocked out of someone. We watched the rotating shadows under and above the door. It lasted almost half an hour. Then we heard Babe's painful, *Ouch!*

"Hai."

○ ◑ ◐ ●

By the time the girls returned, we were all sitting in the main hall. Hanako was helping Babe, who had a black eye and was limping on her right leg; her sweaty, torn kimono was hanging off her.

Hanako looked the same as before, neat and tidy—maybe her hair was messed up a little.

"Don't smirk too much, Tobias. She promised to teach me!"

My face was the most stoic of all of them. Kolachek stood in the doorway of his treatment room and somberly shook his head. By dinnertime, Babe would be fine. Kolachek's herbs and his ancestors' concoctions could heal sore muscles unbelievably fast.

"Hanako, would you like a massage? It will help you relax after a fight," asked young Kolachek with the expression of a medical professional.

"Yes, I would, gladly." She beamed.

"I should have been a headsman! Yes, now I am absolutely sure," said Ripper after the door shut behind them. I was thinking exactly the same thing, and Kamile also looked deep in thought.

○ ◑ ◐ ●

"I am going to change." Hanako walked by the bar wrapped in a large towel with her wrinkled outfit in hand. Her muscles were even more sinewy and her legs longer than I thought—the towel wasn't that big. I would guess that young Kolachek was taking a long, cold shower right about now.

"Don't shit your pants," growled Babe with disgust as she courageously lifted her head and limped away through the aroma of camphor lotion.

○ ◑ ◐ ●

I went to see Theodore and asked him to prepare a weapon for Hanako. He was, however, already almost done with it.

"Bring her here. I have to measure her arm, so I can finish the grip."

Some people would say that a Glock is a Glock, but after Theodore's alterations, an excellent weapon became truly personalized—the line between our lives and another's death.

When I returned to the bar, young Kolachek was sitting at the counter with a faraway look on his face. His wet hair was neatly combed, and every ten seconds, he took a sip of juice from a glass that had long been empty.

In a few moments, Hanako arrived. This time, she wore jeans and a loose-fitting shirt with rolled-up sleeves. The expression on young Kolachek's face changed into something out of a cartoon—except that his tongue wasn't hanging down to his vest.

"Let's go look around the Club, but first, we'll go get your gun," I said. Hanako smiled at me. After that massage, her eyes had a peculiar shine. They were deep, more green than blue. I think that young Kolachek is really starting to hate me.

Theodore let her squeeze two cylinders made from a modeling compound with both left and right hands. He measured around her shoulders and across her back, picked out an armpit holster and harness, and carefully shortened it. Hanako skillfully tried it on.

"Oh yeah, practice, you can tell." He was pleased. He hated it when people got tangled up in the straps. He always said you had to be able to put your weapon on in the dark within two seconds—and he could really do it.

"What kind of pistol did they have you practice with?" I asked, and again, I thought how lucky it was that I brought someone with such elite training into the Club, someone so well-suited for the kind of fighting we did.

"I also had a Glock; it's currently the best handgun."

Theodore happily grunted and handed her the pistol. Hanako deftly picked it up with both hands and bowed.

Theodore almost melted. "What upbringing, not like you guys. You drop your weapons on the floor and don't even say thank you." Hanako checked the Glock with expertise and put it into her holster.

"Try it out. I'll prepare the grips."

"Thank you, Mister Theodore." She smiled. "But is it possible to have two weapons?"

"Why? Glocks don't fail, especially not mine." The *mister* bristled.

"I am trained in shooting two weapons at once."

I raised my brows.

Theodore raised his finger.

"That is merely a misconception from the movies! In reality, firing from only one weapon is the most effective!"

"Yes." Hanako stared at the ground.

Boy, what education! I thought. Always respect your elders.

"Take my six-shooter and show us," I said.

"A Glock is *not* a six-shooter!"

"Yes, Mister Theodore." I stared at the ground.

○ ◑ ◐ ●

Our underground shooting range looked like any other underground shooting range. The air smelled of gunpowder and broken metal. The lights turned on and the exhaust fans began humming.

Theodore attached a target to a moving ramp, and I lay my gun and magazines on the table in front of Hanako. She prepared both weapons and waited with her hands at her sides until both of us put our ear protection on.

Then she demonstrated something I had never seen before. It's true that I should have been prepared for something like this given her performance yesterday when she fired while lying on her back.

She didn't aim—you can't aim while shooting two guns at once—but despite that, all thirty-four rounds made a neat circle, two inches in diameter.

"I can do that while running and rolling, and I have pretty good results from a flip," she said in a matter-of-fact tone after we took off our ear sets. I didn't detect even a hint of arrogance.

"Right," said Theodore, and Hanako gained another admirer. He took her pistol so he could finish it up. She thanked him and asked if he could make the barrel a quarter of an inch longer.

"Will you show me the Club, Tobias, please?" she said after Theodore left.

"That's why I'm here." I turned off the lights and the fans. I don't know if it was my imagination, but when we walked through the door, she leaned her hips into me.

Maybe she just stepped funny on the threshold or something.

○ ◐ ◑ ●

By lunchtime, I had shown her all living quarters on the first and second floor, pointed out where her room was, explained how the exhaust worked even though there wasn't a single window in the Club (our ancestors, already, were clever people), and I took her to a place where nobody was ever allowed to go.

"What is the reason?" she asked when one of John's sons uncompromisingly pointed his machine gun at our bellies. We were in a narrow crooked hallway leading from the bar. "This is the only exit from the Club, the only exit outside onto the street. It's never used. It can't be used, so that the location of the Club isn't given away. Just for the record, not even I know where we are, I think it's somewhere in Old Town, but it could just as well be Josef Square or New Town."

"Yes, nobody can say where it is even in … in an interrogation." She used the less offensive word for torture.

"Exactly."

"How come nobody knows about the Club yet, it must be a large building—" Hanako stopped so abruptly I ran into her.

"You have been in Prague for a while, so you must have seen those buildings in the old districts. They can be one hundred yards long with four stories of tiny, dusty, barred windows and an ancient front door. Usually, there is a sign saying, *Archive*, or something like that, sometimes not even that. They are museum or library depositories built as far back as the fourteenth century. On the other side of the block, in the same building, there is usually some kind of an office or something. Over the centuries, the buildings have been reconstructed and changed a thousand times. They are full of hallways, recesses, and rooms that have been filled in to improve stability. There are stairways that don't lead anywhere and caved-in basements. Businessmen that have worked in those buildings for maybe twenty years usually don't know any other way but the one that leads to their office, and they're afraid of getting lost. Everyone walks on his or her own path, and they all know that maintenance guys sometimes disappear in there. The walls can be as thick as five yards across and everyone—the people who bother to think about it—believes that behind those walls is that archive that they have passed by for twenty years while riding in a tram."

"The Night Club is in there somewhere?"

"Yes, somewhere in there on that lot that was given to Dread's ancestors by Premysl Otakar II."

"Dread, Ripper, those are unusual names." We walked by the bar and followed the spiral staircase down. Hanako was walking behind me and sometimes held on to my shoulder on the worn-out stairs. Even though I was talking, I began to feel a little distracted.

"Traditional family nicknames. Over the centuries, they became names, and there are so few of us that we don't need last names."

"Tell me, Tobias." She fell silent for a moment. "I will never be allowed to leave here? Always just here?"

I turned toward her with some confusion, my head on the same level with her bosom. "Oh!" It took me a little longer than usual to comprehend her question. "No, not at all, nobody is keeping you here. I was just going to show you the exits ... You are a member of the Club, not in prison. If you want, you can leave right now and go back to Japan; you are a free person. Who do you think we are?" I was surprised by my own reaction—restrict someone? Never.

"But I could go to the police and tell them you torture people here, that you have a secret house ..." She twirled her wrist around, and there was something in her eyes that I didn't quite understand.

"You could, but do you think they would believe you? Maybe you could lead them to the lower door, but that would be the last time anybody ever saw them. The tunnels contain land mines, old land mines from World War II. An explosion would seem pretty normal. If you got away, you would have us on your heels for the rest of your life. I admit that you have exceptional training and an excellent establishment in Japan, but we are the Night Club." I paused. "And you better not forget that."

John let us into the outer catacombs. I gave Hanako a flashlight, and we continued on in silence for a long time.

"How is it with accepting new members?"

"Generally, it doesn't happen that often. I have experienced it three times. First, when they brought me in, which I don't remember because I was eight months old. The second time was when they brought in Babe, but even she was still a kid. And yesterday, it was you."

"But there are so few of you ... of us."

"There aren't too many of us, but you don't know everyone. Most of us have lives on the outside, and some are outside right now." We arrived at one of the exits, and I gave Hanako a key and showed her how to open the manhole cover. This was an exit through a garage that everyone in the neighborhood thought belonged to someone else. It had a back door.

"You can use the cars as you like, but you have to ask beforehand. You could happen to take a hot one."

"Hot? Oh, used."

"Yes." I knocked on the roof of a squat, green sedan.

○ ◐ ◑ ●

We returned to the Club just in time for lunch.

"Hanako, you really don't eat anything?" Janie gave her a friendly frown.

"Of course I eat, but only one time in a day, before bed, Janie-san."

"That must be really terrific sushi," remarked Babe.

"It is not sushi, but rather soup from a specific blend of herbs and pureed vegetables. It is also the only drink that I will have all day."

"Really, you don't sweat?" asked Kolachek with a professional interest.

"No, that is why I don't have to drink."

"And you won't overheat because of your hypothermia, of course." Kolachek nodded. "Did they handpick a husband for your mother so these traits would be passed on?"

"Yes, very carefully, and in my mother's case, it was especially difficult; otherwise, an American would be out of the question."

"So you're almost like an Angora rabbit! Good thing you don't have red eyes," said Babe.

"Babe!" young Kolachek yelled at her and immediately withdrew because he realized what he had just done.

"Did you say something, kiddo?" the blonde beauty said with dangerous kindness as her teeth flashed between her full lips. Young Kolachek knew that the massage he'd given Hanako wasn't the only one he would experience that day. He looked around with pleading eyes, but everyone was busy eating and Hanako had no idea what was going on.

After the main course ...

"What is this?! Carrots?! Boiled carrots?! I am definitely not an Angora rabbit!"

"Keep your jokes to yourself, blondeie."

"You're gonna get it too, Tobias!"

After the main course, Dread requested everyone's attention. "So tomorrow we have work to do. It has been confirmed that the city will be pruning the trees around their house, so at nine, we'll be there too. That means me and Ripper up front, Tobias and Babe will cover us, and Kamile will drive. Hanako will come too. It's possible that there will be a chase, and some of us may be injured. Christina will stay here and help Kolachek. Father, call Tony, and tell her to be on the phone in case of a serious injury." Dread glanced at us. "Tobias, tell Hanako what's going on—after we're done here. Questions?"

"Why can't I be in the front?" asked Babe.

"I am afraid that you might enjoy it," replied Dread, and Babe blushed and lowered her head. Dread was the only person she almost never talked back to, not only because he was a father figure to us young ones, but because his family nickname was very fitting.

"We forgot your bulletproof vest. Stop by and pick it up after." Theodore nodded to Hanako and hurried away. Theodore didn't know how to relax. It was all work, work, work. We, on the other hand, were very good at relaxing, especially after a meal.

"Here, Hanako! There, Hanako! A little vest for you, Hanako?"

"Babe, don't be rude!" Father Kolachek frowned.

"Babe-san, would you like to continue our training—perhaps a more rigorous lesson?"

"I don't train after a meal." Babe waved her hand nonchalantly. "Tell me, Hanako, why do you call me Babe-san?"

"In our clan, women hold a high standing, so it is important to show them respect ... Especially, to your elders," she added after a short pause, and her eyes flashed.

"You ...!" Babe jumped up like she was on a spring, and everyone laughed. She let out a childish "Sssss!" and left. She was still limping bit.

"Don't laugh at her," said Kamile.

"She's really edgy!" exclaimed Dread. "It's about time she learned to lose too."

By nightfall, Theodore had prepared a vest for Hanako as well as a second weapon.

○ ◐ ◑ ●

"Very light," she said as she lifted the vest. Again, we were in Theodore's kingdom.

"I invented, designed, and made it myself. It will even take a direct hit from a machine gun—unfortunately only one. It stuns a person somewhat, but I am working on it." With his thumb, he motioned over his shoulder toward his lab. His machines and instruments certainly weren't outdated. He had invented the composite from which the vests were made as well as the directional gel that dissipated a bullet's force sideways. He was one sharp guy.

○ ◐ ◑ ●

At six o'clock in the evening, we held Clara's funeral.

Funerals were the most traditional ceremonies of the Night Club, and black clothes were mandatory.

"All she needs is a sword and a few throwing stars, and she's a ninja," I heard Babe's unavoidable commentary. I happened to like Hanako's black kimono and her unusual shoes with tall, wooden soles.

Our cemetery was in a completely different place than that of the convicts. It was the largest area of the catacombs with arched ceilings, brick columns, an earthen floor, torches, and graves.

Hanako looked around, and yes, the crosses on some of the graves of the First Ones were really made of gold. Even here, there were too many graves, many more than we would like. Fresh flowers were lying on several of the latest ones.

Father Kolachek and his son were already waiting by the grave, and a wooden stand was on the side.

Clara lay in an open casket in traditional white clothes, carefully groomed with a red satin pillow on her chest beneath her crossed hands. Her face looked as though she was alive; the deformity and the hole left by the projectile had disappeared. I didn't know how Father Kolachek did it, and maybe I didn't even want to know.

Our ceremony was traditional but short. There were times when many had to be conducted in one day.

We gathered around the grave.

"The Night Club will never forget you, Clara," Father Kolachek began, and Dread placed the Book of Honor on the stand.

All of our fallen, from the very beginning, were listed there. It used to be called *The Book of Glory for the Heavenly Departed*, but the twentieth century is the century of abbreviations. When the ancestors established it, more than seven hundred years ago, they wisely selected the thickest binding that could still be handled—but even so, it was almost half full already.

"Your actions will live forever, and your soul will find everlasting peace," Dread concluded and wrote on the little line that awaited all of us one day. Then I placed her Glock on the red velvet pillow. It was shiny and loaded—our ancestors were buried with their swords too. Even though Clara wore gloves, the icy, stiff weight of her fingers petrified me. I closed the lid and snapped the latches. I saw the darkness swallow Clara up; the face so familiar disappeared in the everlasting shadow—a sight that cannot be forgotten.

As Dread and Kamile lowered her down, Babe slid her hand into mine, and I saw that even Hanako had noticed the tears running down Babe's face. Otherwise, nobody wept. Then each of us cast a lump of dirt down into the chilly night, and in silence, each one left—alone. Only a few people could handle hearing shovelfuls of heavy earth pounding on a Night Club casket. This job was another cross that Father Kolachek had to bear. His son may have been old enough for executions but not for this.

As I went up the stairs, I thought about all the nice times I had spent with Clara. The higher I climbed, the more I was confused by something that I had forgotten, something that had nothing to do with a funeral, but something important.

A mourning dinner was waiting for us at the Club. Thomas and Janie tossed in their dirt first—you have to be practical even at a funeral. A row of tall glasses was ready at the bar.

"You don't have to drink, just pretend," I whispered when Hanako looked at me with confusion.

Dread poured champagne, and without a toast, we all took a drink. "It's behind us," he said. With that, Clara was buried.

"Ufff, my shoes are too small," said Ripper and took his usual place. "I hope that you will outdo yourself, Janie. No carrots, *I hope.*"

Hanako sat down next to me.

"Don't sit so close to him, you ninja. Those pajamas of yours are big enough to hide your ass, so they must be big enough to hide a sword too. Don't you cut our little Toby."

"The ninja really use swords, but if you are from the Ippon-sugi Clan all you need are your hands … especially for fake blondes."

"Ha, ha!" Babe was obviously in a better mood—after the funeral and after her morning beating. "I am a natur—!"

Suddenly, I saw that thing I had forgotten about.

I didn't even have a chance to scream as a black lightning bolt flashed through the room. A bent fork zipped through the air and stuck in the wall …

(Shock!)

And right in front of Hanako, Cat hit the brakes. Sixteen smoking, coiled wood shavings curled off the tabletop. We all looked like a living picture. Obviously, it wasn't just me who had forgotten about Cat. Sometimes he'd be gone all night or he'd be sleeping someplace warm. He was just a thing that no one noticed anymore. A long time ago, two bricklayers broke through a wall into the Club with a pickax, and we had all forgotten how Cat killed them within five seconds.

He didn't like strangers in the Club.

"Cat, don't do it," I whispered.

Hanako looked at us with amazement.

"Kitty," she said and then made the biggest mistake of her short life—she stretched out her hand and …

I closed my eyes; this, I didn't need to see.

○ ◔ ◑ ●

When I opened them, along with everyone else, the living picture theme continued except our eyes were even wider now. Cat arched like a bow, pointed his tail at the ceiling, and *let her pet him*! On top of that, he immediately rolled over on his back, paws up in the air, and let her scratch his belly! And he was purring! Following that, I just about fell under the table. A rainbow of colors passed over his black coat, and then he turned *pink*!

"Phew!" We all exhaled.

"Oh my god, Cat are you sick?!" I said, and I was serious. "You look like a powder puff!"

"Kitty, kitty! Meow," Hanako said to him and twirled her fingers in front of his eyes. He reacted by extending his claws and scratching at the air while bearing his teeth, like a small kitten. He continued to purr and sounded like a distant tractor.

"Girls, I am stunned!" said Babe with shock.

Dread reached over and pulled the fork out of the wall. Even he had some trouble fixing what Cat had bent with one incidental strike of his paw.

"What is going on, Tobias?" Hanako lifted her eyes. "Animals like me."

"Yes, I see that. They like you, animals do, for sure," I said and thought what would happen to me if I pulled on Cat's ears and stuck my finger between his teeth.

○ ◑ ◐ ●

Some people left after they finished eating. Kamile and Babe discussed dinner in the city tomorrow. Ripper finished watching the weather forecast and mumbled that they should limit the guy on there, and Cat returned to his normal color. He turned green.

"How does he do it?" asked Hanako and blew into his fur. He was on her lap the whole time.

"Who knows?" I shrugged my shoulders. "Possibly some kind of adaptation to his surroundings ... He is really weird anyway." I didn't tell her how close she was to death right then. "He is unbelievably strong, and you must have noticed how fast." I pointed at the shavings.

"Yes, I noticed."

"He can kill a person, and he does it, very easily." Cat knew we were talking about him so he hopped on Hanako's shoulder, wrapped his tail around her neck, pressed his side against her cheek, and continued to purr.

"He can kill a person," I repeated. "He will sit on the person's shoulder, stab his claws into the guy's chin, and break his neck."

"You're such a clever kitty, kitty!"

"Meow?" said Cat. He licked Hanako's nose with his coarse tongue, and she started to giggle.

"Some things are out of this world." I slapped my hand on the table. "Cat, jump!" The animal flowed through space like a drop of green mercury. "How do you feel about invertebrates?"

"Invertebrates?" Hanako frowned. "What is that?"

"Make like a spider," I murmured and watched the Japanese girl. She turned white as a ghost, and it looked like she had a suction cup on her back—as she stopped near the ceiling.

Cat could fold his front legs, back legs, and his tail so he looked like ten-pound tarantula, especially when he added the right colors, stripes, and fake shadows. The person, for whom it was intended, the illusion was perfect.

"Don't take it personally, Hanako, but you shouldn't play with a live grenade either. Cat … the thing he just showed you is implausible—almost unbelievable. With that, I want to point out that he may not be in such a good mood tomorrow. He really does kill people… Enough." The last word was meant for the animal and he turned back into a proud, dark green cat with large paws sprawled on the table.

Hanako slid off the wall and was no longer affectionate—with either the cat or me.

I said to myself that it was high time I wrote something. I didn't feel too comfortable in my black suit, and tomorrow would be a tough day.

"Good night." I got up.

"Night."

○ ◑ ◐ ●

All clean, in my robe and warm socks, I left only a small desk lamp on in my room and hooked my laptop to the local network. Ulrich's operating system accepted my request and downloaded my latest book in progress from the X drive. Thanks to Ulrich's program, nobody could trace who requested the data and where it ended up.

The *latest book* was a pretty strong term; there were barely ten pages, and I'd already run out of stuff to write about. I took a sip of some hot tea. The way Dread and Christina saved that little girl could be useful, but I probably won't be able to work the meat mallet in there.

"Of course!" I got an idea for a four-handed murderer. He could be sitting in a bar full of black guys and tell racist jokes and that girl could be Japanese …

Someone knocked on the door. I knew who it was; she had been knocking like that since childhood.

"Am I interrupting, Tobias?"

"You're always interrupting, Sis." I turned around on my chair. Babe was also wearing a robe over her favorite baggy pajamas, her hair pulled back into a ponytail with a rubber band. The shiner from this morning's fight was already gone.

"What's going on?" I inquisitively raised my brows when she closed the door. Oddly enough, she didn't say a word.

"Why should there be anything going on?" She threw herself across my bed, her chin cupped in her hands.

"Then why are you bugging me? I'm creating."

"Uh-oh! It's Mister Writer! It must be another *Star Trek* … I'm miserable."

"Clara?" I asked even though I already knew that she handled funerals much worse than the rest of us. "I miss her too, but you know …" I didn't want to repeat the same old stuff like death is death and Clara was in a better place and the Grim Reaper dines at the same table with the Night Club. "You see everything so cynically, but you can't do it with the one thing that, in large doses, can't be seen in any other way." I shook my head because she was starting to cry. "My god, what's wrong with you? All you've done lately is bawl. Tomorrow won't be anything easy. We may have to replace you."

"Tomorrow is tomorrow." She pulled a hanky out of her robe and blew her nose. "I am sad today."

I knew what she wanted. When we were younger, we called it *making darkness*. When Kamile's mom died and Kamile turned into a parental figure, Babe lost the two most important people in her life within one week. It brought us closer together back then. Childhood in the Night Club wasn't a piece of cake anyway.

Babe couldn't stand the dark, but she couldn't fall asleep with the lights on either, so we used to sleep together. There was never anything erotic about it, but I must admit as I got older, it became more and more difficult for me. Anyway, we were siblings by upbringing only.

Clara's death must have been harder on her than I thought, because we hadn't made darkness since we were about sixteen.

But I decided to be true to the Night Club.

"Babe, we are way too old for darkness. You should grow up already ... You are a married woman." I grinned and grabbed a pillow.

"You jerk!" But this time, it didn't have the usual sting, even the pillow flew a little slower. That's when I knew it was serious.

I was almost ready to agree to play our old game when someone knocked again. This always happened; when I started to write, everyone suddenly needed to tell me something unbearably urgent.

"Yes?" I said dejectedly.

The door opened inward so you couldn't see the bed right away.

"Am I interrupting, Tobias?" asked Hanako.

Babe grinned and arranged herself on the bed like Madame de Pompadour.

"No, come on in."

Even Hanako was wearing a robe, but my robe—with orange parakeets—looked tame compared with hers. *Oh well, that's Asians for ya.*

She closed the door, and I was looking forward to her awkwardness. Besides her smile and possibly a spark in her eyes, I had yet to see real emotion from her.

"Nice evening, Babe-san." Hanako didn't seem moved at all. She walked over to the bed, took off her slippers, and sensually laid on her back so that her head ended up on Babe's stomach.

"Whaaat???"

"You Europeans take everything so seriously." Hanako sat up on the side of the bed, crossed one knee over the other, and flashed her subtle smile.

"B ... b ...b...!!!" Babe was speechless. She pointed her finger alternately at me then at the Japanese girl and acted like a very upset Madame de Pompadour. I was quietly choking with laughter.

"Tobias, you forgot to tell me about tomorrow's assignment."

"I bet! She crawls in here, right into your bed, and she says it's about work!"

"But, Babe-san, quiet please." Hanako reached back and stroked Babe's calf while looking me right in the eyes.

Babe almost fell off the bed.

"This is sexual harassment! Did you see that, Tobias?! Did you see?!"

"Why should it bother you of all people?"

"I ... I ... I am a married woman!"

I couldn't hold it in anymore, and no one could possibly believe that my cough was real.

"Don't laugh! I don't have to be here!" Babe jumped up, her eyes on fire with anger.

"Please, Babe-san, I apologize for the inappropriate joke." Hanako turned toward her and lowered her head. "Stay here, please."

Babe put her hands on her hips, but instead of another outburst, she sat down. "Fine, since you asked so nicely." She acted conciliatory.

"Tobias, will you tell me then—?" Hanako's eyes focused on my computer. "What are you writing?" she blurted out curiously, something a Japanese person would never do.

"Oh?! Our writer didn't brag to you yet? That's unbelievable!" Babe immediately joined in. "Ask him, and he will write one about a rocket or about a couple of little guys with a very long sword." By then, Hanako was on her feet, and unfortunately, the book was open to its beginning and my outside name was black on white right under the title.

"I know you!" Hanako's eyes almost popped out, and she pointed her finger at me. "You wrote *Vampires!*" In her excitement, she switched to fast-paced English.

"Ohhh! The writer's first fan ever. Maybe even the first one to read the thing all the way through. I should go ring a bell or set off a canon." Babe was paying me back for that laugh a minute ago.

"You really read it?" I felt a demented smile spread across my face. *I* certainly didn't care at all whether or not someone read my books; however, my vanity cared very much.

"Yes, I have a copy in my room. You will sign it for me? Yes?" Hanako even started to jump up and down a little—and they say the Japanese are too stoic.

"You will have to poke him first so he floats back down to us mere mortals."

"I will be happy to. Is tomorrow okay?" As a writer, I always speak with correct grammar—even in English. It was surprising, though, that I didn't even stutter given the way Hanako was looking at me—those eyes, wow those eyes!

"I am studying modern Czech literature, and I was using *Vampires* for my comparison study … just as material, initially, but then …! Not until I had finished reading it, then—"

"Don't butter him up. We won't be able to stand him!" Babe covered Hanako's mouth from behind, but Hanako, sort of incidentally, threw her back on the bed.

"Oh, excuse me! I apologize, Babe-san; that was a reflex."

"Ouch, I hit my head." Babe simply demanded constant attention, and she couldn't stand it when it was given to someone else—or something else—like my book for instance.

"Will you allow me, Babe-san?" Hanako sat down by her and began to feel the top of her head.

I was looking at the two most beautiful women that I had ever seen lounging on my bed, and I didn't know what to think.

"Is that better?" Hanako was massaging Babe's scalp, and my little sister's eyes began to glimmer suspiciously.

"Hmmm," she moaned strangely.

"Girls, girls, don't forget that you are just visiting here!"

"What's the matter, you confused?"

"I see that you are in a much better mood, Sis. Go home." I switched back to Czech.

"You are throwing me out?"

"Yup. Get out."

"And I am supposed to leave Hanako here alone?" She ran her fingers across the Japanese girl's shoulder. I knew they were kidding, but surprisingly, even Hanako had something in her eyes … something … I stuck my hands into the pockets of my robe.

"All right, I am leaving already. Make sure to discuss tomorrow's work thoroughly!"

Babe walked off like the Queen of Sheba, and just before she closed the door, she made an obscene gesture at me. I sighed with relief; there was nothing left of her sadness.

○ ☽ ◑ ●

"Is she really your sister?" Hanako sat on the edge of my bed, pulled the corners of her robe together, and again crossed her legs.

So for the next few minutes, I explained our familial relationships to her and even revealed Babe's real name.

"Poor Carolina." She looked toward the door. "Do you think ... back then ... they hurt her?"

"Given the way she relates to men? Yes."

"That's why she's more into women." She nodded her head with concern. "You are nice, the way you treat her," she added a little oddly.

I shrugged my shoulders. Hanako got up and walked to my desk.

"May I ask what you are working on?" She nonchalantly picked up a book lying on top of some notes and study materials.

I froze.

"*Velvet Pussies* ... I don't know this one." She flipped through the pages, and suddenly, she blushed and looked at me questioningly.

"I don't read that. Well, I do ... How to say this ... ? Readers always want erotic scenes from me. Not that I have problems writing any, but ... but ..." I twirled my hand around. "I'm at a loss for words, descriptive words, you understand? Erotic scenes need description for certain words ... I mean that the other way around." I began contemplating biting my tongue off.

"That's why. Did it help? *Velvet Pussies?*" She was still holding that book in her hand.

"I don't know. They use this terminology ... well, I would say more or less geological."

"Geological? Sorry, but I am not exactly sure what you mean."

"You know ... I'll read it to you." I took the book from her. "Or I'd better not."

"Please explain it to me. I really don't understand, but I am interested ... academically speaking."

She still doesn't get it, dense Japanese girl! What am I supposed to do? Damn it?!

"Okay, fine." I took a deep breath. "I was looking for words, *those* right words, but in *Velvet Pussies*, it's all about erupting volcanoes, hot lava, pouring hot lava, spraying hot lava, rods, hard rods ... Get it?"

"Lava? Rods?"

"Yeah, rods, land surveyors use them," I acted out pounding one in, "when they measure out streets." I was now talking completely off the subject and seriously considering suicide.

"I still don't understand it at all, Tobias. I am sorry," said the captivated Hanako. "Please read me something."

"Okay, you asked for it," I muttered and opened the book. "Here, for example ..." I flipped through the pages and cleared my throat. When it was necessary, we from the Night Club could do anything. "'Her bosom was heaving in front of him like a red-hot volcano, but his rod was moving closer oh so, so slowly' ... You can well image what comes next, but from a geological prospective, the end gets interesting." Again, I flipped a few pages. "... and the hot lava was flowing." I closed the book. "Clear?"

Hanako giggled quietly. "Rod! I get it!"

I took a hanky out of my pocket and wiped my forehead. *That took long enough.* "See, writers don't have an easy life." I tapped on *Velvet Pussies.* "And an orgasm is always called fireworks. What can you do? You can't write an erotic scene with vocabulary like that. I would feel like a pyromaniac."

"I get it ... Do you have another chair here, please?"

"Just the bed ... No! I didn't mean it the way you think I did." I waved my hand, my head filling with applied volcanology.

"How can you know what I am thinking?" she said and stepped so close to me that the hem of her robe tickled my knee. I smelled the faint aroma of her perfume, and Hanako smiled in a way that almost caused fireworks right then.

○ ◗ ◑ ●

"Brrr, you're as cold as ... as ..." I was going to say *ice*, but I decided we had had enough geological terminology for one day.

"Seventy-three degrees Fahrenheit ... but not everywhere." She moaned out loud and arched her back, and the bed quietly squeaked.

"True. I also don't get why people are always feeling someone in *Velvet Pussies.*" I lifted my head. "It's like '... and his hand was feeling her body,' when everyone knows ... hmmmm."

"You think too much, Tobias," Hanako said after a while, a little out of breath. "See, in Japan, we have this saying—a *traditional* saying—why should a man do something that a woman can do?"

I didn't find the answer (I wasn't even looking for one), but it turned out that Hanako really was from a very *traditional* part of the island empire.

I had never seen so many firecrackers and pyrotechnics in my life.

○ ○ ◑ ●

Hanako's chin was resting against my breastbone. She was looking into my eyes, and her breath was tickling my chest. Her look was thoughtful, and I knew she was going to ask me something.

When I was twelve, Dread pulled me aside, but he didn't tell me about the birds and bees and the seeds floating on wisps of air. Instead, he told me about post-copulation release and how at that exact moment, women can make a man reveal things that he would otherwise never tell them. *Don't ever forget that; it could cost us our lives—all our lives*, he warned me. So, I lost the first two girls on the outside because I didn't want to talk to them.

"Tell me, Tobias, what is the hardest thing about writing?"

Sure, a likely approach, I thought. *Start asking about my work*. What could be so mysterious about my writing, especially for a member of the Club? Because I didn't answer, she buried her finger in my belly button.

"Yeah, I'm thinking," I mumbled. "In general, I don't really know what the hardest part is. Personally, I have the biggest problem with names."

"With names?" she repeated like in an American screenplay. To be sure, she didn't pull her finger out of my belly button just yet.

"You are never supposed to name anyone from your immediate circle. I suspect that's why so many authors write stories from distant and exotic places. I broke this rule only once …"

"Clara in *Vampires*!"

"Ouch! Watch that finger!"

"You notice how clever I am, no?"

"True, it was Clara. Even though I gave her name to one of the good guys, she started hating me because of it anyway. You know, ever since then, Babe didn't call her anything other than *vampire*, and even the best practical prosthetic fang joke gets old."

"I get it … but *I* would like to be in a book."

"Hmmm." I pulled on her ear. "So you would like it? Maybe I will write about you someday." I shrugged my shoulders patronizingly.

"That would be very nice." She smiled and very innocently ran the tip of her tongue cross her lips. "How do you come up with these stories anyway? Do you have a plan … an outline? Do you study resources … the library or the Internet?"

"It just kind of comes to me, on its own. I sit and write," I said with uncommon honesty, but frankly, all I was thinking about was that tongue between those soft, crimson lips.

Her finger twisted in my belly button.

"Excuse me?"

"So those *Vampires* also just came to you? Just like that?" she repeated and looked at me admiringly. Nothing has a greater effect on an author than looks of admiration from beautiful women while discussing his works.

"Yes."

The hand by my belly button started to twist the little hairs on my belly. Hanako yawned, stretched, and laid her cheek on my ribs; her hair tickled my skin as I breathed. Her tummy clung to my side, and I could feel her heart beating.

"All those details about how some are affected by silver and others not so much, about crosses, but mainly their reproduction … I have read a lot of vampire books, but nobody wrote what you did … how the teeth extract the blood, which is modified in the vampire's body and then sprayed back into the victim who then turns into a new demon."

"You know, that's imagination." I gulped.

It was harder to talk now because the hand on my belly was no longer twisting my little hairs, and it wasn't even anywhere near my belly. Hanako stretched again. Her smooth thigh slipped along my leg, and her head moved a little lower.

A tongue on your belly does tickle.

And another stretch …

Like I said, a *traditional* upbringing.

○ ◑ ◐ ●

Hanako was returning from the bathroom and wasn't in any great hurry. She had evidently found something interesting on my desk.

"That's a very aromatic tea. Mango, yes?" She leaned over to smell the teapot.

"Exactly, I buy it here on Rose Street." After watching her lean over like that, I couldn't think of anything smarter to say. The lamp on the table was still on, and the yellow ray of light from beneath the lampshade illuminated her from the waist down to her knees. Usually, women look the best when they have a little something on, but Hanako didn't need to wear a thing and she knew it. The dim light bent across her hips and shone through between her long, slender thighs, and when she bent over ...

I gulped several times.

Not that I was exactly a choirboy, but women like that didn't usually notice me—let alone so passionately and only after two days of acquaintance, even though those days were full of strong emotions.

Hanako turned around, and as the golden reflections on those luscious thighs got closer, heretical thoughts dissolved one after another in my head.

○ ◑ ◐ ●

This time, her head, framed by black hair, burrowed into my shoulder and her breath was ticking my neck for a change. One of those heavenly legs lay bent across my stomach. In *Velvet Pussies*, I read that in certain situations, sparks can jump between people. It sounds stupid, doesn't it?

Slowly, I ran my fingers over her soft flawlessness, namely from the knee upward.

After a while, she began to purr.

After another minute, she asked, "Did you really come up with that all by yourself? Even the fact that a she-vampire can only spawn a he-vampire and vice versa?"

"O-oh!" I spanked her a little. "Another loony that thinks I personally know a she-vampire! If only you could've seen all those letters pleading to know where the vampires of Prague get together, where they live ...!"

She leaned over me and buried her elbow into the middle of my chest. "Confess! Where do they meet? Where do they live? I don't want to grow old either, and I want to be young and beautiful forever!"

"Why don't you let them embalm you then."

"Youuuu!!!"

○ ◐ ◑ ●

5

We were sitting in an old, brown, rusty van, parked by the curb near Walnut Street; Kamile was in the driver's seat with Hanako next to her. *Hanako ...*

I shook my head. Babe was next to me, Dread and Ripper behind me. Luckily, by morning, I was able to explain to Hanako what was going to happen ... *Hanako* ... Cat was lounging on Hanako's lap. *Honestly, he's the smartest animal I know.*

"Listen." Babe leaned over to me and sniffed the air. "You have a new aftershave? It's an Oriental scent ... Where have I smelled it before?" Kamile shot me a cheerful look from the rearview mirror.

Babe continued, "Hanako, do you know why Tobias looks like a Tamagochi today? A neglected Tamagochi? He's so pale, almost green ... Could it be an acute case of jaundice?" Babe stretched out her hands along the headrest and began massaging Hanako's neck. That neck, that skin, I could still feel it in my hands ...

"They're coming. Ten minutes," said Dread from the back. We'd been waiting there over half an hour already. When a Czech worker says he'll be there at nine, his arrival at nine thirty is more of a miracle than the rule.

"Ten minutes ..." Babe muttered and ran her thumb across Hanako's spine. I saw how Hanako moved over, lowered her head to the side, and rubbed her cheek against the back of Babe's hand!

I must have made a face because the car filled with laughter—juvenile laughter—from three people. Hanako shot me a look over her shoulder, a look that startled me. In her eyes, there was that something again ...

"Quiet," said Ripper in a serious tone, as if he were preparing to move Mount Everest. "I need to call home."

"Uh-oh," I said when I saw the small cell phone in his hand. Ripper had terrible problems, even conflicts, with modern electronics. Kamile handed me the antenna jack, and I passed it back to him. He was able to connect it to the phone, but considering how simple that was, he looked way too pleased, prematurely pleased.

"Helloooo???" he yelled into the phone—he always yelled into the phone. It was a good thing our Volkswagen was soundproof.

"You have to dial the number first, Ripper," declared Dread.

"Don't tell me what to do, okay!" Ripper snarled. "I know exactly what to do!" He started to dial, but his large fingers were way too big for the little keys.

"Why do those morons make these so tiny?! Those Japanese guys, they stand behind a stump, you can't even see them, and they think they can make these—!" The phone objected with sad beeping and squeaking.

"That phone is from Finland," said Babe.

"Japanese or Finnish, it's all the same bunch of tiny morons ... Helloooo???" he yelled, and surprisingly, the voice of his five-year-old daughter answered.

"Hi, honey, give me mommy!"

"That kid must be traumatized from all that yelling," said Kamile and started the car. In a moment, a van, very similar to ours, passed by. Kamile waited a minute and then took off after it.

I noticed that Babe had left one of her hands on the headrest, as if by accident.

○ ◑ ◐ ●

"My god, what a piece of junk!" Ripper whacked the phone over the edge of the seat.

"You can't pull out the antenna cable while you're talking." Dread pointed at the jack that Ripper had disconnected in the heat of the conversation.

"Don't tell me what to do! Do I tell you what to do?!"

Dread shrugged his shoulders. Ripper wasn't worried about what was waiting for us—mostly what was waiting for the two of them—he was really only worried about the phone. He jammed the little instrument into the breast pocket of his orange overalls. His bald head flushed red, and lightning in his eyes.

From the outside, a faint cough and the sounds of a chainsaw sneaked into the soundproof van. There were more and more of them. The workers started trimming the trees.

"Let's go," said Dread and yanked on the side door.

Dread and Ripper put on their orange helmets with plexiglas face shields and pulled on long leather gloves. From a distance, you couldn't tell they were waterproof. Then Ripper opened the tailgate, and the autumn light revealed two chainsaws—Husqvarnas with a medium-length guide bar.

This was one of the problems we had to deal with. If you wanted to start a war within the Russian mob, then you had to use its distinctive methods.

Two more chainsaws joined the other ones, and the air filled with the smell of gas and burnt oil.

I just hoped there weren't any women in this plain gray house.

I pulled a hat over my forehead and secured large yellow-tinted goggles. Babe had the same ones.

We walked toward the house quickly, but not suspiciously quickly.

"On my signal, we go in," said Ripper and kicked in the door. "Now."

I shot the first Doberman, and Cat ripped the head off the other one.

Ripper jammed the screaming chainsaw into the belly of a guy in a black suit, and the tastefully painted hallway instantly acquired an abstract motif.

Both Babe and I had silencers, so the next guy started dancing without the usual gunshots—both chainsaws acted as a very adequate sound barrier. Ripper's guy finally fell apart.

"My chain is dull or something." With his glove, he wiped the blood and bone fragments off the shield.

When the next guy saw the slaughter, he screamed something and tried to run upstairs. Dread cut him in half from behind. For an instant, I thought about the double meaning of my current thought, "… *And how do I like it? From behind!*"

I turned the corner, and two slugs that hit my vest almost knocked me down.

"Watch out! Camera!" While kneeling, I blasted apart the objective, but the rest of the security already knew about us.

Babe took out the Mongolian thug who shot me.

○ ○ ◑ ●

One minor problem was that we didn't know how many people were really there. Nifontov, the primary Czech faction of the Kaluza Group, was a large animal, so we estimated ten, maybe fifteen guys. The plan was to set the Kaluza Group against the White Brigade. Today would be assumed to be revenge for Vorozin. What we expected to follow was a sharp decline in organized crime forces in the Czech lands.

○ ○ ◑ ●

I was covering Ripper's back.

He kicked in another door, and a short shriek dissolved in the scream of the chainsaw.

Crunch! I heard behind me, more with the nape of my neck than with my ears—Babe and her kung fu. This time, it was me who took out the other guy.

"Don't fool around and shoot," I said. She was covering Dread's back so we each went a different way.

○ ◐ ◑ ●

Ripper was doing exceptionally well until the chainsaw choked up inside a huge, fat guy at the end of the hallway.

"Damn it," he said into the abrupt silence. I couldn't shoot because he was standing between me and the fatso and because I was keeping my distance—I didn't have waterproof overalls. The seriously wounded giant grabbed Ripper's head and started to twist it. Ripper was trying to start the chainsaw, but the thing was flooded.

The Russian fell to his knees and jerked Ripper along with him—still holding on to his head. The chainsaw hit the rug, and even though I was running so fast my feet were hardly touching the floor, I was afraid that the fat guy would break Ripper's neck before I got there.

While I was in midair, someone whacked the door into me with a well-calculated thump. I noticed there was a white plastic figure on it.

The Russians have no taste.

I landed on my back, the Glock flew out of my hand, and my goggles shattered all over the hallway. That was when a short black muzzle peeked out from behind the door with the figure on it. It was an Ingram thirty-five. I finished my backward roll, then did a lighting-fast roll forward and kicked the door as hard as I could with both of my feet. Now the owner of the Ingram was enjoying a free flight for a change.

I reached for the Glock, but at that instant, someone kicked me really hard in the shoulder.

"Ouch!" I said, and again, I was looking at the ceiling with the disgusting blue stars on it.

Who makes paint rollers like *this*!

A black muzzle was aiming at my face. The owner was obviously a much better pilot than me.

I was surprised he wasn't shooting though.

A bloody hand in a long leather glove flashed above my head. To my surprise, it was holding a small gray cell phone.

The Russian with the Ingram rolled his right eye at me. Instead of the left one, he had a gold-plated connector. I bet the antenna was sticking out of his ear.

"Don't hesitate to call me," said Ripper and destroyed the rest of the guy's face by hitting him with the chainsaw's motor. "These cell phones are good for something after all." He stomped on his bloody gadget and tried starting the chainsaw again. "Hey, Tobias, should I have said, *Call me tonight,* like in those late-night girly commercials?" The chainsaw coughed and finally engaged.

In the next twenty seconds or so, I returned him the favor of saving my life three times over. All the while, I was wondering why I didn't watch more TV; by all accounts, it seemed like fun.

"There are a lot of them here, huh?" Ripper revved his saw.

"All this work, how exhausting." I changed my clip, and we ran through the next room into the back part of the second level. Through the window, you could see a calm Prague street—people with shopping bags were getting some bread.

We ran into a guy with a broken neck and deep claw gouges on his chin.

That Cat, he never thinks about what he is doing.

Ripper revved the saw and covered up the tracks.

Next door was the bathroom.

Black hair above the rim of the tub, the smell of soap, and wisps of steam … my trigger finger stopped at the last moment. It was a small boy, about seven, with a showerhead in his hand.

"Say a word into that showerhead, and they'll be carrying you out of here in a baggie … Kolja," Ripper said over my shoulder. I slammed the door shut, and we looked at each other. Rather, I looked into a blood-splattered face shield.

"What's a kid doing here?"

"Don't ask me."

In the next five minutes, the house was clean—well, that depends on one's definition of *clean*. We identified Nifontov's body, and then Dread and Ripper had to finish the job; the saws screamed again.

It was sickening, but the Russians really did this, in addition to dissolving people alive in acid, slowly burning them in the fireplaces, and many other civilized pastimes. Luckily, there weren't any women here—just that kid.

"There is a kid," I told Dread.

He slowly lifted his shield, and the look in his eyes made me weak.

"How old is he?"

"About seven, he's upstairs in the bathroom."

Dread looked at his chainsaw. A foul-smelling white smoke was coming from the red-hot motor. Besides that, the whole house was smoky, and nothing smelled as repulsive as cut-up bones.

"If we leave him, they will know it wasn't the White Brigade ..."

From the outside, he was interrupted by screeching tires and a long round from a submachine gun. Time was running out.

"Cat, Babe, bathroom upstairs. Make him sleep and take him with us. Ripper, splash some blood around in there."

Dread made the right decision, as usual, because we were the good guys ... *The good guys ... that's a good line, I'll have to remember that for one of my books, the good guys.* By then, I was running out onto the front steps.

○ ○ ○ ●

Two cars were parked across the street in front of our van.

My quiet rapid fire disabled the guy with the Uzi in the blue sedan. Hanako stood up behind the other car and with both hands sprayed the back windshield with about twenty rounds. She was delightfully thorough.

I wouldn't sign a life insurance policy for any of the guys inside.

○ ○ ○ ●

The door flew open, and Babe ran through with the sleeping boy wrapped in a towel. Ripper and Dread were shoving their overalls, helmets, and saws into a giant plastic bag. Dread was wearing one of his suits under the overalls, complete with a fancy tie and silver clip.

Two more cars tore up to the house.

How come, damn it?! They couldn't be here that fast! And so many! I didn't believe in coincidences like that.

○ ○ ◑ ●

The tires of the silver Subaru were smoking, and Uzi rounds came from the passenger-side window. Bullets buzzed around my ears, but I was shooting at the other car from which they targeted the unarmed Carolina sprinting across the street with the kid.

The side window, along with half of the driver's head, fell out of the elderly BMW. The car went into a spin, jumped the curb, and ran into a cement bench. The passenger exited through the front windshield with his forehead slamming right into the cement. I ducked behind a low wall and changed my clip. Several other Uzis joined the one in the Subaru, because two more cars came. I would guess most of the soldiers the Kaluza Group had in Prague were here. Someone knew we were coming—not the exact time, but this was close enough.

Ripper threw the heavy plastic bag over his shoulder; in the other hand, he had his gun. Dread nodded to me, and I jumped up from behind the wall and covered their retreat.

At that moment, a deeper thunder joined the clamor of Uzis and rifles—a machine gun.

Babe tripped, and several puffs of dust rose from her clothes as she hit the sidewalk.

○ ○ ◑ ●

Time slowed down again.

I wasn't really covering myself; I was just methodically killing the guys in the Subaru.

○ ○ ◑ ●

Fortunately, that machine gun was one of ours. I was wondering what had happened to Hanako.

She had Ripper's Red Baron.

The Subaru exploded, and a charred hand with an Uzi landed by my feet. As long as you have something to shoot with, there is no point in picking up other people's weapons.

On the other hand, an Uzi is an Uzi.

○ ◓ ◑ ●

Right in the middle of a shower of bullets from the incoming cars, Dread lifted Babe. She still clutched the kid in her arms. Ripper was kneeling, bag in front of him, shielding them with his body. Sparks flew from the asphalt all around him, and our van was clanging and paint was peeling off.

Suddenly, a strange noise, this inhuman screaming, joined the rumbling of the guns. A hole, as if from a cannonball, appeared in the windshield of the front incoming car. I had seen this once before; it meant that Cat was really pissed.

Another car came; I couldn't keep count anymore.

This time, it came from the front side. They were shooting like in the Battle of Kursk. Our machine gun fell silent.

The good news was that Babe, Dread, and Ripper had slipped into the van, which wasn't just soundproof but also bulletproof. The soundproofing was actually merely a side benefit. Theodore had used the same material that was in our vests, except in a slightly thicker layer.

The bad news was that the path to the brown Volkswagen was still ahead of me.

○ ◓ ◑ ●

The burning Subaru covered the street with black smoke. I looked into the Uzi's magazine, but there were only three rounds left. It's always like that. I put the weapon down and pulled out my Glock. The Russians knew about me by the grass jumping up around me and little twigs flying off nearby bushes—.

"Man," I huffed, "I should have practiced my cross-country running a little more." The bushes pulled on my coat. I jumped over a fence and hauled ass straight toward the last car coming in from the back.

It spun around and drove in front of the car where Cat was sharpening his claws. I fired as I ran, but despite the white explosions of glass on the windshield, it wasn't enough. The driver hit the gas; then there was a crash, but he couldn't move the BMW that was entangled in the cement bench and blocking the street.

I jumped over the trunk of the Beamer and landed on the hood. From this close range, my shots had the desired effect. I rolled back over the roof of the Beamer just as Ripper leaped out of the van with the Red Baron.

"Where were you, man? They're trying to hurt me here!" I changed my clip and dashed toward the car where Cat was. He didn't need my help, however. Some things really are out of this world. Like how could such a cute, soft animal kill four adult men in such a short amount of time?

"You okay?!" I opened the door, and Cat jumped on my shoulder.

"Meow," he said.

The tires of the last car—the one in front of the van—screeched. Its transmission rattled, and it started to get away. The problem was that as few people as possible must see us, especially the Russians.

Ripper and I jumped into the already moving Volkswagen, and Dread slammed the door behind us.

"Go, Kamile, go, go, go!" I decided I didn't need to worry about Babe. The coat on her back was torn to shreds, but at that moment, she was trying to hit the swerving car in front of us. I think it was an unremarkable older model Ford, a Mondeo, I think. I also think that Babe was not the best candidate for shooting at moving targets.

"Hanako, shoot!" I pointed forward with my finger. Somehow, I was still tangled up with Dread, Ripper, and a complaining Cat.

We heard the roar of the van's muffled motor. We were going over ninety miles per hour, but Kamile was our best driver. Just then, Hanako blasted out the Ford's back tires.

The Mondeo started spinning and smoke came from the burning tires. Then Kamile hit the breaks. Dread and I jumped out of the moving van, and proceeded to change a standard Mondeo into a perforated one.

Mobsters have a hard life sometimes.

Dread straightened out his tie and put away his gun. We got into the van and left.

It was just another day at the Night Club.

○ ◑ ◐ ●

"There was something wrong. How come they were all swarming like that?" Ripper voiced what we were all thinking.

The van turned sharply, and Dread was thoughtfully looking at Hanako. I knew what he was thinking, but she was at the Club the whole time. If she had attempted any arbitrary unauthorized exit, Ulrich would have told us.

"And she knew about the plan only since this morning, like around six." I just mouthed the words into the roar of the motor, because I knew Dread's and my thoughts were moving along the same lines. Despite that, I had come to the realization that Dread had spent the night someplace other than I did.

Kamile followed all the traffic signs, and around the Victory Square roundabout, we hit a typical traffic jam. Our car looked like it had been in the Prague uprising, but people were likely to think that it was just another publicity stunt.

Nevertheless, we parked in the nearest garage, so the Club was still pretty far away. The youngster, wrapped in a towel, was still sleeping on the back seat.

○ ◑ ◐ ●

"Ripper, give Ulrich a call that we'll be delayed." Dread again made sure that we didn't forget anything in the garage or in the van—the cops might find it here.

"I don't have a phone," a very happy Ripper answered.

Dread glanced inquisitively out of the van.

"One of the guys back there needed an eye contact adjustment."

Kamile had already opened the manhole cover and was beginning to descend.

"You okay, Hanako?" She looked at the Japanese girl from below.

"Yes … Maybe … Not really." Hanako was pale, and her lips looked almost blue to me.

"Cat, jump." I tapped on my shoulder. The animal changed to an unhappy yellow but obediently jumped over. Hanako obviously had enough other burdens to carry around besides his ten pounds.

"Listen." Dread held her face toward a lightbulb. "Have you ever killed anyone? On purpose? So that you saw his blood?"

"Yes ... No ... Today." Hanako blinked, and tears gleamed beneath her long lashes.

"Damn it," I said. I hadn't even thought of that. We'd been carrying this kind of experience with us since our youth; plus, they'd been preparing us for this since we were very little. Hanako's training prepared her for killing too, but preparation was one thing—the dead stare of your victims was quite another, even if they were assholes.

"You can't even have a drink," said Ripper and bashfully squeezed her shoulder.

"You poor thing," said Babe and hugged her.

"Ehm, hmm," I said when it lasted a little too long. "Let's just go." Kamile looked at Babe and Hanako with sad eyes.

○ ○ ◑ ●

It was really far from Dejvice to the Club—especially underground. Luckily, Dread and Kamile had excellent orientation skills. If I had to navigate from there, some archeologists would find our dusty bones a thousand years from now.

"One of your nightmares, huh?" Ripper figured out what I was thinking and shifted the sleeping kid in his arms. So the rest of the way, everyone was, of course, making fun of me. The trip was so long that by the end, even Hanako was laughing.

○ ○ ◑ ●

6

John let us into the Club, and the expression on his face immediately erased our laughter.

"Hurry," he said.

It was the first word I had ever heard him speak.

So we hurried.

○ ◐ ◑ ●

Father Kolachek stood with his back to the bar, and Thomas paced back and forth across the rug. Judging by the light-colored path of matted-down fibers, he had been doing so for a while. He had a gray, worn face.

"Janie has disappeared," Father said.

Dread pointed his finger toward Ulrich's computer shrine.

"He already called everyone in. Tony has surgery, so she'll come a little later."

Dread nodded and turned towards us. "Get cleaned up." We all needed it. Those of us who had been in the house reeked of burnt blood, and the stench of sliced bones must have gotten into our skins.

Theodore took our weapons.

"Get me a harness for the Baron," said Ripper.

"For a machine gun?" Theodore caught my gaze.

"I guess. Yeah."

The disappearance of a any member of the Club was the most serious thing that could happen. Janie knew the consequences, so she would never run away, no matter what, even if she fell head over heels in love. Janie wouldn't run away even for that.

By then, I was running toward the stairs leading up.

"Everyone arm yourself. Theodore, activate the security system and switch on the backup generator—!" I overheard Dread giving out instructions.

First, the Russians knew we were coming. Now, Janie was missing. Something was wrong—damn wrong. I felt my stomach tighten into knots.

○ ◖ ◗ ●

My room was still filled with the faint aroma of Hanako's perfume, but last night was a thousand light years away.

I tore my clothes off, took a hot shower, and scrubbed with a brush that almost scraped my skin off. My denim mingled in with her perfume. Hopefully, that would cover up any leftover bone stench. I yanked out the clothes drawer and grabbed some loose canvas pants with side pockets, a T-shirt, and the vest. There was no time now to look for a new one. I examined at the two sheets of thin metal on my chest then took a shirt, Glock harness, and a three-quarter-length black coat from the closet. Then, I started to rub my hair with a towel, but I was already running out into the hallway—at the same time as Babe and Ripper. Dread would already be downstairs even though he was the last one to shower.

I threw my towel under the stairs.

○ ◖ ◗ ●

Weapons and ammunition were laid out on the bar. I put my Glock in the left armpit holster—a short Heckler & Koch on the other side—and magazines into special little pockets that I had sewn into all my coats.

"Tobias, come here!" Kamile called me. She stood on her tiptoes and combed my hair. "We can't have you looking like a vagabond."

Two eighteen-year-olds ran through the curtain: the Club's small fries. We waved our hellos.

"Conrad, Darius, good to see you." Dread nodded to them and turned to Kolachek. "Anything?" Kolachek shook his head. I knew that right now young Kolachek was being Ulrich's eyes, and both were looking at all the cameras that Janie could have passed by. She had left the underground through the nearest exit to get vegetables for dinner; she'd gone that way a thousand times before.

The knots in my stomach tightened.

"Ripper and Babe, retrace her steps. Kamile, Tobias, Conrad, and Darius will scour the shops and restaurants she passed. Take the other possible route, too. Christina and Hanako stay here. John, have them join your sons. Quickly, please."

Conrad was running in front of me, Kamile behind me, and that spiral staircase had never seemed so long.

○ ☽ ◑ ●

The air smelled of autumn and stank of smog. Dark gray clouds raced across the sky, and the smell of an upcoming rain hung in the air.

I took the left side of the street, and Kamile took the right. The street cars were clanging by. I kept asking the same question, "Was my sister here? She's short, blonde, a little chubby, wears a suede jacket, and carries a big yellow shopping bag. She's sick." I was getting the same answer over and over, "No. No. No."

I would cut in front of people in line, and they were irritated with me, but only until I said she was sick or until they saw my face. If I looked them in the eyes, they turned pale.

I made it all the way to the vegetable market, where she usually shopped—nothing. I glanced up and down the street. It was dark and dreary. I pulled up my lapel.

A kidnapping.

I couldn't see any of our people anymore. I had the most to cover, so it took me fifteen minutes longer. In this situation, there was nothing left to do but return to the Club.

Again, I looked around.

I noticed that next to the market was a narrow wooden door concealing an alley between the buildings—evidently a delivery entrance. The latch was locked, but the wood around the lock was freshly chipped. Even though I knew I was making a mistake, I grabbed the lever that served as the door handle.

The screws were stripped; someone had yanked them out recently.

○ ◑ ◐ ●

It was dim behind the door but not completely dark.

The dirty, leaf-covered, wire-enforced glass panes were letting in enough light. It was a gloomy, damp tunnel with a glass ceiling.

Red and green plastic crates, the rotten smell of old potatoes, a forgotten bunch of carrots … the Glock leaped into my hand … and the metallic stench of blood.

○ ◑ ◐ ●

Janie was all the way in the back behind a pile of folded, rotting boxes.

At first, I didn't understand what I was looking at, but then the sour taste of vomit rose up into my throat.

Her hair was matted with the dirt on the floor, her mouth wrapped with duct tape, her hands bound behind her back, and a look of terror in her wide-open, dead eyes.

Her blood had spilled along the grout lines of the shabby tiles.

I gulped—not even the Russians could do something like this— and at that moment, I was glad that death was behind her. I bent down and closed her eyes, but the terror and pain remained on her face—Janie, happy smiling Janie, a little chubby, a little simple, the nicest person I know … I knew.

Something rustled behind me.

I turned around, and a small gray mouse froze under my stare.

I took the top box from the pile and covered Janie. Those that found her didn't need to see the same thing I did.

I will never forget that sight.

○ ◑ ◐ ●

Some time must have passed, I didn't know how long. I noticed I was crushing a piece of carton in my hand. I knew it was a mistake to let my emotions control me, but I felt a cold, murderous fury.

The mouse fearfully squeaked and ran into the wall like it was mad.

○ ◑ ◐ ●

I tore through the catacombs. The packed dirt smacked beneath my boots, and damp air hissed in my lungs.

When I emerged from the passage, I forced myself to calm down. I carefully closed the door behind me and looked around. A lady in the nearby phone booth stared at me wide-eyed. Dropping the receiver, she left much faster than her dignity and her high heels allowed.

Yes, I needed to make a call.

Using an obsolete number that didn't require a calling card, I connected to the black phone on the bar. For the first time in my life, nobody answered.

○ ◑ ◐ ●

The closest entrance to the underground we had was in an old gray building masquerading as office space. The sign on the door in the basement read *Joza Skalova Endowment*.

Someone jumped out of the way ahead of me in the poorly lit hallway, and I heard the rattling of breaking bottles. Around here, they thought I was the most polite person in the world. I used to be anyway.

○ ◑ ◐ ●

The door from the catacombs was wide open. Old John was lying across the threshold with the flamethrower hoses tied around his neck and his bluish-black tongue on his chin.

One of his sons lay under the spiral staircase, his head turned completely around facing backwards. I checked the pulse in his wrist; he was already turning cold.

I clicked off the safety on my Heckler & Koch, and I felt my face stiffen.

○ ◑ ◐ ●

Along the spiral staircase, blood ran very neatly in a groove by the wall. Many centuries ago, our ancestors chiseled it out so they wouldn't slip with their swords on the stairs.

Roughly halfway up the stairs, I found a bloody ball. It was Kamile's head. By the looks of it, someone had ripped it off. Her shattered teeth were everywhere.

I was aware of one very important thing: there were three dead members of the Club, but not a single enemy body, not a single bullet casing, and no projectile holes in the walls.

I felt that this would soon change.

I wanted it to.

○ ◑ ◐ ●

At the top of the stairs, I found Kamile's headless torso and Dread. I recognized him only by his tie and shoes.

I felt as though it was freezing all around me. I even heard the crunching of ice.

Someone had impaled young Kolachek to the wall with a chair leg. I know it sounds impossible, but there he was, his boots disappearing in a pile of his own entrails.

But still, there was not a single slug.

I ran through the beaded curtain.

○ ◑ ◐ ●

Ulrich lay on the floor wrapped in a ball, a fist-like depression in his bald head and his broken pince-nez glued with blood to his forehead. Legs tangled up in a leather apron were jutting out of Theodore's workshop, and Christina was lying on the bar. Someone had ripped off the arm that held her weapon and slammed her face into the wood so hard that the tip of her nose was sticking out next to her ear. I knew it was her by the bandage wrapped around her head.

Ripper was hanging on a chair. Someone had lifted him high in the air and dropped him down, back first, over the back rest. His arms and legs were touching the rug. An icicle of coagulated blood ran from his nose all the way across his forehead and half his bald head.

I gulped.

"Look here! The Maestro himself! I am very glad to meet you," someone said in English.

○ ◐ ◑ ●

A man walked out of the kitchen. He was polishing an apple on the sleeve of his coat, which was buttoned up over his slight belly. He was smiling at me.

He had pink, chubby cheeks, round wire-rimmed glasses, a thin mustache, and a funny derby-style hat on his head.

He wore black gloves and medium-high leather boots. Both were bloody. Even the apple was bloody. The man exposed his white, square teeth and took a healthy bite.

"Looky, looky, it's our maestro novelist," said someone behind me, also in English.

This man was older, and taller, with a dry, wrinkled face and a hooked nose. His eyes weren't visible under the brim of his gray felt hat. He also wore a long coat and totally unsuitable tall boots with many buckles and rugged soles. They didn't go with his tie at all.

I could see his left boot especially well because he had it propped up on a chair and was polishing it with some kind of rag. No, it wasn't a rag; it was a dead Cat.

"Yes. Mr. Van Vren, our writer." The man with the apple was crunching loudly.

Something knocked the Heckler & Koch out of my hands. It landed on the table far away from me. I stared at my index finger which was still caught on the trigger.

"I apologize," said Van Vren, "a necessary security precaution," and continued to polish his boot.

I think he knocked my weapon out with Cat.

I didn't see it.

○ ◐ ◑ ●

Hanako stood by the wall in front of the bar and smiled at me sadly. I realized that I had been aware of her since I entered, but because of the layers of ice, I only noticed her just then. The men held strategic positions blocking the exits. Blood dripped from what remained of my index finger, and it felt intensely hot.

"Hanako?" I finally managed to say, but it wasn't very loud.

"'Hanako?!' Did I hear correctly?" The man in the derby hat kept on crunching his apple, and a little bit of the white pith splattered on his chin. He took a folded handkerchief out of his pocket and meticulously wiped it off and also swallowed in the meantime. "I apologize." He wiped off his mouth too. "I am just surprised that, hmm, *Hanako* didn't introduce herself by her real name … Do you usually do that, *Agony*? With your victims? Isn't that true?"

"Shut up, Wries!"

"I prefer *Mr.* Wries, a little bit of respect toward an old man." He grinned at her and began spinning the apple core by its stem, between his thumb and index finger.

I had the hollow feeling of being in a dream—that dense, pulsating, out-of-body atmosphere, the ice on top of it all, that crackling ice.

"I bet you didn't tell the maestro here a whole lot of other things about yourself." Wries had a little piece of red apple peel stuck between his front teeth.

Someone in the room moaned, and it wasn't me. It was a gruesome sound. The ice became even colder.

Hanako stood where I couldn't see the table behind her. Come to think of it, she had moved there when I ran through the beaded curtain.

"I don't mean to change the subject, Maestro, but that book of yours about those vampires is really outstanding. Mr. Van Vren and I had it translated into English."

Surprisingly, that didn't make me happy. I was thinking about what was on that table behind Hanako.

"But, Maestro, you're not listening to me." The plump fellow wagged his finger. "Don't do that to me. You won't learn the most interesting thing."

I blinked.

"See, every time something like that is published, *they* send … a kind of accountant. He finds out where such delicate details came from, underlines and adds it all up. In your case, they sent their best—Voila! Agony herself!" With a theatrical gesture, he pointed both arms toward Hanako.

Why is he calling her Agony?

"Who are *they?*" I said, and my voice sounded perfectly normal even through all that ice.

"'Who are *they?*" Wries repeated and raised his eyebrows so much that his glasses slid down to the tip of his nose. "You didn't even tell him that, Agony? You are so secretive, you didn't even show him your little teeth."

Hanako smiled at me again, but this time, her smile appeared painful.

As she stood there, I noticed that something about her seemed strange, but only then did I realize what it was; her pupils. They weren't round, but vertical, like those of a cat.

○ ◑ ◐ ●

"Huh!" I said. The voice, whom every author has somewhere inside him, noted that such a profound expression must be preserved for future generations.

"Vampires don't exist," I said.

"On the contrary!" said Wries. "Why do you think, Maestro, we have been living here in your Prague for almost two months, drinking beer, and being bored by those noble deeds that your club of do-gooders carries out?" He surveyed the dead bodies. "I mean *carried* out."

"Of course, we were waiting to see who they would send after you, you moron," said Van Vren behind my back.

"Exactly," said Wries, "but that Agony herself would come ... *They* are incredibly valuable. You wouldn't believe all the things they can be used for. All their physical attributes ... She probably didn't tell you why she's called Agony? That's a very enlightening story—"

"Shut up, Wries!"

While the plump fellow looked at Hanako, I leaned forward, took three steps, jumped, flipped over the table, and was standing next to her so that Van Vren couldn't reach me.

I landed on my feet, and the Glock found its way into my hand with a move practiced a thousand times over. Even a middle finger is good enough to squeeze a trigger.

In the fraction of a second that I was catching my balance so I could shoot as accurately as possible, I saw the thing that Hanako was hiding from me.

The handgun dropped out of my hand, and I involuntarily bent over and threw up on my shoes.

○ ◑ ◐ ●

"Excellent acrobatics," Wries clapped, "but you should not be doing them if they make you sick."

Babe's hands were nailed to the table with shiny spikes. She was lying on her back. Someone had slashed her face to the bone repeatedly with something sharp—a bloody wire was hanging over the chair.

Prior to that, they had burned out her eyes.

Her ankles were spread far apart and tied to the legs of the table.

Again, I threw up.

They did the same thing to her that they had done to Janie, except Carolina was still alive.

○ ◑ ◐ ●

This time, it was just stomach juices. The wild pattern of the rug floated before my eyes. I wiped my mouth with the back of my hand and straightened myself. Sweat ran down my forehead, but that last convulsion broke the icy shell.

"Ugly, very ugly," said Wries. "Good thing I finished eating." He dropped the apple core and began to drum his black-gloved fingers on the bar. Grooves from the wire were obviously visible in the leather of the glove.

"So, to answer your question, Maestro, Agony came to kill you. She certainly must have joined you through some heart-wrenching circumstance, isn't that true? Before she kills, she interrogates. That's why she's called Agony."

"I would never hurt you," whispered this creature, who was inadvertently the means of, but nevertheless responsible for, the death of the Night Club.

I vaguely thought about all the country cannibals that would start getting fat again.

○ ◗ ◑ ●

Babe moaned again. I tried not to look in her direction. She was not only alive, but also conscious. The bar darkened in front of me just a little.

"Toby ... kill ... kill me!" Her voice gurgled through her slashed lips and broken teeth.

The bar darkened a little more.

I am still alive. I am still the Night Club, and that creature beside me is too. My head churned with thoughts. I had to concentrate on something; otherwise, I'd go mad.

Go mad ... That was an interesting thought and would be pretty easy to do—no dramatic effects, no dramatic poses, simply, *click*, and all problems would dissolve into laughter, long, long laughter.

○ ◗ ◑ ●

One thing was certain; if they hadn't gotten Hanako yet, there must have been a good reason. What kind of reason could they have, these beings that had massacred the entire Night Club without anyone firing a single shot?

My literary theories about the physical endurance and speed of *these beings* must obviously have had some truth to them.

"I will hold them off, and you save Babe," I said in Czech.

"You can't hold them off. They are ... in your book, you called them Hunters, Hunters with a capital H. People are nothing to them."

"Save Babe. I can't do it. Carry her away from here, and save her. I will stall them somehow."

"What are you two whispering about? I am beginning to get bored, and it's rude to speak in a language that others can't understand," said Wries. He wasn't smiling anymore.

"Through the curtain and downstairs, the door to the catacombs is wide open," I said.

"You will die," said Hanako, and despite that inhuman shape of her pupils, her eyes had a strange gleam to them.

"Probably yes, but it won't be for you."

She blinked; it looked like she was hurt by that.

That made me happy.

"When I say *now.*"

"Enough," said Wries.

"Now."

○ ◔ ◑ ●

Just before I said it, I pushed off the edge of the table with all my strength and jumped on Van Vren.

Time slowed to a crawl, as usual.

Despite the fact that both Wries and Hanako turned into long, smudged, shadows, Van Vren disappeared altogether.

In midair, I slowly turned my head.

All that was left on the table where Babe lay a minute ago was a clump of bloody blonde hair, three broken teeth, nail holes, and shredded ropes. I didn't think anything of that—a person can't think that fast.

The next sight was a shadow with something else flying past it. Some super-fast translator in my head determined that the something was Cat's body, this time used as a throwing weapon.

His little body missed the shadow and splattered on the wall. What little fur was left was ignited by the force of the impact.

I wasn't even halfway through my arc.

I noticed that the rug was suddenly ripped to shreds, as if someone had run across it in long leaps with very powerful takeoffs.

In the following moment, I was looking Wries straight in the eyes.

I had just passed the halfway point of my arc.

He was aiming a black Luger at me, and it looked like he had been doing so for a while.

I always wondered what it would be like to die and if there was something after—a light at the end of a tunnel, hell, angels, Hooters' girls, and stuff like that.

A smoking bullet froze in midair right outside the muzzle of Wries's gun.

I always wondered if it was true that your whole life flashed before your eyes when you were about to die.

I must be simpler than most. All I saw before my eyes were today's events and not even all of them—just those since breakfast.

○ ◔ ◑ ●

7

Ripper, still drowsy from sleep slid into his seat, and Janie brought him breakfast: soft boiled eggs with horseradish and toast. He thanked her but was frowning heavily and kept frowning more and more.

"What the hell are we listening to?" He pointed his fork toward the radio.

"The radio," said Babe, and because Kamile wasn't paying attention, she stole her butter.

"Radio? This ... you call *this crap* radio?"

Obviously, we were approaching a favorite group discussion: what music to listen to. Thomas took his usual post by the kitchen door and rubbed his hands together with giddiness.

"Just for fun, what do you think of this, Hanako?" Ripper used an old trick of approaching a newbie in hopes that she would join his side. I poured milk over my cereal, and Janie refilled my coffee. I also wondered what Hanako's opinion was. Anyway, I felt that absolutely everything about her interested me and nothing other than Hanako was interesting. Even my cereal had the faint scent of her perfume.

"Come on, what do you think, Hanako?" Babe repeated, squinting at her. She was eating a breadstick with butter and honey. She licked the honey off her upper lip very slowly, so slowly, in fact, that young Kolachek dropped the knife on his plate.

"Sorry," he said bashfully.

"Well, it's your basic popular music," said Hanako indifferently and gracefully shrugged her shoulders.

"Music?! You call this music …?! Over there in Japan, all you have to do is blow into a bamboo pipe and everybody gets excited!" Ripper protested. "How can you say that?! *Music!*" He made a fencing motion with his fork. "This isn't music; this is … this is basically *shit, out loud!* The only people that can like this are blonde, blonde …!"

"Just finish!" said Babe threateningly.

Ripper just waved his hand, because he concluded that he would refute Hanako with *irrefutable arguments.* "Some filthy rich guy writes a few weepy ballads, then they hire five morons to wiggle on stage, who call themselves the *Happy Willies*, and they end up taking a bunch of money out of the pockets of young girls. When those morons get older or when they begin thinking of themselves as real artists, they throw them out and find new morons. They teach them the same old stuff and Happy Willies, Inc., keeps happily going! Don't you think it's awful just for that reason?"

"I think that's their business," said Hanako. "I have a feeling this music was not meant for your generation. Some people like it and they would miss it."

I wondered if she was a Buddhist, given her peacemaking tendencies.

"Fine, but do we have to listen to it during breakfast! Over and over!" Ripper returned to the heart of the problem.

Babe began singing softly along with the radio.

"Happy Willies, you say?" said Kamile, deep in thought, twisting her blonde locks around her finger. "That must have been a rough night last night, huh, Ripper? Of course, yesterday, instead of Tatyana, there was Johny Zakopcanik. No stimulation there, right?"

Janie burst out laughing.

"Hey, Ripper." Babe batted her eyes innocently. "I saw this nice vibrator in the store the other day. Would you like one for Christmas? It won't make Willy any happier, but the wife might be."

That was when even Thomas began laughing, and Father Kolachek quickly took off his glasses and started cleaning them. Even the corners of Dread's mouth twitched a little.

"Babe! We're talking about music here, not about my … my personal life!"

"Oh! So now it *is* music? You're starting to lose your focus, my dear boy." Babe puckered her lips into a heart shape.

"Don't worry, Ripper, your personal life is interesting too but probably not as much as the radio," Kamile said with a serious face. "But, you know, I always wondered how you can manage your wife as well as Tatyana. I bet you watch the forecast at home too."

"I love my wife, but I adore Tatyana ... Hanako, you really like this wailing?" He desperately moved away from this sincerity.

"Wait a minute, Ripper. Can you please explain the difference between *love* and *adore*?" Hanako asked and smiled softly.

She was probably not a Buddhist.

"Et tu, Brute! Women! They're all the same, remember that." He pointed his fork at young Kolachek, who was slowly choking on a bunt cake, so he didn't react.

"Go ahead and laugh! Just wait until you get hitched, then you'll learn the difference between love and adoration—and then there will be two of us sitting there." He nodded toward the TV and finally began to peel his cooling eggs. "So, anyway," he bravely lifted his head for the last time, "can't we listen to something else? I can't digest anything listening to this stuff." He looked at Dread with an almost pleading look.

"Allllllll riiiiiight then," Babe moaned and dropped the uneaten half of her breadstick on the plate. "You're all the same! Since he's the boss around here means he can tune to something else for your little ass!"

"I am not the boss around here, Carolina!" Dread exclaimed and got up. "But you know, democracy is democracy, and Radio One is Radio One. Listen to Radio One; it has everything," he said together with Ripper. Dread walked to the radio and switched the station.

"That Radio One of yours! All day long they hit some metal with a stick, and they call it performance, and when everyone is drooling by the evening, they put on some heavy metal for a change," Babe growled, but not even she dared to change Dread's selection.

Life is pretty good sometimes, I thought.

○ ◔ ◑ ●

8

Light reflected off the casing leaving the barrel of Wries's Luger. I must be even simpler than I thought; not even that entire last day flashed before my eyes.

As I flew through the air, the bullet burned my chin, ripped open my throat, and crushed my spine.

Big, fat drops of red blood were suddenly hanging in the air all around me.

Time resumed its normal pace.

I landed.

The lights went out.

○ ◑ ◑ ●

9

Thomas was crouching under the sink behind a drape made from embroidered canvas that was normally used to cover big black cooking pots—the ones that no one ever uses anyway. The kitchen floor felt unbearably cold on his knees, but he didn't dare to move. Through a slit in the drape, he could see Father Kolachek's hand—that enormous hand endowed with inhuman strength. Small snakes of blood—red at first, but now they were black—slithered along its broken fingers.

Thomas was holding the small boy tightly in his arms. When Ripper handed him over for safekeeping he was just waking up and rubbing his eyes with his little fists. Thomas didn't understand the boy's Russian very well so he was trying to figure out what the boy wanted to eat by showing him the kitchen. That's when those *sounds* first came from the main hall.

Even though he had no idea what was going on, his hair bristled like that of a floor brush. Then, Father Kolachek's hand flew in through the door.

Without hesitation, he grabbed the boy, and with one swift leap, he was under the sink. Since then, he had been clutching the boy to his chest while kneeling on the freezing tiles without moving a muscle.

When Babe started screaming, he covered the boy's ears with both his hands. He had nothing left to cover up his own ears so he just stared at the stainless-steel drainpipes. Even though there wasn't much light down there, he could still see the hair on his temples change to gray. He figured that being gray at thirty-nine was much too early.

Then, after what seemed like one hundred years, Babe fell silent.

Someone was talking in the main hall; it was English, but it was too muted for him to understand. He heard the voices of two men and the new one, the one that didn't eat, Hanako. From their tone, he could tell that they wanted her to do something, but she had refused.

Then he heard footsteps on the tiles of the kitchen floor. The small Russian boy saw a shadow on the drape, and his eyes opened wide, but fortunately, he didn't move.

Feet in mid-calf leather boots stepped over Kolachek's hand, and Thomas also saw the hem of his buttoned-up coat. Rusty brown footprints were left on the tiles, and Thomas heard that person dig through the basket of apples.

The footsteps grew distant, and again, there were voices, but one of them was new and Thomas recognized it.

"Tobias!"

His chest filled with hope; it really felt that way. Tobias was the most dangerous marksman of the Night Club, Mr. Death …

Then he heard a loud Czech word.

"Now!"

The air whistled, and a shot rang out—one single shot. Then something landed on the floor, and by the sharp crack of teeth, he knew it was a body.

At that moment, Thomas realized he was alone. He held the little one even tighter.

○ ◯ ◑ ●

Another hour passed before he dared to crawl from beneath the sink. He couldn't feel his legs below his knees so he just sat there helplessly on the floor and massaged his calves. The little Russian looked at Kolachek's hand and then pointed his finger at it and looked Thomas in the eyes. *"Chasee."*

"Yeah, watch," said Thomas. He got on his knees and stood up. His legs throbbed like they were about to fall off, but he knew they had to get out of there—those two English voices could return.

He picked up the boy. The kid buried his nose in Thomas's shoulder.

"What is your name anyway?"

"Menia zavud Robin."

"Can you speak Czech?"

"Niemnozhka."

"Robin? Robin? What kind of name is that for a Russian kid?" Thomas took a large meat cleaver from the butcher block. He knew it would be useless, but he felt better holding it.

○ ◑ ◐ ●

When he saw Christina's face smashed on the bar, he clenched his teeth. After the screaming he had endured, nothing could rattle him, but just in case, he didn't look too closely at Father Kolachek's shredded body. There was a strong odor of burnt hair or fur around the bar. It overpowered everything else. He stepped over Theodore, and in his workshop, he exchanged the meat cleaver for a pair of Glocks and filled his pockets with ammo.

"Bolshaia vintovka." Robin pointed at the wall filled with various weapons. Thomas knew that he could survive only if he was as inconspicuous as possible. So what was the point of dragging a machine gun along?

He returned to the kitchen and took out all the grocery money that was left in the drawer.

He walked through the bar and held the boy's head so that he wouldn't see anything. He was afraid that he would see Babe, but luckily, the girl was nowhere to be seen. There was a splatter on the wall that he didn't understand at first, but from the tip of the tail, he recognized Cat.

Another unwanted thought came to him, *So the furball was in reality just a plain old Czech tabby.*

On the floor, on his side, was Tobias.

The blood on the rug by his torn-up neck had already coagulated. Thomas couldn't not look. In the wound, he saw broken pieces of white spine. There were crimson drops splattered on Tobias's face and on his wide-open eyes.

Thomas was surprised that he wasn't throwing up.

He stepped over Tobias and Ulrich too. The beads softly rattled, and only then did Thomas realize how quiet it was in the Club. He had never heard such quiet. He walked around young Kolachek. Upstairs, he saw legs in white boots—so Tony too. She had run over from the hospital almost forgetting to take off her doctor's coat. One private clinic had just lost its best surgeon. Some time ago, the two of them became close, when Father Kolachek was sick. Back then, she lived there and took over interrogation. Kolachek was very proud of his eldest daughter.

Thomas passed Dread's body as well as headless Kamile and began descending the stairs. His legs weren't throbbing so much anymore, and he knew what he had to do.

"I am Night Club. I am Night Club," he kept repeating to himself over and over.

○ ☽ ☽ ●

At the bottom, he put the boy on the ground. "I will call you Volodya; Robin isn't a good name for a Russian kid."

"*Da*," said the boy and studied the body of one of John's sons.

"Get used to it, kid. You'll see a lot more of those—even you are now the Night Club."

"*Da*."

Thomas took the flashlights from both bodies as well as John's set of keys. There were only four of them, but they opened many locks. Then he dragged both bodies almost to the interrogation room. He called Volodya to him, and opened an inconspicuous, rusty access door set in some greenish bricks. Inside was a cobweb-covered detonator. Everyone in the Club knew how to use it.

"See." He picked up the boy. "You have to turn it to the left and push." Despite the cobwebs, Theodore had maintained the detonator in perfect working order, just like all the other weapons.

"Like this." He pushed the lever, and a dull rumble shook the hallway. The pressure wave hurt their ears. Pieces of mortar fell from the ceiling, and the compacted earth jumped beneath their feet.

"*Vot tak,*" said Volodya.

"Yeah, something like that," said Thomas. Hundreds of tons of rock fell on the spiral staircase. The explosives were calculated enough to cut the Club off completely from the underground.

Thomas knew what he had to do next. The plan arranged itself in his head like a grocery shopping list.

He removed everything from his pockets, took off his white jacket, wadded it up, and threw it on the floor—cooking would have to wait for a while. He picked up a spade and a shovel and went to dig his first two graves.

○ ◔ ◑ ●

John's body dropped down heavily. Alone, he wasn't able to lower it with the appropriate honor.

"Forgive me, John." He wiped the sweat off his forehead and went to wash up in the constantly flowing stream of water near the execution hall. He took off his T-shirt and splashed the top half of his body with water. He contemplated his cook's belly and just for practice tightened his right bicep; that looked significantly better—cooks are strong too.

"I am the Night Club," he said and wiped off with a cold cloth used for covering up corpses.

○ ◔ ◑ ●

All clean, he stood on the pedestal and opened the Book of Honor.

"Come here, Volodya," he called to the boy who was quietly playing among the graves. Then he took a moment to remember what Father Kolachek and Dread used to say. "Aha." He grabbed the edges of the podium tightly.

"The Night Club will never forget you, John the elder, nor you, John Junior. Your acts will live forever, and your souls shall find everlasting peace."

When he wrote the first line in the Book of Honor, his hand was shaking.

○ ◔ ◑ ●

117

"Listen, aren't you hungry?" he asked two hours later, after he had erected simple crosses on each grave and with that crossed off another item on his *shopping list*. Somewhere deep within his soul, he thought that he might be acting in the wrong order. First, he was taking care of the dead, and after that, those that were alive.

But a list was a list.

"*Da*," said the boy. He looked sleepy.

"We say *yes*."

"*Da* ... yes."

Within the next two weeks, they had a rhythm going. Thomas got himself a long, worn-out coat and pretended to be a homeless man. Besides, while living underground, he didn't have to try that hard. The boy proved to be very resilient and adaptable. Apparently, he was used to growing up without other kids around, and he did exactly what he was told. He didn't even seem to miss those who had taken care of him before.

The exploding staircase in the middle of Prague naturally didn't escape the attention of the authorities, and that was how the Night Club was exposed. The police spokeswoman tied it to the currently ongoing war between the different factions of the Russian-speaking mob, and she dismissed curious questions from the reporters with the usual, "No comment." The few articles that were published soon disappeared under an ever-growing number of slightly more interesting corpses with missing body parts and severed body parts whose skin was covered with Cyrillic tattoos.

Thomas was most troubled by the lack of money. He knew he'd never be able to access the Club's accounts even if he did know how to use a computer. Ulrich was a true genius, and cryptography was one of his favorite subjects.

The night was falling in the park, and it was beginning to rain.

"I am the Night Club," said Volodya in Russian.

"*Da*," replied Thomas and folded up the newspaper.

During those two weeks, Thomas called every hospital and cemetery until he found out where most of the bodies from the Club were taken.

Lately, there had been a lot of dead bodies in Prague, so the coroners put each one in a different place. The police figured that they couldn't identify them. The medical examiners determined the cause of death, photographers took pictures, and fingerprinters took fingerprints. Everything seemed clear cut, so they buried all the bodies without even performing an autopsy. Who had the time to deal with them when every day a new pile of Russians and their body parts arrived? There was also a desperate, almost critical lack of freezer space. Most citizens didn't appreciate dead bodies being stored at the slaughterhouse between the cows and pigs. Rumors began spreading throughout Prague about pork loins with Cyrillic tattoos.

Fortunately, medical examiners were not allowed to cremate unidentified bodies. What if they had to be exhumed one day?

○ ☽ ☾ ●

When Thomas was digging up his first dead body, he was scared. Throughout those two weeks, he cursed himself for acting so irrationally on *that day*—first, he should have buried his close ones and then blown up the staircase, if at all.

"What can you do?" He sighed as the shovel's shaft bowed in his hands.

The wind blew through the night cemetery, and the leaves rustled. The earth was soft, and every five minutes, Volodya came by and quietly said in Russian, "Good!" For such a small kid, he was a reliable lookout.

Thomas pulled out the casket without any problems; his belly was nearly gone, and his shoulders had grown significantly wider. He exercised up to eight hours a day, and he knew exactly what to eat so that his strength would grow minute by minute.

He dragged the casket to a light blue van and loaded it inside. He had found the car in a garage by one of the exits. The exit was pretty far from the private catacombs of the Club, but none of its hallways crossed those leading to the offices of the Joza Skalova Endowment.

He went there once, but what he saw was enough to make him want to return only one more time. All the doors were shattered and buckled as if an incredibly strong animal had run through them. Curious people from the building wandered through the catacombs, so he waited until nightfall and set off an old German anti-tank mine.

Because he had no practical experience with explosives, he had no idea what the large metal plate could do, so he collapsed the hallway ceiling over many hundreds of yards and disrupted the structural stability of that section of the catacombs. At least he was sure that no one would ever come from that way again.

○ ◗ ◑ ●

It was an unpleasant thing, opening caskets, because he didn't know who was inside and thus didn't know whose name to write into the Book of Honor. He pushed a cart with the casket all the way to the Night Club cemetery while Volodya sat on top and yelled, "Giddy up! Giddy up!"

Thomas sent the boy away to play and wrapped an aftershave-soaked bandanna around his face, but it wasn't really necessary since it was fall and the nights were below freezing.

"So, it's Darius." He nodded his head, closed the lid, and lowered the casket down as carefully as he could.

○ ◗ ◑ ●

Since Thomas always carefully covered up his tracks, no cemetery manager had any clue that bodies were disappearing. As he was dragging the third bulky casket, he decided that next time, he would only carry the bodies.

When he ran into one of the night watchmen, he happened to be carrying Kolachek Junior under his arm. The watchman took off screaming. A broad-shouldered, dirty-haired, pale man with a corpse under his left arm and a small, pale, big-eyed boy would haunt the man's dreams until the end of his life.

Thomas whistled. He knew that this kind of grim work was only preparation for an even grimmer part of his list—revenge.

"I am the Night Club," he said to himself when he felt tired. All he had to say to Volodya was, "Brush your teeth and go to sleep!" and in a minute, the boy was quietly snoozing in a cozy bed Thomas had made for him in one of the holding cells. Every night, he would hear the screams of the tortured girl. When he could no longer remember Babe's real name, that's when he really didn't like going to sleep. There were more and more lines in the Book of Honor.

Thomas also had problems—only two of them, but it was enough. First, he couldn't exhume and properly bury his own daughter. He knew she was dead, but he didn't know how she had died, and that was something he really didn't want to find out. Whenever he thought about her, he could hear Babe screaming, even during the day, and a strange dusk was about. That's when Volodya would look at him inquisitively, and that look brought Thomas back. So he didn't think about her.

The second problem was that despite all his efforts, he couldn't find Tobias—and every day, there were tens and tens more graves.

Others also noticed this growing number—particularly those who knew that Russian gangsters sometimes had gold teeth.

○ ○ ◑ ●

10

"This one has been in there for a while; it's all fucking compacted down here." A man wiped the sweat off his face and crawled out of the hole. He wore a ripped hat and had the husky voice of a heavy smoker.

It was raining, and the raindrops fell quietly on the surrounding gravestones.

"Keep digging, you asshole, keep digging." The other man tried to get out of doing the work, but the first man forced the shaft into his hand without saying a word.

"I hate this fucking work." He slid into the grave, a shallow puddle splashing under his feet. He made sure that his pocket with the stainless steel dentist pliers was securely fastened, and he rammed the spade into the muddy ground.

At least it's not damn freezing, he said to himself and kept throwing the dirt until he heard a hollow thud. The vapor rising from his rain-soaked back looked eerie, almost ghostly in the glow of the covered oil lamp.

"Done?" The first man leaned over the hole. His face illuminated by a cigarette, he handed down a bottle of rum. He looked a little cowardly, but very greedy.

"Another Russian Klondike." The one in the hole took a swig and again struck with the spade, which made the casket crunch under the thin layer of dirt. He took another drink.

"Hey, hey! Slow down." The man at the top reached for the bottle. His soaked clothes reeked like old floor rags, and the rain dripping from the brim of his hat hissed on his cigarette.

"Don't shit yourself." The one below lifted his arm with the bottle but yanked it away at the last moment, and the guy above almost fell in. Flailing his arms, he regained his balance, and along with some chunks of dirt, he sent a stream of profanity into the grave. The one below took another drink and regretted that it didn't work—all it would have taken was one swift whack with the spade and it would all be his. He felt that today he would find a real treasure down there.

"All right already." He took one more drink and handed up the nearly empty bottle. When his buddy saw the status of the rum, he followed with more insults.

By then, however, the man below was digging again, which wasn't easy. The casket had to be uncovered so that you could get at the hands too. Sometimes they left the rings that wouldn't come off. The other problem was that the casket lids were not made for walking on. The wood was cheap, so even only after a few weeks in the dirt, they rotted and cracked.

"… and if I fell through, I would wreck my shoes again." He groaned as he tossed up a square piece of earth. "Get me some light at least!"

The man above lowered the oil lamp down so that he could see half of the dirty casket. The rain washed the dirt into muddy streams.

Cheap wood had its advantages too. The lid had to be cut in half so that you could lift the side where the head and hands were—so even with a handsaw, he did it in a mere twenty strokes.

The smell of sawdust filled the air.

"I hope those bastards didn't put him in backwards again, shit." He used a sharp clawhammer to find the gap between the lid and the bottom. He recalled how last week he had opened the casket from the wrong side, and instead of gold teeth, he was looking at rotten feet with overgrown toenails.

The tip of the hammer finally found the gap. The man made sure it was in place and hit the tool with his hand. He stood up and pensively wiped his hands.

"Rum."

This time, his buddy didn't argue; he'd rather leave this part of the job to his partner. The man poured a swig of the brown liquid into his mouth and swallowed, but he didn't swallow the second one—just in case it got really bad. He'd swallow later. He poured a little bit of the rum on his hand and wiped it under his nose and chin. What if it was another crispy one, man how those guys stank!

"Okay," he gurgled with the alcohol still in his mouth, then he carefully kneeled down, grabbed the hammer, yanked on it, and the top section of the lid came up.

The man above carefully sniffed and then curiously leaned over; this time, there wasn't the usual breath of putrid stench. If it was a young chick, young and well preserved ... *Fresh,* he thought to himself. Right then he heard his buddy down below swear out loud.

"Oh, crap."

"Good evening," he heard a *second voice* say from below.

○ ◯ ◑ ●

11

I was lying on my back and looking at the ever wider eyes of a guy with a dirty face. Sparkly raindrops bounced off the top of his head which was illuminated from above by some kind of lamp. The sides of the grave were claustrophobically closing in on me.

"Huh," he managed and a drop of saliva smelling of rum landed on my cheek.

"How disgusting," I said, and my inner voice noted his reaction along with those other ones that I would someday use in some book.

The man stopped staring, reached behind him, and instantly, there was a spade edge, polished by dirt, thrusting at my neck.

"Not the neck, it's kind of sensitive." I smiled and with unbelievable ease stopped the spade—with my hand. Then all I had to do was push upward, and the man landed on the other side of the hole. I bent my knees and long, white, thin splinters broke through the thin layer of dirt.

From the edge of the grave, another man stared at me wide-eyed. He was wearing a hat, had a cigarette, and was holding an oil lamp at the end of a string. Raindrops hissed on the hot glass cover.

"Hey, look what I can do," I said, and from a prone position, without touching anything, I stood up. *Boris Karloff ... or was it Bela Lugosi?* I thought, but stopped paying attention. I lost my balance and landed face first in the muddy wall. "I'll have to practice a little." I picked the dirt out of my nose and watched the man with the spade. God only knows why he was shaking and why he stank of fresh alcoholic urine.

"Chilly, isn't it? A cold pecker really sucks." I grinned.

"Huh," he said, sounding a little repetitive.

I was wearing a white (what used to be white) hospital gown, and smooth, muddy *poops* were coming up between the toes of my bare feet. Even the one with the lamp was looking at them, but his eyes were strangely empty.

There was the sound of raindrops, and all this silence began to feel socially awkward. That was probably why the one with the spade tried it one more time.

Without any kind of effort, I broke the shaft in half. The force of the strike dislocated most of his fingers. I lightly grabbed his soaked lapels and in an elegant arc threw him out of the grave.

"Wow, I am in awesome shape." I stomped, and the lip of the casket dutifully thundered.

The guy with the lamp didn't care for my bodybuilding technique so he began to get up slowly with an apologetic smile. Suddenly, his head abruptly turned, but because the rest of his body did not follow, there was a loud crunch—his neck without a doubt. He slowly tipped forward and landed heavily by my feet. The rest of the casket broke through, and the flaming oil bit into his soaked clothes. The man was starring at his own back with a thoughtful wrinkle in his forehead and a broken cigarette between his lips as the rain crackled in the flames.

"I told you, Mr. Van Vren, that there had to be a reason why Agony didn't kill him," said Wries as he looked at me with a friendly expression from up above.

○ ◐ ◑ ●

"Oh love, what a heavenly feeling," said Van Vren and threw down the corpse reeking of rum and urine. "Don't take it personally, kid." He wiped off his bloody fingers. "But golden teeth are golden teeth." Bloody saliva was leaking out of the corpse's torn lips.

"What a pity," said Wries. "Have your own teeth made out of someone else's teeth, my kind of guy ... Would you like to crawl out of that hole, Maestro?"

"Of course, with pleasure." I smiled.

All it required was a slight push, and with a long jump, I landed above on the grass.

This time, it didn't even seem like time slowed down. The raindrops fell very slowly, or maybe I was moving very fast.

With all my strength, I landed a punch in Wries's pudgy belly.

○ ◑ ◐ ●

Before my punch landed, however, a hand in a black leather glove closed around my wrist. I noticed that it was actually the skin pulled off the hand of some black guy. The fingernail holes had been skillfully patched. At that moment, an incredible force hurled me down, and I landed on my back six inches deep in the soggy turf, but it didn't really hurt.

Unfortunately, not even this time did I manage to rise effectively. I overdid it a little with the push-off, so I went into a double summersault and landed on my stomach right in front of Van Vren.

"Nice ass, but that won't work on me," he commented on my bare behind, and his fingers wrapped around my neck as he picked me up like a rabbit.

"Don't thrash around so much, Maestro. It's useless ... Anyway, you look a tad bit underdressed." Only now did I notice that my hospital gown, considerably decayed after weeks in the casket, had completely fallen apart from all the beating. As I hung there, I managed to wrap the biggest piece around my hips.

"Shall we go?" said Wries.

"We shall," said Van Vren.

A flash of lightning rushed through my head, followed by thunder and then sudden darkness.

Strange—a thunderstorm in early winter.

○ ◑ ◐ ●

I woke up bound in a fetal position by a thick, black cable. I was locked up in some kind of a square crate which was, by the lack of sounds coming in from the outside, well insulated. So this wasn't much of a change from the past few weeks. Even though I was tied up in a position that would normally drive me crazy in a matter of ten minutes, I didn't feel all that uncomfortable.

○ ◑ ◑ ●

12

That was a horrible feeling, when I woke up back then. I remembered absolutely exactly when the bullet hit my spine and even the final distant thud with which I hit the rug.

It was inescapably, totally, and absolutely dark. I felt a very narrow and constricting space around me. I smelled raw decay, dirt, and damp wood and felt the wriggling of small slimy creatures on my chest. I couldn't move, scream, or anything. I knew that I should remain as still as possible to use very little oxygen, but because it was slowly rising, freezing water that woke me, it shouldn't have bothered me that much.

Even though the water rose slowly, it rose steadily, and those slimy creatures were looking for refuge on higher and higher places of my body. The water wasn't moving at all because the barely perceptible breathing movements of my chest weren't enough.

Then the water flowed over my eyes, and only my nose was sticking up above the water level. For the maggots, it was a kind of localized Mount Ararat. Then, even my nostrils disappeared, and after a while, the little dead bodies of the drowned animals fell down my cheeks like tears.

I think I was nearest to insanity at that point—and no wonder, I was drowning and not able to move, all while buried alive …

○ ◑ ◐ ●

First, there was a slight pressure behind my breastbone. Within a minute, that changed to a burning pain, and then my lungs were literally bursting with lack of air—just like they write about in books.

I began to pray, but that wasn't really making me feel any better. As I was thinking about it, it seemed to me that my lungs had been bursting for a suspiciously long time. As an untrained person, I should have fainted within barely three minutes.

After about ten minutes, I realized that the unbearable pain and bursting were just in my imagination; reading can sometimes be bad for you.

After about two hours, I felt just fine—that is, as far as my lungs were concerned. Otherwise, there was this turmoil of thoughts in my head, so often described in literature. Why didn't that bullet in my spine kill me? Why am I not drowning? Why …?

When the water receded after two days and my nose triumphantly rose above water, I still didn't have an answer—or to be honest, I didn't want to believe it. I wrote about it in my book, how one vampire bites a sick woman (she had AIDS) and the change heals her. I had confirmed many times, however, that books lie—mine especially. The fact that Wries and Van Vren said that Hanako was a vampire didn't mean anything either. You could tell they were psychopaths just by looking at them, and even if she was, why in the world would she bite me?! And when!?

Then I remembered that Babe told me I looked pale that last day, in the car, just before we went after the Russians. Nonsense, I shook my head—and I really did! I realized that I had really turned my head!

A small private celebration followed.

Hanako *was* with me the entire time that night, but then I would have had those two bite marks on my neck …

"Don't believe books, my boy, don't believe," said my inner voice; he was starting to become more independent lately. I told him to note this down—a dual personality, that could be useful somewhere.

○ ◑ ◐ ●

Even though many days must have passed, I didn't feel hunger or thirst. Because the only input from the outside was more and more maggots plus subtle earth tremors as more and more graves were being dug, I kept falling for long hours at a time into a very comfortable stupor.

Then one time, when I was wondering which cemetery they buried me in (I always wanted to make it all the way to Slavin[1]), I had this strange feeling in my mouth. Actually it was in my upper jaw, even more precisely, in both of my upper canines. I still couldn't move my arms, but the unusual pressure on my lower lip, halfway down my chin finally convinced me.

"So it's *tlue*," I mumbled through my new long fangs.

Not only were those my first words, but after that mumbling even I believed it. It may sound a little hokey, maybe even a little amusing, and certainly very stupid; but I became a vampire.

Period.

○ ◑ ◑ ●

Since that time, my physical prowess had improved dramatically. Before long, I began moving my arms and could finally deal with those pesky maggots. They broke their little teeth trying to gnaw on me, but that didn't stop them from trying again and again. It was a tough match, but I won.

The casket was so narrow that I could barely bend my elbow to reach my head. The first good news was that there was no trace of a bullet hole on my neck and my spine was as good as new. Granted it was a little creaky, but that could have just been the dampness. The second piece of good news was that my index finger grew back and so did the tip of my ear that had been shot off during the fight in the passageway. I took off the now-useless Band-Aid.

I was wadding up that little piece of sticky plastic between my fingers, and for the first time, I let my thoughts wander back. Again, I was walking through the massacre at the Night Club. Again, I saw Carolina and her slashed face. Again, I saw ... I gulped several times and tried to lift the casket lid.

Even though it cracked a little, the tons of earth above it didn't budge. I kept the past away and fell into a stupor.

---

[1] **Translator's note:** Slavin is a famous cemetery in Prague where many important historical figures are buried.

○ ◑ ◐ ●

When I woke up, I felt even better. I could move my legs. The creaking in my spine stopped, and all the fillings fell out of my molars. The holes from the dentist's drill disappeared. Suffocating from the accumulation of liberated fillings is not a problem if you don't need to breathe. I felt better inside too, because my future was now clear to me: One day, I would get out of here and seek revenge.

Hanako was the first on my list.

I thought about the effects of decapitation on a vampire's immortality, and I realized that I had a lot to learn. Wries and Van Vren were a close second. Then the casket began to fill with water again, so I started to stuporify again.

"That's a terrible word, *stuporify*," said my inner voice. I had come to accept his stubborn existence and started calling him My Other.

○ ◑ ◐ ●

When I woke up the next time, the water had receded already and I felt good. I stretched, and my beard brushed against the lid. My heels and head bumped into the ends of the casket.

"I hope I don't start growing; that would be trouble," I said out loud, and at that moment, I saw that I could *see*: the structure of raw wood just a few inches above my nose, the hospital gown covered with black mud designs, the pale corpses of dead maggots ... *Black* and *pale* were not very good words ... Human language didn't have names for these colors. I happily wiggled my toes.

"How can you see when there isn't any light here?" said My Other.

"A different wavelength?"

"You mean rays that can go through solid matter?"

"What else, smartass?"

"Don't call me that!"

I wondered if my pupils also narrowed into vertical lines. To be honest, that was always the thing for me—those eyes were enough of a reason to be a vampire. I imagined myself gliding through the night with my face shrouded in a cape and my frightful eyes gleaming in the darkness. Surprisingly, my fantasy didn't proceed to the point where I buried my fangs into the neck of a beautiful woman, but rather to the standard storyline where I rescued her from the claws of evildoers. Then she took me home with her—all grateful—no matter what my eyes looked like.

"Damn it." I squirmed around in the casket and tried to think about something else.

After a while, I started getting hungry. It was nothing serious, just that feeling you get three hours after a good breakfast when you start thinking about what's for lunch.

"I probably won't be able to avoid the bloodsucking, after all." I smacked my lips, and my teeth grew just a little. In my culinary vision, I saw rabbits, geese, and such—not people.

"You wrote about that in that famous book of yours. Do you think it's normal or did it affect you so much that now you think it's normal?" asked My Other.

"How am I supposed to know that? And don't be looking at what I'm thinking!"

"Sheesh, geese and rabbits—how boring. That thing with rescuing a damsel in distress was much more interesting."

○ ◌ ◐ ●

As time passed by, the hunger didn't really become unbearable. I wasn't thirsty at all. I did get bonier though, but lying like this without expending any energy, I wouldn't need to eat for quite some time. I'd have to ask someone when I got out of here—or rather *if* I got out of here! I was really beginning not to like it in this casket, and I was thankful that my new metabolic system was without waste. I imagined all the things that would be swimming at the top of the water when it rose again, and My Other said, "Yuck!"

"Exactly," I agreed with him and again tried to lift the lid, but the water-logged earth resisted even my ever-increasing strength. It was a little frustrating to say the least.

○ ◌ ◐ ●

After several more days of stupor, I discovered the most interesting thing about myself. I was just thinking how I could arrange it so I didn't have to constantly lie in this damn muck, whose only novelty was the splinters constantly trying to jam themselves into my butt.

Then I suddenly realized that I had just hit the lid with my nose—without ever lifting my head. With panic, I felt below me, and there really was a gap between me and the splinters.

"You're levitating!" yelled My Other.

That startled me so much that I fell back down.

"Okay, damn it! Don't yell in here!" I screamed at him.

"You can't levitate! That ... that's impossible!"

"I know that." Again, I levitated a little, but after three seconds, I realized that it wasn't easy at all and I fell back down in exhaustion.

"I said you couldn't levitate," said My Other maliciously.

What could I say to that?

As I tried to come up with a good comeback, the earth around me shuddered with faint but regular tremors.

After nearly an hour (right after the teeth of the grave robber's saw came dangerously close to my waist), half of the lid above me lifted. Even though it was night, I was surprised by the amount of light there was. I smelled rum, then I smiled, and the head above me said, "Oh, crap."

13

Someone was carrying my crate, because it swung back and forth and then it landed hard on top of something wooden, judging by the sound. The crate must have had those arrows on it that said which side was up, because they would always—with persistent consistency—put me head down.

First, I was in a car, then in an airplane (for a good long time), and now on that wooden thing. The crate swung again, and I recognized the wooden thing as a ship. My suspicion was immediately confirmed by the roar of a strong motor and the increasingly faster impact of the waves.

I clenched my teeth and shifted down a little so I was more on my back and not so much on my head. There was a faint shaft of sunlight entering the crate from somewhere. It was so comfortably yellow in there. The box smelled of tea, which I realized only after many hours when I remembered to breathe. Except for the constant standing on my head, this was a considerable improvement over the casket. Most importantly, it was dry. I felt the thin shell of cemetery mud on me crack with the rhythm of the waves.

○ ○ ◑ ●

After an hour, it was clear that we were on the ocean. There weren't too many lakes that big, and I thought that I smelled salt and iodine in the tea. After another four hours, the crooning of the motor stopped, the ship cut a sharp turn (I noticed that from my new position—on my ear), and the wave impacts softened. The motor started to putter, and then the ship hit something. Along the way, the seams of my crate loosened a little so the soundproofing wasn't what it used to be. I heard these strange, high, melodic voices.

"*Where have I—?*" thought My Other.

"Chinese?" I said.

The crate began shaking. It tilted to one side and then to the other. Then, with a swinging motion, it lifted. Several loud shouts followed and then a thud as if it had landed on a barrel. Several metal-on-metal noises followed, and the rusty teeth of a crowbar entered between the planks. They yanked out the nails which squealed, and the lid popped off.

"So what did you bring me, gentlemen?" said a woman's raspy voice in heavily accented English.

"Madam Dao, how glad I am to see you again," I heard Wries say.

"Madam Dao," murmured Van Vren very respectfully.

I still couldn't see anything, except for a square of beautiful dark blue evening sky, the mast tip with an angled yard, the soft scalloping pink clouds dissolving … Damn, I never thought of myself as such a romantic, but after all those weeks in the casket …

I heard the ocean slap against the sides of the ship. I smelled varnish and green bananas, felt a rocking as the waves stretched under the ship's keel, and noticed the calming creak of the wooden frame and roping.

"Vacation!" I whispered. My Other disappeared somewhere before all that blue and the clouds.

"So?" said the raspy voice, the one that my kidnappers called Madam Dao. Someone lifted my crate, and I rolled out onto the deck with the appropriate thud and a pile of dry mud.

It was late afternoon, just before nightfall. The large crimson sun hung above the ocean, and its golden rays died along the ridges of the waves that lazily rolled along after their shadows … I shook my head.

"What is this?" asked Madam Dao. "Not a Negro, I hope?!"

Even though she stood with her back against the sun, it wasn't a problem for my eyes—I could see her perfectly. She was a heavy-set Chinese woman adorned with lots of gold, who wore a loose dress of an embroidered fabric—the kind that they make drapes out of in luxurious bordellos. On her bare feet, she had green flip-flops. I bet they were made in the Czech Republic.

"They sent this cripple to take care of that writer?" She snapped her fingers, and a muscular guy with very narrow eyes and a black ponytail placed a very long brown cigarette between them. He struck a lighter, and a sweet smoke tickled my nostrils. I realized that not only my eyesight, but all my other senses had become much sharper too.

"No, Madam Dao, it is somewhat more complicated than that," said Wries, and he looked very out of place in his buttoned-up coat, derby hat, and black gloves. The evening breeze caressed my cheeks, and if I had been Oscar Wilde, I might have started composing a poem or something. The sun and the horizon had something monumental about them, especially when you saw them after attending your own funeral. I couldn't get enough of it.

"I would like to hear it." Another puff of aromatic smoke took off for the horizon.

"This *is* the writer." Wries pointed at me. "He looks somewhat neglected because he was buried for over a month, but they sent Agony herself after him, so—"

"Agony!" Several surprised exhalations followed. Madam Dao raised her heavily made-up eyebrows and lifted her cigarette with interest.

"Yes, Agony. We almost had her, but—"

"Don't exaggerate, Mr. Wries," Madam Dao interrupted him, and a soft giggle sounded somewhere behind my back.

In vain, I tried to figure out who these people were that they could make fun of Wries.

"Really, Madam Dao, we almost had her," said Wries in a tone that no one dared to laugh at. I noticed that despite the significant back-and-forth movement of the deck, no one had the slightest problem with their balance—not even Madam Dao with her three hundred pounds of live weight.

"Agony managed to escape, but honestly, we were very, very close."

"So you captured this stinker instead?"

"Maybe you underestimate him, Madam Dao. He is the one who wrote *that book*, but more importantly, he is Agony's progeny."

"Really?!" Madam Dao's expression suddenly became very animated. "That sounds more than interesting, Mr. Wries. What have you got to say, stinky?"

"Do you mean me?" I asked.

"Maestro, I suggest that you answer Madam Dao's questions as accurately, as quickly, and most importantly, as politely as possible." Wries smiled at me. "Even though now you must be feeling the invulnerability and strength of your new body, resisting Madam Dao can be very painful even for you. Very painful." His round spectacles glistened with a crimson glare in the setting sun.

I had a feeling he wasn't lying.

"I am not sure, Madam Dao," I said, "but it is very possible."

"Very possible ..." She narrowed her eyes, threw away her cigarette butt, and snapped her fingers. There was the patter of bare feet, and in an instant, a man in yellow, frequently washed garments appeared on the deck. In his hands, he carried a large case made from light-colored wood. Madam Dao pointed in my direction with her fresh cigarette.

"Nothing personal, just a few tests."

The man in yellow put the case on the deck and opened it. He was Asian and had long, sparse sideburns and a ponytail, and even though he looked completely different, he reminded me of Father Kolachek.

I felt uneasy, and the evening didn't seem so romantic anymore. Where was my lovely casket?

"Just lie there, Maestro," said Wries, and Van Vren stepped on me just to make sure.

Mr. Yellow took a small wooden cross out of the case, and I felt a slight twitch in the back of my neck, but even after he placed it by my foot, nothing happened.

"What do you feel?" asked the man.

"It tickles," I said. I heard the waves. The man pulled out a small bottle made of thick glass and splashed me with the stale water. Again, there was that twitch, maybe a little stronger though.

"It could be, Madam Dao, yes indeed ... he is insensitive to Christian symbols, and Agony is Japanese, so her line must also be insen—"

"Do you think I don't know that, Li Pao?!"

"Forgive me, Madam." Li Pao bowed before her raspy voice all the way to the wooden planks. How is it that all some people have to do is speak and others bow?

Li Pao turned back toward me and began reciting. I looked at him with some confusion, but when he started with the Lord's Prayer (in Czech), I realized they were prayers from different religions. The Lord's Prayer made me a bit queasy, but I didn't let them see that. In the end, he took out a Buddhist prayer wheel and spun it in front of my eyes. It was creaky.

"Unprecedented," said Madam Dao and pointed her cigarette at Wries. "Mr. Wries, I am starting to be satisfied." Wries and Van Vren took a bow. My chest slightly groaned under Van Vren's boot.

Li Pao, on the other hand, was frowning—like any expert, who wasn't doing well. He began pulling various herbs, stones, and smooth cylinders of wood and metal out of the case. He would place them by my foot. He had a stopwatch in his left hand and hope in his eyes, which then faded to disappointment.

Some things were slightly itchy, some things a little more, and some things were cold. I recognized garlic by its smell, but mostly, they didn't do anything to me. Li Pao just shook his head.

"Unbelievable, I have never tested anyone from Agony's line, but according to all this—"

"It is so," finished Madam Dao. "Real, Japanese, and possibly a transfer from Agony herself—to a white guy even. Truly unprecedented. Gentlemen," she turned to Van Vren and Wries, "I will be expecting you in my cabin for a celebratory dinner," and sublimely, she lowered her head.

Li Pao enviously flashed his eyes at them and again reached into the case. I was starting to feel like a star. *I am an aristocrat, a superstar among vampires, King Leopardi.* Li Pao again pressed a cylinder against my heel, like so many others before that—

"Argggggh!!!" I screamed, and Van Vren's foot forcefully squashed me. Li Pao pulled his hand away and clicked the stopwatch. I saw that even through the white smoke rising from the sole of my foot.

"Silver always has an effect on you guys," he hissed quietly, glanced at the stopwatch, and continued in a normal voice. "Flesh renewal is proceeding slightly faster than normal; furthermore, if we take into account that he is not fully developed yet ... but we have a whip even for him." As if by accident, he again ran the silver cylinder across my foot. This time, I didn't scream.

139

"Take him away." Madam Dao didn't even look at me, and despite her size, she turned unbelievably easily and floated away into the sunset with her gold jingling.

Wries picked me up. (He was really starting to annoy me with the way he picked me up by the neck like a kitten.) There was a metal clang behind me, and I proceeded to rapidly descend below decks. It didn't seem very tactical to reveal my levitating skills, so I didn't try to slow down. That was why I smashed a nice, even half-moon shape into the wooden planks on the lower deck.

○ ◔ ◑ ●

"What's this?!" said someone behind me—actually, said a *woman* behind me. She had a deeper, somewhat caressing, I would say almost erotic voice. Even though, after a month in a casket … I spit out sawdust and checked my teeth with my tongue—they were a little loose.

"Miss Denise, I'm glad to see you again. Say hello to your new colleague. He is a bit misbehaved, but I think you can handle him."

"Good evening, Mr. Wries." Her voice sounded respectful.

"You as well." Judging by the sound of his steps, I guessed Wries had left.

I turned on my back, and above me, I saw a grate (five by eight yards) and above that an ever-darkening evening sky. There was a hatch in the grate—already closed—and all around, the heads of the Chinese crew were leaning over. I turned to my side and finally saw my companion— first slim tan ankles, then perfect tan calves, soft tan thighs …

"What do you think you're looking at?!" She pulled down her short, white T-shirt. Her hips were slightly wider than Hanako's or Babe's, but perfectly shapely, like the rest of her body. Plus, as she pulled down her T-shirt, her bosom—

"What are you looking at *now*?! Don't you know you're supposed to look me in the eyes?"

"Yes." I was looking at her T-shirt. "But it's pretty hard to look you in the eyes from down here. Could you untie me? Please?" I said and finally looked at her face. As a whole, she was even prettier. She was about twenty-five and had large gray-blue eyes, well-defined eyebrows, a proud nose, sensuous full lips, high cheekbones, black hair pulled back into a ponytail … I gulped.

Her pupils were shaped like vertical lines.

That's when I discovered one of the cardinal rules: If you ever meet a truly gorgeous, twenty-five-year-old woman, she's a vampire. If she's not, you find out she is anyway.

"Well, well." She saw my eyes too. "How did they get you?" Her voice softened a little, but not much.

"Easily."

She leaned over me and scowled with disgust. "You stink!"

Again, a sentence you couldn't really comment on.

"Hey, can you wash him or something? He smells like they pulled him out of a coffin!"

Laughter came from above. "You can—!"

Smack!

The faces above the grate disappeared as if blown away.

"I apologize for the disrespect, Miss Denise," said a melodic male voice. "May I look, Miss Denise?"

"Certainly, Mr. Ho."

"Mr. Ho?" I said with disbelief. "Half the people in Hong Kong movies have that same name."

"Greetings, Mr. Tobias." The shiny, bald head of a fifty-year-old Chinaman leaned over the grate.

"Howdy," I answered.

"Yes, Mr. Wries was right. It will be necessary to work on his manners." The head smiled. "I will lower a fire hose down to you, Miss Denise. Will that be suitable?"

Miss Denise gave me this look, and something akin to a smile flashed across those gorgeous lips of hers.

"Yes, Mr. Ho, I think that will do just fine. And, Mr. Ho?"

"Yes, Miss Denise?"

"Don't be stingy with the water pressure. I think the dirt has really set in."

I began to notice that if there was anything truly international, it was *lighthearted* lines from detergent commercials.

"They even let you watch TV? You must kiss ass nicely, my dear." I couldn't help myself even though I knew that with time, prisoners and their captors can develop a close relationship. For me, as a member of the Night Club, such behavior was absolutely unacceptable.

"Miss Denise." The grating clanged as Mr. Ho inserted the nozzle of a high-pressure hose.

It was a very thick high-pressure hose.

"I appreciate your interest in my hygiene, but don't you want to untie me first?"

"No."

Denise made sure the nozzle was closed and positioned herself so that the water wouldn't splash the hammock hanging in one of the corners.

"Go ahead, Mr. Ho!" she yelled, and the curious Chinese heads again appeared above the grate.

Somewhere, a water pump began humming, and the hose fabric snapped noisily as the water made its way through. I knew that a thing like that could easily whip two grown men around, but Denise didn't even move a muscle.

She smiled and turned the nozzle lever.

"No—!" I managed to say before the pressured air crackled, and instantly, I was pierced by a white thundering flood.

I don't know how long it lasted, but I do remember that the water was cold and salty, and at one point, someone said, "Behind the ears too, nice ..."

The surge easily swept me wherever Denise wanted, and when she tried a little, it lifted me up almost to the grate where it began spinning me. When she stopped trying, I fell down on the wet floorboards. Again and again, this happened.

I was more than ten feet in the air.

Then it was finally over.

"I think that will be enough, Mr. Ho," said Denise. I must have given her an unfriendly look, because this time, the water hit me right between the eyes.

The heads above the grating whistled with delight.

"I apologize." Denise smiled.

"Don't worry about it." I also smiled and put on a pleasant expression. "Anyway, thanks for the shower." Her hand withdrew from the lever.

"Yes, I also think it is sufficient," said Mr. Ho from above. I felt that I was beginning to slowly but honestly hate both of them. The pump fell silent. Denise released the pressure from the hose and handed it up. Even though the below decks area was quite large and even though Denise was being careful, her T-shirt still got completely soaked. The way she extended up on her tiptoes with her hands above her head made me realize that one could find something good in every situation.

I used my forehead to push off the wet planks and sit up precariously. At least this was a more dignified position than slithering around. In the rhythmic rocking of the ship, the last little wave rolled over the floorboards, gurgled in the drainage holes, and disappeared.

"Can you finally untie me? Please?" I spat. Even my sense of taste was keener, and the salt water was nothing pleasant.

"We'll wait until things dry out around here." She tapped on my shoulder and as if by accident pushed me over again.

"You'll pay for this," I gurgled.

"Did you say something?"

"How could I?"

○ ○ ◐ ●

Within fifteen minutes, night fell and the deck dried off. The hot tropical air acted like a hairdryer, and surprisingly, even I felt pretty good. Sometimes a little bit of water doesn't hurt, and even though a cage is a cage, when compared with a coffin, it's the whole world. The whine of Chinese music and rattling of dominos came from within the ship, and the aroma of food with all kinds of Oriental spices filled the air. Even though I used to love Chinese food to death, it didn't really appeal to me now despite the fact that I was pretty hungry.

"Do you need anything else, Miss Denise?"

"No, Mr. Ho, thank you, and I bid you a pleasant night."

After he disappeared, I said, "It's strange that you get along with them so well. They killed everyone close to me, tortured my sister to death, kidnapped me ..." I allowed it to set in.

"Is that supposed to be an accusation?" She stood where I couldn't see her.

"Not at all! A compliment!"

"You don't know anything; that's your only excuse." She sighed heavily. "Let's look at those knots of yours."

Without any problems, she picked me up and carried me to the middle of the cage.

"Where does it start?"

"Do you think I tied it myself?"

"Then I'll just have to find out." She started rolling me around until I didn't know which way was up, down, or middle.

"Here." She found the end by my ankles. I was wrapped up in that cable like a larva in a cocoon; the only things visible were my head and my feet.

After she uncoiled that black snake to about my mid-thigh, I realized with horror that even through all the knots, the surge from the hose had completely destroyed the last remains of my hospital gown.

"Careful! I will need something to—!" Before I could finish, there was nothing left to talk about. I jumped to my unbound feet, but not even my body could handle such a long period of immobility so I just fell over to the other side. Miss Denise had to—naturally—take a break right about then.

Finally, she unwrapped me completely.

I tried to distract attention from my embarrassing situation by stating that, "If we tie that cable around the grate, pretty soon, I will have enough strength to rip it out ... that is, if you have a spare pair of pants lying around."

"You couldn't rip it out, and I don't."

"You try it then—"

"You don't think they're stupid enough to make a cage that we could destroy?" She tapped on my forehead, and the motion was so quick I hardly noticed it. "Let's just go to sleep. You'll sleep in that corner over there." She pointed to a completely empty corner opposite the one with her hammock.

"I don't need to sleep," I said provocatively.

"I don't either, but I recommend that you learn to. Otherwise, it gets pretty dull around here." For a moment, she waited for the predictable tasteless comment that it didn't need to be dull—especially at night.

But I wasn't a vulgar dirtbag.

○ ◐ ◑ ●

So I tried falling asleep, but even that was problematic. I had to lie on my stomach and even though there weren't too many splinters in the floor, there were a few. Moreover, it's not very easy to fall asleep with a constant wind blowing across your naked back, particularly after so many calm days in the cemetery. Simply put, life is more complicated when you have a naked rump.

Denise wasn't sleeping either. Whenever I stole a glance in her direction, she opened her eyes. They shone blue in the black night. I was really jealous of her hammock and sleeping bag.

○ ◑ ◐ ●

The next morning, Mr. Ho gave me a pair of short linen pants, a large T-shirt, and flip-flops. It was the biggest treasure that I'd ever received, mainly because the sun had just come up and Denise had all kinds of stuff to do and just happened to always be around me. Spinning around on my belly or standing around like a soccer player in a penalty kick lineup was no picnic.

I slid the flip-flop straps between my toes, ran a hand through my beard, and finally felt like a person again—I could finally sit down normally after more than a month.

"So?" I said.

"So what?" said Denise and continued to comb her hair in front of a mirror glued above a small sink.

"Tell me who, what, why, and how—everything."

"Why? What you need to know you will experience, and what you don't need to know, I am not allowed to tell you, nor do I want to … Do you have any kind of training?"

"You mean, if I am a hockey player for example?"

"Do you see any hockey sticks around here?"

"That's the thing, I don't."

She put her comb down on the sink and walked up so close to me that she almost stepped on my outstretched legs. "We will have to work together so don't be rude … to me or anyone else."

"That sounded threatening." I smirked, and instantly, I was flying through the air. I bounced off the wall, and even though I usually didn't hit girls, I couldn't help it. While still in midair, I kicked her in the chin.

I mean, I tried to.

145

She ducked and jabbed me in the stomach with her elbow. Even though I didn't have to breathe, I exhaled completely. I landed in a crouch and with a swift whack, kicked her shins out from under her ... but even her shins were no longer where they were supposed to be.

"Ouch," I said with my cheek on the boards, my arm twisted up to my neck, and her knee jammed in my spine. My other cheek was being tickled by the hair that fell over her shoulder. It had a beautiful jasmine scent.

"What do you think of him, Miss Denise?" I heard Wries's voice above the grate.

"He's a bonehead—a slow, stupid, rude, arrogant bonehead." With every word, she twisted my arm just a little more. I would have rather let her break it than say ouch again. I learned that when I was young from my fights with Babe.

"Don't underestimate him, Miss Denise. He is a rare case—apparently a progeny of Agony herself."

Her grip loosened. "Excuse me?!"

I rolled over on my back.

"Indeed." Wries didn't have his coat. Instead, he wore a loose white shirt and a funny-looking short, wide tie. Old-fashioned suspenders were holding his pants up high on his stomach, and his hat was pushed over to the side.

"For hundreds of years now, Agony hasn't ..." She looked at me deep in thought.

"Will you train him, Miss Denise? At least for now?" Wries began cleaning his glasses with a handkerchief.

"Why not? At least I won't be bored." Denise pushed on my chest with her hands and stood up.

"Excellent, excellent." Wries waved his handkerchief and disappeared.

"I don't need any training," I said and also got up.

The reason that everyone is beating me up is because I just haven't learned to coordinate my body yet (I think). My reflexes were set to human abilities, and it was a big change to suddenly consider five-yard-long leaps to be normal. I was not the best martial artist in the world, but my combat with Babe did teach me a thing or two.

"Can you at least wield a sword?"

"Sword? Why a sword in God's name? Guns." I mimicked shooting with both hands.

"Agony didn't teach you that?" She looked at me with surprise. "It's our tradition."

"She didn't teach me a thing, and since you brought it up, can we get something to eat?"

"When did you eat last?"

"More than a month ago—oatmeal for breakfast."

Her eyes widened, and she looked really surprised. As she shook her head, her ponytail fell over on her back again.

"Are you trying to say that you never drank ... you know ..." She made a circular motion with her hand.

"You mean blood?"

"Yes."

"No. I was buried for a month, then Wries and Van Vren shoved me into a crate, and to top off this series of lovely experiences, you gave me a shower yesterday. That's my life, in a nutshell."

"I had no idea ..." She reached her hand out to me—so gently.

"None of that sort of thing." I moved back. "I am not going to exchange compliments with these *people*, nor with anyone who does that with them."

"Yes, you will." Again, she took a step toward me. "You don't know anything; you're just a baby, a newborn. You can't even feed yourself, and you are alive only because they want you to be. You don't even know what they are capable of, and you are wrecking the morale around here!" Slowly, she pushed me all the way to the wall; her eyes were on fire.

"See, Miss Denise, you don't know everything either." I didn't smile, and she stepped back—maybe she saw a little bit of the Night Club in my eyes. She looked up quickly.

"Mr. Ho, could you get us something to eat, please?"

"Of course, Miss Denise, but unfortunately, it will take a while." The small Chinaman was apparently always within earshot.

"No problem ... In the meantime, can you give us two swords? I think the bamboo kind will be enough."

○ ◯ ◑ ●

By the time Mr. Ho brought food, I had been hit on the shoulders and jabbed in the ribs more times than ever before.

A bamboo sword is an awful and unwieldy piece of crap.

○ ◐ ◑ ●

The hatch in the grate opened up, and Mr. Ho lowered down a big basket covered with an embroidered tablecloth. Denise was holding my wrist, and she twisted it so that I couldn't move; it wouldn't have been a problem for me to jump out, and she knew it.

"Why did you do that?" I looked her in the eyes from up close when she let me go, but by then, the opening was shut again.

"It's for your own good. Do you think you could beat Wries on this ship? All of a sudden, just like that? And Mr. Ho? And everyone else? Or that you could swim away?"

"Why not at least try it?"

"Arrogant bonehead—it's no use." She shrugged her shoulders and went to get the basket.

She laid the cloth right on the boards and set the basket on the edge. When she sat down into a cross-legged position, I looked away on purpose even though I noticed from the corner of my eye that she lifted her T-shirt just enough for me to see her white panties.

"So, how do we do this?" I sat across from her, after she pulled her T-shirt back down, and looked into the basket. "Fish? Raw fish??! *Live*, raw fish?!"

"Look here." She took out a cutting board, a glass with a thick bottom, a cleaver, and a large rough glove. She put the glove on her left hand, grabbed one of the wriggling green fish, and with a short *whap* chopped off its head. Skillfully, she caught the blood in the glass and stirred it to prevent it from congealing. She returned the headless fish to the basket, whacked another one, and then her goblet was full.

"Here you go." She handed me the cleaver and the glove and moved away with her drink in hand.

Despite the fact that this seemed somewhat disgusting at first, the smell of fish blood evoked in me the same feelings as the aroma of Chinese food did before. Only then did I realize how hungry I really was.

After a short while, I figured out that Denise didn't move because she wanted to show me how long her tan legs were. I could handle chopping off the head, even though I didn't like it. (Thomas or Janie always did the fish killing, and as far as I could remember, not even Father Kolachek could handle it.) Catching the blood in a glass, however, proved to be a virtually impossible problem. The Chinamen above were betting how much I was going to spill, and Denise smiled cunningly.

"Oh, the man doesn't need any training, hmmm?"

I should have just humbly asked her to do it for me, but I would have rather not eaten for another month than do that. Denise took a drink, narrowed her eyes with satisfaction, lifted a napkin out of the basket, and dabbed her lips.

I killed a second fish and nonchalantly mentioned, "Mine are kind of bloodless." I manipulated the wriggling little body for a little bit and then threw it back in the basket. I had barely a couple of inches of blood in the glass, but I looked like Jack the Ripper after an especially busy night.

"Cheers." I smiled at Wries, who was watching me from above, and I downed the whole thing. Not only did I like it, but I felt this warmth in my veins that was followed by the feeling that I could—and I really did—fly a little, but luckily no one noticed.

"Are you still hungry?"

"I've had enough." I put the glass on the floor. The last little bit of blood was sloshing with the rhythm of the waves. My god, how I would have loved to finish it off!

"But you didn't eat for an entire month—"

"*Enough*, I said." I cut her off so she would understand that I was not going to talk to people who were friendly with the crew—especially not to some vampire chick.

Looking offended, she put everything away in the basket. Mr. Ho pulled it up and lowered down a hose with a shower head on the end. Ah, that was why there was a sliding screen in one of the corners. He even gave me some clean clothes.

"Would you have a toothbrush, please?"

"Oh! I am sorry, Mr. Tobias. How could I forget! I will bring you a whole set." He slapped his forehead, and in a minute, he threw down a canvas bag. It was the same kind Denise had by the head of her hammock. There was a hammock in the bag along with a sleeping bag and a rubber belt with a knife pouch—without a knife of course.

"That's for your leg," said Denise when she saw my confusion as I stared at the size of the *belt*. I didn't answer. In the pouch was a long, hollow needle, whose purpose I really didn't get, but this time, Denise didn't say anything. Soap, toothpaste, toothbrush, a shaving kit ...

I cleaned up (a shave really made the difference). I showered (unfortunately, again only salt water), and then I hung my hammock in the corner and lay down in it. It didn't spin away under me thanks to my levitating abilities. Getting into a hammock was not as easy as it looked, especially on a rolling ship.

"Should we practice?" Denise couldn't stay quiet for more than thirty minutes.

"Why not?" I slipped onto the deck. *The more I learn, the easier I can escape.*

○ ◔ ◑ ●

In the next five days, we destroyed all the bamboo swords on the ship—after all, they weren't made for beings with our strength.

Already on the second day, I noticed my coordination improving, but I didn't make it obvious and I blocked only the most painful blows. Denise's favorite places to aim were my fingers holding the hilt, my head, my stomach, and my crotch.

"That's how it is in a real fight," she would say. "Forget the movies where knights help each other to their feet and hand one another fallen swords."

Because we were constantly active, we got something to eat every night. Denise explained to me that fish blood was not the best-tasting blood in the world, but it was the most nutritious. My strength was growing almost miraculously. Another miracle was the improved flexibility of my joints and muscles. It was becoming harder and harder to keep it all hidden.

In the evenings, Mr. Ho would show me exercises similar to those that Babe used to do, and I was getting a kick out of pretending to lose my balance once in a while.

○ ◔ ◑ ●

"How about real swords?" said Wries on the morning of the sixth day. He was always coming to see us, unlike Van Vren whom I hadn't seen this whole time.

"Only if you join us," I said audaciously. I heard Denise take a deep breath. I supposed I would never get rid of those human expressions either. Besides that, if you wanted to talk, you had to breathe anyway.

"Good idea," said Wries surprisingly, and in a minute, he jumped down, two katanas under his arm. A pile of heads appeared above the cage, and bets began flying.

"Aren't the odds against you a bit too high, Maestro?" Wries tucked his tie between the buttons of his shirt and pulled on his black, human-skin gloves.

"Miss Denise?" He smiled at my companion. She squeezed into a corner, and it looked like that grin made her tan skin turn a little paler.

Oh, well, she won't be helping me—doesn't matter.

I was preparing to kill Wries. I looked into his eyes, behind those glasses, and I saw that he knew it too.

"Please, Maestro." He handed me one of the katanas, hilt first.

In comparison with a bamboo sword, this weapon was obviously heavier, but in contrast to the execution swords—the only kind that I had ever held—it was perfectly balanced.

"Shall we?" said Wries and swung the blade around him impressively. I took a ready stance, just like Denise had taught me.

○ ◗ ◑ ●

Wries attacked. His blow was hard, and my loss of balance looked quite convincing.

Hot pieces of metal flew from the swords, and I was in retreat. *Pacify your enemy, and then destroy him,* that was what Dread had taught me.

I grimaced under the make-believe struggle, but inside, I was preparing. Wries began playing to the audience. After a double strike that *knocked* me to my knees, he turned around in a circle with both hands above his head, the tip of his sword ringing against the metal cage.

The Chinamen cheered wildly.

Another double strike and I noticed that he wasn't lifting his hand to cover himself as he should.

Every killer recognizes his moment.

I used all my abilities.

Time stopped again.

The blade of the katana was nearing the white shirt, fitting tightly over a spare tire of belly fat. I guessed that if I struck the side of the ship below the water line with the same strength, we would be going under. Since my days in the casket, my strength had really increased several times over.

The screaming of the Chinamen changed to a low booing sound.

Suddenly, I realized that the blade of the katana was pointing in a different direction than I wanted it to.

What the ...? I looked at my hand, and saw my wrist holding the hilt. The weird thing was that my wrist and the weapon were pretty far from the rest of my arm.

A foot wearing a black boot came from nowhere and hit me square in the chest. I flew so fast that the sound of my last rib breaking came to me after I had landed.

I slowly slid to the floorboards and saw the katana on the other side of the cage, stuck in the floor, swaying back and forth with the fingers of my right hand still squeezing the hilt.

"He has a lot left to learn; plus, he needs to grow up a lot, but for our purposes, this is just about adequate. Thank you for your patience with his training, Miss Denise." Wries cleaned the blade of his weapon with a hanky and slightly bowed to her. Mr. Ho opened the cage. Wries pulled out my sword and peeled off my fingers one by one as if he was playing that kids' game where the little piggy goes to the market.

"They're holding on tight, I don't want to break them." He smiled at Mr. Ho, who nodded with understanding. Wries threw my hand into my lap, and without any obvious effort, he leaped out of the cage. The Chinamen sighed with awe.

○ ○ ◑ ●

"How are you?" Denise kneeled by me.

"Fine. Leave me alone." I tried to shoo her away with my other arm, but I couldn't. Obviously, my ribs were not the only thing damaged by that kick and looking at my arm stump wasn't helping either.

"Will you need any help, Miss Denise?" asked Mr. Ho from above.

"Thank you, but I can manage, only if you could …"

"Here." Mr. Ho lowered down a jute bag. Evidently, he had had it prepared ahead of time. Denise laid me down on my back, turned my head so I couldn't look, took something out of the bag, and grabbed my severed wrist. Luckily, she refrained from cracking jokes like *Hello, Thing.*

Then my stump began to itch, then it felt cold, then something was poking it, but I had no desire to look at what she was doing to me.

"Done," she said and showed me my right arm—my entire right arm—with my wrist wrapped in a cloth bandage.

"It was a clean cut. You'll be fine in four days. Now the ribs." She pulled up my shirt and began feeling and pressing my chest. I felt the ends of my bones touch and immediately join. "This would have healed on its own, but it's faster this way."

All that time, her hair tickled the bare skin on my chest—by accident, I am sure.

○ ◑ ◐ ●

Even though I tried to make her leave several times, she stayed with me all night. When she thought I had fallen asleep, she even put my head on her lap and began stroking my face. I pretended to wake up, and despite the pain, I rolled away.

○ ◑ ◐ ●

When the stars grew pale, I noticed the feeling return to my wrist. I could even move my fingers, but I made sure no one saw that. I was apparently able to regenerate four times faster than usual.

"What an idea, challenging Wries to a sword match!" Denise couldn't keep quiet any longer.

I didn't say anything.

"He was born around the year fifteen thirty, at a time when firearms were still unreliable and inaccurate. Back then, they killed each other mainly with swords and knives, and Wries was famous for his abilities.

153

He probably killed more people with his sword than you've ever seen."
Because I still didn't say anything, she stopped.

Surprisingly, I was suddenly in a pretty good mood. My wrist was
working better and better by the minute (though it was uncomfortably
tingly and itchy). My ribs were completely healed, but most importantly,
for the first time in my life, I had gotten to fight with a real sword and
against a real killer. It wasn't a bad fight at all.

Privately, I would admit that it was my self-confidence that suffered
the greatest injury.

○ ◐ ◑ ●

When Mr. Ho lowered down the basket-o-fish, I filled my own
glass, even though Denise filled one up for me. I couldn't do much
with just one hand, but the hurt look on Denise's face made me really
happy. She could have told me about Wries anytime before hand. It
would have been appropriate to mention what kind of a sword-fighting
celebrity we had on board during our training with the bamboo
swords.

In the evening, without a word, we began practicing, albeit only
lightly. I had decided that the ability to handle a weapon with my left
hand could be useful.

There was one more thing that warmed my heart; not even in that
difficult moment after the amputation did I let them know—about
the levitating I mean.

One day, when we meet outside of this cage …

One day …

○ ◐ ◑ ●

"How do you feel, Mr. Tobias?" The next morning, Mr. Ho came
to see me personally. He jumped down fearlessly.

Now he stood above me and looked concerned. Even though he
was only a little over five feet tall, wrinkly, and thin, I refrained from
issuing any sort of fight challenges.

"Good, it seems." I sat up.

"May I?" he squatted down, took my hand, and removed the
bandage. The cut was replaced by a red line trimmed with sutures—I

think it's called a running suture. I stared wide-eyed at the black thread.

"Miss Denise did a nice job sewing you up," Mr. Ho commended. He took a pin out of his lapel and began pricking my fingers, my palm, and the back of my hand.

"Excellent, excellent," he mumbled, when I announced that I could feel everything. Finally, he took out small scissors and pulled out the sutures.

"Don't strain your wrist too much, it seems to be completely healed, but total regeneration is confirmed to take four days. Here," he said and pulled a green rubber ring from his pocket, "squeeze this, but carefully." He stood up and stretched his back.

All it would take was just one kick in the stomach …

"Thank you, Mr. Ho. I am in your debt," I said.

He smiled with satisfaction. "I see that you are an insightful man, Mr. Tobias. Thanking someone and showing respect is not just a sign of good upbringing." He stuck the pin back in his lapel and leaped out of the cage—with even greater ease than Wries.

Good thing I didn't kick him, or I'd be counting my ribs again. Maybe it could be even worse, since Madam Dao probably wouldn't let some dimwitted valet guard us.

Mr. Ho closed the cage and nodded at me. I nodded back.

○ ◐ ◑ ●

I stretched out right there on the floor and for the rest of the day pretended to sleep. I had the feeling that the crew wasn't making as much noise as usual. Why were they being so considerate? We had to be either very valuable to them or … Why did they want me to practice with a sword? Why was Denise so loyal to them? Why …? I wasn't finding the answers so—through half-closed eyes—I just watched the shadows cast by the cage slink and sway across the floorboards.

When the sun climbed high enough to shine on my head, Denise hung a towel above me. Then I must have really fallen asleep because I woke up with the delicate taste of fresh fish blood in the corners of my mouth. Denise had my head propped up against her thigh and was feeding me with a straw. It was so pleasant that I didn't even jerk away this time, but I didn't let her know I was awake either. Apparently, vampires can be fed this way; it was hard to choke when the last breath I had taken was this morning. That was another interesting thing—we did have to breathe, even though only once in a while (I am not talking about breathing necessary for speaking). I did so with much less frequency than Denise. It was either that, or she just couldn't resist heaving her bosom.

○ ◔ ◑ ●

A strange silence woke me up the second time around. I opened my eyes abruptly. The towel above my head had disappeared, and instead of a leg, there was a rolled-up sleeping bag under my neck. The sky was growing darker with the first signs of dusk and above the cage stood Madam Dao, her squinty-eyed muscle man, Van Vren, and Wries … in short, everyone on the ship who was important.

"Please get up, Mr. Tobias," said Mr. Ho. Denise was standing already, and because she wasn't showing me her panties, I knew that this was something serious. I got up and politely bowed to Madam Dao.

The enemy must think you are broken, I heard Dread's voice from a distant past. My politeness was acknowledged by a wave from the fat hand wrapped in gold bracelets.

"You have improved considerably since last time. Clean, shaven, polite, you might even be something more than a doormat." The people above me laughed, but I saw that sharp stare from beneath the blackened eyebrows. It was a test of how I would react to an insult. Again, I bowed.

"You can even control yourself," said Madam Dao. "Look up when I am speaking to you." I lifted my head obediently, and Madam Dao nodded to Mr. Ho without taking her eyes off me.

"Madam Dao has decided—on the occasion of her birthday—to invite you, both of you, to the festivities." Mr. Ho paused, and I had never heard such quiet on that ship. I directed all of my mental and physical abilities to my face so that I could maintain an ambiguous, light smile. I was hoping that my eyes wouldn't give me away.

"You will only be invited on the condition that you will not do anything to disrupt the festivities, and when the time comes, you will return here." Mr. Ho pointed to my feet.

My face was valiantly stoic.

"I know that Miss Denise appreciates the value of one's word, but do you, Mr. Tobias? Do you know how we deal with a man who doesn't keep an honorable promise? Who loses face? Even if you escape, this truth will be carried by the wind, and no one—not even your own kind—will speak to you ever again. A man without face is dead, only his shame lives on forever."

"I know the weight of one's word," I said, but I really didn't mean for my voice to have such a hollow tone. However, I really did know what Mr. Ho was talking about. It is—it was—one of the cardinal Night Club principles. You must keep a promise at all costs. Your life was inconsequential when judged against that promise. Again, I heard Dread's voice.

"Yes, it seems as though he knows," said Wries.

"So you promise?" said Mr. Ho.

"Yes, during the celebration, I will not do anything to offend Madam Dao or anyone else, and above all, I will refrain from leaving the ship unexpectedly."

Madam Dao laughed loudly. "I like you. Let them up." She nodded to Mr. Ho and the hatch really opened.

"Miss Denise," said Mr. Ho.

Denise was well aware of how one's exit from the cage was judged and that was why she put on a show. She performed a cartwheel and pushed off with her hands so that she flew through the hatch feet first. Then she flipped into a somersault and landed with taut feet on the grate—with surgical precision. The crew's impressed chatter seemed to have no end.

"Mr. Tobias," said Mr. Ho, and everyone stepped back a little. Apparently, the trust in my word was not as great as I deserved. I pushed off and, not very gracefully, leaped out. The crew hummed with disappointment.

Freedom! thundered through my head when I saw the horizon after so many days. My eyes must have given me away because everyone who could stop me took a step forward. I was most surprised by the movement of Denise's shadow—so even she would be hunting after me.

I dropped my eyes and bowed to Madam Dao. "It is my utmost pleasure to participate in the celebration of your honorable birthday, Madam. May the lucky dragon guide your path through life."

"Thank you." Madam Dao bowed her head gently. "A very nice wish." She snapped her fingers. "We'll start in an hour."

The crew exploded with excitement, and the tension around me disappeared. Mr. Ho turned toward me. "That was wise." His black, impenetrable gaze hit my eyes. "Now it's necessary for you to dress in the appropriate clothes. Miss Denise naturally also." He nodded toward my companion.

"May I ask you for something, Mr. Ho?"

"Yes?"

"I need a haircut." I pulled on my long locks. In the grave, I had turned into a total hippie.

Again, Mr. Ho looked at me inquisitively and then burst into loud laughter. "But of course, I will take care of it myself, Mr. Tobias."

"Why didn't you ask me? I can cut hair too," said Denise.

I didn't answer and followed Mr. Ho to the stern.

○ ◌ ◐ ●

The ship, a traditional Chinese junk, was surprisingly big. It was wide, over one hundred feet and had four masts and a raised stern. The lower deck, that we were walking on, looked like it was in a permanent state of chaos, but I noticed that each thing had its place. Barrels were carefully tied up, as were the bunches of bananas and fuzzy coconuts, and the floorboards were scrubbed clean. Once in a while, the slanted yards creaked and the sail hems fluttered noisily.

The ship sailed in such a way that the wind stabilized it, and I'd noticed before that the helmsman was quite the expert. The rolling was almost indiscernible, and the water along the sides just hissed.

At the stern, Mr. Ho clapped and rattled something off to the man who ran up to him. The man bowed, ran off, and instantly returned with a chair, a large towel, a mirror, a comb, and scissors.

"If you please, Mr. Tobias." He set the chair down so that I could watch the setting sun. Apparently, he knew a thing or two about prisoners.

I sat down, and he wrapped the towel around my shoulders. "How do you want it?"

"Hedgehog style, shorter on the sides please."

"I am afraid that—"

"I mean a crew cut." I remembered the correct English term, and the scissors knowledgeably snipped away. I was beginning to suspect how they broke Denise; no force, no punishment, just courtesy in return for courtesy. They must have known that you get more bees with honey.

I smiled and watched the sun, and Mr. Ho didn't interrupt with any idle chatter.

The thing they didn't know about me was that I didn't like sweets.

○ ◑ ◐ ●

"Satisfactory?" Mr. Ho showed me the mirror. I ran my hand across the back of my head and nodded in agreement.

"Perfect, Mr. Ho. I am in you debt." He looked really pleased. "Could I take a shower somewhere up here? So I don't have to go back to the cage? I can't stand the way the little hairs itch my back." I shivered because I really couldn't stand it.

Mr. Ho issued an order to the man, who was politely waiting in the background. (I noticed that the whole time, he was trying to—in vain—discreetly catch my cut hair. I felt almost sorry for him and his human clumsiness.) The man ran up with a baggie full of shampoo and a bucket, and pretty soon, he was pouring salt water over me. The shampoo wasn't getting very sudsy in the salt water, but you can't have it all.

Mr. Ho took me below decks and gave me a towel and a brand-new, dark blue, long robe with wide lapels and long wide sleeves. He turned around so that I could dry off and get dressed in privacy. That was when I got up enough nerve to ask a second question.

"Mr. Ho, I noticed that there are women on the deck also ... Are they all ... all ... I mean ..." I stuttered and began tying my belt.

"Yes, Mr. Tobias?" He turned around and looked impenetrable. This Oriental mimicry, how the hell was I supposed to know what he was thinking?

"I don't want to insult you, and I don't know how your culture reacts to these kinds of questions." I tied a knot. "But are they all ... I mean ... married?"

Mr. Ho's expression turned even more impenetrable, but then he suddenly burst out with laughter again, but this time much longer than before.

"They are not married, no. Actually married women are not even allowed on Madam Dao's ship." He slapped my shoulder. "I think this problem will resolve itself, in the evening." Again, he laughed. "You are the tallest man here, plus an exotic European ... *Are all women married?*" he imitated my voice and laughed so hard he doubled over.

○ ◝ ◗ ●

Dusk was falling quickly—that's how it is in the tropics—and the crew hung lanterns made from rice paper (not that I recognized it, but I read somewhere that they were made of it) on the deck, which was otherwise strictly dark. With the darkness, even the wind died down. The waves quietly splashed and the sails hung loosely. A big advantage of being on a ship in the middle of an open ocean was the absence of pesky bugs.

The aroma of food came from somewhere, and the cheerful anticipation of a party was in the air. To my surprise, I was exited too—boredom is a terrible enemy—only if this robe didn't have such ridiculously long sleeves. Mr. Ho left me, so I began to slowly stroll up to the bow. I examined everything with great curiosity, and the crew members would politely bow to me and move out of my way. That made me feel pretty good. I would probably make a damn fine slave master.

"Miss? Do you speak English, please?" I stopped by the first good-looking girl I saw. She was scooping drinking water out of a barrel.

"Yes, Mr. Tobias," she said with virtually no accent, but I detected obvious fear in her voice. *Of course, I am a vampire, it's almost night, we're alone ...* I smiled.

"I need to roll up these dang sleeves, and I am having some trouble." I waved my hands in the air, and the girl burst out laughing. Immediately, she put her hand over her mouth and looked into my eyes with alarm. Oh yes, my pupils must have narrowed in the darkness.

"A dragon!"

"Oh, no, I just have something in my eye." I grimaced and tried to rub my eyes, but those dang sleeves got tangled up in each other, and the girl burst into laughter again. I avoided making vampire eyes and looked into the darkness as a human. That made the night much prettier.

"What is your name, if I may ask?" I said when she was rolling up my left sleeve. You couldn't really roll it; you just folded it over and tightened it, almost up to the elbow, then it stayed in place.

"Selma, but they call me Sel." She winked at me, but right away lowered her eyes down to my sleeve. She wasn't nearly as perfect as Hanako, Babe, or Denise, but she was that much more beautiful.

"Selma, that doesn't sound very Chinese."

"I am from Hong Kong, Mr. Tob—"

"Can you just call me Tobias? My ears hurt from all the 'mister this' and 'mister that.'" I grinned and noticed how quickly she looked at my fangs.

"Don't worry, I won't bite," I said, and again, she laughed—very delightfully.

"Yes, Mr. ... *Tobias*." She emphasized the last word. She had been folding up my sleeve for a long time now, but it didn't really bother me. When she folded up the right one, she sadly stroked the barely noticeable scar over my wrist.

She had long, very tender fingers.

Suddenly, the entire ship shook with a bellowing blare that vibrated my teeth and startled me so much that I would have fallen over the railing if Selma hadn't caught me *at the last moment*.

"What was that?! A dying elephant?!"

"The celebration has officially started; we have to go up to the front deck."

○ ◑ ◐ ●

I stood next to Denise and listened to a long, melodic Chinese speech given by Li Pao, who was puffed up with pride like a ... well, like a bloated goat ... maybe not quite that.

We stood in a giant U shape with Madam Dao and her gold in the middle. Closest to her were the most important people followed by less important ones farther away. Lastly, the crew formed the legs of the U. Considering that we were prisoners, Denise and I were not in a bad spot.

At times, I felt as though I was in a dream, or rather a nightmare. I never dreamed that I would be attending a celebration with Van Vren and Wries, and we would be politely smiling at each other.

"Can I fold up your little sleeve? Toby? Maybe the other one too? And we wouldn't want you falling into that nasty water!" Denise hissed into my ear. I continued to politely smile at Wries.

"Such a ... such a ...!" She couldn't find the words.

"Shhhh!" Mr. Ho hissed at her.

When the address was over, everyone began clapping. I always thought that people didn't clap at the thing the person said, but at the fact that he had finally stopped talking. So I clapped loud and long. Then the muscular guard brought an ornamental box, opened it, and held it so that Madam Dao could reach inside. The crew began to file past her. The last deckhand, a kid who was barely eight years old, went first. Madam Dao reached into the box and gave everyone something yellow and shiny.

"Gold coins." Mr. Ho leaned toward me. "A tradition on this ship." Every one of the crew bowed all the way to the ground. The entire Orient is based on the bow. You chop off someone's head, and he'll bow to you just before he dies. After even the helmsman had received a coin, the entire crew lifted their right fists in the air and yelled something three times—maybe the Chinese equivalent of hip, hip, hooray! Then the U fell apart, and the cooks ran off to begin serving dinner.

"Boy, Miss Denise, come with us." A commanding wave from her gold-covered hand invited us to the upper deck in front of the second mast. There, under a canopy, was a soft rug with many pillows. The Chinese know how to do this right; why sit during a meal when lying down is much more comfortable? I waited until Denise lay down (everyone was looking), and I stretched out all the way behind Mr. Ho. Who wanted to listen to her venomous remarks?

The cooks and their assistants started to bring literally tons of goodies. Not being human really sucks sometimes—it all looked so beautiful, with the colors, the aromas ...

"Please, Mr. Tobias." One of the cooks handed me a tall, dewy glass with a slice of lemon.

"But I—"

"Rabbit's blood, chilled, with a drop of soy sauce and a pinch of finely ground white pepper. It is considered a delicacy," he said in perfect hospitality-style English.

"Then all I can say is thank you." I nodded with the elegance I imitated from Madam Dao.

Everyone else continued to bring large bowls of food, and Madam Dao would look them over and wave them away. The cooks would then scurry away to the lower deck where the crew was already sitting in two rows, white linens on the floorboards in front of them. I estimated there to be about fifty.

"You can't begin eating before Madam Dao does," Mr. Ho whispered, and because Madam Dao had just made her selection, he called over a cook to set one entire bowl in front of him. It glistened beautifully (I guessed it was shuang-si), but by the aroma, it wasn't beef but from the typical Chinese chow chow dog. Another cook hurried up with a bowl, chopsticks, and rice.

Mr. Ho shared the rice with Wries.

Then Madam Dao initiated dinner with another speech in Chinese, luckily only a short one. Judging by her figure, she understood that it was silly to let food get cold on account of some chatter. I joined in the ending cheer, and then it was finally time to eat.

That chilled rabbit's blood … well, how to say this … I had sort of gotten used to the fishy kind.

○ ◑ ◑ ●

The Chinese make a lot of chewing and burping noises when they eat—the more the better.

But there's nothing you can do about that.

I sipped my *Bloody Mary* and watched the lower deck. The colorful lanterns swayed in the breeze, and traces of the swinging light stretched into the black ocean. Selma was facing toward me. There must have been something in my gaze because every time I looked at her, she lifted her eyes and smiled at me. The only person ruining the picture was Denise, who just happened to let her hand (in which she held her glass) rest against her hip—right in my line of vision.

Mr. Ho followed nearly every bite with a sip from a porcelain bowl of something that smelled like turpentine. He noticed the direction of my gaze and knowingly chuckled.

Then I realized that more and more girls from the lower deck were looking my way, and I have to say that was not a bad feeling at all.

○ ◐ ◑ ●

After the meal, Madam Dao clapped loudly and that signaled the end the formal celebrations and the beginning of informal fun.

Immediately, a large pile of drums and Oriental noisemakers appeared on the lower deck, and the big band stepped right into it. It was something from the Rolling Stones.

"Do you think I could go down there?" I whispered to Mr. Ho.

"Of course, but don't forget to thank Madam Dao." Aside from his turpentine-induced chuckling, his eyes were completely clear and bright. The servers began distributing water pipes, and the aroma of tobacco and opium stretched across the deck.

"Madam Dao, it was honestly an exquisite dinner. Thank you for allowing me to participate." I got up and bowed almost down to the rug.

"Are all Europeans this polite?" She blew a cloud of opium smoke into my face.

"Only when they meet an extraordinary woman such as yourself."

The heavy woman started laughing so hard the fat began undulating under all her gold.

"Go and dance. Just go. I see that you need it." It was a wonder she didn't die from laughter. She waved me away.

"Where are you going?"

That Denise again.

I stepped over her stretched-out leg. Just a few stairs and I was down there.

○ ◐ ◑ ●

When I approached, the *Rolling Stones* started to screech a little, and the seated people began getting up and parting the way for me. I bowed to the musicians and gave a little wave to Selma. It had been a long time since I had seen so many relieved and understanding looks at the same time.

The people took their places again, the *Stones* caught a second wind, and the opium cloud thickened. People there smoked regular pipes or even rolled cigarettes. Two kids with large jugs and ladles were tirelessly pouring turpentine.

"May I sit here?" I stood behind Selma. It was only a formality, since the place was already empty and the pillow fluffed.

"I would be delighted," she said courteously.

I squeezed myself into the row of sitting people, and Selma softly leaned into my hip. Immediately, a kid ran up with a jug and pulled a bowl out of a bag, but at that moment, she realized who I was and froze in her tracks. The band was beginning to lose rhythm again to the point where it wasn't clear if they happen to be playing 'Help' by the Beatles.

The kid with the jug was a girl of about ten with black braids and thin slits for eyes. I grinned at her and lengthened my fangs.

She squealed delightfully. I caught the jug and ladle that she dropped and returned them to her.

"Please run over to the cook. He knows what I am drinking." I was laughing so hard I could hardly speak—to see that face, truly unforgettable. Selma leaned even closer to me, and the band regained their rhythm. The stiff faces loosened up a little, and they didn't mind me so much anymore—joking with a kid always works like a charm.

The linens and dinner leftovers disappeared. The band ripped into another hit, and the dancing started. The Stones were replaced by Britney Spears. When I heard the musicians' singing, I almost broke my promise and ran far away. My Other noted that Britney's songs could be used as a very effective torture device.

○ ○ ◑ ●

I clapped and swayed to the rhythm along with everyone else, and Selma turned to me several times as if she wanted to ask something, but was too afraid to. She would follow it up with a sip of turpentine, and I suspected that a dance was unavoidable in the near, but gloomy, future.

"Shall we dance?" She finally got up enough nerve to ask and quickly dropped her eyes to the deck.

"But of course, gladly," I said (with a stick-on smile) and dreaded the effect that the floor-length robe would have on my dancing abilities. The band had just ripped into a fast one. They were dripping sweat. The drums pounded. Strumming hands fluttered …

What I wouldn't give for a slow one right now.

Robe or no robe, I began to boogie fearlessly. Among the vertically challenged Chinese, I looked like a watchtower in an earthquake, and they started to fall over too—with laughter.

"I was never a good dancer," I said to Selma with apologies. Those jerks formed a circle around me, clapped, and let me burn there by myself. I hiked up my robe and began gyrating until my flip-flops flew off. When the band began to miss beats again, I simplified my moves.

The next song was a slow one. Those I could handle, to the right and even to the left, though I probably wouldn't win any Mr. Tango contests. Selma nestled into my arms, and her eyes sparkled—that's what it's all about.

After the next song, the band took a beverage break, so we sat down. There was a new embroidered pillow in my spot, and behind it, a girl stood at attention with a tray and a tall glass.

"Thank you," I said and took the drink (I mean food). The girl was staring at me scared stiff, so Selma rattled something quick in Chinese and the kid ran off. Gently, I lifted Selma and put the embroidered (and obviously more comfortable) pillow under her fanny. That was when my neighbor on the other side considered me so commonplace that while gesturing wildly, he dumped his turpentine all over me.

The ominous silence indicated that I was still being carefully watched.

"No problem." I clinked my glass on his empty bowl. Everyone exhaled, and the conversation exploded again. *Good thing I don't speak Chinese.*

I put my hand on Selma's knee very discreetly just as she was using a scarf to wipe the turpentine off my lapel.

"Why me, Tobias?" She looked into my eyes. "When you have …" She glanced in Denise's direction. "She is so beautiful, perfect …"

"On the outside maybe, but I don't like what she has here." I tapped on my forehead.

"Misterrrrr Tobiiiiasssss?" I heard an opium-slurred voice behind me. "May I aks … ask you for something?"

"Of course. What?" I turned around, and one of the musicians was standing there.

"Wo … won't you play some Eu … European music?" He handed me a chubby thing vaguely resembling a guitar.

"Not enough strings," I murmured. *How the hell does he know I can play?* Everyone was staring at me again. I tried a chord, and surprisingly, it sounded pretty good.

Play, play, but what?

I suspected that a Czech camping song wouldn't impress anyone, so I ripped right into a classical three-chord Elvis tune. It wasn't exactly European music, but who was going to notice?

I realized that being a vampire had other great advantages too. I had so much time to figure out and position my fingers on the next chord. There may have been only three chords, but playing them one right after another was no picnic. When you can put all your wind into singing, it sounds damn loud. In my younger days, my guitar playing stalled with one problem: how to synchronize the melody and the words. One thing was always getting ahead of the other, so I solved that problem by maximizing the speed of both. Even now, my Elvis sounded crazy, and the furious rattling of the chubby instrument only exaggerated that. In other words, I was screaming and yelling loud enough to make the ocean shake.

Surprisingly, the Chinese jumped around like mad, hands above their heads, asking for more and more.

Weirdoes.

Then I realized that there was a very similar situation in that cursed book of mine, and from there, it was only a skip and a jump to the Night Club.

I made 'Tutti Frutti' a lot shorter.

○ ◐ ◑ ●

"Are you sad?" Selma asked after I returned the instrument.

"I remembered … freedom."

"We are not allowed to talk to you about anything like that; the punishment would be severe," she said and with fear pulled away.

"Don't worry, I won't ask." I gently squeezed her above the knee with my thumb and forefinger. "I am just kidding around."

"You!" She slapped me on the shoulder and gazed into my eyes. People on the deck were whirling about again, so we disappeared unnoticed.

○ ○ ◑ ●

Selma had her own cabin. It was small so I felt like a midget, but a casket was a lot smaller. After I banged my head on the ceiling for the third time, I just sat down on the bed. The ocean hummed from outside. The swaying light from the lanterns reflected off the round window, and somewhere downwind someone was throwing up—how very romantic.

That Japanese proverb about men not doing things that can be done by a woman was apparently known in China too.

○ ○ ◑ ●

I must have dozed off for a minute because my robe disappeared and my T-shirt and shorts, laundered and ironed, appeared on the shelf. Selma purred from her sleep and dug her nose into my shoulder. She felt really hot to me, and I must have felt cold to her.

I smiled as I remembered how she froze the first time I kissed her neck. I lifted my head, made cat eyes, and exposed my fangs. "Draculaaaa!" Selma also had a wonderful scream.

Because it was almost morning, I grabbed my clothes and slipped out on the deck. The air had grown cooler and a white fog was rolling around on the ocean surface. Mr. Ho was sitting on a stool, not far from the door that I had to use. His water pipe was giving off soft, gurgling sounds. He smoked tobacco rather than opium, and the blue smoke was mixing in with the fog.

I laid my clothes on a rice barrel and jumped into the ocean.

○ ○ ◑ ●

The water was warm, and to my eyes, it wasn't black, but rather a bluish gray. I saw the shadows of large fish deep below me, which didn't make me feel too good so I swam closer to the keel and stared at it with some surprise. I was expecting it to be as chubby as above, but from below, the ship didn't look at all like a junk. It had a perfectly streamlined profile, a forward-extending sharp naval ram, and two—currently closed—openings, definitely for drawing in water into the jets.

"Well, look at this," I said, and instead of words, a stream of silver bubbles left my lips. After examining the seam between the junk and the speedy underbelly (which seemed to be made from honest-to-goodness steel, several inches thick), I realized that the wood on the outside must be just camouflage.

I wasn't in the water, however, so that I could peek under the ship's skirts, I wanted to find out how fast I could swim.

I quickly dismissed standard swimming styles such as the freestyle and breaststroke. Those were invented for people who had to breathe and who didn't have so much strength in their arms and legs. Immediately, I discovered that the fastest way for me to move was a in wavy style like a dolphin. Now, if I could only get my hands on some diving flippers …

Because I was underwater for a while now, I caught up with the ship and pulled myself onboard. Mr. Ho was still sitting in the same place as before.

"You wouldn't have a cigarette, Mr. Ho?"

He raised his eyebrows but got up and in a minute returned with a box of Camels. Not that I ever smoked, but there are those moments where smoking just belongs. I put my shorts on over my wet body and puffed little clouds into the wind until I dried off. When the cigarette died in the ocean with a soft hiss, I said, "Now?" Mr. Ho nodded.

The hatch closed with a steely clang.

○ ◑ ◗ ●

Denise was already in her hammock, and if anyone has ever seen a back that is lethally pissed off, it was me just now. I spread my sleeping bag right on the deck and fell asleep.

Knowing how to sleep really is a good thing.

○ ◑ ◗ ●

"My god! What stinks in here?!"

Denise's words woke me up. By the sound of it, she was standing right above me.

Last night, I noticed that Selma had sprayed a strong, sweet-smelling perfume on my T-shirt. I remembered that Oriental women did this so the man wouldn't forget them.

I pleasurably sniffed the air, stretched, and as if from a deep dream, I made a face that I assumed would make Denise mad as hell.

I was right.

Practice began early that day.

○ ◯ ◑ ●

Because I had gotten all tangled up in my sleeping bag while I slept, I was at first just getting beat up—with hands only, probably due to the lack of bamboo swords.

"Careful, Miss Denise, he isn't completely healed yet," said Mr. Ho from above.

"Isn't healed yet?!" She hit me on the head so hard I saw colorful circles. Finally, I freed myself from the fabric octopus.

"Hi, Selma!" I waved up to her. Spectators, some of whom were still very pale, gathered in much higher numbers than usual. Nothing stays quiet for long on a ship, so they were expecting a tough match.

I was disappointed that the odds were in Denise's favor.

○ ◯ ◑ ●

Today was the first time we didn't hold back, and I discovered how dangerous kung fu could be with beings like us.

The boards pounded, the cage rang, bones screeched, and strikes hammered. Even though the audience could only see us when we jumped apart, they cheered frantically; eyes bulging out of their heads, pieces of paper with bets in their fists. In one of the quieter moments, I noticed that even Wries had brought over a chair. I bet he saw everything, just like Mr. Ho, so I doubled my efforts to resist the urge for any levitation tricks.

Another short pause came when the elastic in my shorts broke. Denise did wait until they brought a new pair and until I got dressed, but if it wasn't for the audience, she would have continued to pound me, shorts or no shorts. During our hard physical exertion, we were breathing about once in fifteen minutes, which for us was almost breathlessness.

The next round lasted about an hour. Then I managed to hit her in the solar plexus with my heel. It didn't knock her breath out, but she had a bunch of nerves there just like everyone else. She wobbled. I threw my fist hard, which she ducked, but I used a trick that Babe taught me and hit her with the elbow that followed my fist. It was a damn good strike. It didn't toss her away, but it did knock her down to the floor. I didn't hesitate and smashed my left fist into her plexus again.

With that, it was over.

Slowly, I got up and felt tired but happy. This was the first time I had beaten Denise. That was not bad after only about ten days of training. I congratulated myself. Simultaneously, I realized that even we can be knocked out and not just by a blow to the head.

I looked at Denise and threw a towel over her. Her clothes were in tatters, just like mine, and her favorite panties (light yellow today) hung on only by a few threads.

From above, I heard the excited shouts of those who had bet on me. Selma was jumping up the highest.

Because Denise not only didn't get up but didn't even move, Mr. Ho clapped and the crowd reluctantly dispersed. He lifted the hatch and jumped down with his jute bag.

"Good fight," he praised me. "You will make a valuable soldier, Mr. Tobias, if I consider that you are only a month and a half old ..."

He leaned over Denise and began examining her chest. It hurt her enough that from unconsciousness, she waved her hands around.

"Can you hold her down, please?"

"With pleasure." Gently, I grabbed her unsteady wrists that were, just like mine, covered with a continuous layer of bruises, which were disappearing right before my eyes.

"She doesn't have anything broken." Mr. Ho lifted his head. "But you should be careful, two such hard blows to the same place ... She never hit you full force in a sensitive place, even now she held back." His voice had a scolding tone.

"I thought I couldn't hurt her." I was a little stunned, and instinctively, I began feeling the pulse on her wrist.

"You can, of course. Even you are mortal. Invulnerability is only from fairy tales, not reality." He waved his hand around. "Turn around," he ordered and pulled her torn T-shirt up to her neck. A moment of medical murmuring and then the smell of camphor—a lot like the salve that Father Kolachek used. I heard smacking noises as he applied the medicine to her skin, and then Denise sighed and opened her eyes. When she saw me leaning over her, she jerked.

"Easy, Miss Denise. Easy." Mr. Ho pressed her against the deck. "You will be fine." He placed a white linen over her glistening chest and pulled her shirt back down. "You must lie on your back until evening, no hammock, only floorboards." He knocked on the wood and sounded just like a doctor.

"And you, if you ever hurt her like this again," he looked at me sternly, "you will be fighting me next time."

I will admit that the black look of this five-foot-tall little man made me uneasy.

"And today, you will take care of her." He grabbed his bag and jumped out.

So, take care of her, huh!

A mischievous smile flashed across Denise's face. She thought I didn't see her.

"I really did it this time." I lifted her and gently laid her on the sleeping bag.

"Could you change my T-shirt? I hate wearing ripped things." This was the first of about a million modest wishes of the day. Around lunchtime, I was cursing myself for not getting knocked out.

"I have a craving for a cocktail from those two types of small fish … Mr. Ho knows which ones," she said in a dying voice. So I spent the next hour chopping off the heads of tiny little fish, like those from an aquarium, and then ones even tinier, before I got the usual full glass. By then, it was too warm, so I had them bring some ice, but then it was too cold …

What a spoiled prima donna! I clenched my teeth. Then, she made me feed her even though there was evidently nothing wrong with her hands, and she was probably just fine otherwise too.

Mr. Ho appeared above the cage once in a while and asked how it was going, and when she answered, she complained, of course. Her voice wasn't nearly as weak as when she asked for a pillow to elevate her legs or for me to brush her hair or complained that the fold in the sleeping bag pressed against her back … Mr. Ho frowned at me, so I didn't complain too much. He was probably serious about that fight, and I really didn't feel like getting my hand chopped off again or something.

Another problem was that the threads on the sides of Denise's panties kept on breaking, and she knew it and insisted that I stay close to her. (I happened to be creating a shadow at the moment.) The night before, I found out that vampirism caused not only my sight and hearing ability to grow more sensitive and intense, but other bodily functions as well.

Interestingly—important and pleasurable feelings intensified and pain and uncomfortable feelings became significantly duller.

Around four o'clock, I couldn't stand those panties anymore and asked Mr. Ho if I could go see Selma about something important and promised not to run away.

He looked down and said that I had to take care of Miss Denise.

That squinty-eyed asshole.

○ ☽ ☾ ●

At that time, I realized that with Selma, I had braided a nasty little whip for myself and handed it right over to them. I had a lot to learn.

Because the sun set beyond the rim of our porthole and I didn't have to be a sun shade anymore, I flopped into my hammock and started to concentrate on deep meditation. It was very calming.

○ ☽ ☾ ●

When it got dark, Denise, who was now miraculously healed, demonstrated what getting Australia means. That's when a person, who is meditating in a hammock, gets spun around, his hands and feet get tangled up in the netting, and the poor guy ends up belly down.

"Is this what I get for taking care of you?!" I fumed.

"No, not for that." She brushed her hip against my shoulder and glided off.

○ ☽ ☾ ●

14

In about two hours, I learned why we were so valuable and why Mr. Ho didn't like it when we hurt each other.

"Get up." Denise shook me. I expected some trickery, but there was a tension in her voice and something similar permeated the entire ship. "Get dressed." She threw a velvety bundle on my stomach. "But put this on first." Something that looked like a set of rubber gun straps landed on the package. "This is how you put it on ... Hurry up a little, will you? Please!"

I put on the straps. They were kind of snug in the back of the neck. Denise tightened them and snapped on a metal clasp in the front. "You can't take this off until I say so, understand? For any reason." I saw that she wore the same thing as she stood there just in her bikini. She bent down and pulled up a pair of loose pants. They were so black that they seemed nearly invisible even to my eyes. The bundle she had thrown at me earlier contained a pair for me too, along with a loose, black ... I don't know what it's called but probably a kimono top. When I tried to tie a wide belt around it, she said, "Here!" and skillfully wrapped it twice around my waist and tied a knot. With a sharp stare, she asked, "Do you need your sleeves rolled up too?"

"Are you sure you are all right, Miss Denise?" I heard a worried Mr. Ho from above.

"Yes, Mr. Ho," she said but winced a little with pain, probably to make me feel guilty.

"So." She tied her hair back into a loose bun and pulled on a hood. Suddenly, the only thing visible was the area of light skin around her eyes. "That thing pressing against your spine in the back of your neck is a small explosive. If you don't return to the ship by the time they tell you, it will blow; if you try to take it off, it will blow; if you attack anyone of the crew, it will blow. The only time it will not blow is if you do exactly what they tell you to do." She pointed her thumb at the upper deck. "I am sure I don't have to explain to you what happens if you try to escape."

"It will blow up," I said in a muffled voice, because I put my hood on backwards.

"Exactly. So don't get your hopes up. It certainly won't kill you. The charge will destroy a few vertebrae and sever your spinal cord. That means you won't be able to move for a week. It also means that they will have plenty of time to find you. You don't even want to know what they'll do to punish you."

"Did it ever happen to you?" I straightened my hood, and Denise tucked the hem under my lapel.

"No, it hasn't. I just had to watch when they did it to others …" She paused. I saw what flashed in her eyes, and she didn't have to continue.

"Ready?" asked Mr. Ho from above.

"One moment," said Denise, "those are boots, you moron."

"They did seem too weird to be gloves." I pulled my hands out of something that looked more like thick satin socks rather than boots. They had little unidirectional hairs on the bottom so my feet adhered to the floorboards almost completely. Denise showed me how to tie them.

"What is this anyway? We look like black ninja," I said, my laugh sounding muffled under the mask.

"These clothes were first created in the eighteenth century in the Japanese kabuki theater, and in Europe they are associated with ninja movies. However, here they still conjure up deadly fear … By the way, if you ever run into a real ninja, despite all your abilities, run … Now Mr. Ho." She raised her voice, and the hatch opened.

"Did Miss Denise explain the nature of our straps? I mean, *your* straps?" Madam Dao asked.

"Yes, Madam," I said and felt a little uneasy, and not because of the clothes. The ship raced through the darkness. There were no lights anywhere, only the sharp hiss and splashing of the waves. So far, Madam Dao had only used the wind, but judging by a certain detail, I determined that I would hear the engines soon.

That certain detail was a double-barreled machine gun, looming up on the upper deck under the second mast right where we had had our opulent feast the night before. Madam Dao, dressed in a fluttering black robe, was nonchalantly leaning against it, not a piece of gold on her. Her bodyguard was behind her and Van Vren and Wries beside her, both of them in black coats and hats set low on their brows. The tips of their coats quietly fluttered around their knees.

"Pirates! They're pirates!" I turned to Denise.

"You didn't think this was some sort of vacation, did you?" Blood gurgled in her raspy voice.

"Why didn't you tell me this either—?!"

"It's not Miss Denise's fault, Mr. Tobias," Mr. Ho interrupted me. "It's the number one rule on this ship, which you didn't need to know until now: *Don't ever divulge anything to anyone that they don't absolutely need to know, until they absolutely need to know it.* Yes, we are a pirate ship, and unless you submit to the commands that follow, you will suffer ... actually, *until* you submit, you will suffer. We will never kill you. Your abilities are much too valuable to us, but the suffering is so great that in the end, everyone always submits."

"Okay, enough with the scary stuff, what I am supposed to do?" I said, and in my head, I heard Dread's words: *Eat shit when you have to if it helps you learn more about your enemy. The better you know him, the easier you can destroy him—when the time comes.* That swearword was the only swear I ever heard Dread use, which was why I remembered this lesson especially well.

"Your weapons." Mr. Ho handed us two short katanas ... These swords were probably called something else, but who could think about terminology at a time like this?

"Kill them all, Mr. Tobias. Dead people can't surprise you from behind. You will recognize the captain and the officers by their clothes, they will be similar to those on this ship. Knock them out or wound them only lightly. If you use a captured weapon, you must leave it on the other ship before you return; otherwise, you will be punished. One more thing ..." He handed me something that looked like a giant wristwatch. "It's a compass, chronometer, and depth gauge. If you have to dive, stay above ninety feet. If they injure you, try to jump into the ocean; we will find you. They have this ugly practice of chopping up a wounded enemy into small pieces, very small pieces."

"Finished, Mr. Ho?" said the raspy voice.

"Yes, Madam Dao."

○ ◐ ◑ ●

"To the bow, quickly." Denise shoved me.

"So we're supposed to hook onto them, swing on ropes, and yell yarrrrrrr, or something?" I remembered the colorful pictures from my boyhood books.

"These jokes will ... Have you ever killed anyone?"

I shrugged my shoulders.

"You don't have to feel guilty. Apparently, we are attacking another pirate ship—a *human* pirate ship." She emphasized *human*. "They're animals. If you'd only seen what they do to their captives—" She shrugged.

"I am sure we don't do anything bad to our captives," I said innocently.

"We don't ... *I* don't," she corrected herself and winked at Van Vren and Wries. "They will cover our backs. They've saved my life about fifty times."

"Why us? I mean vampires, why don't they do it themselves? They're for sure better than me." I tried to draw my sword.

The deck began to shudder. Several quiet commands were issued. The sails fluttered and slid down. The engines roared. The bow lifted upwards, and the impact of the waves stiffened. The wind began to howl around my katana so I put it away.

"Why us?" Denise pressed her fingers into the hilt of the sword which she skillfully swung onto her back. "Probably because of our eyes. We can see better than any of them at night, not even a shot from the blackest darkness will blind us or make us blink ... plus our regenerative abilities. Why should they suffer what usually befalls us?" She looked at me, and I realized that she was scared. She hid it well, but she was almost shaking from her fear. That thing about chopping people into little pieces must have been true.

She had probably seen it too.

It didn't bother me, with my Night Club upbringing. Besides, I already knew what death was like, and it wouldn't be any worse the second time around. A slug in the neck or chopped into pieces, what does it matter? You can't make peace with death, but you can get used to the idea.

My Other made a note followed by a big exclamation mark.

○ ◑ ◑ ●

"More to the left," Denise whispered over her shoulder, and in a moment, the ship leaned a little.

I also saw the target pretty clearly.

"One hundred yards." Out of habit, I began to quietly call out the distance.

"Hold on, we'll ram them," Wries whispered behind me.

"Eighty," I said, and Wries passed on my quiet words. I hung the sword on my back, and Denise checked that it fit well.

"Sixty," she said this time, and the ship slowed down to lower the noise.

○ ◑ ◑ ●

At thirty yards, they noticed us. The bow of our junk was a hell of a lot higher than their deck. I saw the faint reflections off the naval ram as it shifted forward underwater.

"How is your long jump?" I asked Denise. I missed that no one here was cracking jokes before the battle.

"Twenty yards," she said quietly, and it wasn't a joke; her teeth chattered.

On the ship in front of us, someone was yelling disjointed commands. I slapped Denise across the butt. "Don't be wound up so tight! Ten yards!" I screamed and pushed off.

Show initiative, and the enemy will begin to value you and be less likely to expect treason from you: Dread.

I landed, and the planks rattled under my feet. My sword swished, and the first beheaded corpse, a machete in hand, fell over. I had a feeling that there would be a lot of people on this pirate ship, since they attacked cruise ships and must be able to subdue masses of people.

I kicked in the nearest door and knocked out the officer with my fist. I had the advantage since he didn't even see me. I jumped over the body, and suddenly, the ship was hit by our ship. The impact was followed by really massive creaking and a huge roll. All I had to do was put my weapon in front of me, and when the rolling stopped, I had three pirates skewered on the blade. Only at that moment did I appreciate the ninja boots. They didn't slip even on blood. I ran through the little hallway, and at that point, some genius turned on the lights.

I took down the blinded guy, buck naked and tattooed from head to toe. He had one of a dragon with an extended tongue around his wiener.

"Yahhhh!" screamed a second guy, and I had to defend myself against something that looked like a pointy meat cleaver. He was no match for my speed. He stared with confusion at what was left of his chopped-off hands, but he didn't enjoy the stump left by his head.

I grabbed onto a short ladder and swung upward. Hello, bridge! I mean, I tried to swing up there, but midway, someone smashed a baseball bat over my head—but that was nothing compared to Denise's fists.

Speak of the devil, she just pushed off my stomach (I was lying under the ladder) and jumped up, sword first. Her maneuver was rewarded by a loud gurgle, and blood instantly flowed down the rungs.

By then, I was up there too.

A second man was holding a short Uzi, and even though he couldn't have known where we were because of our speed, he squeezed the trigger.

Plus, he had his eyes closed.

Click! Click!

I jumped in front of Denise, and both slugs went through the kimono on my belly.

○ ◑ ◐ ●

That's what I get for saving others instead of taking care of myself, but Night Club reflexes are not easy to forget.

I probably wouldn't be able to run very easily after that, and to be honest, just simple standing wasn't so simple anymore either.

○ ◑ ◐ ●

The equipment on the bridge started jumping around when someone from outside chimed in with something significantly bigger than an Uzi. To make things worse, the door on the other side flew open and a guy with a shotgun started his running target practice on us. Even though, in my case ...

Denise's sword wedged itself into the guy with the Uzi (unfortunately, she destroyed his weapon too), so she grabbed an automatic revolver from the first guy she killed. It was a classic Colt forty-five millimeter, model A1.

It had seven, maybe eight, rounds, I thought. I saw more and more orange balls of flame explode from the end of the shotgun and sprays of splinters coming closer and closer ... *Why is everyone always shooting at me?*

Bang! Bang! thundered the forty-five.

It was hard to miss from only a few yards away. Denise, however, managed to do so. The bullets made two light-colored holes in the wooden trim.

During those few moments, however, my body was able to adjust to the double stomach wound ... not completely though. It adjusted enough for me to jump and yank out Denise's revolver.

While still in mid-flight, I wedged my index finger on the trigger and performed the exact same maneuver as Hanako had in the passage of the Blanik theater, but now I was able to do it while *flying*. I was also discovering that my shooting skills had improved several fold thanks to vampirism.

Bang! Bang!

Right eye, left eye, the guy's brains splattered all over the wall.

Bang! Bang!

This time, I was shooting through a cabinet on the wall, guided only by sound, but I silenced the heavy automatic weapon outside.

While still in flight, I watched the four rotating casings and the slow recoil of the handgun slide.

Glock! I want a Glock! I want two Glocks!

I landed and rolled onto my knees. A sword that Denise kicked to me along the floor slid into my left hand. With her aim, I was surprised that it didn't skewer me through the belly.

That was when, katana in hand, she ran through the door and jumped to the lower deck.

I wasn't nearly as quick as she was.

○ ◐ ◑ ●

On the mast, a large floodlight was shining downward. So many people were running around beneath me. Luckily, they were dressed differently than our crew; otherwise, I would be really confused about why there were so many of them. They weren't just running around either—they weren't a bunch of wussies. In spite of the fact that the bow of our ship was sticking out high above the broken railing, they were already attacking it.

That was none of my business, though.

I swung, chopped a guy in half (I overdid it a little with the swing), and broke the blade on something inside of him. I dropped the hilt, grabbed the upper half of the corpse by its hand, spun around, and smacked another guy in the face with it. I was left holding only the hand; the rest of them flew into the ocean.

Now what? No sword? I grabbed the Colt from my belt.

One, maybe two, shots.

○ ◐ ◑ ●

Denise dashed along the railing and with short, efficient chops cleared her way. Speed was our biggest advantage and she didn't have two holes in her belly.

○ ◐ ◑ ●

Another guy, an officer, approached. I couldn't finish my kick so his slug singed my kimono.

Fist.

"Knock out the officers?" I looked into his smashed face. Maybe they'd be able to revive him. The good news was that his weapon was a good old nine-millimeter semi-automatic CZ 75, according to some people, a handgun made from the best materials ever. I was happy to see that it was a fifteen-rounder and three clips were still in the officer's belt.

I knelt down behind the mast and began learning to shoot single instead of double rounds. My accuracy got so good that the second shot was just wasteful.

○ ○ ◑ ●

There were really a lot of people on that deck. I tried to cover Denise. I didn't understand where she was rushing to, but I was no expert on ship attacks.

At that point, the first of the pirates clambered onto the bow of our junk. From my high vantage point, I saw Madam Dao. She was just lighting a cigarette. As soon as the pirates appeared above the bulkhead, she grabbed the handles of the machine gun and the slaughter started.

My high vantage point, unfortunately, also meant that I was within range, and now I understood where Denise was hurrying off to: out of the twins' way.

The muscular guard held the ammunition belt for Madam Dao, and both of them were having a good ol' time. I, on the other hand, really wasn't anymore. As I watched what was happening over there, I stopped paying attention to what was happening over here.

When I heard the clamor behind me, I managed to turn around, but not duck. The arrow hit me in the right shoulder and pinned me to the mast.

The little guy, who looked just like Mr. Ho's twin, was placing another arrow into the string of the bow. On his head, he had a Chinese hat, the kind that looks like an upside-down gold-panning bowl.

I couldn't quite lift my right hand with the nine millimeter.

"The left one then," I said in Czech.

His hat, full of the most precious liquid flew off into the distance. Strange, I didn't even fire.

○ ○ ◑ ●

"Maestro, I wouldn't hang around here," said Wries. The whole front of his coat was covered in blood and dripped on his boots, but I couldn't say I wasn't happy to see him.

I broke the arrow, pulled myself off the mast, and followed up with a head-first leap to the deck below. Madam Dao's activities up in the upper atmospheres were becoming somewhat dangerous to one's health, somewhat rapidly.

The corpse of the little man with the bow didn't even have time to fall over. Against the glow of the reflector, I saw the rounds from the twins scatter him into the air.

The cloud of crimson aerosol was so thick it looked like it might throw lightning bolts.

Crack!

I hit an officer with my gun. He had the same embroidery on his lapel as our helmsman, and I began limping my way to the rear deck. The pirates in front of me were jumping into the water.

"I wouldn't do that, guys. I really wouldn't," I said. Unlike them, I saw those triangular fins in the water, lured in by all the blood. You could see that the precious liquid was just gushing off the deck.

In the next three minutes, the remaining crew surrendered.

○ ◐ ◑ ●

Our men lowered a plank, and Madam Dao, cigarette in the corner of her mouth, descended to the captured ship.

"The captain?" she said, and Van Vren brought the guy that I knocked out under the bridge. "Good work," said Madam Dao. I didn't even try to own up to it. I had a little problem with the arrow. It was so disrespectfully sticking out the back of my shoulder, and I felt foolish—a tough guy like me needing help from someone with such a silly thing. I tried to wedge the tip in the jamb of the cabin and yank it out, but it didn't work.

"Vampires?" said Madam Dao again.

Denise immediately stepped forward and stuck her sword into the deck. Up above, on our ship—above Madam Dao—Mr. Ho was standing with something in his hand that looked like a walkie-talkie. The explosive charge behind my neck began to itch a little.

I stepped out of the cabin's shadow and placed the revolver on the nearest corpse.

"Good," said Madam Dao. "Any other officers?" Wries dragged over another three; except for one, I had knocked out all of them.

"Excellent," said Madam Dao. Even through there were barely six of us on the deck of this pirate ship, the thirty kneeling captives didn't dare to move a muscle.

"Cargo?" Madam Dao pointed her cigarette at one of them, and Van Vren lifted him high in the air with one hand. Madam Dao calmly spoke to him in Chinese for a bit, then she nodded at Van Vren and he threw the guy overboard. The sounds with which the shark's jaws tore up the screaming meat didn't make me feel good at all.

Not even for a moment did I forget who *my* enemies were.

Van Vren lifted another pirate, and his dialogue was significantly longer and more colorful. Only at that moment did I realize that my clothes were soaked with human blood. It was cooling off in the evening breeze. Surprisingly, I found the stench disgusting. In no way was it appetizing to me.

My Other made a note to himself: *The notion that vampires drink human blood is crap.*

○ ☽ ☽ ●

Despite the other pirate's talkative nature, he also ended up in the churning ocean. The sharks really had a field day.

The rammed vessel was taking on water and started leaning. The crew, loaded with their loot, was winding its way back over the plank. The guard found the ship's safe, and Wries and Van Vren tied up and carried away the captain and other officers. Mr. Ho remained on the bow, the walkie-talkie in his right hand, and I understood that it was thanks to me and Denise that the prisoners were kneeling there staring at the deck.

Everyone must have understood that English word for *vampires*.

Wries had just returned and was saying something to Madam Dao when a giant man charged out from below decks—for a Chinaman, he was a super giant. In his hands was an Uzi with a black perforated cover over the barrel.

In the movies, these last fighters generally scream wildly and spray bullets all around them. This one was completely silent, and by the looks of it, he didn't know how to operate that nasty weapon and was going to use it as a club.

He was charging toward Wries and Madam Dao.

Without thinking, I reached for the nine millimeter. The giant, now with a hole in his head, lost direction and stepped right into the jaws of the nearest shark.

Left handed! I twirled the gun around my index finger and realized with disgust that I just saved Wries's and Madam Dao's lives. The giant probably wouldn't have had time to beat them up, but he could have at least thrown them into the ocean. Then again, why should some sharks have all the fun instead of me?

One day ...

"Thank you, Maestro," said Wries and frowned at the bloody froth beyond the railing.

"Don't worry about it. I was aiming for you," I murmured under my breath and put the pistol back on the corpse.

Unfortunately, he heard me.

○ ◑ ◐ ●

For that insolence, I had to go check below decks, since the giant had beat up several members of our crew.

I didn't find any other pirates, just the rising ocean, and ... I sniffed the air ... the unmistakable stench of people that have been held captive for too long.

All the way in the back, with the water up to my waist, I found a low door behind which were apparently hostages. Hostages might not be the right word, rather what was left of them. I felt my stomach tighten.

Those that still had eyes looked at me, pleadingly, and I knew what they wanted.

I had no choice but to shoot them all. They were grateful, but I hated myself. Better to hate myself than to let them drown or get torn up by sharks. I stood there, and the bloody water was rising up to my chest.

These were the kind of people that I would have otherwise saved, those that always mattered; the victims.

I realized that I really, really hated those who had forced me to do this.

It's always easier to hate someone other than yourself.

○ ○ ○ ●

I struggled against the current, which wasn't an easy thing on the ever-more-slanted floor. I suspected that the pirate ship would soon slip off the ram and sink to the bottom like a rock. I clearly heard jaws snapping and heavy bodies rubbing up against the outer hull.

No one was left on the deck, not even Madam Dao, and the plank was pulled up. Only the pirates continued to kneel on the leaning deck boards, and Mr. Ho was perched at the tip of our ship with a transmitter in hand.

"Mr. Ho, catch." I threw the nine millimeter up to him. It would have been a sin leaving such a fine weapon for the ocean to take. Any compassion I might have felt for the pirates was gone after what I saw below deck, and I wished those jaws on them.

I grabbed the railing with my left hand and pulled myself up. Water was gurgling out of the holes in my stomach.

Somehow, I couldn't quite scramble up. At that moment a hand wrapped around my wrist and pulled me up like a rat. For his size, Mr. Ho had oomph.

I stood next to him until the pirate ship slipped off. Those guys were hardcore. Not one of them begged for mercy; not one of them tried to climb up on the mast.

There was just this hissing splash!

I would have never believed it if I didn't see it, but the ocean literally teemed with shark bodies, and foam that was as scarlet as well-aged red wine splashed all the way to our feet.

○ ○ ○ ●

"There will be a victory celebration. Will you join us?" said Mr. Ho casually as we walked down from the bow. He hid the transmitter in the folds of his jacket and twirled the nine millimeter.

186

"Thank you for the invitation, but I'd prefer to rest today." I held my hand so that he couldn't see my holey kimono. "I broke the sword," I said, completely out of context.

"Doesn't matter. You are obviously much better with one of these." He lifted the gun. I wondered if he could trigger the explosive before I had a chance to shoot him—probably yes.

"The crew will prepare a hot bath for you on the stern. You did a good job." He let me go on by myself.

A good job, he says ... How many hostages were there? Seven? Eight?

I stopped some guy and asked him for a cigarette. He gave it to me and all but ran away. When I tried to put the filter between my lips, I realized I still had the ninja mask on. When I took it off, I knew by the stretching of my skin and cracking around my eyes that I was covered with blood where the opening in the mask used to be. Even the cigarette had red marks on it. I put it between my lips and clicked the trusty lighter. I noticed that I was wobbling a little, and the owner of the lighter was looking at my shadow. That arrow was still sticking out of me.

○ ◑ ◐ ●

I walked all the way to the stern where, behind an embroidered curtain, they were just scrubbing off Denise.

A hot bath in exchange for murder.

○ ◑ ◐ ●

I sat on the railing, and even though bloody water was dripping from my feet, I wasn't afraid of some shark grabbing me. Even sharks are smart enough to not commit suicide. I realized that my thoughts were strangely swirling and wandering, and then Mr. Ho was standing next to me.

"Why didn't you tell me about your injury, Mr. Tobias?!"

I didn't answer. I was thinking, *Why not just fall in the water...?* when suddenly I was on the deck and someone was pulling the arrow out of my shoulder. I felt weak.

"These arrows are poisonous. Everyone knows that! Otherwise, why would anybody shoot from a bow these days?!" Mr. Ho fumed. "Of course it can't kill you, but as your body destroys the poison, it makes you weak … What in blazes is this?!" The holes in the back of the kimono, where the bullets went through, must have been a little bigger than those in front.

"That's nothing." I started to get up. Removing the toxic stick really helped. "Is the tub free yet?"

And never make a weakness obvious to your enemy, I heard Dread's voice in the distance.

○ ◯ ◑ ●

"What is the matter with him? What a pansy!" Denise looked at me from above as she brushed her hair. She was dressed in a ceremonial robe, and besides jasmine, she smelled of rose oil too.

I sat on a box and watched as they belted the loose robe at her waist. Lanterns were starting to light up all over the boat.

"Buzz off." That was the best comeback I could manage. I didn't feel that great. They even had to help me to my feet. When I remembered that those bullets were meant for her …

In the meantime, they changed the water in the tub (which was really more of a large wooden vat). It really was warm, and even better, it was fresh.

A small celebration.

"Could you call Selma over?" I asked the people who were getting ready to scrub my back. She was already waiting behind the curtain. Mr. Ho removed the explosive harness and taped up the bullet holes with little squares of waterproof tape. Then everyone left, and Selma pulled the curtain.

○ ◯ ◑ ●

The wind was drying off my crew cut as I sat in deep darkness next to the deck cabin. Behind me was a coiled rope; my feet were up. As listened to the happy clamor of the band , I definitively decided to escape, not right away though …

"A cigarette, Mr. Tobias?" a deck boy, who brought tobacco and opium to the other dignitaries on the ship bowed in front of me.

"Cigarette? Why not?" I took another Camel. A dancing little flame illuminated my nose.

"You smoke?" Because of the cigarette smoke, I failed to notice the aroma of jasmine and rose oil.

"I don't." I released a blue cloud from my lungs.

"Smoking is an obvious sign of suicidal tendencies." Denise pressed her thigh against my shoulder—accidentally—as the ship rolled.

"Thanks for the psychoanalysis, *Mr. Freud*." I moved away and gazed at the cigarette glowing in the wind.

"What do you see in her?" she asked, her voice remaining the same. Mr. Ho's bong was bubbling somewhere on the left. She certainly wasn't referring to the cigarette. "She is just a plain whore," she continued when I didn't answer. "She has slept with everyone onboard, including Madam Dao!"

"Yes." I blew at the orange ambers. "I would say so. She has had many pleasant experiences." I tried to make a smoke ring, but in the wind, it was useless. Suicidal tendencies ... probably.

I felt how Denise stiffened.

"Why should I care that she is a whore? What else am I?" This time, the ring held for a little bit. "She opens her legs and gets food in exchange. I kill people, and in return, they let me live." I got up with difficulty and began limping toward the stairs leading to the lower deck.

"But ..." Denise said behind me.

"Don't worry. I didn't mean you."

○ ◑ ◐ ●

At the cage, I discovered a minor problem. Somehow, I couldn't get myself to jump those ten feet down; two bullet holes in the stomach do hurt quite a bit.

Luckily, Mr. Ho was very vigilant and lowered me down without anyone noticing my weakness.

I had a dream, I don't know what about, but it smelled like jasmine and expensive rose oil.

○ ◑ ◐ ●

A terrible shrieking woke me up.

I fell out of my hammock and still tangled up in my sleeping bag rolled into the middle of the floor. The sun had been up for a while.

"That's nothing, it's just Wries and Van Vren interrogating a prisoner," said Denise.

Again, I heard a scream of unbearable pain.

Despite hearing this a thousand times before, this time, Janie appeared before my eyes—and Babe—and I realized that I couldn't take it.

Again, there was a scream, this time a really long one.

It was I who had captured these guys, and now they were suffering because of how well I followed orders.

"Pirates usually have hiding places on shore and bank accounts, of course," said Denise.

Again, the screaming. Just then, I realized that I was hearing the familiar chatter of the crew. Apparently, they were watching the torture and placing bets as usual.

Screaming.

"I can't take this," I said.

She looked me in the eyes and without a word rummaged through her canvas bag. She took out a stick of wax that she used to make her eyelashes shiny, broke it, and quickly kneaded both halves between her fingers.

"Stick this into your ears."

"Song of the Sirens," I said and plugged up my ear canals. Then I wrapped my sleeping bag around my head, Denise added hers, and then it was finally quiet. In that quiet, My Other came out, so we chatted for a bit.

To the decision that I would escape, I added another: *One day, I will return. I am still the Night Club.*

○ ◑ ◐ ●

Denise held my hand, and when the interrogation was over, she unwrapped the sleeping bags. I scooped the wax out of my ears and heard only the last words of Madam Dao. She was standing above the cage looking at me.

"What's with him?"

"Poisoned arrow, it was in his body for too long. He needs to rest," said Mr. Ho.

"I was almost worried that he couldn't take a little bit of screaming," she said and disappeared.

After a while, I heard four loud splashes off the starboard side. It's strange, but I could tell the sound of a falling body no matter where it landed.

○ ◐ ◑ ●

Two days later, for the first time during the voyage, I heard the cawing of seagulls like they always mention in sailor books, but in reality maybe seagulls don't actually caw. I don't know.

By then, I felt good. The wounds had disappeared. Only my shoulder throbbed a little. Mr. Ho examined me every six hours, and I'd have to say he looked pretty amazed.

"You regenerate damn fast." Denise confirmed his astonishment.

As a reward for the way we murdered all those pirates so nicely, they lowered down a small rechargeable TV. To my utter horror, I discovered that Denise loved to watch soap operas and in Chinese, those are even worse than normal. I liked to watch Hong Kong action flicks and *Star Trek,* which was also pretty amusing in Chinese. Unfortunately, I saw a lot more soap operas because despite being healed already, I wasn't strong enough to defend my channel. Denise got into the habit of sitting on me, and when I squirmed too much, she tickled me.

I suffered valiantly, especially after Selma stopped by to say hello; that's when Denise would routinely give me a painful back massage.

Even worse, though, was the music channel. Denise must have had an even more perverted taste in music than Babe. When she discovered how much I despised the sweet, sentimental dribble, she even started skipping her soaps, so I could enjoy it to the fullest. I patiently lay there (in all honesty, those back massages were nice, and my shoulder throbbed less because of them), and in my mind, I spun a story about a tough yet fair fellow who was forced to do evil, completely against his will, by conniving evildoers and their alien technology. It could even be a brand-new book, someday.

○ ◐ ◑ ●

Two days later, I felt so well that it was me sitting on Denise as we watched an action flick with Chow Yun-Fat.

When she squirmed too much, I tickled her.

○ ◌ ◑ ●

An hour later, next to the TV, two bundles of black satin clothes landed with two rubber harnesses and exploding charges. In my mind, I had started calling them chastity belts.

○ ◌ ◑ ●

"Here." Mr. Ho handed me the nine millimeter and five clips. The weapon was clean and smelled of oil. Again, we stood on the bow, it was a dark night, and again, the engines hummed below us.

This time, even Mr. Ho wore a ninja getup. Wries and Van Vren were behind us in their coats and hats. Behind them was the entire crew, all dressed in black kimonos, with blackened faces, Uzis, and machetes.

"We are attacking a pirate village. It is apparently very large, and our task is to attract as many defenders to us as possible," said Mr. Ho.

○ ◌ ◑ ●

A hundred yards from shore, we got into rubber rafts with outboard motors. Half the crew remained on board because the people in the village had little boats too. Madam Dao stood behind her machine gun, an unlit cigarette between her lips.

"A village—women and children will be there," I said into the silence when the motor on our raft started humming. Its exhaust went into the water, so it was very quiet.

"Yes, don't kill them. They will be sold to slave traders," said Mr. Ho.

I was glad to hear that a human life did have some value.

○ ◌ ◑ ●

After a few minutes, the sand hissed under the bow.

It was a semi-large island with a rugged shoreline among thousands of other semi-large islands with rugged shorelines. No wonder the pirates left barely twenty men as defense. Five were handicapped, half were elderly, and all of them were so drunk they could barely stand. I could understand the pirates' reasoning: This place was hard to find by accident, and they couldn't imagine even in their wildest dreams that someone would betray them. Only an officer from their ship could do that, and why would he, right?

We captured the village without a single shot fired. (That's true if you don't count the execution I performed on a big-ass spider that climbed up on my shoulder by one of the huts.)

"You're not afraid of spiders, are you?" Denise's gray-blue eyes twinkled speculatively under her mask. Never again could I get hurt so much that she would have an advantage over me. I didn't know if there were spiders on the ship, but …

"Why should I be afraid of spiders? It just spooked me." I shook my head.

We gathered all the residents in the village square without any problems. I couldn't understand why, but they were genuinely horrified by us. Kids cried, teeth chattered, and fires crackled—since we used their wooden huts as light for our work.

While our crew carried the loot in from hideaways in the jungle (way too much silver for my taste), Wries and Van Vren performed a selection—young women and older kids on one side, everyone else on the other.

"Don't look," Denise whispered.

Well, sometimes it's important to confirm why you hate someone, especially when that someone you hate the most saved your neck. Instantly, I discovered that the value of human life varied: those that were too old, too young, or too sick had none.

Wries and Van Vren pulled out their swords and didn't quit until the last baby stopped crying. I read once that this was how the execution squads of the SS behaved. I wondered if they enjoyed it as much too.

○ ○ ◐ ●

We corralled the remaining forty souls into the biggest ship in the harbor.

The women who had lost their children cried quietly; otherwise, nobody else made a sound. They walked like sheep. The sand crunched under their feet, and the stars were shining.

I was glad that I had a mask on my face.

○ ◖ ◗ ●

Madam Dao, who meanwhile arrived in a speedboat, stood on the beach, smoked a cigarette, and examined the flow of prisoners. Once in a while, she stopped someone and examined their teeth. She separated out three young women and then began a discussion with Wries about how much he should charge for the whole lot.

Obviously, both of them knew something about people.

The burning village felt warm at our back.

○ ◖ ◗ ●

Van Vren and several sailors boarded Wries's vessel, tied a speedboat to the back, and sailed into the darkness.

The rest of us returned to our ship, where things were busy because it was necessary to carefully put away a lot of stuff. Precious metals are very heavy.

"Aren't you interested?" asked Madam Dao and nodded toward the three new ones who stood in the middle of the deck encircled by the crew (who were betting on something again). I was surprised to see that the women were smiling, and I realized that they understood they weren't too bad off.

"Thank you for your kindness, Madam Dao, certainly later." I bowed.

We sailed out on the ocean, and again, there was a celebration. I sat on the cabin, leaning up against a rope, smoking Camels, and listening to the ship's band and the gurgling of Mr. Ho's bong. When my social obligations were fulfilled, I returned home to the cage and for the rest of the night watched the stars. They were large, bright, and foreign. The screams of children being slaughtered couldn't be silenced by a couple of wax chunks and a sleeping bag around your head.

○ ◖ ◗ ●

15

Right away the next morning, I learned another reason why I was valuable to them. The exploding harness hit the planks and the cage opened.

"Please take your gear," said Mr. Ho. I watched what Denise did, and then I also strapped the knife holster around my calf, tightened the strap around my ankle, and tried to pull out the hollow needle—no one had told me yet what it was for.

"Leave your shirt here and take your swimsuit," said Denise and took off her own shirt; today, she was wearing light green panties. I pulled on my board shorts, the clasps on our chests clicked, and we checked each other's remote controls.

Up on the deck, it looked like some advertisement photo for *Visiting Tahiti!*—a cobalt-blue sky, an azure ocean, romantic mounds of white clouds on the horizon, plus little bushy, emerald-green islands.

The slaughtered children couldn't be seen from here.

"How deep is it?" asked Denise.

"I estimate about five hundred meters," said Mr. Ho.

I had no idea what they were talking about, and I watched the crew as they built a small crane on the port side, lowered some kind of a floating bamboo raft, attached a ladder to it, prepared plastic buckets with holes on the bottom—

Mr. Ho tapped my elbow. "Mr. Tobias, I am talking to you!"

"Excuse me, Mr. Ho." I bowed. The thing he tapped me with was a knife with an eight-inch-long, stainless-steel blade, rubber handle, and a wrist strap. I guessed it would fit perfectly into the holster on my leg.

"Is this against sharks?" I figured out pretty quickly that we'd be diving.

"No. Sharks attack vampires only rarely," said Mr. Ho. "That knife is in case something pins you down there and you can't free yourself. Then you can cut off your hand or your foot."

"Cut off…?!" I lifted the instrument in front of my eyes. That was why this thing had a serrated edge at the top of the blade.

"Yes, your appendage will grow back in a couple of weeks. We have special food additives to make it grow faster."

Cut off my foot, that's great! My Other noted.

"Below us is a shipwreck." Mr. Ho folded his arms behind his back. "Your assignment is to search the cargo and find the ship's cash box and possibly other valuables. Pay special attention to antiques. Madam Dao has extensive collections. You will receive a reward for antique armor or weaponry."

"Five hundred meters is pretty deep, isn't it?" I said, and the skepticism in my voice was *very* obvious.

"Your body can handle even five thousand meters without major damage … after some experience and after certain preparations."

Judging by the way Denise clenched her teeth, one's view of what *major damage* means probably varies from person to person.

"Thank you for the reassurance, Mr. Ho." I bowed, and Mr. Ho handed me a pair of black fins.

"Some important advice—just before diving, you have to oxygenate yourself well. It's demanding down there, and you should last at least two hours. Second, around ten meters," he tapped on the instrument around my wrist, "you should begin filling your lungs with water."

"Filling my lungs…?!" I must have looked a little frightened.

"You just breathe in some water," said Denise, "through your nose, so that all your respiratory tracks get flooded."

"Through my nose?! That's just great."

"You can't drown, Mr. Tobias, just don't forget to open your mouth when you are coming up, and relax here." Mr. Ho patted his neck.

"What about the needle?"

"If you feel your bones deforming," he tapped on my forehead, "then you shove it up here," he stuck his knobby index finger into my nostril, "maintain this angle, and push until it's enough. You'll know when."

"Right, sinuses and equalizing pressures," I said with apparent calm, but inside, I got all twisted up. I'd rather die than undergo this kind of *acupuncture.*

"Isn't diving a beautiful sport?" said Denise.

"I can't wait." I put the needle away.

"Oh, and initially, your eardrums will pop, but that will go away with time." Mr. Ho stroked his chin.

"I won't hear anything."

"But you will; with the resonating of your skull."

Damn, I thought.

"Damn," said Denise, "let's do it." She leaped over the railing onto the floating raft. I didn't say a thing and jumped after her.

"Take this too." Mr. Ho dropped some kind of milky candy into my hand—correction, more like earrings. Candy doesn't have stainless-steel clips on it.

"What is it?"

"Let's call them flashlights." Denise stashed one piece of candy in a little pocket on her wrist instrument.

"Flashlights?!"

"Yup, flashlights. Inside a wreck, it's too dark even for us. They make 'em out of glowworms!"

"Out of glowworms?!"

"Yup. Hide it for now, and attach it when you're down there—here." She tugged on the strap from the explosive charge.

"One more little thing, if you don't return within two hours ..." Mr. Ho raised the transmitter. "Of course, it works underwater also."

"Thank you for the information."

Denise was already breathing like she was preparing for labor. "Don't laugh and start too, I don't want to have to drag you as well." She pointed at the endless blue beneath us. It no longer seemed as azure as before.

I hate Tahiti.

○ ○ ◑ ●

Mr. Ho swung out the crane's arm and handed me a large dented chunk of lead with six handles on it. It was attached to a thin rope that dangled over a pulley and it had 550 lbs stamped on it.

"Aren't I a Hercules?" I held it in one hand with no problem. However, the bamboo below me didn't, so in the next instant, Denise was pulling me out along with the weight; she was smart and stood in places where the support beams crossed.

"Grab on to the handles, and don't let go until we reach the bottom. If something were to happen to you down in the ship, tap on something metallic with your knife. Two taps means danger; three, you found something; four is trouble. Watch the time, and ..." She turned her head toward Mr. Ho. "Two hours, starting now!"

Mr. Ho squeezed the stopwatch. A whirl of bubbles, and we dropped like a rock.

○ ◑ ◐ ●

Diving is no joke. The current was pulling off my swim trunks.

A little while after my left eardrum burst with a whining crack, Denise tapped me on the chest. I didn't want to, but my deformed ribs forced me to. Someone who has never inhaled water can never understand what I am talking about.

Then my right eardrum ruptured too.

The lower we dropped, the darker and colder the water was. The first to disappear was the red part of the spectrum, then the green, and that was when everything turned blue. I noticed that Denise already had her vampire eyes and was keenly staring down. I, on the other hand, was staring up; it was a more comforting view. The rope above was at a steep angle from the current that carried us.

Denise jammed her finger into my belly and looked very annoyed. For some time, she must have been trying to point out something to me on the bottom. I figured out that the vague shadow was our wreck. Denise put her free hand around me and hugged me tight, so tight in fact that the water in my lungs splashed around. I was thinking how I could strategically indicate to her that I didn't even want to think about sex right then. Only after she jammed her finger into my kidneys, for a change, did I get the point and began helping her to steer so we would land as close to the sunken ship as possible.

At two hundred and fifty meters, I began having problems with my sinuses. There was a nasty cracking inside my head, and it hurt more and more with each meter. Even Denise must have heard the cracking, and when she realized that I couldn't handle it myself, she took it upon herself to skewer my nose—disgusting, truly disgusting.

○ ◑ ◐ ●

The weight landed and raised a cloud of white sand. I always thought there was mainly mud at the bottom of the sea, but here it was sand. Our surroundings looked like a desert covered with ripples, stars, and trails from creatures that looked like prickly Big Macs. Even though it was dark, to our adjusted eyes, it was an acceptable purplish dusk. The pressure deformed my eyeballs so it was damn hard for me to focus.

"It's not the pressure!" My Other exclaimed cunningly. "It's a different index of refraction. Get it, you're used to the air, but here it's—"

"Water, I noticed."

Offended, My Other didn't say anything else.

I watched how quickly the cloud of sand moved; the current here really was strong. Then I watched how Denise matter-of-factly adjusted and tightened the strings on her little bikini. With those straps across her chest and that knife on her ankle, she looked a little S-M. I realized that the pressure didn't affect her bosom at all.

Neither did the angle of refraction.

She pointed at her eyes and then at the rope, and I understood that this was our primary point of reference. Some fish were swimming around, and they had the same purplish color as everything else—no brightly colored TV scenery here. I was so looking forward to it.

Slowly, we swam to the wreck.

○ ◑ ◐ ●

It was a metal ship, maybe a three hundred feet long, whose age I didn't dare to guess. It was all covered with a grayish brown-green sludge and small clams. I realized that I had only imagined that grayish brown-green color—even the sludge looked purplish. The ship sat a little crooked; on the side where the current came from was a high

199

bank of sand. The deckhouse and the bridge were in the back. I really didn't want to go into those gaping black holes left by broken windows, but Denise attached her glowworm and slid in just like that.

We had to move around carefully, because inside, there was sediment, and when it was disturbed, it looked pretty impenetrable even to the beams of light. The all-natural Chinese mini flashlights appeared to me like the strongest halogen bulbs; the nice thing was that the colors returned.

We separated.

I swam from room to room, and I started to enjoy myself—if it hadn't been for that stainless-steel needle sticking out of my left nostril. But even with that, it was more fun than the cage up there.

The kitchen was a terrible mess; everything was piled up in the corner. A withered skeleton in a raggedy apron was grinning at me from ear to ear, its hand on a rusty cleaver.

Tap-tap-tap.

For the life of me, I couldn't remember what three taps meant. So just in case, I returned to the hallway and started in the direction of the sound. (As Mr. Ho explained, you had to press your forehead against the wall and then you could tell where the sound was coming from; otherwise, it seemed like it was coming from everywhere and nowhere at the same time.) Anyway, whoever thinks that it's quiet underwater is dead wrong. With the acoustics of my skull, I sensed all kinds of interesting things; the murmur of drifting sand, the scratching of small creatures scurrying somewhere, the crunchy munching of something as it crushed the little clams growing on the ships hull ...

Tap-tap-tap.

All right already! I swam near the ceiling, avoided the hanging lamps, and watched the sediment disturbed by Denise's fins.

○ ◔ ◑ ●

She was in the captain's cabin and had tapped her knife on a metal strongbox. *Oh, so three means I found something.*

I closed the door behind me.

Judging by the décor, the ship was from the sixties—apparently American. The captain's bed was carefully made. Everything was held in place by two wide rubber straps that had decomposed and almost dissolved a long time ago, but they served their purpose. The cabin was pretty nicely decorated: an armoire, a desk, a bath corner ... A round paperweight filled with spirits was floating near the ceiling. When I shook it, snow began falling inside. *Christmas in Montana* was written on the log cabin, and the stark light of my glowworm gave the scene the feeling of a freezing winter morning.

I swam to a mirror that was still reflecting despite being covered by a thin layer of fine silt. Little squares of paper were tucked behind the frame, but the pictures from the photographs had long disappeared. A comb and a shedding toothbrush were sticking out of a holder. A porcelain cup with a broken handle lay on the floor.

Finally alone, I wrote in the dirt on the glass with the sharp end of the comb.

Denise put her knife away, and with a questioning look, she put her fingers behind her bikini strings.

I calmly analyzed the situation—so much cold water, the pressure of five hundred meters—and wrote under *Finally alone*:

Escape?

Denise emphatically shook her head *no*, swam to the mirror, took the toothbrush, broke it, and in small letters described all the means of escape that were ever attempted. No one had ever escaped. All the vampires that she had ever known had died in the services of Madam Dao. With surprise, I discovered that she had been a captive for more than twenty years.

You are a pretty old hag, I wrote.

With lightning quick speed, she pulled out her knife and placed it against the elastic of my swim trunks.

Very, very well preserved, I quickly wrote.

Agony is more than six hundred, she scribbled, *and for maybe four, maybe even five hundred years, she hasn't had a descendant. Why you, such an ordinary little person?"*

I am not just an ordinary little person! I wrote infuriated. *I am a writer, and girls really dig that!*

Ha-ha-ha! she wrote and then thoroughly cleaned the mirror. Then, just to be sure, she broke it. She pointed at the broken pieces, then up, and made a slitting motion across her throat.

She was more afraid of them than I had thought.

I took the strongbox, and then for a while longer, just for sightseeing purposes, we swam around the ship. In the ship's freight compartment were some huge steel things—pieces from a power plant or something like that. The water in there was brown from the rust and tasted metallic.

Slowly, we started to return, and thirty-five minutes before time was up, we swam out into the open ocean.

Open ocean ...

The charge behind my neck again felt uncomfortable.

○ ☽ ◗ ●

We put away the glowworms, grabbed on to the handles of the lead weight, and Denise yanked on the rope. For a normal person, it would have been impossible to try to pull on a rope held taut by the current, but the crane above must have rattled.

In a few moments, we began ascending. It was a feeling similar to being in a balloon.

The purplish fish swam above a purplish desert in the middle of which a purplish ship had capsized.

○ ☽ ◗ ●

Our ascent was a lot longer than our descent, and I have to say that was a good thing. The decrease in pressure didn't really make me feel good.

Suddenly, we were out of the water, and someone was yelling at me, "Close your eyes!"

I couldn't hear very well. Water was gushing out of the needle, and again, that yelling, "Blow your nose! Blow your nose!" That really helped. The pressure in my head decreased, and my eyeballs no longer bulged out of their sockets. Instantly, someone grabbed me by the ankles and lifted me into the air, pouring the remaining uncoughable bit of water out of my lungs ...

Simply hell.

I lay on the bamboo raft. The railing above me was swarming with slanty-eyed heads. Mr. Ho was standing next to me with his arms folded, and Denise was in a handstand coughing up the last bits of ocean. Then, she was more or less just in a handstand. Now I knew why the Chinese weren't chattering or placing bets, but just staring.

"What about the bends?" I said and was able to hear a lot better than a minute ago.

"You can't get the bends, Mr. Tobias," said Mr. Ho. "You would have had to breathe out of pressurized cylinders down there." By the looks of it, it was he who had poured the water out of me.

"So, did you bring me a treasure?"

The crew dispersed.

"I hope so, Madam Dao." I handed the box to her muscle-head. Second by second, I felt better, so one last spit and then I climbed up. Denise was already sitting on the cabin ringing out her hair.

"You okay?"

"Just peachy."

Mr. Ho jumped up after us and with a somersault landed in front of me. "It will tug a little." He pressed his left hand against my forehead, and with his right, he yanked the needle out of my nose.

"Thank you." I grimaced while peeking at Madam Dao and the rusty strongbox. I admit, there was something romantic about retrieving treasures out of sunken ships.

"Aren't you interested in what's inside?"

"Sure."

"So, come and take a look."

Li Pao brought a bag with his instruments and got to work on the lock.

"It's waterproof," he said after a moment, and after another, something in the lock crunched and the lid popped off. I didn't want to make my curiosity too obvious, and besides, since my eardrums hadn't healed yet, I was losing my balance a little on the rolling deck.

"Boy! You bring me luck!" Madam Dao reached inside and pulled out a fat wad of hundred-dollar bills. "Luck and gold too." She threw a small brick of yellow metal to me. "You can pay the Indians with that." I respectfully examined the heavy currency and returned it.

Because we worked so hard, we could take a bath in fresh water again. How comfortable when a perpetual layer of salt isn't constantly crackling all over one's body.

Even though no one was rushing me back into the cage, pretty soon, I was hanging out in my hammock. Needless to say, it was an exhausting morning.

○ ○ ○ ●

By noontime, I was feeling quite well, and my ears were as good as new.

"Your eardrums didn't burst?"

Denise was watching TV.

"No, with time, even yours won't; your body will adjust and learn to equalize the pressure."

"What about the *Titanic*?" Diving had caught my interest, and I thought about this legend the whole time down there.

"We raided the *Titanic* a long time ago. Don't even remind me."

"Tell me! Exaggerate!"

"I am watching TV. Can't you see?!"

"This stuff is always the same. Why don't you tell me about the *Titanic*! Denise, honey! What did you find there? On TV, I once saw Telly Savalas triumphantly opening a fished-out safe."

"Savalas? Oh, Kojak ... *Always the same?!* How can you say that the soaps are always the *same?!*" The episode had just ended. "How about we practice a little?" She obviously didn't want to talk about the *Titanic*—she never wanted to talk about anything.

"You'll get a whooping again, little girl." I tactfully reminded her how she had to find medical assistance last time.

"That was just a temporary indisposition on my part. I can always beat a pansy like you." That was when she put the TV away in the corner and tied the strings on her bikini tight.

"Full contact?"

"Otherwise, what's the point, you pansy?"

"How original."

○ ○ ○ ●

Even though it had only been a few days, I had improved so much that Denise didn't have a chance. *Why not?* I thought. *Changing into another species doesn't have to end with two-inch-long extending fangs. I can continue to evolve. Having Agony for a mother must mean the best vampire genes that* …While deep in thought, I got a wallop in the chin so hard that my head jumped back. I blocked her next kick with my forearm, whack, and I stopped my blow just in front of Denise's neck.

"You're dead."

"That'll be the day!" Another series of hard blows followed, but it seemed that our dear girl was getting weaker, or I was getting stronger. I tried a few moves that Babe had taught me, but I could never do them fast enough to be effective. Because I didn't have them internalized, I couldn't put the brakes on the last one and so Denise flew across the entire cage.

"Ouch," she said.

"Damn, I didn't mean that." I helped Denise to her feet, not really because of her, but because of what Mr. Ho said. But what can that old man do against my ever-growing attributes?

"You okay?"

Denise was buckling a little at the knees, and her eyes were all over the place.

"No."

"Don't pretend. You just want a cocktail made out of those tiny little fish, don't you?!"

"My back hurts."

I propped her up against my chest and looked at her shoulder blades. The grain of the wooden wall was impressed onto them—very clearly. I realized I could kill her.

"A massage?" I lightly ran my finger along her spine, and she relaxed.

"No. Yes, but I want to watch a show while you're doing it … Mr. Ho, please." Denise raised her voice, and our guard chased away the crew along with their tickets.

"Mr. Tobias, here." He threw me a porcelain dish with the camphor cream.

○ ◔ ◑ ●

For the next five days, we sailed along a barrier reef where shipwrecks were a dime a dozen. Usually, they were fifty meters deep, so we spent long hours underwater, and I learned all about diving. The wrecks were mostly untouched—not really because of the large number of sharks, but because of incredibly strong currents and unbelievably cold water. The only problem we had was silver coins, but that was resolved with rubber gloves and a bit of care. It was important not to mess around in the disturbed sediment. (We generally fizzed a little after that.)

Every evening, Denise and I practiced, but she had practically no chance. She beat me only when she wanted to watch her soaps.

Mr. Ho watched everything attentively.

○ ◗ ◖ ●

On the sixth morning, Mr. Ho said, "It's time."

Denise gave me a sly smile, and one of the crew, who had heard the words, started running around the deck and chattered so much it made one's ears ring.

"What's going on?"

"It's time, my boy, like Mr. Ho says," and again, that smile.

Mr. Ho opened the hatch.

○ ◗ ◖ ●

On the bow, behind the first mast, a space was cleared, but it didn't look like there would be any celebrations today—no drums, no noisemakers, and it was too early in the morning.

"Good luck, boy." Madam Dao was sitting on the upper deck, a side table with a tall glass on hand, in her eyes a pleasant tension in anticipation of pleasant entertainment. The entire crew was pressed around the clearing, and as always, they were frantically placing bets.

"What the hell?!"

"Yup, yup, you shouldn't beat up girls, my boy." Denise pushed me into the temporary arena.

"Oh, shit." *Now I get it.*

Mr. Ho came over and reverently bowed, his hands folded across his chest. He wore a simple black kimono bound with a black belt, the sun reflecting off his bald head.

"I am going to make a bet." Denise slapped me on the shoulder. "On Mr. Ho, to win," she said, to make sure I didn't miss it.

"All right," I whispered and thought about which of my growing abilities to reveal. Mr. Ho was surely quite good, but he simply couldn't keep up with me, not anymore. My goal, however, was not to beat up Chinese senior citizens; my goal was to escape from here, so ...

"Kumate," said Mr. Ho.

"I don't want to injure you," said I.

○ ◗ ◑ ●

It was a quick fight. Never in my life had I gotten my butt whopped so badly. I used everything except levitation. Mr. Ho was faster, stronger, truer, simply way better. When I stayed lying down, he said, "To a wise man, it should be clear what I just conveyed to you, Mr. Tobias."

It was clear to me. I should know my place, and most importantly, I should stop thinking about escaping.

○ ○ ◑ ●

Mr. Ho himself took care of my broken bones, and Selma took care of my broken spirit. They knew that I wouldn't escape in this state, so they left me alone all night and the entire next day.

"It's no good fighting a master of ninjutsu. It's definitely no good telling him that you don't want to hurt him before the fight," said Selma in a wise tone and carefully laid her head on my chest. Great care was very appropriate given the state of my ribs. I thought about how many of the last strikes there were, three, maybe four, or even five. They were so fast that I really didn't know, but they made my ribs into a puzzle. That was why I couldn't get up. On the flip side, though, four hours later, my chest was as good as new, although it did hurt a little.

That gave me an idea.

○ ○ ◑ ●

"Mr. Tobias, I hate to interrupt, but could you please return home?" Mr. Ho was really a polite guy. You couldn't refuse him. I patted sleeping Selma on the fanny, and after a short bath in the ocean, I was snug in my hammock.

○ ○ ◑ ●

The following day, I heard the growl of a speedboat, and Wries with Van Vren came back. A while later, the ship left the barrier reef and took off into the open ocean.

I behaved very politely the entire time despite Denise's chastising me with intolerable jokes, and the Chinese music channel running from morning till night.

On the next night, we attacked a huge cruise ship called the *Iron Cinderella*, that's when I escaped.

○ ◑ ◐ ●

16

"Why didn't you tell me Mr. Ho was a ninja?" Again, Denise and I were driving in a rubber raft, and this time, the night was pitch black, as only a night in the tropics can be. Clouds concealed the stars and the moon. Something unsavory hung in the still air.

"Who told you …? It was *her* wasn't it!" Denise said, and I realized it wasn't tactical to let her know that Selma had told me Mr. Ho was a ninja. I glanced behind me, but the driver of the boat couldn't have heard our quiet voices. Even though it was so still and unpleasant, the air whistled in our ears and the waves hit hard under the raft's flat bottom.

The ship we were approaching looked like a lit-up skyscraper from the back; it was a really *big* ship. In the briefing before the attack, Mr. Ho explained to me how I should behave. Most importantly, never kill a white guy, and if you have to, then don't let it be an American.

"After something like that, they always start waving their flag, rattling their aircraft carriers, and pretty soon, half of their fleet is chasing us," said Madam Dao.

"Your job is to frighten the passengers. Do a few flips, take down the usual heroes, and hold everyone in the main game room."

"How many are there? Passengers," I asked.

"Around fifteen hundred. Our crew will take their money and valuables."

"Be careful of the security guards, Maestro," said Wries. "They shoot without warning."

"Yes," said Mr. Ho, "the security force will be taken care of by the gentlemen here." Van Vren and Wries bowed. "But you too can kill them as you please."

○ ○ ◑ ●

We came closer and closer to the *Iron Cinderella*, and as the stern grew higher and higher, I became uneasy about how we would clamber up there. See, the fact that a person ... a vampire could do certain things—like levitate in my case—didn't mean that he lost his fear of heights ...

"Now!" said Denise. She threw something. There was a metallic click, and our taxi driver put it abruptly in reverse. The rope between the magnetic anchor and the raft was pulled taught with a loud snap.

"They have ladders, if someone falls. Not that anyone was ever saved that way, but it calms the passengers. They aren't as afraid to get drunk, and business blossoms," said Denise as she started climbing. I bent my knees and started after her, but a wave still got my boots all wet.

"Braaap!" we heard above us when we were barely six feet below the railing. I was thankful for the wind that blew the stream of puke to the side.

"What a pig!" whispered Denise. The man went off to have more fun while singing loudly. Cheap, duty-free alcohol was the main attraction on these cruise ships—cheap alcohol and gambling, of course. A thousand times of what one saved on drinks was lost in the ship's casinos and slot machines, but everyone was happy and the ship's safes became loaded with cash. These ships usually belonged to the Triads; that was why the anti-pirate security was tough and numerous.

I leaped over the railing, and the roar of the music and hum of the crowd scattered behind the glass windows got abruptly louder. I heard the rattling of little balls in roulette wheels, the ringing and whistling of slot machines, the metal clanging of pachinko, the meaty slapping of playing cards, and the never-ending rustling of paper bills.

Denise didn't even turn to me. She took off—the goal was clear.

Wries's hat appeared on the opposite side of the stern. We were late. The crew would begin to swarm behind Wries, and by that time, the passengers should already know they couldn't defend themselves.

I took off too and was appalled to hear that even here they listened to Denise's favorite Chinese music channel. On top of everything, about one hundred fifty drunken Japanese were just performing a group karaoke.

Even my goal was clear: the navigation room. See, it's really hard to escape, if you don't know where you are—especially if you're also in the middle of the ocean.

I had absolutely no idea where the navigation room was on a ship like this, but I suspected it was somewhere very high. So I pulled myself up on the next deck. It was all lifeboats up there, and the roar of the music grew fainter.

I jumped one level higher ...

"Hey! Yeah, you in the Halloween costume, hand me that ball!"

"Me?" I poked myself in the chest.

"Do you see anyone else here in a costume?" A man with meticulously combed gray hair spread out his arms, and the rest of his company laughed. I was on the exercise deck, and there was a bunch of white Americans in white shorts and white shirts playing a ridiculous white American game in the glow of white lights.

"Don't just stand there. Get the ball!" The lady's eyes showed she was slightly inebriated. Even a real American democrat like her starts to feel like a master pretty quickly among all these subservient Chinese.

Again, everyone laughed.

"There, yes, over there! It's not that hard." Another lady showed me.

Because I didn't want to attract attention, I leaned over and threw them the ball. But as it usually goes with these kinds of people, at night, in the Orient, they wouldn't leave you alone—especially when they were wearing white and you were wearing black.

"Hey, frieeend, we neeeeed someone to cheeeer." The first man imitated a Chinese accent.

I plucked at my ninja getup. *Do I look like a cheerleader?!* For a second, I saw myself jumping around with orange pompoms in my hands screaming, "Yayyyyyyy, go team go!"

"What is it gonna be, you Chink!?"

I stood up, and the man who had taken a step toward me stopped.

"Fred, isn't he standing up a little tall? What if we poured some ice down his pants?"

"Good idea." Fred took the champagne out of the ice bucket, picked it up, and at that moment, a woman's scream and a round from an Uzi came from the lower decks. Someone was shooting at the ceiling, and bullets were shredding the boards beneath our feet.

"Beware of the pirates," I said and chopped the neck off Fred's bottle. "This is how they open champagne." I ran around them, pushed off the railing, and before any of them could turn their heads, I disappeared into the darkness.

A bubbling geyser flowed across Fred's hand.

○ ◑ ◐ ●

The wide glass structure above couldn't have been anything other than the bridge, and the navigation room would be nearby.

I suspected that *our guys* were probably starting to miss me.

○ ◑ ◐ ●

"Hello, boys." I opened the door to the bridge. "Where are your maps?"

"Map ... what?" said the officer in a white, gold-embroidered uniform, with disbelief. He was white.

"Maps."

"Are you a pirate?"

"Why couldn't a pirate want maps?" Because I was pointing my nine millimeter at his belly, he nodded, and one of the Asians, in a less-embroidered uniform, ran into the adjacent room.

"What maps exactly?" He stuck his head out briefly.

"Hmmm ... surrounding and nearby area." I twirled my wrist. Then I pinned the next man's hand to the console, with my sword..

"If you don't want anyone dead, please don't call security," I said and refrained from revealing my vampire eyes; the less they knew about me ...

Blood ran down the console, and everyone stared at it in disbelief.

"Here." The Asian man put a large roll of wax paper on the map table. I was sure they had a computer version, but on paper, it was easier to see.

"Oh, crap," I said. Not that I was all that ignorant about geography, but neither the surrounding or nearby area was familiar to me and all the labels were in Chinese.

"Where are we?"

"Here," said the golden one and pointed to the center of a large, blue blob.

"Aha. Please start with the name of the ocean around here."

Suddenly, the man who brought the maps used a karate chop to whack me across the hand in which I held my gun. I didn't have to do a thing; he broke his own arm. From that moment on, everyone was very nice and helpful.

"We are in the South China Sea, roughly eighty nautical miles southwest of Macau."

"What is that in regular miles?"

"About ..." The embroidered one clicked the little beads on an abacus next to the radar screen. "About ninety-three miles."

What do you know? Good news, I should be able to swim that like nothing.

"Watch your eyes," I said and kicked apart the radio. A poor one, but an excuse nevertheless, in case I ran into Mr. Ho on my way. I couldn't leave the ship just yet, my plan was missing one very important detail. "Where is the nearest kitchen?"

"Kitch ...??? Two levels below the main deck."

"Great. Oh." I stopped with my hand on the doorknob. "There are a lot of pirates on this ship, so just steer and don't rush into anything. They're not exactly nice—like me."

They looked at me with some confusion.

○ ◯ ◐ ●

I jumped down about forty-five feet to the exercise deck, then to the deck with the lifeboats then ...

"Shit!" I pulled away from the window. Wries could have seen me even in the darkness. I glanced over and saw that they were robbing the passengers just fine even without me. I opened a door and slipped into a narrow hallway—sized for a Chinaman—and raced by the glass door of the main game room so fast no one could have noticed me.

Now I hope I don't meet … I thought about the part of the crew that went with Van Vren, Madam Dao, and her guard to rob the ship's safes. They carried pretty ugly persuasion instruments intended for the safe clerk.

○ ◑ ◐ ●

"Kitchen, kitchen, where are you?" I muttered and sprinted along the gray runner as the lights were shining unusually brightly. It was these eyes … I smelled burnt oil, but in this maze of hallways, I couldn't tell from where.

A small bellboy crouched behind a plastic palm tree at the nearest intersection.

"To the kitchen, move it!" I slapped him across the back with my sword.

The kitchen was flooded with bright light and completely empty. All kind of food was being burnt on wide stoves, and a greasy soup had been spilled on the floor. The shots from the Uzi could be heard even here. I shut the bellboy in the food storage locker.

"Start making some noise in an hour, not earlier, clear?" I made vampire eyes at him, and I think he understood.

I leaped over the puddle of soup and in the increasingly thicker smoke ran to the table for preparing raw vegetables.

"So where do we have it, knife, knife … here!" Almost immediately, I found the thing I was looking for. Only now did I realize that my plan simply *didn't have a single fault.*

The thing I needed was a large Chinese cleaver. Local cooks used it to cut everything. True, it didn't have to be a cleaver, but I needed something wide, flat, and of quality metal—and where there was a Chinaman, there was food, and there was also a cleaver. Not even today did they let me go without my harness, and the charge on the back of my neck was seriously itching me from my very first step in the wrong direction.

I figured it this way: if the harness could not be removed without the charge exploding, what if something was inserted underneath it, something sharp, hard, and wide, like a cleaver for example? The

214

charge would of course explode and of course would take me down, but it wouldn't disintegrate my vertebrae. The rest would be left up to my ever-improving regenerative abilities. The main problem was that they must not find me while I was out. So I would do the following: I would insert the cleaver between the charge and my back and use levitation to get as far away as possible from the ship. When my signal grew weak, the charge would automatically explode, and I would fall into the ocean. For that reason, I was now stuffing my kimono with pounds of stainless-steel silverware until I had a nice jingling spare tire. That should—and pretty fast—pull me down *really* deep. I was hoping not too deep. "Good-bye, my friends." I smiled into the black smoke from the burning groceries and thought about Madam Dao and her goons. The cleaver was really nice. The wedge-shaped blade would deflect the explosion a little to the side so I wouldn't get the whole thing in the back, but a part of the energy would change into rotation—my rotation. I hoped it wouldn't twist my neck off.

Now, only to get to the deck unnoticed.

○ ○ ◑ ●

The hallways were full of stench and smoke, but for me, it was the smell of freedom. From the game room, I heard two shots and the fall of a body; on a metal ship, you can hear everything. I even heard a distant screaming. The clerk probably didn't want to reveal the safe codes.

"I will return one day," I whispered and thought about the ship where I'd spent the last month and all those *pleasant* people that I met.

"I will return and invite you to the Night Club, *my friends*."

○ ○ ◑ ●

Intense gunfire came from somewhere on the ship. Apparently, the security got involved.

All the better, I thought, at least no one would notice me.

I peeked out on the port side. This side of the ship wasn't lit. There was no one in sight, only white screaming came from the upper exercise deck. I closed the door behind me and stood under the staircase, just in case. There was lightning in the clouds, and a few moments later, the thunder clapped. There was no better time for an escape than during a storm, I thought, but it was more likely that My Other was doing the thinking rather than me. In the flash, I saw (unintentionally) my height above the surface and began to question the quality of my plans.

Oh, well.

I took off my hood and ripped open the kimono; the steel of the cleaver felt very cold.

"Theeere …" The tip slid smoothly under the edge of the charge. "A little more …"

It thundered again.

This time, however, it was suspiciously close.

○ ◔ ◑ ●

17

Something wet was tickling me on the left cheek. I opened my eyes, and instead of the iron stairs of the *Iron Cinderella*, I saw some kind of planks directly above me.

Planks? Where the hell …!?

I tried to move, but I couldn't feel anything, not a thing, let alone move.

Instantly, I understood everything; the creaking of the hull, the hissing of the waves, the smell, the flapping of the sails …

Promises are supposed to be kept. Keeping a promise makes a man a man.

I really did return to Madam Dao's ship; I just didn't expect it to be so soon.

○ ◑ ◐ ●

It was an ugly disappointment, even though my plan was so good, so perfect. Judging by my inability to move, the charge had destroyed my spinal cord. Fine, that I was familiar with. It was much worse in the grave, but what the hell was tickling my cheek?

I rolled my eyes downward.

A big rust-colored rat was sitting on my bare chest and that tickling was its pink snout. Surprisingly, it was really a plain old rat, not a sewer rat. I spent a lot of time in the sewers, so I knew that a rat living in the wild was truly a rare thing. This rare animal, a little startled by the movement of my eyes backed up, and I realized that I was literally covered with rats. I don't know; they usually say that rats stink, but these smelled like wheat. I was hoping that there was an adequate supply of grain, because we could have a slight problem if they got hungry. As far as I could see, there were no marks on me from needle-like teeth. Just like anyone with a (freshly) severed cord, I couldn't feel my body from the neck down, but because all I had on was a pair of torn kimono pants, I would notice any bite marks.

I was lying in a small closet no bigger than a coffin. Gray light was coming in between the planks, the wind was blowing a lot more than usual, and the ship was really leaning. The nice weather must have ended with that storm on the *Iron Cinderella*. Momentarily, I heard the drumming of rain on the deck.

The rat started to sniff my cheek again. I couldn't speak just yet, or breathe, so I just blew all the air I could fit into my mouth at it. The animal began to rub its snout in this funny way. When I blew at it a second time, the rat quietly sneezed, turned away pouting, spun around twice on my chest, and nestled down to sleep—all the critters around me were also sleeping.

Of course! This was also a pretty good guess in *Vampires*—animals like us. That was why Cat was so friendly with Hanako!

In a moment, I realized another thing—much more important—spine or no spine, I wasn't in limbo for more than three days (according to my sense of time). That was a big improvement over several weeks of death-like unconsciousness in a coffin.

I wondered how long it would be before I could move again.

Instead of idle thoughts, I made like the rats and fell asleep.

○ ☽ ◑ ●

When I woke up and saw an even thicker flood of little rusty-colored fur coats, I wondered with horror if this attraction worked on spiders too! I remembered very well the big-ass hairy one that climbed on me in that village …

Sometimes being helpless is really horrible.

However, not even the cuddliest tarantula could squeeze through so many pointy white teeth.

I love rats.

○ ◑ ◐ ●

There was nothing else to do so I studied the social relationships in the rust-colored community, and My Other and I took turns thinking up a book. We continued the one about the roughneck who is forced by alien technology to do things he doesn't want to, except that the roughneck, unlike me, will have luck. A chance shot accidentally frees him, and with that, he even gains a cool yellow eye.

We were just arguing whether or not to give the roughneck some kind of super vehicle to start with and how to name it, when the rats dispersed all at once. In a moment, the deck above me lifted—Mr. Ho.

I had my eyes closed and played dead. He lifted my leg, then let it fall and knocked on my knee with his fist. Oh, he was testing my reflexes. Apparently, he didn't completely believe my unconsciousness. He had been monitoring my improving regenerative abilities this whole time.

○ ◑ ◐ ●

On the second morning, my hands began to tingle, and when I wanted, I could breathe in. Rusty, the name I gave to the big rat camping out on my chest, jumped all the way up to the ceiling when I really huffed at him deep from my lungs for the first time. Then he ran around on my stomach all upset, and I had a feeling that I could sense his paws.

On the next day, my feeling changed to certainty—and I could move my fingers too. Of course, the storm was the biggest attraction.

The ship sailed at an angle, so that I rolled into the corner, then it sailed straight, but it was so fast that it literally jumped over the waves. The rats were smart enough to move away from me; otherwise, the path through life would have ended under my body for many of them. It was fun—a wave would kick us up above the boards. All the animals would spread their legs in the air, and then we would all fall back down. The noise I was making was thunderous. Rusty sat on my chest; his little eyes glistened, and he looked like he was enjoying himself.

The storm lasted three days, and the plank massage did me a lot of good because after those three days, I was almost fine for someone who had had a bomb explode on his spine.

On the fourth day, the weather settled down.

I was just scratching Rusty behind the ears, when he took off and hid. In a moment, Mr. Ho tapped me on the knee, and my leg cowardly twitched—not even we can control this reflex.

The hatch closed above me, but judging by the excited hollering and strange banging on the deck, not for long.

"Let's go, Mr. Tobias," said Mr. Ho as he pulled me out. To be honest, I was not looking forward to this moment. When I planned my escape, the next time I was supposed to meet Madam Dao was in a situation where she was kneeling and begging for her life.

It didn't look like that was going to be today.

○ ◑ ◑ ●

The ship sailed on a broad reach tack, so she was leaning a little but wasn't rolling too much. The ocean was gray and dark clouds swelled low above the masts.

Everyone was on the deck. From the corner of my eye, I saw Denise; Selma, I didn't see. I was trying to look tough, as much as possible in tattered and flapping kimono pants. What really sucked was that Mr. Ho stood me upright; I wasn't all that well yet.

"You disappoint me, boy," said Madam Dao, and I didn't get a very good feeling from the tone in her voice. "Because of you, eleven members of the crew died, and we even lost one raft with money."

"That really tears me up inside," I said and realized that my position did have one advantage: I no longer had to pretend to be a polite lad. I could talk to them how they deserved to be spoken to.

"You are going to be rude?!"

"What would you say …?" I couldn't remember how to say *head cheese* in English so I at least made a face.

"You will be sorry."

"Kiss your ass if you can reach it," I growled, and the crew dropped their gazes down toward the deck in fear. I looked Madam Dao in the eyes and gave her a particularly obnoxious smile. She stood up, and I saw the knuckles on her tight fists turn white.

"Boy, no one ever escaped from my ship, and in the end, you will all do what I want. Sometimes it takes longer, sometimes even longer than that, but in the end, you will break. You will be glad when I allow you to kiss my feet."

"I would love to see that degenerate ... Wait a minute, you really have feet under all that fat?"

Bam!

Suddenly, I was on my back. The planks, so smooth from long years of scrubbing, were quite remarkable close up.

"It isn't necessary to dirty your hands with him, Mr. Ho. Our boy is only trying to get me riled up so that I will lose my temper and kill him. I never lose my temper, my boy. Never."

I slowly got up, and her voice caused something to cramp and then churn in that place where humans usually have a stomach—something very cold.

"You're shitting me," I said and concentrated on remaining upright. When her guard took a step toward me and she stopped him, I added, "Don't have the guts, Fatty McFatface?" and I made a universally well understood, yet not very polite gesture. Maybe he could throw me overboard.

The meathead's face dimmed.

"Believe me, boy, we're going to have some fun too, and a little longer than you," said Madam Dao. The crew laughed obediently, even though my jokes were definitely a lot better. Even Denise laughed. The thing that alarmed me was a strange contraption that I had noticed behind me when I got up. That must have been all the banging I heard down with the rats.

"So, boy, what you have done will be followed by a punishment ... a *strict* punishment." She emphasized the word *strict* and was looking at the contraption behind me. "Oh." She waved her hand as if she'd remembered something very important. "I know you don't know our language, so I will divulge to you what my people are betting on in this case: how long will it take before you start screaming." Again, she waved her hand, and again, she smiled. The smile didn't look very encouraging, and the gesture meant something like *begin*.

I must say that I have lived through several nicer moments—like my entire life so far.

○ ◑ ◐ ●

"Don't fight it, Mr. Tobias. That only makes it worse." Mr. Ho twisted my arm and turned me toward the contraption. It looked like a bed with high headboards but without the part that you would normally lie on. The whole thing was made of really massive beams, and on top of the posts were iron shackles with a ratchetting handle.

"A rack? Piece of cake," I said, and even though Mr. Ho held my head down I saw several admiring looks.

What a tough guy I am!

Maybe they weren't admiring, but full of pity.

With routine motions (that I remembered well from Father Kolachek), Mr. Ho put me in the shackles and pulled the ratchet taut between the headboards. I felt my spine crackle quite pleasantly. The stupid thing was that I had nothing to rest my head against, and since the explosion, the muscles on my neck weren't yet what they used to be. As I twisted around, I caught Denise's glance—it seemed to me that her eyes were tearing up.

"It's probably from laughing at those *jokes* of yours, you fool," said My Other.

"Hey, fat lady, is this all?" I raised my voice.

"No, this isn't all. You wouldn't believe it, but everyone asks that the first time around. In the end, even the toughest of you cried, so they wouldn't have to return to the bed. It's a kind of tradition here, after every escape attempt ... Only one guy tried it four times." Again, that smile. I would be very interested to know what happened to him. Even in this situation, it was unimaginable for me to think that I would live out the rest of my days on this ship. In my case, that could be hundreds of years, hundreds of escape attempts, hundreds ...

Li Pao approached, tested the chains, and surprised me a little by placing a metal basin underneath me.

At that moment, the usual betting frenzy started. Li Pao raised his hands. In his right, he had a stopwatch; in his left, something that I couldn't see.

Then I saw it; it was a large but otherwise unremarkable coin.

The coin was silver.

Li Pao placed it on my stomach.

○ ◑ ◐ ●

It wasn't really all that dramatic. Just imagine that someone placed a coin that was a steady six hundred degrees on your stomach.

It hurt so much that after just five seconds, I thought I'd go insane.

After ten seconds, I knew that the fact that I wasn't screaming was the biggest achievement of my life. The coin, in the meantime, burnt through my skin and was working its way down. It hurt more and more.

Dread once told me that in such a situation, it is necessary to act the way your enemies expect you to. *If they want you to scream, then scream; if they want you to cry, then cry, but don't overdo it because they might start to enjoy themselves.*

Really damn good advice.

After fifteen seconds, I realized that no one had ever experienced fifteen seconds this long—but still, I didn't scream.

When I saw, as in a fog, the wanting faces of the crew, I decided to wreck their bets—not for bravery, not for higher principles, just simple spite. I decided that *I* would not scream with pain.

I noticed that their faces were not *as if* in a fog, but they really were in a fog, actually in smoke that was rising from my stomach.

I was like, *What the hell stinks around here?*

After a moment, Li Pao added another coin—probably because his ticket fell through. It didn't get much worse.

I never thought I would be bothered by someone giving me money.

○ ☽ ◗ ●

When dusk began to fall in the sky to the east, I was glad for some reason. Night or day, it still hurt like hell. There were even bets on when the coins would burn through. At least now I knew why that metal basin was under me—so that the coin would make a noise.

I still didn't make a sound, and the admirable gazes increased. *I will kill each one of them with my own hands. I have hundreds and hundreds of years to do it.*

Truthfully, I was able to not scream by cheating. When the pain became unbearable, I gave my body to My Other and he screamed the entire time; you just couldn't hear it.

223

Around noon, the first of the coins clanged in the basin.

The other one fell out toward the evening. It took a while. I got my body back from My Other. He didn't look too good, poor guy.

○ ◑ ◑ ●

The entire crew was around again.

"I hate saying this, boy, but I admire you. I have never seen anything like this before."

Kiss my ass, you fat cow! I screamed at the top of my lungs—to myself. I didn't want to piss her off while I was still on the rack. I didn't want to piss her off period, since an eternal service on a pirate ship seemed to be a pretty tempting option for my future.

Mr. Ho pushed the basin aside and lowered me down. The jute bag was on his shoulder, so he dressed my wounds right away and carried me home to the cage.

○ ◑ ◑ ●

At first, I thought that once the coins fell out, it would be fine— big mistake. The pain stopped, but a little bit of silver must have gotten into my body because I felt really, really rotten. The graceful movements of the ship rocked me rhythmically in the hammock, and even without that, I felt like I had drunk a pint of pure grain alcohol yesterday—on an empty stomach.

"Are you hungry?" Denise asked.

○ ◑ ◑ ●

When I came to, I felt better. I was wrapped up in both of our sleeping bags, and above the cage was a canvas tent on which the rain was falling.

Denise was practicing shadow kung fu.

"Please tell me how we vampires can commit suicide," I tried to lift my head.

"It can't be done." She didn't look at me and slowly executed a corkscrew fist strike, the muscles on her forearm like ropes.

"A wooden stake through the heart?"

"No."

"Getting your head chopped off?"

"It will grow back together."

"Silver bullet?"

"Nope."

"Getting chopped into pieces?"

Denise didn't answer, and her muscles tightened a little more. Getting chopped into pieces, with our viability … probably a pretty dumb idea even for suicide.

Again, I fell asleep.

○ ◑ ◐ ●

The next day looked the same as the previous, except I felt a lot better. I peeked at my stomach and saw that all that was left of the burns were two round red spots.

"Something to eat?" Denise snuck up on me from the side, grabbed both of my wrists with one hand, and even though I resisted with all my strength, she threw apart the sleeping bags and began—very slowly—massaging my burns with Mr. Ho's salve.

"I would take some pants first, if you don't mind."

"Of course." She unwrapped the sleeping bags completely and pulled on my shorts.

"I could have handled that myself," I said when the waistband snapped on my belly button.

"I am not so sure about that."

Me neither.

She called up top. Mr. Ho lowered a basket with fish, and she prepared a meal. When I wanted to climb down from the hammock, I discovered with astonishment that I couldn't. Denise lifted me, laid me on the deck, sat behind me, propped my head up against her thigh, and began feeding me with a straw. We'd done that once before already.

"It will be fine, even silver metabolizes with time. You just have to get plenty to eat right now." She rapped on my ribs so hard it made me choke.

I wasn't in any hurry after eating, and Denise wasn't either. She turned me to my side and started massaging my neck. "This part looks pretty good already." She stroked the places where the charge had exploded. I felt smooth, fragrant skin under my cheek and felt fine. It

appeared that she had given me a shave when I was out—probably so
that I was not prickly in situations like this.

○ ◑ ◐ ●

Three days later, I could feed myself, and three days after that, I
started to practice shadowboxing with Denise. I felt a lot better than
I let on, but it's nice when you don't have to prepare your own food.
Even Mr. Ho raised his eyebrows (again) at my regenerative abilities.
He treated me as if nothing had happened, as if there were no escape
and no coins on my belly.

"Denise, tell me what they are?" I waited with my question until
after she had handed me the glass of blood. It was absolutely clear who
I meant, and it couldn't have been such a great secret that she couldn't
reveal it to me. Regardless, she didn't say a word, except to remind me
of the ship's number one rule that everything was on a need-to-know
basis. Even while we were down in those sunken ships, she refused to
discuss (or write about) this topic. She always shook her head so much
that her hair whirled around her head.

That was a problem.

How was I supposed to make up escape and revenge plans if I
didn't know what my enemies were, I didn't know what they could do,
and I didn't even know what to expect. Even though I had made some
unbelievably accurate guesses in my *Vampires* book, I couldn't count
on the fact that Wries, Van Vren, Mr. Ho, Madam Dao, her guard,
and God knows who else on this ship had the abilities that I attributed
to my so-called Hunters. In the book, the Hunters and vampires had
very similar physical assets; they were just distributed differently. In
reality, my senses were significantly more acute, but the Hunters were
faster, stronger, and generally better at the important stuff. Maybe I
just had to wait until I finished evolving? What about Denise, though?
She was for sure all grown up for a vampire, and even now she was
weaker than me (true, not exactly *right now*). Surely I wouldn't, as I
added on the years, get weaker? Why, even Hanako, despite her blessed
six hundred, looked to be twenty-five and her conditioning certainly
wasn't lacking.

Denise didn't want to say a word about this either, not even about
whether Wries and Mr. Ho, for example, were the same species, not

even about how old Madam Dao was. (Just once, she unintentionally spoke about our buxom leader fighting during the First Opium War and mentioned that she hated the British.) I didn't know when the First Opium War was, but I suspect it had something to do with the cessation of Hong Kong from China and that was pretty long ago.

In short, because Denise wouldn't tell me anything, I stopped talking to her—completely.

○ ☽ ◑ ●

After eight days of silence, she looked very unhappy. I didn't know why, but that delighted me.

"I really can't tell you. Really," she said and sounded a little weepy. I was sitting with my back to her pretending to meditate. She had tried everything already. I ignored the Chinese music channel over which we always argued before whenever it was on. It cost me a lot of strength, but I prevailed. (The silver coins were good practice.) I didn't even watch the movies that she tuned in for me, and I ate alone too. Then she acted like she wasn't talking to me either, but she lasted exactly until the, "I really can't tell you. Really."

I continued to act like I was meditating, because I had a plan. Since I couldn't learn anything about my captors from Denise, the only ones that I could learn from were my captors themselves. When the relations in the cage got sufficiently thick, it could be expected that they wouldn't leave it that way. Even a vampire is a social creature, and when he doesn't speak for eight days, it could be a symptom of some problem that needed to be investigated. A vampire with problems certainly wasn't as effective as a vampire without problems.

Decreased effectiveness brought financial losses.

It lasted two weeks.

Then Mr. Wries came by for a casual chat.

○ ☽ ◑ ●

Denise no longer got up from her hammock, and she no longer changed her clothes. Sometimes, I felt her looking at me, and more than anything else, there was hate in those stares.

I was glad that my plans were working out.

"Maestro, how's life going?" Wries put a chair up top under the rain tarp. He sat, a pipe in hand, and threw me a box of Camels and a lighter.

"Mr. Wries," I said with *surprise* and turned so that I could see him. "Truthfully, not that well." I lit a cigarette.

"What's the matter? Difficulties? Discomfort? Illness?" He sounded really worried.

"Don't know." I released a smoke ring. (I had gotten much better at doing that.)

"Your girlfriend, Selma, she died, but no one would object if you found another. Just say so."

"Died?! What happened?"

"Oh, it was nothing." He waved his hand, but then he remembered that today, he was playing the good guy. "During that huge storm, when you escaped, she fell into the ocean and no one noticed. Everything was in disarray here. They were shooting rockets at us from the *Iron Cinderella*. On top of that, the weather, the night … plus, she was somewhat sick, threw up all the time, that happens quick." He packed the tobacco with his thumb. A whirl of air grabbed the ashes from my cigarette and for several long seconds held them almost in one place. I relaxed my concentration, and the ashes flew in all directions— probably just coincidence.

"Physically, you are all right? I can obtain a typewriter for you if you'd like to write?" He struck a match and puffed.

"True, I am a bit bored. You don't have too many books around here, do you?"

"Not unless you read Chinese or wish to read the English version of *Vampires*." He looked really unhappy, took off his glasses, and in a very human gesture, began rubbing the base of his nose.

"Though …" I paused.

"Yes?" He put on his specs, and his gaze pierced my eyes.

"You probably wouldn't want to do that."

"Speak your mind, Maestro. Let's hear it." He smiled, and I felt the sharks in the depths beneath the ship disperse in all directions.

"Good … Could you train me? With a sword?" I said it quickly and bashfully. A request for teaching in anything usually seems like ego-stroking of the one you're asking. Wries looked at me with great scrutiny. He was for sure familiar with this approach too.

"The fact that you want to kill me is no secret to me." He paused. "True, not that I forgot what you did in Prague, never. But …" I paused. "What would I get out of it? I can't escape … and some kind of feeling of complacency? Satisfaction? Revenge? It'll be swordplay just for the sake of swordplay. It would be more fun than this." I motioned to Denise's back.

Wries didn't say anything and studied the horizon (which was invisible to me). I lit another cigarette.

Suicidal tendencies?

"I guess we can try it." Wries bit down on the shank, cast a sharp gaze my way, and left.

In a moment, a sailor ran up and took away the chair. The lighter and cigarettes remained.

○ ◗ ◑ ●

On the second morning, I received a loose black kimono from Mr. Ho (*A noble match requires appropriate clothing, Mr. Tobias*), and after I promised not to try and escape, they allowed me up on the deck. I considered jumping in the water, and no one would ever see me again, but a word is a word. Interestingly, whenever they gave me my remote control, they never wanted a promise; maybe it was some kind of a strategy.

"So, Maestro, what weapon would you like to learn?" Wries stood by the front mast, again only in his shirt, his necktie tucked in between the buttons of his shirt, derby hat low on his forehead.

"Katana? It appears to be appropriate for the East."

"A Japanese style, good then." He snapped his fingers, and a Chinaman hurried up with the swords.

○ ◗ ◑ ●

He taught me how to stand, how to defend, how to back up, what strength to use so I didn't keep on breaking blades, and of course, we also engaged in combat.

After a week, I realized that I was looking forward to these all-day clatter sessions. Not only was nothing else happening on the ship (we maintained our course and hurried someplace), but I was beginning to enjoy swordplay, and a physical workout doesn't hurt anyone. Let's not delude ourselves, Wries was probably the best person to learn from on earth.

"If you can wield a sword very well, then no one with a firearm has chance against you—in hallways and rooms of course," he would always say. Even though we practiced on a rolling and perilously leaning deck, he never injured me. He could always stop the blade. Only when I made a serious mistake did he slap me, in dissatisfaction, with the flat part of his sword.

Then, after fourteen days of intense training, it was he who made the mistake.

○ ◑ ◐ ●

I knew that I was getting better day by day. The coordination of a vampire body really was several times better than a human one, but as of yet, I wasn't good enough to beat Wries. The speed and flexibility of his movements were truly unbelievable; plus his size and apparent clumsiness confused me. It would always seem to me that there was no way he could pull off a certain move, but he always did—I mean, up until that day.

I knew that it must happen one day. Everyone makes mistakes.

○ ◑ ◐ ●

Twice, I struck against his neck, and as always, he parried without a problem. Then I used this amateurish attempt at a trick I had come up with the night before. I pretended that the force of the defense threw me off, and he naturally attacked. I acted as if I had tripped, but as I fell, I got him in the knee with my heel and at the same time used the energy of my fall to do a corkscrew on the ground. While he was wavering backward, I pushed off the deck and still had enough speed in the right direction to unexpectedly attack him—which I naturally did.

Wries would have probably blocked it, but just then, he made a mistake.

○ ◑ ◐ ●

It wasn't really a mistake, but the fact that the deck could roll in the opposite direction from what you expected was something you must simply count on.

A hard chop against the cross-guard and a vigorous stab at his unprotected neck …

How easy.

Wries looked into my eyes.

"Sir?" I said and lowered my blade.

He continued to look into my eyes. He knew that I knew that I could have at least seriously injured him right then.

"You could have killed me, Tobias." That was the first time he had called me by name.

"Who would I sword fight with then?" I grinned.

"En garde!" he said, and the swords rang again.

○ ◓ ◑ ●

Apparently, nothing had changed, but in the evening, when he got into the habit of smoking a pipe above the cage, he invited me up for the first time.

"Is the promise on?"

"Yes."

He brought me a new box of Camels, and a sailor pulled up a chair for me. We were silent as we watched the stormy gray horizon. The clouds had sulfuric-yellow edges.

Our nightly smoke turned into a new ritual—observing the horizon had a lot to it. On the fifth day, Wries leaned toward me, and in a quiet voice, he asked, "What do you have against her?" with his eyes motioning to Denise. In the whistling wind, she couldn't have heard anything.

"Nothing … I hate her." I shrugged my shoulders.

"Hmmm … that happens." Wries nodded his head, and we continued the silence.

When night had nearly fallen and Wries packed an untraditional second pipe, I said, "May I ask you something?"

Rain began drumming on the canvas above the cage. Wries puffed, and the pipe lit up his face. He slightly nodded.

"Why did you torture that blonde back then in Prague? In the bar?"

Wries was silent, so I thought he wasn't going to answer.

"When we walked in, Mr. Van Vren noticed that she and Agony had ... that they were *intimate*. I think he said something about a hand on the knee, almost under her skirt." He paused and not a single muscle moved in his face, but I knew that from the corner of his eye, he was watching me just as closely as I watched him. "And Agony didn't run away even though she could have before I took a position at the second exit." His teeth gnashed lightly on the shaft, and the rain wildly intensified for a moment. "So the objective was to force Agony to come with us voluntarily ... nothing personal." He turned his head toward me abruptly.

"She didn't go," I said.

"She didn't."

"If she had gone, would you have left the blonde alone?"

"Why are you so interested?" He was still looking at me.

"She was my sister."

"Of course we would have left her alone," he said.

Now I knew what his face looked like when he was lying.

○ ◯ ◑ ●

"We can't work out today, Maestro." He apologetically raised his hands the next morning. "Because we will reach port," he replied to my questioning look. "Moreover, they're going to box you up for a couple of days, so you should get plenty to eat. Later." He flicked his derby hat.

I looked at Denise, but she hadn't even turned on her side for the past two days.

Not that we wanted it, but Mr. Ho lowered down some fish and even Denise ate. Not even once did we look at each other. Could she have heard me even over the whistling wind?

A little while after noon, they covered the cage with a false deck. Before that, they took away our TV and my lighter and cigarettes, and Mr. Ho carefully reminded us to keep as quiet as possible. Li Pao was standing next to him and was flipping a large coin. In the murky light, it gave off greasy pale reflections.

I knew that I wasn't going to make a peep.

○ ◔ ◑ ●

For the next three days, we were docked.

From the deck, we heard the pounding feet of servants carrying out treasures and bringing in supplies, the banging of crates and barrels, and sometimes rain. We saw the green dusk in the cracks between the planks and smelled the spicy aroma of trees and the stench of sweat. I had absolutely no idea where we were because no one said a word in a normal language; it was all just chatter. On the second night, the glutinous smell of cooked rice and fish was coupled with the smell of gasoline, and somewhere around the cage, the fat pipes bubbled. So we were probably not in a public port. Madam Dao probably had no urge for anyone to know that our inconspicuous wooden junk had gas afterburners.

I wanted to ask Denise where we were, but I was not going to risk my laboriously implemented plan because of a little bit of curiosity. It didn't matter anyway. I simply had no chance of getting out of the cage.

Then we finally set sail again.

○ ◔ ◑ ●

"You all right?" The deck lifted, and Mr. Ho was looking worried.

"I am, but she is a little stinky, so I am not sure." If anyone had ever received a murderous look, it was me right then. I smiled at Denise kindly. Mr. Ho furrowed his eyebrows with discontent and left, and Denise again took up the position of a rotting corpse.

When Mr. Ho returned, I was expecting him to bring food, but he surprised me. "Miss Denise, would you be so kind and come up on the deck?" The hatch opened.

She was so kind.

After about an hour, the regular janitor lowered himself into the cage with a bucket and a mop and scrubbed the already squeaky-clean floor. When he finished, he handed his utensils up to Mr. Ho, then packed up Denise's hammock, sleeping bag, and canvas bag, and threw them up top.

"What's going on?"

No one answered.

○ ○ ◑ ●

"Practice?" The next morning, the derby hat appeared above the cage.

"Looking forward to it."

Wries didn't even ask me to promise that I wouldn't run away. He must have considered my commitment to sword-fight training as permanent.

The swords started clashing, and I discovered that I wasn't really concentrating. Wries frowned, and whacks from the flat blade rained down on me. Instead of swordplay, I was focused on any sign of what they did with Denise. They couldn't have …

"Ouch!" I said. It hurt on the back of the hand.

"Don't let your mind wander, Maestro, because otherwise …"

He was interrupted by loud yelling from the lookout. Something resembling organized chaos broke out on the deck.

"What the—?" but Wries was already long gone. Surprisingly, I was left alone on the bow, sword in hand.

But a word is a word.

Because the lookout was pointing somewhere east, I gathered that he probably saw a ship, and judging by the hoopla, it wasn't just any old ship. I walked over to a barrel of rice, jumped up on top of it, and looked in the indicated direction.

It wasn't a ship, but rather three ships, speedboats, judging by the tall, white wings under the masts—and they were coming our way.

They were pretty big, and the stark boxy deckhouses looked *very* military. I came up with one acceptable explanation: We didn't do a very good job hiding the fact that our junk was in port.

So it was a police anti-pirate unit—or the army.

Or the Triads were really upset by the way Madam Dao had raided the *Iron Cinderella.*

○ ○ ◑ ●

The crew began to swarm and take their positions on the deck—their favorite Kalashnikovs in hand, machetes on their backs, and knives on their belts. Still, no one was paying attention to me, and the enemy ships were approaching awfully quickly.

I felt as though I should also be doing something. Despite my recent suicidal thoughts and self-destructive tendencies involving smoking and other theories about death and feeling sorry for myself, I too valued my life.

A flash came from the middle ship.

I thought that the tube pointing in our direction looked kind of suspicious, and what do you know? It was a cannon.

○ ◑ ◑ ●

Zoom!

A projectile missed us by three yards, and after a moment, a tall white geyser bloomed in the ocean behind us.

Crack! The sound of the blast reached us. Considering how far away it was, even the first shot was awfully accurate.

"Distance?" An obese, raspy voice came from the upper deck.

"Two point seven miles," said Van Vren. I'd almost forgotten what his voice sounded like.

Another little flash of fire.

Zoom! Smack! Crunch!

I looked up and saw a perfectly round hole, about three inches in diameter, in the sail above. The surrounding canvas was smoldering.

Another geyser erupted, this time much closer.

Why wasn't anyone from here shooting back? Damn it?!

Zoom!

This time, the shell gouged a chunk of wood out of the railing on the bow. If the ship just happened to be going up a wave …

Crack!

A fountain rose a little too close to the side and collapsed on the stern. I stuck the sword into a barrel and leaped up to the upper deck next to Madam Dao. Now we were all in the same boat.

"Why aren't we shooting?" I quietly asked Wries. He stood there along with the entire ship's elite. Van Vren was looking through binoculars with a prehistoric range finder, and was wearing a striped sailor T-shirt.

How shocking.

"We haven't got anything," Wries answered from the corner of his mouth.

"Rockets?"

"Don't have any."

"At least a small cannon?"

"No."

Son of a bitch, I said to myself in Czech. When a person is in trouble, he always starts thinking in his mother tongue.

Thump! Thump! Thump! Little, but nasty, fountains began jumping up from the ocean. A little orange light blinked rhythmically on the boat to the left.

Thump! Thump! Crunch!

It must have been an anti-aircraft gun, maybe a thirty millimeter. Its rounds were too short and it fired too slowly and too accurately to be a machine gun. Also, the crew member who went *crunch* was in bad shape. The round had almost cut him in half, and a scattered image of bloody tissue splattered all over the scrubbed deck.

It smoldered.

"Two point two miles," said Van Vren, and Madam Dao lit a brown cigarette.

"Why don't we have rockets? A few Stingers, or whatever they're called ..." I didn't finish.

"Madam Dao is a little conservative in these matters," Wries whispered.

"I heard you, Mr. Wries ... But you're right, I am conservative, but I have a right to be at my age."

Another row of little fountains bloomed, and this time, two of them jumped on the ship. Two men with a fire hose doused the holes where they hit and where little flames already slithered around. I wondered dejectedly how much gas we must have.

"The gas tanks are below the water line and are surrounded by reinforced steel." Wries was apparently reading my thoughts. "But that eighty-eight ..."

He was also reading my worries.

Zoom!

If the helmsman hadn't maneuvered out of the way, we would have gotten a direct hit. I clearly saw the swirl of bubbles behind the shell and the way it exploded a few feet below the surface.

The fountain missed us this time.

"One point nine miles," Van Vren announced as if he was at a boring golf tournament.

"How about a long rifle of some kind?" I asked.

"How about a long rifle of some kind?!" I said a little louder.

Madam Dao turned toward me, eyes squinting, looking like she was sleeping. We didn't really chat a lot since my rude comments preceding the torture.

"Mr. Ho?" she said, and it could have meant anything—even that he should kick my ass back into the cage. Mr. Ho ran off and returned with a plain old hunting rifle that had a scope and two five-round clips.

Correction, that rifle wasn't so plain. They hadn't made barrels that long for over a hundred years. Even the caliber was massive. The rounds didn't have lead tips, like I expected, but copper with something blue at the tip—it looked hard.

I shoved one clip in and rattled the bolt handle. The rifle smelled the same as Theodore's workshop, and on my back, I felt this long, cold touch. Mr. Ho would chop my spine in half way before I could even begin to aim at anyone on the deck.

"To the railing please, Mr. Tobias."

I didn't argue with him because another round of anti-aircraft fire was marching toward us.

It cost us two more crew members. One wasn't dead yet and screamed like crazy.

I shouldered the weapon, looked into the scope, and realized that this wasn't going to work. I undid the clasp and removed the objective. My eyes were really damn good.

I stood with my legs firmly planted shoulder width apart, and I synchronized my hips with the rolling of the ship.

Thump! Thump! Thump!

This time, the round flew at our height. A bunch of green bananas splattered to all sides, a severed rope rattled, and a barrel of rice ripped apart. Projectile shrapnel killed another man.

Bang!

The bolt rattled.

Bang!

Again the bolt.

Large casings dropped on the deck.

I thought that the weapon didn't kick at all. My vampire muscles absorbed the recoil almost completely.

It took the bullets a little longer than the shells from the cannon. I put both of them in the windshield of the middle boat. I clearly saw a set of spiderweb cracks running outward. Unfortunately, it seemed to be very bulletproof.

Bang! Bang! Bang!

The gunner at the eighty-eight wasn't as bulletproof—even though I hit him purely by accident. Blood splattered all over the speedboat's windshield, and the wipers started moving back and forth.

"Magazine," I said. Mr. Ho handed it to me and began filling the empty one with ammo.

○ ◗ ◑ ●

The gunner was the only person I took down, but my shooting forced the other boats to zigzag so the accuracy of their gunfire deteriorated quickly. Then I hit the base of the rapidly firing anti-aircraft canon, and it started shooting completely off target.

"Nice, boy," said Madam Dao.

I was surprised how they could have survived without me since the Opium Wars.

I heard the roar of a strong motor. I turned around and saw that a boat was just taking off from the stern with Wries, Van Vren, and the guard. It was the exact same boat that had brought me here. The sailors called it a fifty-seven.

The helmsman took a sharp turn and sent the bow of the junk directly against the attackers. Madam Dao was already clutching the handles of her double-barrel machine gun.

"Fourteen hundred yards." I took over the announcer's job, and my estimates were about as true as Van Vren's range finder.

"Last five." Mr. Ho handed me a magazine.

"We'll save those." I returned the weapon to him. "Can you hand me a Kalashnikov?"

"Sure," said Madam Dao.

"Thirteen hundred."

Zoom!

Crash!

The ship shifted under my feet, and with a somersault, I landed on the lower deck. Madam Dao spun all the way around the machine gun stand—she didn't let go.

The shell from the eighty-eight swept off a piece of our deckhouse and the rear mast. Shredded bodies lay everywhere, and the men with the hose began dutifully putting out fires.

"Eleven hundred yards."

I returned up top. The planks were riddled with shrapnel, and there were several holes in Madam Dao's loose dress. Apparently, the holes were not just in her dress judging by the pieces of flesh, but the fat lady ignored it.

"Did you say eleven hundred, boy?"

"Yes, ma'am."

"That's a good distance." She lifted the muzzle of the gun upward, and steel rain began drumming upon the incoming boats.

Besides being demoralizing (the noise inside must have been terrible), it also had a secondary, unexpected effect: The roofs of the boats weren't as reinforced as the bows, so once in a while, a *drop* snuck through.

Then the fifty-seven arrived by the left boat, and despite an angry barrage of small arms fire, it managed to hook on.

After about ten seconds, the rapid-fire cannon rattled again—the one from the hooked boat—but this time, it wasn't aiming at us, but at the boat with the eighty-eight. From such a close range, hitting it was very possible. The stricken boat rapidly slowed down and went into an uncontrolled spin.

I saw how the deckhouse became covered with smoking holes and the inside of the windows with blood.

The last boat, however, was still attacking. So it wasn't the army or the police; those guys would have strategically retreated by now.

The Triads never retreated.

I was a little surprised that these guys didn't reveal their full arsenal yet. They were too close for indirect gunfire, so Madam Dao's projectiles sparked harmlessly off their steel.

"Three hundred and fifty yards."

"A Kalashnikov, Mr. Tobias." A sailor ran up and hung a bag full of green magazines on my shoulder. Mr. Ho wasn't guarding me anymore, but I would have to be crazy to shoot at anyone other than the actual enemy.

"Two hundred and fifty."

A large orange light rose from behind the deckhouse of the attacking boat, and I glimpsed a pointy shape just before the boat that Wries occupied exploded in a ball of fire and smoke.

After a moment, I almost went deaf from the whoosh of a rocket and the crack of an explosion.

At one hundred yards, even the crew began firing, but it wasn't very effective—actually not at all—and not just because our helmsman was zigzagging like crazy. The ocean around the attack ship bloomed under the strikes of hundreds of bullets. An amazing rainbow appeared in the sloping rays of the sun filtering through the clouds. Vampire eyes are really something.

I jumped down to the lower deck and yanked my sword out of the barrel. I didn't have anywhere to put it so I stuck it through the kimono on my back. I just hoped I didn't cut myself too much. I returned up top, shoved a magazine into the Kalashnikov, and pulled back the charging handle. The way the ships were speeding toward each other, the thing that I suspected would happen became inevitable.

○ ◓ ◑ ●

Our crew stopped shooting because the deflected bullets were buzzing all around and collected a bloody tax from us (as they write in those romantic novels).

When the ships were passing each other, I took a running start and … What's fifteen yards?

○ ◓ ◑ ●

The trigger of the Kalashnikov just about squeezed itself, and the rocket man crouching behind the deckhouse began flailing around in a bloody mess.

Swishhhh!

His last rocket missed me by only a few inches, and the flames from the engine set my hair and kimono on fire.

I screamed and began rolling on the ground.

At first, I thought that the ringing was the sword on my back, but instead, it was someone shooting at me with a pistol. Projectiles bounced off the steel plates, and gray paint peeled off in long strips.

With the Kalashnikov at my side, I changed his mind, but the fire drill would have to wait for later. I jumped up, all aflame, burst into the cabin, and ... the Kalashnikov jammed.

Wries was right, though: Inside a room, with a sword, no one has a chance against us.

○ ◑ ◐ ●

A little dazed, I looked at the slaughter all around. Blood from the raised katana ran down my arms and filled up my sleeves. Not that it bothered me, because a minute ago, there was so much of it in the air that it put out my flames.

I grabbed the red, slippery handle and pulled it all the way down, and the boat stopped.

I didn't feel too good.

I scanned the situation and discovered a small hole in my chest—just who could have done that. As the boat stopped, it began rocking back and forth turbulently. I wiped off the sword with a towel from the small bathroom and walked outside. I thought about escaping, but the word I gave to Wries was still on. I really didn't feel good anyway.

Two streams of smoke came from our ship—apparently, not even the rocket that had set me on fire had missed.

In about five minutes, three rubber rafts took off from it. One roared to my location. The sailors greeted me politely; two of them got out, started the boat, and drove the attacking vessel back to the ship.

I scrambled up to the deck and looked over the devastation. The rocket had had a similar effect as my sword except on a much bigger scale.

That's progress for ya.

"So, boy, is it you that stinks? What kind of a hairdo is that?" Madam Dao laughed. Mr. Ho was just using gauze and duct tape to wrap up the folds of fat that were ripped off her by shrapnel. Aside from the pieces of flesh all around, there were also pieces of gold jewelry. The fat lady was smoking a cigarette, and from several holes in her chest, smoke was escaping. I reached up to touch my head, and true enough, except for a few flaking scales, I didn't have a lot of hair left on the right side.

"A bitchin' Mohawk," I growled and went to help the other rubber raft that had arrived with whatever was left of our squadron and towed in the fifty-seven.

Wries, all black from smoke, carried his own legs, and Van Vren held in Wries' insides, but only with his right arm because his left was between Wries's legs. Or better said, he carried it along with his own legs. The shoulder joint gleamed among all the soot like a white star. They all stank to high heaven.

"Hey, Tobias, you don't look so good." He cheerfully waved his legs at me.

"Mr. Wries." I decided I'd rather not comment on his appearance. Madam Dao's guard was in the worst shape. The rocket had blown off all his appendages. A flap of skin off his scalped head was hanging down to his nose, and he couldn't move it. He was fuming that he couldn't see anything. He cursed his rescuers and warned them that if they left behind a single one of his fingers, they were going to get it.

I jumped down to the raft and began handing them to Mr. Ho.

Madam Dao was leaning up against the railing shaking her head; the smoke was no longer coming from her torso.

"Tobias, don't you think about running." Wries laughed and handed me his legs and Van Vren's arm.

○ ◐ ◑ ●

By noon, the ship looked almost the same as before. The deckhouses were repaired; the rear mast erected, decks washed, sails sewn, and burnt places painted.

A funeral for the fallen ones was quick and modest, as it is in places where death is frequent.

Mr. Ho and Li Pao sewed together Wries, the guard, and Van Vren, and all along, Madam Dao joked with them about not getting their legs mixed up.

I asked one of the ship girls to shave the other side of my head (she was pretty and sadly winced over me), and Mr. Ho slapped some camphor cream on it. Pieces of flesh were falling off me a little, but after a few hours, only red scars remained. What was a jet engine compared to silver? I didn't even mention the bullet in my chest because it went clean through. Even if it hadn't, my immune system would have probably dissolved it.

○ ◑ ◐ ●

"Boy, see if there is anything interesting in those dinghies," said Madam Dao after I had eaten lunch. Mr. Ho threw the harness with the explosive into the cage.

We towed in even the boat that Wries skewered with the anti-aircraft cannon, but there wasn't much there, or more accurately, there wasn't much left in there. Even the eighty-eight was destroyed. However, the boat that I captured had two rocket launchers and fourteen crates of rockets. In the kitchenette, I found some cans and fresh vegetables.

Then we sank the boats and sailed off.

Just another day at the office.

○ ◑ ◐ ●

In the evening, the derby hat appeared above the cage, and during swordplay, there wasn't anything unusual about Wries—except maybe his new glasses and a singed mustache.

During the following night, we attacked the *Iron Cinderella's* sister ship with a similarly poetic name, *Iron Beauty*.

The Triads must get off on fairy tales.

That was when I saw Denise again.

18

"It's payback time," said Madam Dao. As usual, we stood on the bow. The ship hurtled through the darkness as usual, and the diesels pulsated (as usual). The stern of the *Iron Beauty* looked like a shining skyscraper, exactly the same as the stern of the *Iron Cinderella*.

"... Boy, are you listening to me?!"

"Yes, ma'am."

Good thing she didn't ask me to repeat what she'd said.

"So, one more time: You kill the guards, personnel, and passengers, except for the white folks ... However, that doesn't mean that here and there, you can't knock some sahib's teeth out. We'll see what the Triads have to say to an unexpected, yet rapid decline in interest for hazardous games."

"I'd say they'll start paying up again," said Van Vren as he skillfully swung the sword. So the Triads were probably paying Madam Dao *protection* money, and they were probably behind on payments.

"If they don't start, we'll pay a visit to shore." The fat lady smiled darkly. "Today's youngsters have forgotten how I took care of their ... When was that?"

"Sixty years ago?" The guard thought about it.

"... grandparents too. Boy? Please don't run away today; that would really make me mad." Madam Dao blew smoke in my face; no one dared to remind her about the blackout rule.

I didn't answer, and over the smoke, I smelled a faint aroma of jasmine.

Denise stood behind me, and no one said anything, so why should I? Where the hell was she this whole time?! And why—?!

"To the rafts, quickly!"

I slid into the inflatable raft, and Denise descended in after me. It was not like I was going to start talking to her now!

○ ◗ ◑ ●

I swept through the game room, bloody sword in hand. Denise disappeared on me; everyone else disappeared on me too. The passengers were pressed against the carpet, and the slot machines exploded in fountains of sparks and glass. Never in my life did I have so many automatic weapons shooting at me at once.

The Triads had stepped up the level of their security. It wasn't just the traditional uniformed men or the conspicuously inconspicuous meatheads in black suits, but also completely covert and unidentifiable random players.

"Shit!"

One of them just shot at me—from my immediate proximity— and the bullet grazed my side. He must have known that he wouldn't make it, but the punishment would probably be worse if he didn't at least try.

I yanked the blade out of the bubbling body and hurried forward. Most of the gunmen were somewhere behind a mirrored wall on the other side of the huge hall divided by rows of slot machines and indoor planters. Because they could get a glimpse of me only when I changed course, they covered all the angles. Sure, they had no problem shooting here; it was only coach class and there wasn't even a single white person or a rich Chinese.

Smack! Finally, someone hit me straight on. The strike turned me around and made me run into a game machine. The following projectile caused the steel balls inside to spray out like a geyser.

Smack! Smack! Another two. This time, it kinda hurt. Again, I took off running. I hoped they didn't have …

Crunch!

The projectile ripped up the rug and with a whine bounced off the chandelier. The plastic flew out in all directions. Two more giant leaps and I flew through the center of the mirrored wall.

They apparently didn't expect me to run through the hall so fast, and even if they did, they certainly didn't expect me to jump through the wooden divider behind the mirror. I was, to be honest, pretty surprised by it myself, but it couldn't stop me considering my momentum. I wondered how long it would take for my upper incisor—that had gotten knocked out—to grow back.

I landed in a heap of broken two-by-fours and chunks of glass. My shoulder roll didn't turn out so great, but surprisingly, I didn't even jam the sword into my stomach.

I was starting to get lucky.

○ ◯ ◐ ●

No one could survive the gleaming whirlwind of my blade. There were quite a few of them. Hacked off pieces of human bodies froze in the air …

What's this?!

The last one alive was a woman, a tall, thin Asian woman. Even though her moves weren't nearly as fast as mine, they were considerably faster than those of even the best-trained human.

She was all the way on the other side of the space (a hallway) with a wall of mirrors. Behind her was a wide, five-step staircase with wooden statues of the Buddha instead of a railing.

How kitschy.

Unlike me, she had a shotgun.

So close, the tip of my sword was aimed at her throat, just a couple more feet. Not only did she aim the barrel in the right direction, she also managed to squeeze the trigger.

I said to myself that nothing would happen because she hadn't done that click-clack to cock the gun. However, unlike the gunmen in the movies, she had already done the click-clack earlier.

The shot slammed into my stomach like a battering ram as I was in mid-leap; it bounced me off the ceiling. The collective energies of my running, the shot, and the ceiling spun me around in the air. Now the Asian woman did do that click-clack.

246

A smoking green casing rotated through the air where some of my parts were rotating too. I felt rather empty.

She didn't miss me even with her second shot; apparently, she practiced on clay pigeons or something.

I landed on my knees and whacked my forehead on the floor.

Click-clack.

I wondered how many shells fit into a shotgun.

This time, it went into my left shoulder. If I hadn't moved, I would have seriously needed a handy dermatologist—an expert for rebuilding my kisser.

I swung my right arm.

My plan was to throw the sword like a spear, but I kind of screwed it up so the weapon impaled her chest hilt first. Even the round cross-guard disappeared inside her.

The next shot went into the ceiling for obvious reasons, and a chunk of the woodwork fell on my back.

Bright red blood foamed at the woman's mouth, and she had some trouble manipulating the gun around the jutting sword, but she managed a click-clack one more time. She staggered, fell backward on one of the Buddhas, slid to the ground, and her movements became elegantly slow. I realized that I couldn't even do that; my movements were elegantly nonexistent. I scanned my surroundings, and even though I had chopped up more than ten people in the hallway, there was no weapon within my reach.

"What if we made some kind of deal?" I grinned at her.

She probably didn't even speak English.

Again, the shot went into my left shoulder. Smoke came off my arm, which hung on only by a few shards of skin.

Click-clack.

This woman was like the Energizer Bunny.

"I hate to do this." I reared up in a super-human effort and chucked my left arm at her.

"A slap and a half," I commented on the crunching of her spine as the shotgun fell to the rug with a thud—and so did I.

○ ◐ ◑ ●

Not that I was suffering or anything like that, but I couldn't move or speak. Only a hiss came from my lungs when I tried to call for help.

I hope some snake hunter doesn't skewer me, I thought incoherently. My left cheek was stuck to the bloody runner, and I watched tiny leggy animals mulling around on top of the matted fibers—probably dust mites.

Then, suddenly, the blood was just about dry. I must have dozed off. Maybe not, maybe it wasn't sleep. I remembered people running around, unfortunately none were our guys. Other people didn't pay any attention to one dead body among all the other dead bodies.

I suspected that our people were looking for me, and I thought I knew what they'd do if they didn't find me.

Oh, man.

That thunderclap inside a ship seemed out of place to me.

○ ◑ ◐ ●

This time, I woke up that same night. Actually, it was closer to the morning. Still drowsy, I thought about how I would write this if I was writing this. These passages always started something like: I arose … I came to … I woke up. I should think of something original.

Then I remembered *Iron Beauty* and began to devote myself to more important things. The thunderclap was, of course, the charge on my spine so I couldn't move, as usual, but now, instead of looking for novel phrases, I surveyed the damage.

Surprisingly, I wasn't lying in the space under the deck, but in a cabin similar to the one Selma used to have—on a bed with sheets. I rolled my eyes and saw my left arm where it should be, the even stitch suggesting Mr. Ho's skillful fingers. I was clean. My stomach and chest were bandaged, even though it appeared at a glance that I used to have a lot more stuff in my belly. I imagined how my insides must itch as they regrew, and I was thankful for a severed spinal cord.

Okay, so it's cool; they know I wasn't trying to escape. That's the main thing.

But one point worried me: Why the hell didn't they at least put some underwear on me?

After a while, the girl who had shaved my head came by to check on me. I didn't remember her name, but I couldn't talk anyway. I smiled at her. She sat me up and gently removed the bandages. There was the ding of porcelain, and the smell of camphor filled the room. That was quite the cream. No matter what happened, they slapped it on you and ...

The door creaked again.

I thought it was Mr. Ho, but it was Denise.

When you're immobile, women that you have mortally offended should not have access to you—when you're immobile, naked, and can't call for help, then absolutely not. Denise forced my nurse out with a stern look.

After half an hour, she massaged the rest of the camphor cream into her hands and smiled deviously. It was a damn long half hour. Neither of us broke the vow of silence; I unfortunately couldn't.

Then I slept for twenty-four hours, and when I woke up, I already had feeling in my body, the incisor that got knocked out was as good as new, and I could very slowly move my fingers. That was when Denise returned.

"Underwear," I whispered. "Please!"

○ ◑ ◐ ●

By the evening, I could sit up and even stand up (when I clenched my teeth), and when I walked out onto the deck (wrapped up in a sheet), I heard several words of amazement.

Denise was on a rice barrel, wearing a black kimono, sitting cross-legged, and she certainly didn't cry out in amazement.

"Grrr!" I growled in her direction, hobbled to the cage, and was really afraid that the rolling of the ship would trip me up. An arm wrapped around my waist. "Madam Dao said you can stay with me, Mr. Tobias," said the barber girl.

"That's not a bad idea." I still couldn't remember her name so I at least stroked her hair. She was really pretty. "But get me some clothes, please. Mainly underwear." I pulled a corner of the sheet to my shoulder.

"Hey, boy, are you pretending to be a Roman?" Madam Dao called at me.

"Hail, Caesar!" Even the guard expressed his classical education.

○ ◑ ◐ ●

Two months later, during another big assault, I escaped a second time.

○ ◑ ◐ ●

It was a huge cargo ship full of containers that were later transported by semitrucks. I didn't get how Mr. Ho could have known that I was escaping. I was pretty much alone on the deck.

That didn't change the fact that it thundered again, which sounded like it might be fireworks from *Velvet Pussies*—but it wasn't.

Rusty had grown up since the last time, and I was glad to see him too.

The wooden bed didn't get any more comfortable since last time either. Only I tactically refrained from any rude chatter, not that it helped me any. I discovered that there was, on this ship, a bunch of silver objects more interesting than coins—like a sizable cross for example.

It took three and a half days, and I think that My Other, who was again put in charge of my body, went a little crazy. They didn't get to hear a single scream though—assholes.

○ ◑ ◐ ●

I stopped practicing with Wries. I stopped speaking, and they stopped letting me out, except for pirate business and battles with the Triads. After that cross, I (gladly) let my appetite for escape disappear. Madam Dao told me that the next on the list was a silver chain. "It's laid across your belly, or across anything else, boy."

Time marched on.

The only interesting thing was that Denise had joined them. I discovered that she didn't wear the explosive harness on our missions, and when we were in port or hiding by the islands, I heard her light steps above me—while I was alone locked up in a cage.

Then the weather improved. Then it got hot, and I wasn't even surprised when Mr. Ho invited me again to Madam Dao's birthday.

I politely declined and delighted myself with the thought that they would be sorry about losing such an unsurpassable companion. They put a false deck up above the cage and partied till dawn. In the clamor of the noisemakers and drums, I didn't hear too much regret, except for Denise's exulted hollering.

I thought about why it bothered me *so* much.

○ ☽ ☽ ●

With some simple testing, I discovered that I had stopped evolving. I was a big, grown-up vampire. The testing consisted of slitting my hand with a razor. Not that I was becoming a masochist, I was just concerned with my regenerative speed. Over the past few weeks, I hadn't seen any improvement in these abilities; the cut closed practically right behind the blade.

○ ☽ ☽ ●

A harness and a clean satin kimono hit the planks. It was two days after the birthday and time for work again. As I suited up, I realized that I too must have had a birthday during the year, but I didn't even know what month it was, let alone the day.

I also missed the anniversary of the Night Club annihilation, the death anniversary of Dread, Christina, Ripper, Kamile, Babe, Ulrich, Janie, Father—

"Hurry up, Mr. Tobias." The voice of Mr. Ho brought me back to reality and to slavery.

I wasn't listening at the briefing. No matter what the instructions were; for me, it was always the same. I ran. I killed those that pulled out their weapons. I frightened the other ones. I did everything as an afterthought, but so effectively that my captors left me alone and didn't try to distract me. What I could find out about them I did, so why should I continue to waste my time?

The motor on the rubber raft bubbled at the surface, and I smelled gasoline and burnt oil. Denise reached under my kimono and checked the clasp holding the harness together. A former prisoner turned snitch is the worst kind.

Jiri Kulhanek

We'll see what happens to me after twenty-one years.

○ ◑ ◑ ●

That not-so-big ship was a trap.

The Triads refused to submit and hired these women, one of whom got me on the *Iron Beauty*. I overheard Madam Dao and Wries discussing this a while back. They talked about the Japanese Ipponsugi Clan, the one Hanako lied about being from. Somewhere far away, I heard Ulrich's question, *Are you Straight Branch or of Leaning Cedar lineage?*

Anyway, I was thinking about the Night Club a lot lately. I talked to the dead, and sometimes even My Other joined in. After a several-month silver-induced silence, he was beginning to come around.

○ ◑ ◑ ●

I knocked one of the warrior women out with my fist. Why kill them? From the moment that someone shut off the power, we started winning despite the fact that there were ten of them for each one of us—that meant fifty absolutely cold-blooded professional killers. In the dark, they didn't have much of a chance against us. They knew it, but they didn't back off. They didn't surrender. They didn't beg for mercy. They would have made good Night Club members.

I kicked the pistol away from another one and knocked her out too. I followed a short hallway through a door, and I unexpectedly ran out on the deck and … I realized that I was alone. None of our guys was watching me. Today, even Mr. Ho joined the fight. Usually, he dealt with the runaways, both enemies and slaves. I figured that I might never have a better opportunity than this.

"What about the silver chain?" I asked My Other, and he just howled. I don't think his horror was at all fake. I slipped to the railing, a last look back. I needed at least half an hour, then just …

My last look was interrupted by something. In the shadow of an exhaust chimney, a figure in a black satin kimono moved. So someone *was* watching.

Denise.

○ ◑ ◑ ●

252

In her left hand, she held a remote transmitter.

"You wouldn't?" I sat on the railing and began to lean over the thundering ocean and at the same time saw her stroke the control button.

Her eyes were impenetrable.

Then two things happened unbelievably quickly in succession.

Actually three:

A shot rang out from the door.

Denise's neck exploded.

Then there was the standard thunderclap behind my back.

○ ◑ ◐ ●

19

I was floating in dark blue water, and the pressure was crushing my chest. Apparently, I was about six hundred meters below the surface. The charge did a number on me again, but this time, there wasn't anything amateurish in my plan, because I had no plan. I just knew that I would wake up four to five hours after the explosion, but most importantly, I knew that, underwater, my levitation skills would allow me to really fly, despite my motionless body. I concentrated and began to rise. I considered forty meters to be a comfortable traveling depth.

Because I floated face down, I focused on the bottom. It was about five hundred meters beneath me, and for a moment, I felt an intense dizziness. As my gaze slipped through the cold emptiness, a bit below me—about two hundred meters lower—I saw something else.

A fish?

I stopped rising.

A body in a black kimono was carried by the current in the same direction as me, but it was descending very gradually.

Denise.

For a short moment, I analyzed my feelings toward her and again began rising; the ocean would save me some work. Without preparation, not even we can survive the pressure that was waiting for her down there.

Then I remembered that we were of the same blood (as they say), and most importantly, I didn't know anyone else like that except Hanako. Again, I stopped rising.

Hanako was the enemy ... but so was Denise.

I began to drop.

A person doesn't save someone else for the sake of saving them, but because he thinks that if he is ever in trouble, they will save him in return. It's called unselfishness.

I descended and swore that one day, I would write this down somewhere—maybe a little more dramatically. These kinds of stupid acts deserve to be immortalized. The pressure was crushing my chest, and I couldn't inhale water because of my severed spine. When I came within fifty meters of Denise, I felt my skull caving in.

Fortunately, it didn't crack.

Denise looked significantly worse than I did. The pressure really did a number on her. Her chest bone was caved in, and her face and forehead were hideously deformed.

I was paralyzed so I drifted beneath her and began rising.

At forty meters, I picked a heading.

I didn't see my compass because my hands were spread wide to the side, but that didn't matter. The most important thing now was to get as far away from there as possible. So I drifted in the same direction as the white particles that floated along the bottom. Here, in this ocean, I was bound to reach some atoll no matter what direction I took.

The bottom began to sickeningly drop (vertigo is ugly). Still if I could have, I would have sung out loud.

Freedom, it's a beautiful thing.

○ ◐ ◑ ●

I didn't float very fast because Denise was really slowing me down and pulling me to the left. On the other hand, though, it wasn't that much work. It would have to be really rotten luck for Madam Dao to find us. The odds of really rotten luck were becoming increasingly lower with every second. Moreover, I suspected that the three of them probably had lots of problems on that ship, even though Wries, Mr. Ho, and Van Vren certainly would win in the end. It could have taken them a while so they hadn't been looking for us that long.

When the ocean began to shine with the morning, a shadow passed over us. It was hard to tell how big and what was casting it. I felt it rather than saw it in the water. It's a horrible feeling not being able to turn. I descended just in case and tried to force my tingling fingers to twitch at least a little.

By evening time, I was mobile enough that I could tie Denise's arms to her body and somehow make her a little more hydrodynamic. I tied a shard of my kimono top around her neck—it was her floppy head that was pulling me to the side—and tied her to me with what remained of my harness after the explosion.

All I had to do then was hold a steady course, stop levitating, and start swimming. How did I write it in *Vampires*?

First, you must catch a dolphin and drink his blood then swim faster than the sharks, heading to the nearest shore—even if it was a thousand miles!

What a foolish idea.

○ ◐ ◑ ●

I always surfaced before sunrise and thoroughly oxygenated myself. Oxygen use while swimming was pretty high, even though my body could manage it considerably better than in my *younger years*. Denise didn't move even on the eighth day, didn't even wake up, but the deformations in her head had already disappeared. Her chest was as good as new, and that ugly gash on her throat had also disappeared. Her regeneration time must be normal; only I was superhuman—I mean super-vampire.

I was really sick of swimming.

On the next day, just after daybreak, I saw a barrier reef, and a few hours later, I landed on a small emerald-green island.

○ ◐ ◑ ●

There really is something good about having firm land under your feet after more than a year.

"Hoorayyyyy!" I pranced on the beach as the white sand splashed up around my feet.

○ ◐ ◑ ●

I hid Denise in the jungle (I hung her on a vine in the crown of a tree) and went to scope out the area. I had some trouble with the earth not rolling, but I quickly got used to it.

My first discovery was that the island wasn't so small; my second, that it was inhabited. A calm native village seemed like a miracle to me. A post office stood by the harbor, and in the same building (hut) was a grocery store with an old Coca-Cola sign (so not just natives, but civilization!). On the other side was a bar with a palm-frond roof, and the circular, pounded-down area in front of it was apparently for dancing.

I let go of the waxy leaf from under which I was peeking out of the jungle, and my thoughts weren't as happy as after my initial excitement. I didn't have any money; the shards of my satin kimono pants were dangerously noticeable. Not even in nine days could I have gotten very far. So if Madam Dao was looking for me, she would certainly look for me even here. I had no doubt that she would look for me. She had lost both of her attack vampires so Wries and Van Vren surely set out hunting.

I remembered how she said that no one had ever escaped from her ship. It was a question of honor, and she wouldn't give up easily— wouldn't give up ever.

What a happy prospect.

In the growth behind me, I heard yelling and the loud whipping of canes that the natives used to fend off snakes, so I pulled back.

○ ○ ◑ ●

My other problem was what to do with Denise. I couldn't drag her with me but couldn't leave her hanging up in a tree. Plus, she had joined them once, and I doubted that having rescued her would somehow convince her to leave me alone. Well, well, that thought could have saved me a lot of work if I had figured it out in the ocean.

I was looking for the tree with Denise in it until afternoon. The jungle was probably even more confusing than the catacombs in Prague, but at least I had an idea of what to do with her.

○ ○ ◑ ●

"I don't get how they can write that you can dig a grave with just a branch," I fumed out loud. The branches were breaking in my hands, and I couldn't dig anything with them. Hands turned out to be the best tools in this damp soil. The hole wasn't too deep because I quickly dug down to the coral bedrock, but three feet was enough. I laid Denise down in there and threw soft dirt on her. I did it so that no one would find her, and Madam Dao would think that she ran away too. It would be Denise's decision whether she chose freedom or not.

If she chose freedom and they caught her, then some silver on her belly might give her the right perspective about who the good guys were and who were the bad. If she didn't choose freedom, then the question would be whether they'd believe her that she tried to return on her own. It would be obvious that someone must have helped her out of the ocean. Me. Not that I would wish the *bed* on her, but it might do her some good.

"There is nothing better than the freedom of choice, dear Denise." I pushed some rotten leaves and chunks of wooden vines on top of the grave. *Tomorrow, you won't be able to tell it is here, unless some wild pig parks himself here tonight.*

I washed myself in the ocean and discovered that I was really, really hungry. For the first time in my life, I went hunting.

○ ◑ ◐ ●

I was running through the jungle like an idiot and despite hearing the rustling, quacking, stomping, and squeaking of little animals everywhere in all that greenery mixed with golden reflections of the sun, I didn't see any of them. Then I realized that it probably wouldn't be as easy as it was sometimes written *"… They lowered the rafts, landed on the island, and while the crew filled their barrels with crystal-clear water from a babbling brook, the boatswain caught a few peccary."*

"Peccary are nowhere to be seen," I uttered into the noisy jungle and thanked my lucky stars there weren't any big spiders here. In the end, I caught an orange fish in a shallow stream, probably like a trout only a third of the size, but how to get a meal without a hatchet or a glass? I realized that without modern utensils, I was lost.

○ ◑ ◐ ●

I washed the salt stains out of my kimono pants, put them on inside out, and rolled the tattered pant legs up above my knees.

I looked like I was wearing a pair of tattered kimono pants rolled up above my knees and inside out. I decided to improvise. In the worst-case scenario, I could always swim away from here, but it might be a good idea to figure out a direction first.

I returned to the beach and pretended to jog casually. I ran toward the village.

○ ◑ ◐ ●

Because it was four in the afternoon, the bar was full. I was jogging at an easy pace, the sand crunching under my feet and little green lizards running off to the sides. The surf hissed and crashed.

If I thought I could blend in, I was sadly mistaken. The last time they'd had an attraction of this caliber must have been during World War II when they were bombarded by the Japanese air force.

"Nice day." I jogged up to the bar. As part of my improvisation, I gave my English an accent that I thought could well have been Swedish. Everyone stared at me like I was a ghost. They were a mix of blacks and Asians. They wore tattered, colorful T-shirts and shiny Adidas shorts, and judging by the smell, they were drinking strong white rum.

They wore necklaces with little crosses around their necks.

"My name is Sven." I finally remembered a Scandinavian name. "I arrived on a surfboard, but unfortunately, I lost my sail and in the night also my board … in the tide." My Other began falling over with laughter because he had never in his life heard anything so dumb. What else was I supposed to come up with? That I swam over here?

"Oh," said the bartender. He had a curly beard. His thick hair was pulled back into a ponytail, and he wore a dirty tank top. "What you're saying is that you are alone, no one knows you're here, and you have no money, Sven?"

It took me a moment to realize he was talking to me.

"I have this." I lifted my combination depth-gauge-compass-watch.

"What do you want from us?" asked a guy wearing a faded red baseball cap. He had hairy shoulders, the whites of his eyes were completely yellow, and his pupils and irises blended into one black spot.

Hmmmmm, I thought. *What is it that I want from them?* "Oh yeah, I need to get outta here."

"That instrument is nice, but it won't be enough to get you a boarding ticket, Sven." They laughed, and I realized that in these parts, people were routinely sold into slavery. Although it's written in all kinds of books that the natives are polite and friendly—especially toward castaways.

"A ticket, an interesting idea," I said. "Where to does it sail from here?"

"I am afraid that for you, nowhere." Mr. Cap pushed his hat to the back of his head, and everyone started finishing up their drinks and standing up.

"Could I at least make a phone call?" I motioned toward the post office.

"Yup, sure, but you didn't answer, Sven. You were alone on that surfboard? No friends? Only you and Mother Nature?"

"Yes." I smiled politely.

"So, what can you do, Sven? I mean, if you've ever worked." Mr. Cap was the one talking, and everyone else formed a circle around me. This close up, they smelled fishy and I could see the little white crystals of salt glistening on their eyebrows. A barking and screaming bundle of children, dogs, and piglets charged from of nearby houses which sat on stilts.

"Are those peccary?" I watched the piglets.

"I asked you first, Sven." Mr. Cap poked me in the chest with his finger, and his breath reeked of rum.

"I used to work, yes."

"And what did you do?"

"I killed people." I grinned and threw him over the circle of gawkers.

Honesty, above all.

○ ◑ ◑ ●

The guy returned and straightened out his hat; a layer of gray dust stuck to his sweaty back.

"Okay, Sven, let's not argue right off the bat. Tell me what you need, and maybe we can help you."

Needless to say, natives are friendly to castaways. Who says books lie?

"A shirt, shorts, shoes, knife ..." I shrugged my shoulders.

"Hey! Show me that watch!" The bartender called attention to himself by banging on the counter. I threw it to him without a second thought.

"Sven, have a seat." One of the men slapped the chair next to him. The circle was sitting back at the bar already and looked friendly. The dirty kids were staring at me. The dogs were yelping at me, and the little piglets were mulling around my legs. I noticed that everyone else noticed too.

"Animals like us Scandinavians," I said in the tone of a museum tour guide.

"Come, and we'll get those things next door." The bartender waved toward the store. "Hey, Mumu, watch things for me."

"Sure, Pop."

Mumu?! Someone here is actually named Mumu!?

○ ◔ ◑ ●

At the store, I even had a choice. When I pulled a pair of black canvas shorts from the shelf, the bartender grumbled a little, but the price of my instrument was significantly higher than the shorts plus the T-shirt, the tennis shoes, and the switchblade. I clicked the release, and the steel jumped out quietly. To my surprise, the knife wasn't some chrome-plated junk that you find everywhere in European stores, but a weapon from decent four millimeter steel.

"Nice." I folded away the blade. Here, people didn't carry these things around for fun, but for the reason they had always been carried around. I smiled, and the bartender got a little nervous. He began stroking the little cross on his chest. "You can have dinner at my place, so we even things out."

"I don't eat."

"Fine ... Whatever you drink then, it's on the house."

"I don't drink."

"And … and …" he said, became pale, and squeezed the cross in his fist.

"Are you the postman here?" I pulled on a loose, dark green T-shirt.

"Yup. Yes."

"So if someone was asking about a guy that looks like me, you would know about him, right?"

"That's for sure. For sure!"

"And?"

"What?"

"And was someone asking?"

"No," he answered much too quickly. For a bartender, he was a really rotten liar. Or was it because he was scared? Or was it because in the shadow of the shop I forgot myself and made eyes at him?

They don't believe in vampires around here, do they?

○ ◔ ◑ ●

I sat at the bar and watched the ocean. There is something monumental in the never-ending waves that roll toward the beach. No one bothered me, except the bartender brought several coins. I made sure they weren't silver and put them in my pocket.

When he closed up, long after midnight, I reached over the counter and took one of the less-smudged glasses.

○ ◔ ◑ ●

I discovered that the night was the perfect time for a hunt. Sleepy animals were blindly blundering through the jungle, and all I had to do was pick them up, like I was at the supermarket. I caught something small, fuzzy, and fat. The knife clicked … but it gave me this *look*.

"Breee?" it said and licked my wrist.

I just can't.

"Go, my friend. I don't know how to kill you anyway. Maybe a croc will eat you." I let the little animal go in the grass and set off in the direction of a stream that I had heard. Plus, I didn't feel like drinking warm blood anyway.

After I caught three fish (they were too slow for me), something struggled out onto the bank.

"Breee?"

"Someone is needy." I watched the fuzzy animal. It was probably an anteater of some kind, because while I was eating, he rooted around in the dirt and hunted little white creatures with his sticky tongue.

I discovered that the blood of freshwater fish is not bad, and I spent the rest of the night up in a tree listening for anything uncanny in the whispering of the wind, whistling of the bats, and snorting of the fuzzy one. The villagers recognized me for sure, so a visit from Wries and Van Vren wouldn't take long. The phone here was a satellite one. I could steal one of the boats in the harbor, but they resembled overgrown canoes with implanted motors that looked like leftovers from World War II. I'd have no chance against a fifty-seven on a dinghy like that. I might as well continue my career as a long-distance swimmer.

○ ◑ ◐ ●

With the sunrise, I left the greenery behind, sat in my place at the bar, and returned the freshly cleaned glass. I had had a few fish for breakfast too, and now I was happily belching.

"Good morning, Sven." The bartender nodded at me.

"Mornin'." By the strange gleam from a ray of the rising sun that caught his eye, I could tell that the news had already been passed on. *So, Curly, whatever will you buy in exchange for me?* I smiled, and he stroked the cross around his neck. Maybe he'd build a church in the village.

These Christians.

○ ◑ ◐ ●

Around eight o'clock, the local fishermen set out on the ocean, which meant all the friendly people from yesterday. Mr. Fuzzy, all soaked with dew, clambered up on the bar and began catching cockroaches.

"Useful little animal," said the bartender.

"Looks like it."

Within ten minutes, Mr. Fuzzy looked a little stuffed. I glanced at the clock hanging on a tree that supported the roof. Then I tried to coax a tourist map out of the bartender. He made excuses that tourists didn't come there so he had no map.

"So what is this place called anyway?"

"Tolpang."

"Oh."

○ ◑ ◗ ●

At one thirty, in the rumble of the returning boat motors, I heard a multiple-stroke one, strong but turned down to a minimum. That was fast. Madam Dao's ship must not have been far away. However, the boys were underestimating my vampire senses.

"I have to take a leak." I stretched my back and wandered into the jungle. As soon as I disappeared behind the green wall, I took off like a deer. If I could sweat, I would have done so—from fear.

○ ◑ ◗ ●

When the group of boats reached the harbor, I was ready. I crouched underwater at the bottom behind a rotten wreck of a ferryboat, the planks of the dock above my head and little crayfish tickling my ankles.

I ran through the jungle so they wouldn't see me from the boats, jumped into the ocean (they really had gorgeous waves here), and swam back along the shore (wonderful little coral fish, if only the electric eels weren't so affectionate).

The fishermen arrived in a clump so the fifty-seven could hide behind them. Of course, it was a group effort, the entire village was hoping for a church. I watched the whole thing from below, and due to the rumbling of the surf and the motors, I couldn't hear anything else but the surf and the motors.

The keel of the speedboat looked noble, almost aristocratic, among the keels of the fishing boats.

I waited for the vessels to move as the men got out, then I counted to one hundred and began to rise. If Wries and Van Vren didn't see me, they wouldn't be dumb enough to leave a single escape route open. One of them would surely return to guard the boats.

I surfaced behind the boat's stern, an open knife between my teeth. I couldn't see inside, but sometimes, you just have to take a risk.

"Rambo," I mumbled and leaped up.

Empty.

○ ◗ ◖ ●

I saw the derby hat and Van Vren's sailor shirt at the bar. The bartender was just pointing to the jungle, but Wries's glasses already flashed toward the fifty-seven.

Immediately, I realized that I had a slight problem.

"How the hell do you start one of these things?"

Before my knife fell out and clanged on the lacquered floor, I realized another thing: Even speedboats used keys for starting.

They weren't there.

Wries and Van Vren were already running.

○ ◗ ◖ ●

Just like each member of the Night Club, I had completed difficult, sometimes even brutal, training. Our forefathers had learned to steal and ride horses; for us, it was cars. Retreat was the most important part of a mission, and anyone who couldn't start and drive off in any car within twenty seconds wasn't allowed into action. Instead, he became a cook, medic, or an expert in ...

○ ◗ ◖ ●

Junction boxes are all the same except the wires can have different colors.

"Blue or red?" I uttered the Shakespearian question common to all action movies.

Immediately, I knew that it wasn't the blue one.

The dock was shaking under Wries's long leaps.

"Could it be the red one?"

There was a spark, and the warm motor turned over right away. *Now where is the reverse on this thing?*

Wries jumped on the bow, sword in hand.

"Oh." I understood the labels by the control lever with the shiny handle and put it from N to R and gave it a full throttle.

While making an awful racket, the boat stood almost on its tip, then the tie rope broke, and not even Wries could handle that. The derby hat flew into the air.

"Watch out for the sea rays!"

At one point, the wave lifted him so close that he took a swing at me. That was when I abruptly stopped and even more abruptly turned the wheel to get the front of the boat away from the island.

○ ◌ ◑ ●

That morning, I had watched carefully which way the fishermen left because around these atolls, there were miles and miles of coral reefs, and a channel had been broken through only to the harbors. When I arrived the day before, I nearly tore my belly open several times. Those limestone edges would cut through the fifty-seven like butter. So when they started shooting at me, I didn't dare to zigzag; I just crouched behind the seat.

Bullets were zooming and pitter-pattering for a long time, but with every yard, they dispersed more. In a few minutes, all that was left of the island was a small green hill trimmed by white beaches.

I straightened up. Freedom on a speedboat was even more free than freedom with a severed spine in the middle of the ocean.

Zoom!

A bullet from a gun made a hole in the windshield, so I crouched again and didn't let down on the throttle until the island blended with the horizon.

○ ◌ ◑ ●

I put the boat into neutral and let the engine cough at low rpm. The fifty-seven began rocking chaotically. Needless to say, the waves were pretty high and the boat not too big. Strange, when I swam in the wide-open ocean during the week, it didn't bother me, but now I was worried—about being alone, about capsizing ... It must have been an ancient dread inherited from my ancestors.

As a first order of business, I checked the gas tanks. They were on the stern along the outer hull, and their size filled me with satisfaction. I guesstimated the dimensions, and with a simple calculation determined that they could hold two hundred gallons of gasoline.

"Two hundred little gallons ... I wonder how much is in there now?" I screwed off the cap and peeked inside. Wries and Van Vren were prepared for a long trip; the tanks were nearly full.

Because I had heard at least five hits against the hull, I began looking. As I expected, a boat used for raids had armor-plated gas tanks. Even if they didn't hold up, the foam material in which they were sitting would seal an even bigger hole than one from a rifle bullet.

I love technological progress.

Three slugs were in the back of the chair. The fact that they didn't go through meant that there had to be something bulletproof inside— which was practical, especially during a retreat.

"All righty then." I picked the knife up off the floor, snapped it shut, stashed it away in my pocket, and used a small hand pump to get rid of a few inches of water. The floor mats were already starting to float, and I was hoping that it was water that just splashed in.

During all that, I kept one eye on the horizon. Madam Dao's ship couldn't be far away, and it was me personally who loaded it with rockets. The pump gurgled on empty, so I sat down and looked over the controls. There was nothing that I hadn't seen before; plus, I had satellite navigation with the error removed which was accurate to a few feet. However, even the best navigation system would be useless without ...

"Here." I sighed with relief and pulled out a map from the passenger-side compartment. The map was waterproof, had naval markings, and was pretty detailed. I turned on the GPS, waited for it to acquire a satellite signal. After a moment, I understood the numbers and how to use them to determine my position.

"Hic sunt leones." I made an indicator on the map with a black marker. "And to the shore it's ..." There was a ruler on the marker. "Again these nautical miles." I tried to remember the conversion factor. In the end, though, nautical miles or regular miles, it didn't matter because I didn't know what kind of mileage this boat got anyway.

"So which way." I scanned the horizon, and a dark spot appeared in the direction of the island. Wries and Van Vren must be returning on a fishing boat. I leaned over the map, and three waves hit the side of the fifty-seven in quick succession. Not to China, the Communists were always causing problems. A vacation in Cambodia? I was not too crazy to see the Khmer Rouge either. Vietnam, there, they would think I was American militia, and I would spend the rest of my life whimpering in some labor camp tending vegetables. "So, all that's left is Thailand." I punched in the course on the GPS keyboard, put away the map ...

Zoom! A slug zoomed above the boat. Apparently, Wries had a rifle with him, and apparently, he wanted his fifty-seven back.

"No, no, my boy." I shifted the gear into D, gave it gas, and turned the wheel until the red and green arrows on the display lined up. All that remained was to watch out for any reefs (the GPS warned me about most of them), dodge islands, and pray that I didn't run out of gas and for good weather.

A vacation.

○ ☾ ☽ ●

Because I drove efficiently, I could easily make it all the way to Bangkok, but someone there would for sure notice me despite the Oriental chaos—either the police that may want papers or, more likely, one of Madam Dao's snitches. Someone had to tell the fat lady when the ships that she later attacked left port, so her people could be expected in most of the major ports around. A reward for my capture wouldn't be a small one.

In the distance, I watched the arms of the giant cranes illuminated with floodlights and shrouded in a cloud of dust and smog. In a port for large ships, such as this, they worked even late at night. According to the clock on the dash, it was just past midnight. Bangkok itself lay some eighteen miles up the river ... river ... Menam, it was called. I turned the wheel and went up along the left shore.

I knew that an uncomfortable night was waiting for me, but I had no choice. Even more dumber trackers than Wries and Van Vren would find me if I stayed with this boat.

"Let's do it." I gave myself encouragement after the glow finally disappeared behind the stern. I was one and a half miles from shore and about seven from the port. I checked to make sure that I had everything I wanted to take with me (it didn't take long). I had the knife and my few coins in my pocket wrapped in a piece of seat cushion so they wouldn't jangle and I wouldn't lose them while swimming. For the last time, I looked into the ocean below me. Those hundred meters should be enough to hide the boat. I grabbed the emergency hatchet (it was spray-painted bright red and had a float on it) out of its holder and began chopping holes in the bottom of the boat and its air chambers.

I tied all the things that could float to the steering wheel or shoved them into the passenger-side compartment. There wasn't much—actually nothing except for the floor mats, a flare gun with an unsinkable handle, and the hatchet.

I felt sorry for the noble machine.

I sat on the stern and listened to the bubbling and gurgling of the rising water. As the boat became heavier, it stopped rocking. I used a whistling hand pump to flood the gas tanks with ocean water while the opening was still above the surface. Then I put the cap on so that the tell-tale rainbow blobs didn't reveal the boat's location.

A wave rolled over the side, and the fifty-seven slid underwater stern first. I sank with it for a little while to make sure nothing floated away, and then I let her take the final trip alone.

There was something to having a tombstone out of a whirl of bubbles.

Ten meters under the surface, I headed for shore. Down here, the loud groaning of the surf was even louder.

○ ◑ ◑ ●

I could tell I was approaching shore by the rising bottom and the water becoming cloudy with mud. Also, I could tell that I was approaching a metropolis by the tons of garbage on the bottom. Plastic bags were swimming everywhere. They looked like giant jellyfish and were pretty disgusting if you happened to stick your hand into one of them.

I surfaced. The water tasted of gas and oil and reeked of the sewer.

I cursed myself. I should be swimming to the other side, away from Bangkok. Those weird blue lines on the map were coastal flows that pull all the crap this way.

Too late.

The shore was covered over with mangroves, and their barren tangled roots were covered with plastic, brownish-green streaks of algae and dissolved toilet paper.

I swam as far as I could, but there was so little water that I had to stand up. The next wave slammed me right down into the stuff I was standing in—not white sand, but disgusting, horrible-smelling, salty mud.

"Yuck!" I scraped the stuff off my face and was so glad that I didn't forget to put on my tennis shoes—I bet this stuff had tons of glass chunks in it.

"Tennis shoes won't save your kisser from getting all cut up," said My Other.

Yes, he was always talking, when I needed him the most.

The mud pulled me down like the gulping mouth of an endless putrid monster (copyright My Other). I remembered Papillon; he had similar problems.

"But he didn't have this." I crawled up on top of a mangled and rusty wreck of a small car.

"Or this! Yuck!" There was a fresh layer of bird droppings on the roof. If the tide didn't occasionally wash it off ... better not to finish that thought.

After considering the situation, I decided to fly the remaining fifty yards to the mangrove.

○ ᴐ ◗ ●

The decision was easy, but carrying it out wasn't. I had practiced levitating, but on Madam Dao's ship, all I could manage was to float just above the hammock so no one would notice, and even that was damn exhausting. Floating in the ocean didn't count because buoyancy was a substantial help.

I thought about which position to fly in. That may appear trivial, but it wasn't anything easy. Should I walk normally or do a Superman? I raised my fist to practice, but unfortunately, I couldn't remember what the Man of Steel said just before takeoff. So I just took a *walk*.

I probably wouldn't have made a very good superhero. When I peeled myself (literally) off the mangled roof, I used half my strength just compensating for that weird feeling of hanging in the air and not falling. It really was necessary to concentrate hard during levitation, especially if you were trying to levitate in a certain direction other than straight down. For a little while, I just rocked back and forth in one spot and then drifted down rather than flew. I saw my face planted in that salty muck again, but then I got help from what must have been vampire reflexes. Vampire or not, who would want to fall into that shit?

○ ◐ ◑ ●

The only problem was that when I floated to the mangrove roots and grabbed them, I was so exhausted that I almost couldn't hang on.

○ ◐ ◑ ●

"Holy shit," I said in about an hour when it got better, but not by much. I also knew why movie vampires, who lurk in the night, always howl like they do. I was so hungry that I quietly howled too. That hunger really hurt. My whole body hurt as each cell demanded energy that had been depleted by the levitation.

"I am done with flying … owwww." I wrapped myself around a root, and the seaweed and toilet paper sludge didn't bother me at all.

So, by the way, I discovered another way to commit suicide, but I'd rather choose anything but that.

The fifty-yard-long flight depleted enough of my strength for a month's worth of very active pirate life—without food.

○ ◐ ◑ ●

Not that I was any better in the morning (I fell helplessly into lethargy), but I had to get out of there. First of all, I was visible from the ocean, and second of all, I had higher ambitions than to become part of a mangrove forest. The sun rose slowly, and as the surroundings warmed up, the rotten, fishy stench became thicker. Flocks of seagulls bombarded the surroundings with the products of their metabolism, and in huge sticky cobwebs, the little bodies of their unlucky brethren decayed. The smell wasn't too pleasant either.

Why didn't my nose get tired too?!

Every single movement hurt, and my vampire effortlessness was long gone. I couldn't even pull myself up with both arms, and my calves trembled so much I could hardly stand. So, I was in the ideal condition for traveling through an environment where even Tarzan himself would have had problems. All the branches were slippery from the bird droppings. Small and big snakes were everywhere, and I am not even going to mention the spiders. If some of those specimens crawled on me, they could easily push me down into the squishy, bubbling mud where not-so-big, green crocodiles were running around … I wondered how crocodile blood tasted. I felt drool running down my chin; it was probably very, very good.

If I was a human, I could try eating leaves or something. There were lots of them in the tops of the mangrove trees. Vampires had a distinct disadvantage in this regard. My muscles lost not only strength, but speed too. In the increasingly warmer air, the snakes were getting away from me easier than from a child and the seagulls and crocs might as well have been on Mars. If I were human, I might even start on the spiders; they were so fat and juicy …

My Other made a literary notation; something so gross would fit nicely in our next novel.

The sun dimmed and abruptly moved.

I blinked, waved my arms, and at the last moment caught myself. Not that I was afraid of the fall itself or of the toothy lizards. I was just scared that without help, I simply wouldn't be able to get out of that muck. I imagined myself drifting lower and lower, the slimy substance crushing me like a hydraulic press, for a long, long time … Even a branch covered with bird shit would be nice at that point.

○ ○ ◑ ●

The sun was already setting when in the tangle of leaves, roots, and cobwebs in front of me, I saw something other than leaves, roots, and cobwebs. It took me all day to go three hundred yards—okay, maybe two hundred. Under normal circumstances, it would have taken me just two minutes.

There really was a lot of cobwebs, but I was in such a condition that I wasn't sensing anything. I don't know if a human can feel such complete exhaustion and hunger, but I was literally feeling myself buckle and fall inward.

○ ○ ◑ ●

Deep in the night, it was sheer willpower that forced me to get to that thing I saw between the branches. It was the end of the mangroves, and the ground was rising in a steep, thirty-foot-high, grass-covered bank.

When I crawled all the way up, there was a dirt road and beyond it a cornfield.

I don't know what I was expecting, maybe a vampire bar where they served chilled rabbit's blood with a pinch of pepper and a drop of soy sauce ...

I knelt on all fours, red dust sticking to my hands which were covered with bird doodie, and my head wobbled back and forth. A little over a foot from me, I saw a small, brown lizard. I saw it well even in the dark, so my eyes weren't affected by the exhaustion. Suddenly, there were two lizards, then four, then eight, and then I couldn't count them quickly enough.

○ ◑ ◐ ●

I really wasn't feeling all that great in the morning either.

I was covered in yesterday's cobwebs which sparkled with dew. However, even worse, I heard this weird ringing and human voices. They sounded a little different than Chinese, but still undecipherable.

"Get up!" I ordered My Other, and he really did it. So, I was standing in the middle of the road when about a dozen people, dressed in black nightgowns, appeared around a turn on noisy bicycles. I don't know why, but they started screaming, turned their bicycles around, and disappeared.

These Asians, who is supposed to make sense of them?

Because I had used all the strength I'd gained overnight just holding my balance, I just stood in the middle of the road when a small pickup with peeling paint drove up. It stopped after the turn, and five men with Kalashnikovs jumped off in an orderly fashion. They spread out in the cornfield, and in a crouching huddle, they ran toward me.

This was how I always pictured an attack by the Vietcong.

Because I didn't move, they surrounded me, and the faces behind the brandished weapons looked a little uncertain. They were a foot shorter than me and had large straw hats on their backs.

One of them yelled something at me.

"I don't understand," I said quietly in English.

This invisible, but very obvious, wave of relief passed over the men. I hoped they didn't mistake me and all my cobwebs for some demon.

However, if you say, *I don't understand* and you say it in English, then you must certainly be human, because demons speak Thai fluently.

"Hands up!"

I didn't feel good. How could I explain that I just couldn't do it. I knew that I couldn't let them shoot me because in this state, my regenerative abilities were useless. There was nothing left. I wouldn't regenerate.

The weapons were aimed at me threateningly, so I tried it anyway. For a moment, I felt as though I wasn't lifting just my hands, but the entire earth. One minute, it was beneath my feet, and the next, it was falling on my face.

○ ◑ ◐ ●

While on the rickety pickup, I gained consciousness for a moment. No one was aiming anything at me anymore. What a relief.

○ ◑ ◐ ●

The second time I came to, I was in a house with no walls, apparently built on stilts with grass mats on the floor. I was clean, dressed in a black, native shirt, and someone was trying to feed me a greasy soup. Just the smell alone made me cramp up and gag so badly that four of them had to hold me down so I didn't fall out of the room. When it didn't work with the soup even the third time around, they realized that food was of no use to me. I could comfortably faint again.

In a daze, I heard the beeping of a cell phone and an English conversation with someplace far far far away … The doctor would be able to come in the morning. Overnight, they were supposed to keep me warm and moisten my lips.

With that, the faraway voice saved my life.

The only way to keep someone warm around here was to spoon. Because the nights were surprisingly cold this time of year, they didn't consider it anything out of the ordinary.

The noise of people settling down to sleep woke me up. They slept in a man, woman, man arrangement. They were farmers, really poor people, and only the oldest ones had a bed—one for all of them. So I got to spoon with one woman on each side. One was old. The other one was about eighteen. They covered me (us) with a coarse and really itchy blanket. They smelled of earth, some herbs, and toothpaste. I still stunk like I'd just crawled through some mud in a mangrove forest while coming in contact with a million bird droppings, where the birds followed a strict fish diet. That was even after they'd scrubbed me down at least twice already.

The older woman dipped a scarf in a porcelain bowl and moistened my lips.

I knew that I couldn't faint again, not this time. I commanded My Other to make sure I didn't because otherwise, I would kill him. He wailed but endured. I had to wait until the heavy breathing and moaning stopped (now I know why there are so many Asians). After a moment, the girl turned to face me, and after a half an hour, the house was filled only with rhythmic breathing and irregular but quiet snoring.

I saw the girl smile from her sleep. The other thing I saw was her hand as it slid onto my chest.

Denise said that human blood was disgusting, but if you'd ever considered spiders to be gourmet, then you wouldn't be put off by much. I concentrated on my upper appendages until they began moving. My skin was pretty wrinkly because my body used muscle cells to stay alive. My forearms looked like broomsticks.

I took the girl's arm and stroked the inside of her wrist. She squirmed and smiled a little more.

Well, shit, how do I do this? In the movies, they always showed a frightening grimace and exposed fangs, which was followed by some screaming and then just two holes in someone's neck. I needed some kind of a cookbook, like *Sleeping Asian Girl: Quick and Easy.* I pulled her arm to my lips and still didn't know what to do. I couldn't just start gnawing on her and when she woke up, act like an ambitious bedbug. Drool was dripping down my chin again, and this indecisiveness was killing me.

Then I remembered how the doctors did it. I snuck my left hand into her sleeve, wrapped my fingers around her bicep, and gently squeezed. She purred and continued to smile, and after a moment, several dark blue veins popped up in the crook of her arm.

My fangs had came out already a minute ago. You couldn't see it, but they were unbelievably sharp. They were not pointy, like in literature, but they had this short, inward-facing edge. When pulled in, they looked like regular human canines. It took me a while to get used to them and not cut my lower lip on them. With my tongue, I felt for the vein, and my teeth cut into it almost intuitively—must be another vampire instinct. The girl sighed and thrashed around a bit, but didn't wake up.

It looked like we were sleeping, and she had her arm across my face. I sucked in the life-giving liquid and wondered how much I could drink so it didn't hurt the young Thai girl. *Damn it, how much do they take when you give blood? One cup? One pint? It's probably based on the weight of the donor.* I drank and drank. With one hand, I held her arm by my mouth, and with the other, I monitored the girl's pulse. At the same time, I carefully watched the color of her skin—mainly her lips. When pink started to turn blue and beads of sweat appeared on her forehead, I stopped.

The girl sighed again when I bent her elbow like the nurses always do.

○ ○ ◐ ●

Within half an hour, I noticed a distinct improvement. My skin began to firm up, and my strength was returning. Not that I was full or anything; on the contrary, I was still hungry (very hungry). But I felt I could do almost anything, as before. I carefully wiped off my beard and licked my lips. Human blood really was disgusting.

○ ○ ◐ ●

I woke up when my bedfellows began getting up for work. Someone was loudly coughing; someone else was yawning. It was still almost completely dark. Only in the east the clouds were slowly turning red.

I wouldn't want to be a farmer.

I didn't know what to do. The only thing clear was that I had to discreetly disappear, but … At that moment, I realized something that I had neglected to remember last night within the scope of my mortal hunger. What the hell would happen to that chick?! She wouldn't turn into …!

Someone lit a kerosene lamp, and one of the women began rousing the heavy sleepers. The yawning and coughing intensified, and in the glow of the lamp, I saw that the girl next to me not only wasn't getting up but didn't look good either. Her tan skin was ghastly pale, almost blue, and she had black circles under her eyes. Except for me, she was the only one who hadn't gotten up yet.

Apparently, I overdid it a little.

A bright orange beam flashed across the room as an edge of the sun popped up over the horizon. The older woman who slept next to me shook the younger one, who finally got up. Presently, she wavered and fell, like a sack of potatoes.

That's when the older woman screamed bloody murder. Everyone in the room was staring at her, so even I peeked out from under the blanket. She murmured something inaudibly and was looking at the scarf she used to wet my lips during the night. Apparently, I didn't lick them as well as I thought because there were tell-tale rusty lines on the yellow fabric.

"Son of a bitch!" I swore quietly.

God knows why, but everyone was staring at me.

The girl sat up and hugged her knees. She was shaking all over, and her teeth chattered. She was the only one still staring at the scarf. I had never seen eyes so wide on an Asian woman before. This would be a good time to say something. I threw off the blanket and stood up.

"Does anyone here speak English?"

No one answered, and some of the men were eyeballing the shiny sickles hanging on the wall. The oldest one of them, a wrinkly man with teary eyes, one of those who slept in a bed, shook his head almost imperceptibly. With a quick movement, he reached under his shirt and aimed a small leather satchel at me.

It was quiet; only the morning hooting and hollering came out of the jungle. Because the house didn't have walls, I could see that the fields were to the left. To the right was the untouched greenery of the rain forest from which the road crawled out like a red tongue. The building was remote and surrounded by several palms with bushy tops, probably for shade.

The old man began speaking slowly in Thai, and it sounded like he was putting a hex on me. After a minute, one of the younger men interrupted him and for a little while explained something and waved his arms around. The old man listened and in the end nodded. He again began speaking, and the younger one translated. It doesn't makes any sense to curse a monster that doesn't understand you.

"Leave our house, blood demon. We helped you, so don't take revenge, blood demon. Our house is protected by powerful gods ..." He uttered several indiscernible names. "So leave in peace or a dragon will carry off your soul and cast it in the fire, where it will suffer for eternity." The old man paused, to see what I had to say.

I didn't say a thing.

"Blood demon, you took the daughter of my daughter. We will give her to the gods, so that she may be cleansed. The gods will seek vengeance, so flee as quickly and as far as you can!" The old guy ripped the satchel off his neck and waved it three times in my direction.

I thought about what to do. The tale about the blood demon very clearly pointed toward me and such stories spread much faster than the speed of light. Madam Dao's snitches would certainly be paying close attention. Also, I didn't want them to sacrifice the girl because of me.

"You see, my friend ... please translate." I nodded to the young man. "I am not a Thai blood demon, so this hocus-pocus won't work on me." I pointed at the satchel. "Your gods won't work on me either." When the translator finished speaking, everybody took a deep, frightened breath, and I saw that it wouldn't take much to send them jumping helter-skelter out of the house. "But I am not an evil demon." They obviously didn't believe me. "I needed the blood of your family to live, old man, and that means you truly saved my life. So you needn't worry; I know what gratitude is." Now this sounded a little more credible to them: one thing in exchange for another, a trade. "You too don't need to fear." I picked up the girl, who just about fainted when I touched her. "You won't turn into another blood demon, and in three days, you will be well again ..." When all this was translated, the people murmured, and the older woman began to cry—it was probably the mom.

"And not only well. You will never be sick, and your children will be strong. There will be many of them, and they will live for a very long time." I didn't know how, but I knew I wasn't lying. Vampire reproduction couldn't be as simple as the formula: one bite equals new vampire. The earth would be overrun by vampires because we probably drank human blood more often than necessary. Humans are the most prolific and therefore the most accessible resource. Second, I noticed that the bite marks on her arm had almost disappeared, which was impossible for a human. Something from my saliva must have caused that, something that for sure got into her bloodstream too. So that thing about the health and the kids couldn't be a complete lie.

Even though I paused for a long time, everyone still stared at me without moving a muscle. It also seemed to me that I saw an ever-increasing fright in their faces.

Why the hell? It looked so promising.

Then I saw it too. A mirror hung on a post in front of me. As the sun came up, sharp beams of light stretched through the room; in the moist air, they were clearly visible. As I fell into deep thoughts, my eyes adjusted to the barrage of photons on their own. Even though I stood in the shadows, my eyes were shining like spotlights from the reflected sunrays. I even startled myself.

Why not take advantage of this? I thought.

"Everything will be fine, but only if you don't talk about me. You will call off the doctor and tell the others that I got better and left—that way." I waved in a direction opposite of Bangkok. "We demons from the West, we are more modern than the local demons, and we can keep our word—in good times and in bad." I changed my eyes, and everyone breathed a sigh of relief. I laid the girl down on a mat and covered her up. "Give her some soup, and let her sleep. She will know when to go back to work … Don't delay anymore. Act like I am not here." As soon as that was translated, everyone dispersed, except for the old woman. It was a wonder they didn't break their legs in the process.

I found my clothes and checked the pockets. The knife and coins were in place, despite having been unwrapped from the piece of cushion cover. Of course, they thought I was a shipwrecked tourist, and robbing a tourist in Thailand was considered one of the most serious crimes. They had other, voluntary, ways of taking a person's money. The tourism industry guaranteed big profits, so pickpockets and other riffraff weren't tolerated by either the police or organized crime.

My presence made the old woman really nervous. I looked over the girl's wounds. The remaining pink spots were almost gone so I changed my clothes and left.

With time, someone will not be able to hold their tongue, and I could already see some European scholar interpreting the legend of the *white blood demon.*

○ ◗ ◖ ●

Despite being quite well, I still felt an uncontrollable hunger. "Fishies, fishies, where are you?" I ran along the red path through the jungle, jumped over muddy spots, and hid in the greenery twice; once when I heard a motorbike and a second time when I heard a car. I was a little worried about my footprints because I was barefoot and even the poorest people around here had at least flip-flops. Plus my feet were significantly bigger, but hopefully no one would notice before the next rainfall. I remembered the last time I had my tennis shoes was yesterday morning in the mangroves. The left one had the sole torn off, and the remaining muddy top was somewhere below my knee, with the tip facing back. The farmers must have taken off my right one for the sake of symmetry.

After three miles, I finally reached a small river. It was murky, about ten yards across, and was also the jungle boundary. Green, wet rice paddies stretched beyond it, followed by corn, and some tall trees. In the distance against the blue-colored mountains, a cloud of smog hung above Bangkok.

I ran a little ways against the stream and with the knife between my teeth began fishing. The river was barely three feet deep, and even though I knew they put fish in the rice paddies and canals on purpose, I couldn't feel a single one from the bank. So I dove into the murky waters—also because the stench coming off my clothes was, in the growing heat, increasingly more appalling. Not that it got any better, but I did catch three, eighteen-inch-long gray fish … Okay, but they were twelve inches for sure.

Instead of a glass, I used an old coconut shell and had a drink in tribute to my body since I couldn't get any kind of infection.

After the first three fish, I caught three more. Then I lay on the refreshing green grass, listened to the water splash and watched the sky.

Being free and full is a wonderful feeling.

○ ◗ ◐ ●

The clouds rolled in, and when it started raining, I set out again. The red dust turned into a red ice rink and I into a red-ice-skater.

The raindrops pattered loudly against the bubbling mud and the water in the rice paddies. Except for a few hunched backs clad in black shirts and a few water buffalo with big, pointy horns, I didn't see anyone.

I had to reach Bangkok as fast as possible. Even covered in red mud, here in the country, with my height, I stood out like the Leaning Tower of Pisa ... well, maybe not that, but I was very noticeable. Bangkok, on the other hand, was flooded with tourists and would be just fine, which was also one of the reasons I had turned toward Thailand.

○ ◗ ◐ ●

20

Around three o'clock, I reached the slums of the outer city (getting up with the sun has its advantages—the days are longer). You could smell the slums miles away.

I was in top form; I even tried to fly a little—well, maybe the thing about my form was only half true. To put it more accurately, I was in top shape from my skin inward. On the outside, I looked like a cajun chicken. You couldn't wash off red mud with water from a rice paddy, which was also swirling with red mud. That fishy smell from my shirt and shorts probably wouldn't ever come off.

So, I was more like a cajun fish—a rotting one.

○ ◑ ◐ ●

I marched down the muddy road, the ditches around me oozing with garbage, sewage, and playing children. The intermittent rain showers drummed to the rhythm of my stride on corrugated steel and hanging plastic tarps.

As I walked, the stench of rotting feces and urine somewhat receded, the clouds of metallic green flies thinned out, and patches of asphalt appeared here and there on the road. With the asphalt came thousands of scooters, mopeds, and motorcycles that sometimes carried up to five people. With the first real houses, the asphalt won, and the people—who used to gawk at me, but otherwise ignored me because I looked and smelled a lot like them—were now starting to move away from me.

When ornamental palm trees appeared next to the sidewalk, elegant multistory buildings appeared behind the sidewalk, and fancy neckties appeared on the sidewalk, a policeman stopped me. His clothes were pressed, and he wore a snow-white helmet, snow-white gloves, and snow-white straps across his chest.

"Is your hotel in this area, sir?" he asked in very decent English.

"No," I said after a brief thought. If I said yes, he would for sure try to help me—a tourist in obvious trouble. Then if he found out I was lying and I didn't have any money, it probably wouldn't end well—tourists, yes, but only the rich ones. They had enough of their own homeless here.

A golden Rolls-Royce with black windows sailed by on the perfect pavement.

"Excuse me, Constable," I said in the most distinguished tone I could muster, "which way to the port, please?"

"The entire center of the city along the river Menam is a port." He spoke like a tour guide. "The older part is against the flow; the modern with the flow." He waved his arms in the appropriate directions. Even the palms of his gloves were snow white.

"Thank you." I bowed slightly, and the policeman sniffed the air a little, trying to figure out if it was really me that reeked so badly.

○ ◗ ◖ ●

When you don't know what to do next, the best thing to do is to make a list of priorities, Dread used to say. I didn't feel too comfortable with the crowd around me. Somehow, I had grown less used to people in the past year. Someone could have followed me already; I stood out like a sore thumb.

So, my priorities were: become a little less visible; get some money; wash up; get more money; become a lot less visible; see ya, Bangkok. I found the airport on a large metal board with multilingual descriptions. It was to the northeast, a little ways beyond the city, and it was called Don Muang.

Freedom has wings.

○ ◗ ◑ ●

I walked more toward the old port than the new one and instead of humming limousines, again there were mopeds, scooters, tricycles with unbelievably tall loads, rickshaws, buffalo, and donkeys. Everything was honking, bellowing blue smoke, or occasionally taking a dump on the pavement. Add millions of people, screaming music, lanterns, porn theaters, neon, and ten thousand smells … Visit Asia!

The closer I got to the port the narrower the streets became, the darker the corners were, and paint peeled more and more off the fronts of the wood homes. The air reeked of putrid water, the sewer, and fish guts. I didn't see too many other tourists. Because it hadn't rained for over an hour (a record for today), the thin layer of red mud on me had dried and was cracking while I thought about how to get some money. I walked by many bars with boxing rings in them. A brave tourist could try kickboxing against the local champ. However, tourists only won in the movies; in reality, it would be very suspicious, and popularity was something I really didn't care for right now.

"Come in, stranger, come in!" A guy was luring me into a brothel. Apparently, I must have been in a really seedy place if he would call out even to me. It started to cloud over, and there was a hint of evening in the air. I squeezed the coins in my pocket and walked into the first dive behind the brothel.

○ ◗ ◑ ●

It was unbelievably noisy inside with the clamor of slot machines, Asian disco, a boxing match, and girls screaming. There were topless waitresses, clouds of cigarette and marijuana smoke, the smell of burnt oil and toilets, sweat, and alcohol … standard stuff.

I sat at the bar.

"Beer, sir?" The bartender glistened; his shirt was completely soaked with sweat.

"Hmmmm … yup," I said. "Do you take these?" I threw him one of my coins.

"You'll get change too." He quickly rattled on the abacus, wiped the counter, slapped down a coaster, and thumped a bottle on it covered in local lettering—no glass. Foam bubbled over the rim and ran down the bottle to the coaster. I was beginning to see a problem: How could I pretend to drink and not drink anything?

"You look lonely, handsome."

Of course, a beer comes with a hooker—standard scenario. So, I had to act in a standard way too.

"What will you have, miss?"

"I am Miriam, but you can call me Mimi. Champagne?"

"How about a beer?"

"Okay, beer then." She shrugged her shoulders, and the bartender's eyes narrowed. A beer?! Is that how a gentleman treats a lady?!

I leaned my back against the counter and scanned the bar. I was looking for something that should be in every dive near a port—I hoped.

"What's your name, handsome?"

"John."

"John, like John Lennon." She laughed shrilly.

"Yup. Except my singing is a little worse." This time, she almost fell over with laughter. She did her job well, Mimi.

"John, I see that you are a strong guy." She ran her hand over my shoulder. "Would you like to place a little bet?"

What's this?! Could Lady Luck be smiling upon me? For the first time?

"What's it about?"

"You call it arm wrestling."

Really lucky, this was exactly what I was looking for a minute ago. To rip you off in these parts, they used either pool, cards, the shell game, or this.

"Arm wrestling? Of course." I pretended to take a sip of beer and purposely spilled it on myself. The fact that I didn't sweat could be suspicious. Everyone had triangles of sweat on their shirts. Now I did too—at least in the front.

"Come on." She grabbed my hand and pulled me toward a door that I thought led to the bathroom.

○ ◔ ◑ ●

They even had these little portable arm-wrestling tables. The stench of sweat and cigarette smoke almost knocked me over, but at least my fishiness would blend in. Around me, they played cards, dominos, dice, mahjongg, slots … whatever you could think of. Mimi dragged me over to a table where two guys were guzzling beer—one was big and fat, the other one small.

"This is John," Mimi introduced me.

"Hi, John. You wrestle?" The bigger one went right to the point.

"Sure."

"How much bet?"

I dumped all my coins on the table and pushed half toward them.

"Hmmm, so ten dollar." He slapped a ten-dollar bill on the table. I knew exactly how this kind of rip-off would go down. They let you win twice, then they make you bet everything (*You wouldn't fleece us!* They say), and in the fifth round, they take your wedding ring too.

"This everything you have?" He pointed at the rest of the coins.

"Not at all." I waved my hand, and Mimi snuggled up to me. The way I looked and the fact that I didn't have any shoes didn't seem to concern them at all. White people are weird, everyone knows that.

"To table?"

"Yeah."

In the meantime, the smaller guy brought over the aforementioned sports equipment and placed it next to our table.

We stood up, grabbed the handles with our left hands, and locked our right hands together. Muscles rippled underneath a layer of fat.

"When Mimi say start. Okay?"

"Okay."

People rushed up to the table and began betting—apparently just for my benefit, so I would gain a sense of authenticity.

"Three, two, one, nooow!" Mimi shouted.

Both of us went for it. Fatty was dripping sweat and groaning, "Ummm!" He almost pinned me, but when I started to wane, despite his increasingly louder "Ummm!" he started to wane too. After five minutes, I had him. Mimi was jumping up in the air; there were congratulatory shoulder slaps for me and Thai taunting jeers for Fatty.

"A rematch, John?! But left hand!"

"Fine."

"But we double bet!"

"Fine."

Fatty put another two ten-dollar bills in front of his buddy, who was keeping the bank. Judging by how used they looked and how their color was nearly identical to the dirt on the table, they must have been working money.

We locked left hands, then Mimi counted down, followed by "Ummm!" and at the moment when he almost had me, he suddenly screamed out in pain, his arm relaxed, and I smacked it down to the desktop.

"What happened?" I looked surprised.

"Back cracked—spine bad. When I young, pirates bang, bang!" He mimicked a pistol and looked crushed.

"Well, I can't accept this kind of victory," I said, just like they would expect from a white moron. "I will return your money."

"No! My pride not allow!" He would have made a good actor; I almost believed him. The circle around us murmured with appreciation, but maybe just a little too soon, just *before* he began speaking—extras are always just extras. The last wave of pain ran over Fatty's face, and he said, "You, John, arm wrestling with my friend Ji. I trust he."

"Whatever you want." I smiled dismissively at the short stature of mister Ji. He wore a traditional black garment that was tailored to minimize his *really* broad shoulders.

Mr. Ji carefully rolled his sleeve up to his wrist. He even had a rubber band so not even a piece of his forearm showed. His palm wasn't too big and his arm so short that he had to prop his elbow up on a pillow.

That 'Ummmm!' and the gritting of teeth started again. When I waned after seven minutes, Mr. Ji let up slightly, panted like a dying donkey, and finally succumbed.

"You take everything, John! Mimi, you bring he, so he rob us blind! You bad, bad girl!" The fatter guy raised his voice, and Mr. Ji rubbed his sore hand dejectedly.

Again, I spilled beer on myself and put on a sloshed, invincible face.

"How about we double up again? And I'll add this." I pushed the rest of the coins along the table.

"Okay," Fatty agreed after a brief and truly honest-looking hesitation. Then he really convincingly hobbled over to the table. "Forty-five dollar, I even to fifty, okay? If lose, you pay five?"

"Sure," I said in an arrogant I-never-lose-you-dumb-ass tone, exactly as they expected.

"Left hand," said Mr. Ji. Judging by his accent, his English was much better than Fatty's, but playing a simpleton was all part of the game.

I wobbled a little. The beer was strong, and in this awful heat, it would have certainly acted like a sledgehammer. Maybe there was something else in there besides hops; it tasted suspiciously sweet.

Our left hands clasped, and short Mr. Ji began acting again. He yanked, snorted, bulged his eyes, and looked like he was going to pop a vein. I let him almost pin me, and then I started to groan loudly and bring my hand back up. When I reached vertical, Mr. Ji tried for real. The muscles under his shirt stiffened and ... and nothing. I just smiled with my eyes, and he realized that this time, they were the ones being scammed. Briefly, I remembered how I lifted the five-hundred-pound lead diving weight without any problems. By vampire standards, I was just a toddler back then.

Mr. Ji really had enormous strength for a human. He must have done some special training—no surprise there, if he made his living by wrestling money away from tourists. The surrounding huddle detected that something was wrong and began to drop away from the script. Streams of sweat ran down Mr. Ji's temples, and I breathed and groaned noisily. I would make a pretty good actor too. I just had to be careful not to crush his hand.

After fifteen minutes, I won. I couldn't allow myself to win any faster because that would make Mr. Ji lose face.

○ ◔ ◑ ●

"Wow, John." Mimi was having difficulty staying in character, since she'd just lost her cut.

"Ha ha, I am the best!" Again, I spilled beer on myself and dribbled some foam on my hands, as I gathered up the money.

"One more time," said Fatty. His spinal pains had suddenly disappeared. Mr. Ji grabbed him by the sleeve and murmured something. Asian languages are difficult because they express emotions with a slightly different intonation than European ones, but in spite of that, I recognized that Mr. Ji understood the smile in my eyes. The thing about good players is that they know when they've been beaten.

"You're good, John." Fatty slapped me on the shoulder. "Would you like to work with us for a few days?" His broken English was suddenly perfect.

"Maybe I'll stop by, my fat friend. Don't take it personally, but I need this money more than you do." We grinned at each other, and I gave one of the island coins to Mimi so she smiled at me too. When I left, all three of them shook my hand.

What real pros.

○ ○ ◑ ●

It was almost dark outside, and it was raining again, but Bangkok never sleeps. (I read that on a sign in one of the travel agencies.) I made my way out of the narrow maze of streets and found the local shopping district and a cheap, all-night supermarket.

I paid ten dollars for a shirt and underwear and twenty for a pair of pants with zip-off pant legs and some socks. The boots that I needed were one hundred and ninety-nine, so I stole them. As a member of the Night Club, I knew exactly where the cameras were, and with my vampire speed, no one had a chance. Who could tell that the big paper bag was a little fuller?

"Come again, sir." A girl by the exit smiled and bowed. Of course I'd come back—if I got the wrong size.

In the personal hygiene section, I bought some soap (Purple Passion), shampoo, a toothbrush, sinfully expensive deodorant, and scissors. Then I stole a hundred-dollar pair of shades and returned to the port.

○ ○ ◑ ●

The cheapest hotel with a tub and warm water was called Pink Dream and was seriously overpriced at twenty dollars a night—being white has its disadvantages too.

"I need towels."

"Yes, sir, they are in the room. A girl?"

"No."

"Yes, sir. Please sign in, sir." The desk clerk pushed a worn, smudged guestbook in front of me. The hotel's décor looked like something from the clearance section at an Ethiopian IKEA, but it was clean—except for that guestbook. I had prepared my alias ahead, so without thinking, I wrote John McGregor.

"Mister is Scottish?"

"American."

The clerk understood and stopped asking. Part of my twenty dollars paid for not having to show my passport.

○ ◐ ◑ ●

The room was small, but the bathroom had a real and big tub in it; nothing else would fit. They had to build the wall *after* the tub installation, and the sink was on a hinge so one could either use the tub or the sink. But who would want to use both at once?

Not only were there towels (clean ones), but a single-use scrub brush and bath salts.

○ ◐ ◑ ●

I destroyed the brush pretty quickly, but it was enough to get the red mud off. A two hour bath with salts and Purple Passion took care of even the fishy smell. Here and there, I added more hot water and reminisced. When I took a similar bath a year ago, I would have never thought that the next time would be in Thailand, one year later.

In the end, I showered off all the soapy stuff, and instead of shaving, I just clipped my beard. That changes you a bit, and now I looked like a true adventure tourist. That afternoon, I had carefully observed how bearded they were. Then I combed my hair back, pulled it into a ponytail with a green rubber band, and critically evaluated myself.

"I look like an asshole." I grinned at the mirror, but on the other hand, I didn't look anything like myself. I tried different grimaces, but the temporarily-permanent contraction of facial muscles that could change one's appearance—used by the vampire hero in my book— was unfortunately all made up. I took the square, narrow, mirrored sunglasses out of their case and put them on—a total assassin for hire, just like in the movies. No self-respecting killer looked like this, but as a tourist, I would pass nicely.

A lizard was sitting on the wall, flicking its tongue and looking at me. So I thought I'd better get dressed. The shirt was pretty ugly, but it's not supposed to show sweat. So in my case, it meant it wouldn't show that I wasn't sweating. I rolled up the loose sleeves and pulled out that last pin that you always forget in a new shirt. I unwrapped the pants, shook them out a bit, pulled them on, and stashed the knife and the pitiful remains of my money in the pockets. Then I pulled on the socks and finally the boots.

"I got it right." I walked around the room and tightened up the laces. The boots came up to the middle of my calf. They were made of thick, black leather, with a steel-reinforced sole and toe. I could kick through a car with these, no sweat. Boots are the foundation of success; everyone knows that. These squeaked a little and smelled beautifully.

I thoroughly slathered myself with deodorant, so people weren't surprised when they didn't smell sweat. I untucked my shirt so I'd look relaxed, and now I could finally get to making some real money.

"Okay." I put the glasses in my pocket for now, and my old clothes and everything else I stuffed into a plastic bag. I'd throw this away outside. I swept up my beard hairs, flushed them down the toilet, and wiped down any fingerprints.

○ ◐ ◑ ●

"I wish you a good time, Mr. McGregor."

I laid the key on the counter. "Thanks."

The desk clerk couldn't know that I had no intention of coming back. I glanced at the clock. *Nine, the whole night is ahead of me.* My gaze fell on a small TV. The news was on, and the clerk's eyes were wandering toward the screen even while he was hanging up the key.

On the screen, several black things were floating in a rice paddy. Policemen and spotlights were everywhere. The reporter spoke excitedly. Judging by the position of the sun, it appeared to have been shot just an hour before sunset.

"What happened?" I nodded toward the TV.

"You don't know?!" The clerk's eyes lit up. "Someone killed a whole family of farmers, barely eighteen miles from Bangkok. They say they were tortured, and they say some white guy did it!" He raised his eyebrows. Why does everyone love to pass on terrible news? I stroked my beard.

"A white guy, you say?"

"They have a sketch of him, if you'd wait a moment … See?! They're showing it now!" He pointed at the screen.

In reality, I looked a lot better. They gave me a short crew cut, low forehead, and a square, wicked jaw.

The clerk stole a quick glance at me and looked distrustful. Luckily, all white folk look alike to the Asians, just like they do to us.

"It's probably some Russian or Ukrainian. See that nose and that jaw?" I said with authority.

"Really?! Maybe you should tell the police."

"Maybe I will … What else was on the news? About this?" I expressed the standard bloodthirst.

"It must have happened just after noon. They tortured them—something nasty—then they executed them with a sword. Probably having to do with drugs. They grow poppy in that area … The clerk paused and stole another quick glance at me. Even though drug possession carried the death penalty in Thailand, the drug trade here was extensive and everyone knew about it.

"Okay, good night then." I tapped on the counter. Unfortunately, I couldn't tell him that what excited him so much on TV, he might experience for himself real soon—torture included.

Wries and Van Vren were on my heels.

○ ◐ ◑ ●

"Now to point number three; more money," I mumbled and slammed the trash can lid on top of my fishy clothing. I put on my dark shades. This was pretty common in Bangkok at night.

It didn't rain. The air had cooled off comfortably. A slight breeze was blowing, and even the moon was shining above the never-ending neon.

When I reached the place of the whispering limousines, the police didn't even notice me. There were plenty of guys just like me walking around.

"Hi," said a freckled girl with an ample bosom that swayed in a daring T-shirt.

"Hi." I indicated my empty pocket. Instantly, this beautifully unfolding friendship was over. Prostitutes of all types, colors, tastes, beliefs, sizes, and genders were everywhere, and hoards of German-speaking tourists were grabbing them up like a charging platoon of marines.

I was looking for something else: Tall, fancy houses of the local filthy rich; tall, fancy houses with underground garages. I needed a scenario that happened several times every night in every large city: a robbery or better yet, an attempted sexual assault. I figured out the money situation already when I was in the bathtub: stealing boots and sunglasses, when life is at stake, yes—but violence and robbery, never.

○ ☽ ☾ ●

I chose a pompous building—almost a skyscraper, with shiny thermo-glass—not because it stood alone in a small park, but because it was easy to sneak into. I was surely not the only one to notice. The night guard had probably been bribed. That was how it was usually done, and if it was well organized, the guard gave out tips when a potential target drove in.

○ ☽ ☾ ●

The parking ramp had five underground levels, numbered from top to bottom; most of the top half was full of wire cages with mopeds and heavy, expensive motorcycles.

Because the top level was too full and had an unhealthy number of cameras, I settled on the second one, hiding in the shadow behind a yellow Datsun. Then all I had to do was listen and wait.

At eleven thirty, I heard the luxurious purring of an eight-cylinder engine, and a dark blue Mercedes convertible sailed into the lower levels.

That's it.

The cameras down here were scarce and immobile, so I could walk pretty normally, without hiding. I took off my glasses and put them away in the case. As the Mercedes turned, its tires squeaked noisily on the special green paint.

I was always glad when my plans worked out. As soon as the vehicle's purr stopped, I heard the quick steps of several pairs of feet, then a muffled cry, and the noise of a spilled purse. *A woman! I* am *damn lucky.* The rough soles of my shoes squeaked a little too, so I slowed down.

I peeked into the lowest level. The back of the dark blue Mercedes glistened in the glow of a single lightbulb. The other bulbs, all the way to the back wall, weren't on, and the single camera was *amazingly* pointed in the opposite direction from where it should have been.

Three men in dark face masks pressed a young woman to the hood of a car just a few feet beyond the edge of the light. Her skirt was down already, legs far apart, and now one of them was almost lovingly running a pointy pocket knife along her calf—actually, he was cutting off her black pantyhose. The woman had a gag in her mouth. She quietly sobbed, but was being smart and didn't fight back. The knife looked very sharp.

Her high heels cast long shadows.

I realized that even after those many murders I had committed over the past year, violence against the unarmed bothered me just as much as before. Night Club was deep beneath my skin.

The knife slipped past her knee.

I waited a moment longer and then the tearing sound was interrupted by a quiet squeaking—as if from the sole of a boot.

"Fuck off, whitey!" The one pressing on the girl's shoulders yanked out a revolver and aimed it at me. The woman wasn't just young, but pretty too.

"That sounded quite racist." I kept walking. People usually don't shoot other people. That requires either practice or some kind of a mental defect. For people who just aim, the gun is usually only in the way.

When I stepped over the light boundary, I used vampire speed. It must have looked like I disappeared and in the next fraction of a second appeared ten yards somewhere else.

"Nice piece," I said, the revolver already in my hand. The one with the knife was startled, stopped cutting her hose and took a stab at me. They were complete amateurs. He was holding the knife like a fork.

"It's a knife, not chopsticks," I scolded him. By then, two of the guy's fingers were already out of their sockets, and I was closing the blade.

The third attacker was smart and tried to run away. "Let's go back there, boys. I need to tell you a secret." I held the third one by his twisted arm so he almost scraped the floor with his forehead, and the other two I kicked over there. When I asked them politely, they took off their masks.

They were just boys, eighteen or even younger, and judging by their clothes, from wealthy families. Robbing and raping was the best thing for fending off boredom. I knew that from Prague.

Just by *coincidence*, I stopped paying attention, and the one that had the revolver before *unexpectedly* tried some kung fu. He was apparently the leader. Surprisingly, I was standing in such a bad position I was literally asking for it. I got a swift whack on the chin. I wavered, and the twisted arm slipped away from me. I knew the girl was watching, with eyes like saucers, so I stood in a place where she could see me get clobbered. Victims who were just rescued are usually in shock so they don't call for help; they don't run—plenty of time for a show.

For a while, I fought the boys, three against one. It ended with them running away, supporting one of their buddies. After several uneasy steps, I fell to my knees, the pocket knife deep in my shoulder.

The girl couldn't have noticed how I stuck it in there myself, or the way I first opened my shirt and pulled it out of the way so it didn't get ruined.

"Are you all right, sir?!" She switched to English after a rapid-fire round of Thai. I tried not to not look at her bare legs too much.

"I … I don't know." My voice was raspy. "And you, miss?"

"They didn't hurt me, not enough time." In her hands, she kneaded her tattered pantyhose. In her eyes appeared exactly that thing that appears in the eyes of every princess who has just been rescued by a knight in shining armor.

"I will call an ambulance and the police." She batted her eyelashes and turned to her spilled purse—her elegant cell lying in the middle.

"No, please, not the police … This is nothing." I waved my hand, stood up with some difficulty, and wavered. As I expected, she jumped up to support me.

"You have a knife in your shoulder." Her eyes were really gorgeous.

"That's just …" I wanted to say just a scratch, but that would have been too much. So I just wavered again. "I'll give you my shirt; those assholes wrecked your …" I bashfully turned my gaze away from her legs.

"That's …" She sniffled a little. "That's all right, I have an overcoat in my car … Why don't you want an ambulance?! You'll bleed to death! You'll go septic!"

"No, I'll be all right. Good-bye, miss." I took a step toward the stairs, smiled for the last time, and made sad doe eyes at her.

"No! Wait! I will take care of you myself!" I didn't even have time to waver three steps when she caught me again.

I grinned to myself. I really loved it when my plans worked out. She just touched me, and I again fell to my knees—carefully, though, so I didn't rip my pants. The girl helped me up, propped me up against the back of the Mercedes, slipped into her coat, gathered the things back into her purse, and closed the roof. The locks clicked, and in a moment, we were in the elevator.

A knight in shining armor, a mysterious knight in shining armor, and a wounded knight in shining armor—no girl can resist that.

○ ◑ ◐ ●

"Please have a seat." She lowered me down to the rim of a round tub surrounded by tiles with Chinese dragons painted in light blue. Each one was different, so that meant they were hand painted. The apartment, what I saw of it, was worth a million bucks. It was on the top floor and unbelievably huge by Asian standards.

"I won't surprise your husband, will I?"

"I am alone," she said without hesitation—so she was either a pricey prostitute or an emancipated woman, who sacrificed family life for a career. Apparently, she was very successful, no matter what she did. In the bright yellow light reflected off the mirrors and polished tiles, she didn't look so young anymore. Actually, she didn't look like a girl. She could have been just over thirty—but excellently maintained. A fashion designer, lawyer, TV reporter … but for a designer, she was dressed much too conservatively.

296

"Antiseptic, dressing, bandages." She turned away from the first-aid kit and laid everything on the counter next to the sink.

I looked at her with a tired smile. In the elevator, I had tried to smudge around what little blood dripped out around the pocket knife so that it looked more dramatic.

"That knife must come out." Even though she stood there wearing just her jacket, panties, and high heels, her voice had the authority of a person used to making decisions—so the emancipated version.

"I can do this myself," I said when she reached for the black handle without hesitation. "Get the gauze ready, please ... Now!" She listened to me, and as soon as I pulled out the blade, she pressed a square piece of dressing on the wound—so she couldn't have seen that within a second, the only thing left was a quickly disappearing scar.

I winced, groaned loudly, and narrowed my eyes with *pain*, and the bloody knife fell on the tiles. When she caught me so I wouldn't fall into the tub backwards, I reached over and held the dressing in place myself.

"That's good," I said valiantly.

"You almost fainted!"

"No, no ..." I closed my eyes and wobbled.

"Sir!"

"I'm okay, I'm okay ... Can you please ... a little of that peroxide, a fresh bandage, and some tape?"

"Yes, right away." As she cut the tape (her hands were shaking like those of a hundred-year-old alcoholic), I *disinfected* my wound. When I winced again, she squinted sadly. Then I held the square gauze in place on my shoulder as she clumsily taped it with white strips that were much too long.

"How about you? Do you need a doctor? Did they hit you?" I showed interest.

"No, they just grabbed my purse and then ... and then ..." Her tension released in a stream of tears. She put her hand in front of her face and sank to the tub next to me. For a moment, I held her around the shoulders with my healthy arm and then began to put on my shirt. I didn't even have to pretend that I couldn't do it well with just one hand.

"Thank you for your help, miss. If they hit you, you should see a doctor ... Anyway, you should talk to someone about this. Don't hold it in. Hmm." I shrugged my shoulders. "Good-bye."

"Please?" She lifted her teary gaze. "Where do you want to go?!" She must use high-quality makeup because it wasn't smudging at all. "Well …" My eyes darted around the room bashfully. "I thought that I would sleep here in the garage. That's why I was there in the first place. I lost my papers, credit cards, backpack … but you needn't worry about that. Good-bye." I ran into the door frame with my shoulder, quietly winced, and with quick, wobbly steps rushed toward the door of the apartment. It took her a little longer than I expected (I guess, thirty-somethings don't believe in Prince Charming as much), but she caught up to me just before I could remove the door chain.

"You will sleep here. I have a guest room. No arguments."

Despite being a little slow, the conviction of her decision was praiseworthy.

"I cannot accept that."

"You must!" She almost twisted my arm.

I was surprised that people still fell for these ancient tricks.

○ ◑ ◐ ●

"How rude of me, I apologize." She stretched out her arm just after she pulled the covers over me. "Helen Trang."

"Helen, nice name." I managed a tired smile. "Stuart, Stuart J. Samuel."

Really, high time we introduced ourselves. I took off my own shoes, but she helped me (she wouldn't be denied) with the rest and in the end dressed me in a men's nightshirt (also for guests). I was afraid of overdoing it, but apparently, my acting was very convincing.

"I hope you sleep well, Stuart. Don't hurry anywhere tomorrow. I will prepare breakfast for you in the morning and something for lunch too. I will return early from work, around two, so wait for me, all right?"

"Yes," I said with my eyes already closed.

○ ◑ ◐ ●

At night, she checked up on me three times. Luckily, I always heard her so I began breathing in time. I would rest better after she left for work. Despite being *that* well, I still felt tired after the swamp flight.

I wondered if she was checking up on me to see if I'd died or if I was cleaning out her place. The third time, though, she sat on the bed, stroked my forehead, and whispered something in Thai. It sounded pretty nice.

So, even emancipated Asian thirty-somethings believe in a shining knight. All those soaps must have some truth to them.

○ ◑ ◐ ●

She came to take a quick peek at me before she went to work, and the room filled with the pleasant smell of an expensive perfume. I slept for two hours, woke up, pulled on the guest robe, and went sightseeing around the apartment.

There was a big aquarium in the living room, filled with strange fish, a bookcase stuffed with legal literature, and a desk that certainly wasn't there for decoration. Next to the phone, stacks of bills, papers, and newspapers lay a fancy laptop with an Internet connection. Next, I discovered that the view from the windows was amazing: skyscrapers in the center of the city surrounded by a charming medley of original wooden houses bristling with antennae and satellite dishes. The park far below me looked luscious with small ponds, water fountains, and grinning statues of the local gods. From up here, they looked like colorful, symmetric ornaments.

I didn't find any cameras or listening devices, only the security system controls; it was off.

"What am I supposed to do with this?" On the breakfast counter separating the super-modern stainless-steel kitchen from the living room, she prepared for me the ever-favorite cereal. A note was propped up against the ceramic bowl.

Milk is in the fridge; otherwise, eat what you wish.

H.

I poured milk over the cereal, made coffee, waited a moment, and flushed it all down the toilet. I contemplated this shortcut over the swirling water, but there was no other way of dealing with such situations. I stacked the dirty dishes in the sink.

I took a shower and washed the knife. First, I made a spot on my skin with some dry blood and then put the bandage back on. Then, still in the robe, I plopped down on the sofa, grabbed the remote from the coffee table, and turned on the TV. A bed is not the only thing that is magical after a year of sleeping in a hammock.

I channel surfed over to CNN, nothing interesting, then to Thai News Line—a Thai channel for foreigners. The investigation of yesterday's massacre drew bigger and bigger waves of interest, since they had discovered three more bodies in the fields. Some handy cameraman with a long telephoto lens filmed them just as they were being revealed to a detective, who was covered with red mud. The bodies had become bloated overnight and were crawling with insects, but the signs of a cruel interrogation were clearly visible. Within ten minutes, they showed that clip three times.

I was wondering how Wries and Van Vren could find me so fast, and the thought of an airport and a speedy disappearance from Thailand was slowly dissolving in a fog. Even with six million people living in Bangkok, barely several hundred resembled my description, maybe even less. Guarding the terminals was pretty easy to do. A ship would be safer. Moreover, I needed a passport to get on a plane, and trying to find one would be the same as getting up on a pedestal and screaming: *Here I am!* I even dismissed a trip to the Czech consulate pretending to be a tourist who had been mugged. I couldn't do anything that would be easily anticipated by Wries and Van Vren. The fact that they found my trail so quickly proved that they either knew what they were doing or everyone who escaped from Madam Dao's ship took the same route. Or their network of informants was much more extensive than I had imagined. Or it was all of the above. The thought of Madam Dao's ship sent shivers down my spine, but it wasn't the ship as much as the punishment that awaited me there.

The silver chain.

I wondered what was up with Denise.

○ ◑ ◐ ●

Around eleven, the phone rang.

"Yes?" I said carefully.

"Stuart, how do you feel?"

"Stu ...?"

"That's you, you fool," said My Other.

"Aha, yes, much better than yesterday. Thank you for breakfast, Helen."

"It's the least I can do for you. I will return a little earlier; if you can wait, I will make you lunch."

"That would be wonderful." Despite the happy tone of my voice, I grimaced with discontent. What a moron! I should have made up something like Hanako did, something about allergies. But now, like an idiot, I said I'd eaten breakfast, so ...

"Stuart, are you there?"

"Yes, of course. Helen, may I please use your computer and take a peek at the Internet?"

"Why not? If you can figure it out." She laughed cunningly. "I have to go, so around one thirty."

"Bye." I put down the receiver and pulled the laptop to me. Why should I need to figure it out. I shook my head and flipped open the display. *Who does she think I am?!*

Instantly, I knew what she meant: Windows in Thai looked all but inoperable.

○ ○ ◑ ●

Before Helen returned, I got dressed and put on my boots too. Even though I initially thought I could stay here for a few days, I realized that I would have to take off soon. Wries and Van Vren certainly found out from the farmers that I was wearing only a T-shirt and shorts, and I was dirty and without money. There weren't too many ways of cleaning up and quickly getting your hands on some money without calling attention to yourself. If you bribe some detective, who calls around the cheap hotels, another one who finds out about the unusual things that had happened in the past few days involving a white guy ... In other words, Wries and Van Vren could already be on the elevator. Moreover, they had it easier now that the locals were watching single foreigners especially closely after yesterday's murders.

There was a camera in the elevator here, which I noticed a little too late when I played wounded last night.

Just before one o'clock, on Thai News Line, a reporter was announcing a late-breaking story from a news van. He spoke in Thai, and English subtitles ran along the bottom of the screen, but I didn't need them; the picture was enough. The black body bag that they'd just carried out of the Pink Dream Hotel couldn't have contained anyone other than the clerk. A sketch of my likeness appeared again—this time with a beard. I turned off the TV and opened the door into the foyer so I didn't miss any noises from the hallway.

The only noises in the room were the bubbling of the aquarium and the faint sound of traffic somewhere far below. The fish rhythmically flapped their fins, stared at me, and moved their little mouths. I stared at them too, but with considerably more hunger.

At one thirty-seven, Helen came back. I hid the six-shooter—the one I'd taken from the crook—under a chair. It was a snub-nosed thirty-eight, completely useless against Wries and Van Vren, but the feel of a gun in your hand is calming. I watched as Helen carefully locked the door, and because I had already looked it over, I knew it was pretty strong—a so-called safety door.

When Helen saw me, her face lit up with a smile, but she controlled herself right away.

"I bought caviar and champagne and … how do you say it in English … lobster, I think. Do you like lobster, champagne, and toast with butter and caviar?" Again, she smiled at me from behind a huge paper bag.

I do! I wanna be humaaan again!

By those smiles, I realized that I must have woken some deeper feelings in her. That made things even worse. Just my presence alone here exposed her to mortal danger.

"I like it, but I won't be eating." The eyes behind the bag widened not from what I said, but how I said it.

"Why not?" she said in a hurt tone.

I suspected there wasn't time for deceitful games. It was barely five and a half miles to here from the hotel, and they'd gotten the clerk last night.

"I don't eat!"

"But breakfast—!"

"Please listen." She gasped at the expression on my face. "Yesterday wasn't a coincidence. I was waiting for someone to get attacked so I could rescue them and get into their apartment." The spot on my neck, where the explosive charge used to be, felt a familiar itch.

"But—!"

"They attacked you for real. I helped you for real, but I only did it because I needed you for something."

"What?" she sobbed.

"Two thousand dollars, in small bills if possible."

The paper bag hit the rug and busted open. She'd bought real French bubbly, three bottles of it. The lobsters had a beautifully orangey-red color and their antennae moved around. Finally, there must have been two pounds of caviar. One of the bottles rolled to the leg of the table and dinged against it, and Helen began to cry. It's not easy for emancipated thirty-somethings when their last Prince Charming rides away.

It wasn't easy for me either.

"I would have finished it to the end, but my being here puts you in danger ... Did you see the dead on the news, those farmers? And the clerk?"

Horrified, she covered her mouth, and I could almost hear her wheels spinning: *He is white! That guy is white! This is him!*

"Those looking for me did that, not me, but it's true, that I met all those people recently. The ones looking for me set not only the police after me but all the Thai people too. It's very likely that they will find you too. When they ask you, tell them everything; don't lie and don't hold anything back. It's important because you won't help me, and you'll only hurt yourself. You have no chance to escape. Not even the army can protect you, not even running across the border, nothing. If you act as I am telling you, you will survive." Now I was lying, but maybe they would kill her mercifully in exchange for quick answers. "Now the money. Of course I will return it, not now, but in a year and with 10 percent interest."

She cried and tried to pick up the lobsters as they crawled away. I didn't feel good about it, toying with people like this ...

I heard the elevator.

"The money, please!"

"What about ... your wound?"

"It's fine."

"But you couldn't fake that!"

"I could."

"But ..."

"Hurry, please."

Surprisingly, she got up, threw the lobsters into the sink, washed her hands, and opened a little safe behind an Indian painting. I knew it was there, but an electronic lock was too much even for me, having no tools.

I heard two sets of footsteps in the hallway. I'd heard them so many times, walking above my head on the deck, so there wasn't any doubt.

"Here." Helen handed me a wad of dollar bills. "I don't know, it probably isn't exactly two thou—"

"They're behind the door," I whispered and hid the folded bills in my pocket. "Remember what I told you, don't lie to them; you won't help me by that, but you'll hurt yourself." In my mind's eye, I glimpsed a girl's face, without eyes and slashed up by wire.

The doorbell sounded like a Chinese music box.

"What ... what do you want to do?" Again the tears.

I stood by the window and looked down. It didn't open; the ventilation system took care of air circulation.

I swallowed.

Again, the doorbell rang.

Wries and Van Vren were the best medicine against vertigo that I knew.

Doorbell.

I closed my eyes, took a deep breath, and opened them again.

The door shook under the heavy strike. The bricks slid out a bit, and half the door frame was ripped out of the wall.

"Thanks, Helen." I smiled, kicked out the glass, and jumped.

Close your eyes. I am leaving!

○ ◐ ◑ ●

I was always afraid of heights, but it's nice if you can command yourself and overcome it. With Wries and Van Vren at your back, it really wasn't anything difficult. I realized that I was honestly afraid to death of them.

I was falling along a shiny, coated surface. Around me, pieces of glass swirled and the air roared. I felt like I was speeding up more and more. After briefly deliberating the idea that I couldn't fall faster than one hundred fifty-five miles per hour, My Other just screamed.

Ten yards above ground, I initiated a levitation braking maneuver. I didn't even have to try very hard; it happened on its own. Nevertheless, I still landed ankle deep in the sod. Lucky for me, the pieces of glass beat me down here. Lucky because they massacred a couple of bushes and turned a little ornamental tree into a skinhead.

I wasn't as exhausted as I was after the horizontal flight across the mud, that's for sure, but I was pretty worn out.

○ ◔ ◑ ●

I stepped out of the luscious green carpet and knocked the red dirt off my boots. The good news was that my bones and boots made it through that fall. The bad news was that I'd become as weak as a child.

The street chugged along next to the park.

"Taxi!" I put on my glasses and waved at the passing vehicle. With tires squealing, he zigzagged out of the traffic and stopped.

"To the port." I crumbled on the back seat.

The people who had seen my landing were still staring in disbelief; their mouths gaping open.

The guy behind the wheel leaned on the horn and violently turned—apparently a standard maneuver here in Bangkok.

"You don't look so good, sir." He glanced at me in the rearview mirror.

"Are you a doctor or a cabbie?!"

○ ◔ ◑ ●

First, I let him take me to the fish market where I bought four large four-pound fish. They were live and swam in a large, clear plastic bag.

"You're not getting into my car with—!"

"Drive!"

"But—!"

I slid my glasses down and made vampire eyes at him in the mirror. His maneuvers became even more violent, but he scrunched his head down between his shoulders and didn't say another word. Three blocks away from the bar where I arm wrestled those two yesterday, I threw a ten-dollar bill on the seat. The vehicle skidded to the curb.

"I wish you a good day, my friend." I knew that within thirty minutes, Wries and Van Vren would find him.

○ ○ ◑ ●

I stepped into the bar, not that I found it as easily as it sounds here—with my sense of direction, it wasn't three blocks, but at least ten.

The same auditory and olfactory scene dominated here as yesterday.

"John! Hi, John!" Mimi cheerfully waved from the bar. I leaned on the counter next to her, and the fish restlessly splashed.

"Beer?" The bartender was the same too.

"One for the lady, just a glass for me." I dropped another bill.

"Big John, good to see you. You look good today—especially that ponytail." She stroked my hair.

"How about another wager, Mimi?" I grinned. "Do you think the boys can take it?"

"The boys can take anything ... except arm wrestling." She grinned at me with her yellow, lipstick-stained teeth.

○ ○ ◑ ●

Fatty and Mr. Ji sat in the same spot as yesterday. The room was half empty but smelled the same.

"Mr. John." Both of them slightly (and cautiously) nodded and watched my fish.

"Good day, sirs. How about a bet?"

"On what? How much?"

"This much." I threw three one-hundred-dollar bills on the table.

"Interesting." Fatty's eyes lit up. "What are we talking about?"

"I bet you that I can kill these fish and drink all their blood within two minutes."

"Rubbish! Bad! Stupid! Is this what you wager on in Europe?!"

"In Europe, no, but where I come from, yes."

"He can't possibly make it," Mimi said.

"We let him get us once before, and we know he needs money ..." Fatty looked me sharply in the eye, then he took the bag with the fish and looked them sharply in the eyes too. "Minute and a half."

"You're on."

We shook on it, and they added their three hundred to mine.

"Get me a cutting board, a cleaver, and some towels!" I shouted into the gathering group of onlookers. They were excitedly pointing at the fish and at me. They tapped on their heads and placed bets like crazy.

I knew that he would bite. If I drank blood out in the open, someone would immediately report me, and I didn't have time to look for dark corners. But as a wager against a foolish white guy, it was legit.

"Three, two, one, go!" Fatty squeezed a stopwatch.

○ ○ ◑ ●

I made it in two minutes twenty-six seconds. If I'd tried a little harder, maybe I could have pulled it off in under a minute and a half, but then I could get sick, gulping like that.

"You won, damn it!" I slammed the glass down on the table, burped, and felt strength coursing through my veins. Now, for a few hours of rest …

The circle gradually dispersed. I gave the fish to the cook, and someone came to clean up the bloody mess on the table.

"Aren't you sick, John?" Mimi looked sympathetic.

"A little. A little too much."

"What an idea, drinking fish blood! You Europeans!" She shook her head.

○ ○ ◑ ●

"I need one more thing." I plopped down on a chair after I returned from an adventurous trip to the establishment's toilet. They did have a sink and even some soap.

"I thought that you might want something." Fatty nodded, and with anticipation of more profits, he leaned over the table.

I peered into his eyes, and even though he couldn't have seen anything through the mirrored glasses, he turned a little pale—maybe a player's instinct. I leaned close to him.

"I need a gun, a Glock seventeen, six magazines, and one hundred shells. Then I need a spot on a ship heading for Europe. I will work for free, and no one will ask me anything."

"Two thousand dollars."

"Fifteen hundred."

"Two thousand."

With a gesture that was meant to seem like desperation, I squeezed his hand. He had nice and flexible bones.

"Okay, fifteen hundred."

"In two hours."

"Tomorrow evening at the earliest."

I wrapped the thumb and index finger of my left hand around a thick-walled beer bottle and squeezed. Fatty looked at it with fear; it cracked like nothing. Then he looked at his own hand still concealed in my right palm.

"Is two and a half hours enough?"

"I love you, Fatty."

○ ◌ ◑ ●

Mr. Ji ran off, and when he returned in two hours and four minutes, he carried a package with him. I moved to the wall, and Mimi sat so that no one would see anything. The Glock was brand new so it was a little stiff because of the conservation grease, but a rag and a bit of oil could fix that.

"Shells, magazines ..." I tried the springs. "Excellent. How about the ship?"

"It's called *Courage* and is headed for Calcutta; there is no other option headed for Europe without questions being asked. The captain is either French or Italian, a slave trafficker; that's why he agreed so fast. You, Mr. John, he won't be able to sell without difficulty." Mr. Ji giggled. He was smart enough not to lie to me because he figured I might return one day.

"How long can it take to get to Calcutta?"

"It depends on where it stops and where business is headed; he carries cargo as it comes."

"Fine." I reached into my pocket and counted out sixteen hundred. I had eighty-two dollars left, so I took back a fifty.

"Okay?" I waited for Fatty to count it over.

"At your service." He grinned.

"Where does *Courage* leave from?"

"I will take you there." Mr. Ji looked at his watch. "We still have time."

○ ◑ ◐ ●

We sat around for about an hour and chatted about nothing. I helped them fleece a fat Chinese guy. He came by, claiming that he was an expert at something similar to a Chinese shell game. To my eyes, his hands were moving about as fast as a band of drunken snails.

In the last round, when he tried to clean us out, we cleaned him out. He cursed me and left. I got a third of the take, and Mr. Ji exchanged my Thai bills for dollars. A hundred could always come in handy.

"Would you like to work with us, John?" Fatty asked me for the hundred-and-fifty-sixth time.

"Let's go." I nodded to Mr. Ji. As someone walked from the game room to the bar, I saw the characteristic shape of a derby hat in the clouds of smoke.

Again, that fear, I couldn't control it. I grabbed Mr. Ji by the arm. The time for finishing his drink had passed, and I pointed toward the bathrooms. He shook his head, but I was already dragging him behind me.

"Oh," he simply said, when I ripped out the bars that were there in place of a window.

Behind us, we heard the cracking of doors breaking down. I threw Mr. Ji out the window and jumped after him, the little package with the Glock in my hand. Mr. Ji landed on his toes lightly like a ballerina.

"Could we fight them?"

"Not a chance."

He seemed to get a little pale. (He'd also seen me break the bottle.)

"Then we should run really fast."

What he said, happened.

○ ◑ ◐ ●

309

Mr. Ji had the local urban chaos perfectly mapped. I, on the other hand, was completely lost after the third turn. We raced through gaps between wooden houses (where they were so narrow I had to run sideways), packs of sewer rats scattered underfoot, and something went smack, smack, with each step and I really didn't want to know what it was. Everything reeked of rotting fish, rotting vegetables, and decomposing urine.

We dashed out onto the street, where the standard flow of mopeds, buffalo, two-wheelers, motorized tricycles, and donkeys ran in both directions. Above the street, clothes were drying on lines stretched from house to house and embroidered advertisements in Thai were hanging around. This wasn't a tourist district anymore; this was authentic old Bangkok.

Mr. Ji slowed down to a fast walk; both of us lowered our heads, and we disappeared in the crowd.

○ ◑ ◑ ●

"They will know we're heading for the port." I dodged a salesman with tiny bottles full of a deeply purple stuff.

"In Bangkok, you can't head anywhere else. The port is many miles long." Mr. Ji bowed apologetically to a woman he bumped with his shoulder.

"Okay then."

Again, we were on the little streets that ran somewhat downward this time. The houses along them started to be built on stilts. Reed mats were hung out everywhere to dry. The mud reeked, and old sampan boats were falling apart.

After some time, we reached the water.

Because it was an hour before dark, the river market was still going on.

Going on was an understatement; it was overflowing, fermenting, boiling. I'd read about it yesterday in the shop window of a travel agency, but this never-ending, unstable, tangled mess nevertheless surprised me. You could hardly even see the water surface. Wide straw hats were everywhere and so were mountains of products several times higher than the boats themselves. The boats had rear-mounted oars and coughing two-cycle motors. Adding to this were shrill screams, peeing kids, clouds of blue smoke, smiles, and legs dangling over thresholds that hung way over the water.

"Beautiful."

"Yes," said Mr. Ji. He stood on his tiptoes and was looking around. Then he waved and yelled something in Chinese. It was a miracle that the someone he was calling heard him over the hubbub and hollering, but the requested dinghy started to make its way to shore. It had a side motor with a long axle that was seriously out of balance.

"This is my cousin, Mr. Wong," he introduced me to a hunched Chinaman.

"John." I extended my hand out to Mr. Wong. He had broken, fungus-deformed fingernails and a palm like sandpaper.

"Sit on the bottom, sir, and don't move too much. This boat is really unstable for someone who is not used to it."

I stretched out on the mat, so you couldn't even see me over the packages of dried and disgustingly stinky gross things displayed on some pitchforks.

"That's seaweed; makes very good soup." Mr. Wong patted his belly.

"I believe you." I nodded politely and thought about getting a clothespin for my nose.

"How long is it going to take, Mr. Ji?"

"Wong?"

"Hour and fifteen minutes, maybe longer."

"Fine, would you have a rag, Mr. Wong? A clean rag, a piece of straight wire, and a little bit of motor oil?" I pulled out five bucks.

"Yes, sure." He began digging through a rusty steel box that he used as a footrest while he drove. He didn't slow down, even though he couldn't see where he was going.

"A rag, oil, the wire needs a little straightening out." He threw me a wadded-up piece of yellow canvas with red poles, a half-empty plastic bottle of two-cycle Castrol, and something that looked like a delirious brass snake. With a little bit of effort, I could make a cleaner out of it.

"Thanks." I pulled out the Glock, took it apart, and cleaned it with the motions that I used to practice until my fingers bled—really, I could do it blindfolded.

I threaded the magazines, loaded the eighteenth shell in the barrel, and stuck the gun into my pants and the rest of the stuff into the pockets on my pant legs.

Mr. Wong acted like he didn't see anything.

"Is someone following us, Mr. Ji?"

"No." Mr. Ji looked around periodically.

"One of them wears a derby hat and round glasses."

"No."

"The other one has noticeably tall boots."

"No."

○ ☽ ☾ ●

21

With sundown, we made it to the *Courage*. The ship wasn't anchored in the port, but at a buoy with a Chinese symbol and the Roman numeral 78. Even though we were still on the river, the giant cranes weren't far away. *Courage* was an all-metal ship, about one hundred and fifty feet long, black, with wide peeling sides. It had a flagpole on the bow, and in the back, a tall deckhouse painted white with brown stripes of rust. The name was peeled into illegibility, and the ruined tire bumpers indicated many sharp maneuvers—maybe that was the reason for the lonely buoy.

Mr. Ji yelled something in Chinese, and a bearded guy wearing a dirty red turban with a mini-Uzi in hand peered over the side. Mr. Ji instructed me already that he sort of sold me into slavery so I shouldn't be surprised.

"Come on, climb up, you white crow." A rope ladder rattled, and the mini-Uzi was aimed at the top of my head. I faked some scared babbling, and between the curses was able to sneak in, "Thanks, Mr. Ji."

○ ☉ ☽ ●

I held on to the ladder and acted like I'd rather jump in the water than go up there. So another bearded guy in a turban climbed down and handcuffed me to one of the rungs. Then they pulled me up like a fish and threw a wad of bills to Mr. Ji.

They kicked me along the deck, which was cluttered with merchandise, all the way to a hatch hidden under some boxes. They didn't even check my pockets; they probably needed to get me out of sight as fast as possible.

"And be nice and quiet, one loud word and …!" The bearded guy with the mini-Uzi ran a finger across his neck. I must have looked adequately horrified so he just kicked me down into the darkness.

I expected a suffocating unwashed stench—how slave ships are described in books—but all that reeked here was grease and oil. The hatch closed; boxes slid into place.

I scanned the space, which ran along the right side of the ship. Five … no, six people blindly blinked in my direction. The darkness was pretty thick so they couldn't have seen me. There were two girls around ten years old, an old man, and three young men just about twenty—all Asian.

Cargo.

"Is someone here? Does anyone here speak English?" I tried to be sociable.

"Quiet!" the old man whispered at me.

Okay, if they want quiet, I'll be quiet. I stretched out as far as I could from the dry toilet, which needed serious emptying. The bottom of the ship was bumpy from peeling paint, scaly from the rust, and at the lowest spot had several inches of water covered by a layer of black oil.

I folded my hands behind my head and listened to the outside buzz. The only thing that could make me uneasy was the arrival of a boat with Wries and Van Vren. Otherwise, I was completely relaxed. I was getting out of Thailand without a passport, maybe even to Calcutta. I had over two hundred bucks in my pocket as well as a reliable gun, and I was wearing pretty decent clothes. I was moving up.

○ ◔ ◑ ●

I began dozing off. There weren't any waves on the river, just a slap against the keel once in a while. Then someone turned on the TV. The sound was really low, but it carried clearly—for my ears—along the metal construction. It was the always favorite Thai News Line.

"... lawyer Helena Trang was found brutally murdered in her apartment. Description of the murderer is the same as in the previous two cases, and our reporter was even able to obtain a picture from a camera in the elevator of Miss Trang's building. It appears as though she knew her killer ..."

Luckily, I'd turned sideways to the camera, that I initially overlooked yesterday, so that I was less recognizable. I just needed to get rid of my ponytail. I undid the rubber band and shot it to the other side of the cargo hold.

"... Miss Trang's killer brutally tortured her. The signs are the same as those on the bodies of the farmers and on the body of the clerk from the Pink Dream Hotel. Witnesses say that after his horrible act, he jumped out of a twentieth-story window and drove away in a taxi. Police discovered suspicious shoeprints on the grass in front of the building. We will report any new facts as soon as they become available. Stay tuned."

So I'd become a first-rate journalistic attraction. I also figured out the message from Wries and Van Vren: Whoever helped me during my escape would suffer and die—no exceptions.

So I'll stay by myself. I hate them. I really do, with a deep-seated hatred. I hate that they kill. I hate their decision to forever enslave me on Madam Dao's ship. I hate ... Unfortunately, my fear of them was even clearer and deeper.

This didn't surprise me, and My Other wasn't surprised either—a silver chain burning through your insides ...

Around midnight the generator started humming and the hull began vibrating. A maritime pilot took his place and in half an hour we were out on the ocean.

After the sound of the pilot's boat motor disappeared in the distance, the only thing I heard was the familiar slapping of the waves and whistling of the wind. The clapping noise of the heavy diesel turned into silence within that half hour.

○ ◑ ◐ ●

We had apparently sailed out of some kind of bay, because the *Courage* began rolling a bit more, and both girls got seasick. I stopped breathing and tried to visualize a map. Calcutta was somewhere in India. *How the hell is it ...?* We had to sail around Malaysia, and there was Singapore on the tip. And what kind of a businessman wouldn't stop in Singapore. From Bangkok, it was an estimated—I tried to remember the scale of the map on the fifty-seven and for a while multiplied and divided miles—six, maybe nine hundred miles. That was about a four-day trip, unless we stopped somewhere, so four days of peace.

I felt the fish blood splash around in my stomach a little bit, so I stretched out comfortably and digested.

○ ◯ ◑ ●

Toward the morning, the hatch opened again, and down came another passenger. There was a thick piece of foam under the hatch so even an unconscious person didn't get hurt too much. Those guys up there obviously had practice throwing people down here.

It wasn't a *he* passenger, but a *she* passenger. She was Asian, barely twenty, and a bit too voluptuous for my taste. She was unconscious and smelled strongly of semen. The crew must have amused themselves all night. The old man and one of the youngsters felt their way toward her, wrapped her up in a blanket, and carried her to the others.

Half an hour later, a second one landed. Her face was all bruised and her left eye swollen shut; otherwise, all the same signs of group entertainment were there.

Because it was completely light above the hatch, I took all the stuff out of my pockets and hid it behind one of the ship's ribs.

But they didn't come for me until just before lunch.

○ ◯ ◑ ●

"Whitey!"

The square beam of sunlight was blinding, and as the hot air wafted out of the opening with a myriad of whirling, rusty flakes, a bamboo ladder clunked on the floor. Judging by the shadows, four of them were waiting for me up there.

I obediently climbed out, squinted my eyes with fear, and pretended to be a poor wretch.

The same guy in the red turban as yesterday (an Indian judging by his yellow eyes) lowered down a bucket with some pretty decent-smelling food. It looked like a stew mixed with risotto. I guess they didn't want their merchandise to get too skinny.

"Pockets," said a clean-shaven man in a white turban. He was white, by his accent probably French or Italian, and except for his head-covering he was dressed in European-style clothes. However, on his wrists, he had thick gold bracelets.

I didn't even have to try; the other two knocked me to the ground and turned me upside down. Their turbans were red too.

"I should have known, Ji and old Wong fleeced him already. Open your mouth!" The white turban leaned over me.

I obediently went, "Aaaaaaah!"

"Not a single cavity, or a good dentist. Where are you from?"

"Poland."

"You should say Poland, *Captain, sir!*" One of the turbans kicked me in the ribs.

"Poland, Captain, sir!"

Then for a little while, they let me know who was the boss on this ship, and I, meanwhile, counted. There were these four, someone must be driving, probably a cook, for sure a mechanic, maybe another two on the lookout. So altogether, there must be about ten guys, all of them armed with at least an automatic handgun. The captain had an AutoMag forty-four in a holster on his belt, a weapon suited for hunting whales or, if need be, for a small intercontinental firefight.

"Get up!"

I did as he said, and because they were kicking me just hard enough (they weren't going to devalue me), I didn't even whimper too much.

I couldn't see the shore; it should be somewhere off the port side, but there was this strange fog.

"... Are you listening, Poland?!"

"Yes, Captain, sir!"

"Do you understand me?!"

"Yes, Captain, sir!"

"Good, then back in the hole with you."

"Where are you taking me?! I am a free citizen, and I have my righ—!"

The foam exhaled under my back, the hatch slammed, and camouflage boxes slid into place.

"Are you all right?" The old man came to see me. How sympathetic.

"Thanks. Pretty good."

"We left you some food." He helped me up, and I noticed his hands were all calloused.

"Thank you, really, but this rolling ..."

The old man nodded with understanding. The holes around the hatch let in enough light for him to see my face so I tried to look crushed.

"Do you know where they're taking us?"

"Lin heard them talk about Calcutta, but she doesn't understand the language that the ... *the pirates* speak." He lowered his voice.

"How is she?" I nodded toward the beat-up young woman. There was enough light for me to see her too.

"They won't hurt anyone too much. They're slave runners, so they're not going to damage their own merchandise," he repeated my thoughts.

"Slave runners." I reacted with the appropriate fear, as expected.

"You're lucky; you're white. The Red Cross will buy you within a week ..." The old man waved his hand and went to sit down. Then, along with the unbeaten young woman and the boys, he finished my share of the food. One of the girls got some water from a hanging clay pitcher and brought everyone a drink. She brought some for me too, so I thanked her, spilled it on myself, and gave her back the deformed can. The stale liquid must have been over 100 degrees Fahrenheit.

"Do you think they'll stop in Singapore?" I initiated a conversation.

"Who knows?" The old guy burped loudly. "We might go to Africa first; that's where the biggest slave markets are ... That wouldn't be too good for you. White slaves are in demand."

"Thanks a lot for the reassurance," said My Other. Good thing he didn't speak out loud.

I reached behind the ship's rib and returned the stuff into my pockets.

Nothing happened until the evening, when they came for the girls. Instead of the beat-up one, they took one of the kids.

Almost the entire night, I heard her screaming, then she just cried. I didn't hear the news because of that.

The ship sailed faster than I expected, and I decided not to wait four days (I didn't want to go to Africa at all), so on the next night, it was time.

It didn't really matter whether it was sooner or later; they wouldn't have released me voluntarily anyway.

"Can any of you drive a ship like this?" I asked into the squeaking of the sliding boxes. The girls pressed together, and their teeth chattered. The boys and the old man shook their hanging heads. I saw them tighten their fists, and their eyes fill with tears of helplessness. They were all related. The old man was their grandpa or even great-grandpa.

That little girl didn't wake up until noon. I zipped off my pant legs so they could use them to tend to her wounds.

The strong stench of blood still hung in the air.

The squeaking of the boxes meant that the sailors were coming for another round of evening entertainment. The ladder thumped, and this time, the red turbans took away both of the young ones. From their conversation, I picked up that they had enjoyed last night's screaming a lot more than any profits they might be losing.

"Ehm," I said.

The darkness was made thicker by fog. Neither the moon nor any stars were out, and the ship was under a blackout. They didn't even notice that I had jumped out before they closed the hatch. They didn't even react to my *ehm* and just carried away the kicking and screaming girls.

"Do I have to start singing arias or what?" I shook my head and followed them to the stern between the boxes and bags. Slivers of light escaped from the tall deckhouse, and in the fog, they looked like big yellow razors.

A door opened and then closed, and the moment of brightness looked like an explosion. I waited for a bit until everyone inside focused their attention on the girls. I put on my dark glasses and checked the Glock. Most importantly, I didn't leave anything to chance. A bullet in the head or in the spine would take me out like anyone else, and I couldn't say that now would be a good time for that.

"Nice evening," I greeted them politely, but amidst the screams and laughter, no one heard me again. I found myself in the mess hall and lounge for the crew. It had a long table, benches bolted to the floor, whitewashed walls, lots of nudie pictures, two round windows with drawn shades, a whole lot of beer cans, and a whole lot of marijuana smoke. All three red turbans were there along with the captain and three more men that I hadn't seen yet.

The unused girl was already stretched out on the table, and the used one was getting a pretty indiscriminate instruction in oral sex.

"Sex and violence," I said, and due to the fact that a moment before, I had put two bullets through both knees of the turban with his pants around his ankles, the others were now paying the appropriate amount of attention to me.

The falling turban screamed, cracked his head on the table, and shut up.

Unfortunately, they weren't just armed, but also drunk, so they didn't take me up on my friendly request to surrender.

○ ◗ ◑ ●

I crouched by the door. The captain's AutoMag was chomping out large holes in the steel wall unpleasantly close to my head. I tried not to harm the girls. The bullets from the smaller guns were bouncing and zipping around as they shredded the room's décor.

"Shit."

One began shredding my shirt as well as the muscles on my ribs. *Not like this.*

I changed the magazine and raced through the room like I would during an attack on a pirate ship, even though I knew that the girls would be able to easily identify me by this, when someone asked them.

Except for the captain, I killed them all even before the first man hit the ground. Holes in the turbans smoldered, and the quiet after that incredible racket was electric.

"Hi, ya, Captain, sir."

As an answer, he clicked his empty pistol at me. How rude.

The girls crouched in the corner, hands over their eyes, which was a pretty good reflex for their age.

"How about a little chat, Capt—"

The window blinds exploded with the roar of a machine gun, and the room was again filled with projectiles.

Bullets from the Glock couldn't penetrate the steel wall even though I shot as perpendicularly as possible. The machine gunner stood with his back to the deckhouse and poured bullets in through the window over his shoulder, without aiming.

What dangerous behavior!

"Allow me?" I took the AutoMag away from the captain and pulled an extra clip out of his holster. The slide of the pistol made a noise, as if I was loading a Long Gustav.

Bang! Bang!

Two forty-four millimeter bullets chomped two holes as big as dollar coins in the metal; blood splashed into the room through both of them, and the machine gun fell silent.

"That was number seven. How many more, Captain, sir?"

He stared at the bullet holes rigidly. It looked like the white wall was bleeding.

"Hello!" I waved my hand in front of his face, but he was completely deaf from the firefight. I picked him up and pushed him out the door where I stopped in the light that poured from the doorway.

"Hey! I know you can hear me!" I yelled into the night. "Everyone except the helmsman here; otherwise, I'll start shooting parts off your captain here!" I clicked the pistol's hammer.

"Listen to him!" the captain continued in Chinese or whatever. Looky here, he wasn't all that deaf.

○ ☽ ☾ ●

I didn't even have to shoot off his third finger before two bodies appeared on the deck. They wore canvas pants and Indian shirts down to their knees. The helmsman waved at me from the bridge. I waved to him too.

"What's the matter, Captain, sir?" I shook the fainting fellow, and his golden bracelets clattered. "You two speak English?"

The long shirts shook their heads. That seemed a little obstinate to me, and instantly, I discovered an interesting phenomenon: A hole through a guy's hand dramatically improves his language skills. It's the right kind of speedy course.

"I am glad we understand each other, boys. You." I pointed at the one kneeling with his hand pressed between his knees. "Inside." I pointed the gun to the deckhouse. "You," I said, pointing at the other one. "Bring the cargo."

○ ◗ ◑ ●

I discovered a sad fact in the mess hall. One of the girls didn't survive the machine gun fury. I helped the other one to her feet, but it appeared as though she wasn't registering much.

The white walls were splattered with blood all the way to the ceiling. The nudie pictures got wrinkled. Bodies shot into pieces—or pieces of bodies—were everywhere. The ends of broken bones rubbed against one another in the rhythm of the waves. After the work I had done for Madam Dao, such pictorial spectacles seemed common to me.

Others apparently didn't have as many opportunities as me to witness such scenes.

"Okay, we'll go someplace where it's clean." The captain puked on his shoes, but then took us up to the bridge. After a while, the long shirt brought everyone else. Because the soles of their flip-flops were squishing with blood, I knew I didn't have to explain anything.

"Singapore, please," I said to the helmsman and tied the captain and both long shirts to one of the sturdy pipes running under the ceiling. It's probably not much fun to stand on your tiptoes in a rolling ship, but at least you don't get bored. The captain whimpered that he needed a doctor; the blood from the stumps of his fingers was running down his arm and soaking his shirt.

"You'll be better in the morning; you'll see." I slapped him on the shoulder.

The old Chinaman arrived last, looked over the situation, and immediately disappeared. Then he returned with several knives and had this look that made the captives scream. The boys grabbed the captain and ripped off his pants. I wasn't sure that I wanted to be present during such an unsanitary castration.

"We won't be torturing anyone," I said.

"Who is going to stop us?!" All the former slaves looked at me threateningly. Even the girls looked at me threateningly.

"No one will stop you. I am just asking nicely. And you owe me your freedom," I said in a conciliatory tone.

"They raped my nieces and my grandnieces; they murdered one of them! They ... they ...!" The old man's voice broke.

"Torture without questioning is revenge, and revenge is out of the question." I raised my finger. "A punishment, now that is different. If you like, you can participate ... actively ... tomorrow ... In the meantime, I will ask you to watch them while I search the ship for anyone else hiding." I gave the old man and one of the boys the Uzis from the red turbans. No one complained, and they accepted my way. It's interesting what a soothing tone and an explanation can do. If I had started arguing with them, we would have probably ended up shooting each other, in this tense atmosphere.

As I was leaving, the tied-up pirates cast pleading glances at me.

"Don't leave us here with the ...!"

Crunch. A rifle butt in the teeth is painful.

○ ◑ ◐ ●

My experience of raiding shipwrecks came in handy and allowed me to search the entire *Courage* within half an hour.

In the captain's quarters, I found the thing I needed the most: a passport. The captain was Italian—Francesco di Torro—which didn't sound too Italian to me, but he probably had Spanish ancestors. The important thing was that the passport was old, so it could have been anyone on that picture, and he had a beard too.

I showered the blood off of me, took a clean shirt out of the hamper, and packed some clothes and common tourist paraphernalia into a large leather bag. At the bottom of the sock drawer, I found twenty or so rounds for the AutoMag, a single stage press, and a tin can with gun powder, plus two plastic baggies of cartridges and bullets. Interesting.

"What to do with you?" I weighed the almost a four-and-a-half-pound chunk of deadly stainless steel. On one hand, it was a thousand-dollar rarity and its effectiveness appealed to me, but on the other hand, how would I get this on a plane? I knew how to go about it, but ... Anyway, I had to transport the Glock, so what difference did it make? I decided that this huge hand cannon was worth a little bit of time. I wrapped it in a T-shirt and threw it into the bag along with the cartridges and accessories.

"Now it's your turn." From beneath the bed, I pulled out a standard portable strongbox (they're always under the bed), grabbed the bag in my other hand, and returned to the bridge.

○ ◗ ◑ ●

Screaming was echoing in the hallway.

"What are you doing here?" I opened the door and was looking into the barrel of an Uzi.

The weapon lowered.

"Nothing," said the old man; he thought I didn't see the wires in his hands. Burnt flesh reeked in the room, and the helmsman stared out the window, his back muscles cramped with fear.

"Electrotherapy?" I smiled. "See, my friends, the fact that I freed you doesn't mean I will tolerate you disobeying my orders."

"Who are you to order us around?! A plain old stupid white man!" The Uzi gave the young man an unhealthy sense of courage; again, he was aiming at me. The remaining girl leaped to him and yanked down his weapon. A short, accidentally released round missed me by a fraction of an inch and flew out the window into the night.

The wind whistled through the bullet holes, and the helmsman crouched a little lower. I didn't move, and the little girl explained to everybody in Chinese what had happened down there. She must have been watching through her fingers.

So it was calm again.

○ ◗ ◑ ●

During the night, I had taken the money out of the strongbox and divided it. I myself kept a few British pounds and American dollars and a few French francs. The remainder, the bigger remainder, including the gold, I gave to the Chinese. I think they even started to like me from that point on.

○ ◑ ◐ ●

"How much further?" I tapped the helmsman on the shoulder when the sun started coming up.

"Two hours, if the weather holds, sir." I too was eyeballing that unhealthy purplish-crimson color with which the sun popped up over the horizon. The air was heavy and sounded weirdly muted, and the shore of the Malaysian peninsula was still in a fog that seemed be getting thicker and thicker. I'd be dammed to catch a typhoon on my last day in this wretched ocean!

After the Chinese family finished their breakfast, it was time again. (I knew how they were related more than adequately since they became very chatty after I gave them the money. The dead were forgotten—the family was now rich.)

○ ◑ ◐ ●

"You first." I released the man with the hole in his hand.

"Where are you taking me?! What do you want with me?! Let me go!"

I thought about it. "Let you go? Yes, you could say that."

"Would you like to watch?" I turned to the family who were finishing up their Coca-Colas and planning a trading company that would export tea from China to Singapore, a special mountain variety that grew only in a village where their uncle lived—*delicious!* They even had a name for it already. They figured that the more unpronounceable the name, the more the Europeans and Americans would kill to get it. They kept asking me what I thought about it.

"Watch what?"

"Punishment time."

○ ◑ ◐ ●

"For kidnapping, rape, human trafficking, and murder, I sentence you, you …" I forgot the long shirt's name, but that didn't matter. I was speaking Czech at him. He knelt on the deck, cried, and spoke

Hindi, but through the sights of the Glock, we understood each other perfectly. And they say that guns divide nations. "… you in the name of the Night Club, to a penalty of death ." From the tone of my voice, he discerned that talk was over and closed his eyes.

I motioned with the gun barrel for the Chinese folks to move back. They giggled quietly because they thought I was just scaring the sailor.

Bang.

They should have moved back a little more, because now they had pieces of brain between their toes.

"Now you." I released the second long shirt. Because he had heard the shot, he was thrashing around. The boy with the Uzi, who was watching the helmsman, observed me with a question in his eyes.

Down below, I repeated the Club statement, flipped the gun butt first, and one by one offered it to the Chinese. They all, one by one, lowered their eyes and put their hands behind their backs. Everyone can cut off someone's balls in the heat of the moment, but something more is necessary when it comes to punishment.

Bang.

○ ◐ ◑ ●

I left the captain for last.

On the way, he tried to lie to me that he had a treasure. The number of treasures I had heard about in the catacombs beneath the Night Club, no one could count. The closer someone is to death, the more treasures they have and the more generous they become. That's another one of life's basic rules. The Chinese either believed him or lost their stomach for it, but either way, they tried to dissuade me from my intention.

Bang.

"Clean this up," I said and watched the smoke from the Glock rise nearly straight up. Bang bang bang, a faint echo came back from the fog over the shore.

I thought about whether I felt better or worse, but I realized that I felt the same, like I'd just taken out the trash.

The filth was where it belonged.

○ ◐ ◑ ●

When Singapore was within sight (within my sight), I made a deal with the Chinese that they would give me a five-hour head start. We lowered the motorboat. The boys held the ropes for me. I threw the bag on the seat and jumped in after it.

"Maybe you can keep the ship. I think the helmsman will gladly serve you." I coiled up the ropes.

"We thought about it, yes, sir, we did," the old man answered. After the executions, they were very respectful, yet somewhat standoffish toward me.

The motor started on the third pull. I grabbed the handle and headed for the skyscrapers whose tops glistened above the haze. The Chinese family stood on the port side and waved until I disappeared.

I *am* a nice guy.

My Other made a note to himself.

○ ◯ ◑ ●

After a moment, I discovered one relatively important thing: When you drive into a thick enough fog, you can't see the tops of any—not even Singaporean—skyscrapers.

I gave it some gas and drove blind for about ten minutes, but I had a really bad feeling about it. So I killed the motor and listened for a bit. It's true that, as they say, in a fog, it seems as though sounds come from nowhere and everywhere at once, but not to my ears. I clearly heard the belching and chewing of a large creature that in one instant, both threw up and swallowed a hundred thousand tons of cargo and people. The combined bellowing of numerous foghorns in the port actually did sound like that.

"A little to the left then," I said, and suddenly, I felt a whole lot better. I pulled a pair of pressed black pants, patent leather shoes, a white shirt, and a jacket out of the bag. The captain was a little smaller than me, so everything was snug and short, but you can't have it all.

The tie turned out to be the biggest problem, or rather tying it was. This wasn't an element of clothing required in the Night Club, and on the rare occasions that it was, Babe or Kamile or even Dread tied it for me.

The snake comes out the hole, around the tree, and jumps ... Where the heck does it jump to? I thought with the skinny end of the cloth creature between my fingers. Even without a mirror, I figured that a bowline knot was probably not the right knot for a necktie. Waves were slapping at the sides of the boat; every seventh and eleventh was bigger. The fog was getting thicker and stickier and clung closer and closer to the black water surface. Judging by the way the noise of the port moved to the left, the current was carrying me away, and I'd really hate to end up in the mangroves again, especially because of some tie. Finally, maybe out of pure rage, I tied the thing, even though they probably wouldn't let me into the House of Lords.

I was just straightening out my collar when I heard something. There were a lot of ships sailing by (I heard their faint foghorns in the distance as they sailed far away), but this was significantly quieter and significantly closer.

Instinctively, I crouched down and my right hand became heavy clutching a gun.

Fifteen yards to my right, a ship appeared: four masts, slanted yard, irregular cabins, a raised poop deck, a very quiet hum of diesel engines …

I felt the hair on my head and face stand up. I recognized it. Oh god, how I recognized it. I had spent one year of my life on that ship, and I could have easily spend the rest of it there too. The groaning of the wooden hull and the creaking of the yards sounded the same. The way sounds carry in a fog can be deceptive, so for an instant, I felt as though I was back in that cage.

On the deckhouse in front of the second mast stood two figures—the shorter one was morbidly obese and leaned up against a double-barreled machine gun.

"Shit!" I whispered after the apparition disappeared in the fog. They couldn't have seen me, vampire eyes are better, but if they sailed a few yards closer … I pulled a comb out of the bag and combed my bristled mane.

My hands were shaking so much I almost couldn't do it.

I waited ten more minutes. (If I hadn't heard the surf and hadn't smelled the intense stench of mud, I would have definitely waited longer.) I started the motor and headed full speed toward Singapore.

The entire time, I clutched the AutoMag—safety off—in my right hand and thanked my lucky stars that'd I kept that dreadful weapon.

○ ◐ ◑ ●

Driving a tiny boat (that you can't operate very well) in a fog into one of the biggest ports in the world, which is full of quarter-mile-long cargo ships going every which way, certainly isn't the best idea in the world.

The booming roar of the foghorns ripped apart the dense fog, and I zigzagged like a madman. I discovered (relatively late) that a boat definitely doesn't react to the turning of the wheel like a car. There was one good thing about all this; no police or border guards. Apparently, no one anticipated that somebody would risk doing something similar in weather like this.

Another cargo ship!

As someone from the middle of Europe, I would have never guessed that ships could be this gigantic.

I landed at a dock that was probably for ships a little bigger than mine because it was maybe sixty feet above my head, maybe even ninety. The black side of the adjacent ship was disappearing in the fog and looked more like the foot of some mountain.

The water surface around me splashed under a gray layer of raw crude; ladders with iron rungs were fastened into worn-out concrete—apparently, people sometimes fell off ships while in port.

I hid the AutoMag inside the bag and put on the jacket. Everything, including the tie, was black except for the white shirt. The captain must have been preparing for his funeral. With the bag handle between my teeth, I pushed the boat away and started climbing.

When, after about twenty-four feet, one of the rungs stayed in my hand, I realized that some safety measures aren't as safe as one might assume.

○ ○ ◑ ●

"Welcome to Singapore." I greeted myself at the top and wiped the rust off my hands with an extra pair of socks.

There were huge pipes around me, the pumps hummed, and the stench of diesel grew even stronger. The steam coming from the machines thickened the fog into mush, and not even the lamps on the posts were helping.

Taxi, airport, Europe—a simple, but beautiful plan.

I love simple plans.

22

The workers and security guards were indeed looking at me, but if you're wearing a suit, you look occupied enough, and you walk with enough swagger, then they leave you alone.

It took me a good hour and a half to find my way out of the industrial part of the port. I jumped over a fence so I didn't have to go through a guardhouse combined with customs, and freedom was again a little sweeter.

First, I found the public restrooms (they were amusingly clean), washed my hands, dusted off my suit, and shined up my shoes. The captain's funeral shoes were way too big so I stuffed the toes with paper towels. In front of the mirror, I straightened out the knot on my tie (it was pretty nice, looked innovative) and put some of my money into the breast pocket.

○ ◐ ◑ ●

I walked around for a bit, so whoever was following me didn't have it so easy, and the first taxi I waved down stopped for me.

"To the airport, please." I plopped down on the seat and shut the door. The side windows were so foggy you couldn't see through them.

"Which one?"

"Hmmm … from where does the earliest plane leave for America, the East Coast?"

"One moment." The cabbie, while still driving, ran his fingers over the keyboard of the onboard computer, and two columns of green letters appeared on the windshield in front of his eyes—surprisingly in Roman characters.

"Here." He pointed to the topmost row. "New York, in an hour and fifteen minutes, a Lufthansa Boeing leaving from Changi."

"Excellent."

At the next intersection, he made a U-turn and merged into the fast lane. I knew that we would drive every which way except the shortest one. This was a good thing, because if anyone was following us, there was a much better chance that we would lose them in the thick fog and even thicker traffic. Judging by the presence of Madam Dao's boat, Wries and Van Vren already knew how I got out of Thailand, and Singapore was the first in their sights, so the airports would be monitored. But even if they did see me there, they couldn't just grab me. I was a respectable Italian citizen, Mr. Francesco di Torro, and I just really wanted to go to Europe. I had to go there. I was too much out of place here. I couldn't make out the signs or anything else. There, I would swim in millions.

The engine of the taxi hummed. The air conditioning hissed and in vain tried to defog at least the windshield. The windshield wipers rhythmically squeaked as they swept aside the condensing fog. Nice. I imagined the last time I rode in a car. I was not counting the trip in the crate, the little Thai pickup, or the escape from Bangkok with fish in a bag. It was after that shootout with the Russians, in Prague, in a van. Afterward, we walked through the catacombs to the Club where we found out that Janie …

I chased away the memories; they were still painful.

A more painful thought was, that I couldn't punish the death of the Night Club and that I was even running away from the murderers.

A coward.

A coward.

That word hung in front of my eyes until the taxi stopped in front of the airport's glass building. I really didn't see much of it since the fog grew even thicker.

○ ○ ◐ ●

"That's all right." I handed a ten-dollar bill through the window. "Thank you, sir. Have a safe journey, sir. The airplane leaves from terminal two; that's to the left of here, sir." The fellow was turning out to be very accommodating. Hopefully, he'd remember that I wanted to go to New York and the departure time. That should slow Wries and Van Vren down at least a little.

I walked in the suggested direction as long as the taxi driver could see me, then I turned, and the glass door slid open before me. One more set of doors and I found myself in an endless, air-conditioned hall that smelled of palm trees and perfume dispersed by the ventilation system. Apparently, that smell decreased one's fear of flying. I didn't see a derby hat anywhere, or anything similarly unhealthy, but among those crowds of people ... There really were *thousands*, humming and meandering back and forth between the mirrors, indoor gardens, gangways ... I looked at the square miles of polished glass, clever lighting, chrome, monitors, TVs, multilingual announcements, bars, restaurants, duty-free shops ... and everywhere, it was impossibly clean.

At the self-service information terminal, I found the earliest flight to Europe—to Rome of all places. It's generally expected that a person with an Italian passport does speak a little more Italian than *una pizza signora*. Actually, I was not even sure about that one.

"Here," I whispered. Air France ... Airbus 340 ... Marseilles ... France ... millions of tourists ... the Riviera ... Monaco. I glanced at the clock above the display. *So I have almost forty-five minutes to kill.* I ran my fingers over the keyboard, reserved my ticket, and on purpose, messed up the captain's name to Dit Oro.

Now the gun.

I walked across the hall and tried to stay out of the cameras' fields of view, but there were so many here that I would look suspicious if I tried to avoid them. So I just put on my shades—lots of people had them because the halogen lights bouncing between the glass and the mirrors really burned your eyes.

I took the elevator to the second floor and began studying the stereos behind a spotless window of an electronics shop. They had exactly what I needed. Of course, I was in Singapore. By chance, I looked at one of the TVs, and it took me a few seconds to realize what I was looking at, *whom* I was looking at ... It was me!

It was our favorite Thai News Line, and Singapore apparently carried their most interesting (most disgusting) clips. The clever fellows in Thailand combined my sketch with a computer-enhanced and rotated image from the video camera in the elevator. I guess I wasn't as careful as I thought I was.

Like I said before ... disgusting.

The beard had to come off, right now.

The worst thing was that according to the map that illustrated my path through Thailand (pretty accurately) with a red line, the police over there thought that I had left the country. The map suddenly jumped to a larger scale, and the places where I could appear blinked with red question marks. Near Singapore, there was a really fat one. Instantly, I realized that I didn't have to worry about the beard; they had many more sketches of me. The computer created one of me without a beard, with short hair, with no hair, with colored hair, bald, with a ponytail, from profile ...

I hate technology.

It was gonna be a long forty-five minutes in the glare of the lights.

The main thing was that the man with the derby hat wasn't participating.

○ ◑ ◐ ●

"Yes, sir?" the salesgirl smiled at me, her teeth so white they would glow in the dark. The store smelled of electronics, and all the employees had navy-blue uniforms with name tags and pressed collars.

"In the window there, I saw this stereo, a Panasonic, a portable tower, I think it's called." I pretended ignorance (and I didn't even have to try too hard).

"Did you have the forty series or twenty series in mind, sir?" The smile grew even broader.

"I had the larger style in mind." I stretched out my arms and smiled too.

"An excellent choice, sir. One moment." She went to the back and returned with a box that could hold a rocket launcher and a decent supply of ammo. When she opened the top, she had to get a stool so we could see each other.

"A 3-D equalizer, four band speakers, *super subwoofer!*"

"Excellent!"

"It is possible to run it on batteries; environmentally friendly disposal of the stereo is guaranteed ..."

"Excellent!"

"Of course, even after twenty years—"

"Excellent!"

In the same manner, we made our way through the sound testing and karaoke sample all the way to the payment. I noticed that one of the customers was eyeballing me funny, but maybe he was just a bit gay. I smiled at him warmly and bowed. He returned the gesture.

The printer of the cash register buzzed. "Here is you receipt, sir."

I looked at the final figure. "Excellent!"

"Excellent, sir!"

"Do you take British pounds too?"

"Of course, sir." She calculated the exchange rate on the cash register, and I handed her a portion of my pounds. Money with strong purchasing power is great; everything seems inexpensive.

I moved over to the restrooms with my giant box. On the way, I took a quick look at the X-ray machines.

They say that it's impossible to get a weapon onboard a plane, but all you have to know is which way (which ways) the luggage is X-rayed, and with a little practice, it's not a problem—with a little practice and the biggest toy box possible.

I waited a moment (the restrooms here were snow white and stainless steel), and when no one was coming, I climbed into the handicapped stall. They were bigger, and this one had the sides all the way to the floor so if a handicapped person dropped something on the floor, it wouldn't roll out.

How thoughtful.

I had to take the AutoMag apart. The Glock fit into the right spot entirely, even with the magazine. I carefully sealed the box shut with the brand-name tape, which I conveniently nabbed from the store. No one would be able to tell that I ever opened it.

"Hello, sir, do you need help?" Someone knocked on the door. I couldn't avoid several embarrassing noises.

"Thank you, I am fine."

"I can help you with anything. I am a nurse at the hospital." By his voice, he was either a nosey American or an especially nasty thief.

"Thank you." I made this polite phrase sound as annoyed as possible. I waited for the quick footsteps to disappear and then moved out awkwardly.

"I didn't want to leave it alone, and I could fit in there with it," I said to the surprised look in the mirror. The tall Asian man nodded with understanding, shut off the faucet, and began wiping his hands with paper towels. I washed my hands too and copied his futile efforts. Whoever came up with paper towels was a sadist. We tried to get the wadded-up balls of pink paper off our still-wet hands and multicultural sparks of understanding jumped between us.

The man left, and I glanced at the clock above the mirror. It was high time to pick up my ticket.

○)) ●

Fifteen minutes until takeoff.

I stood in line. I was hoping it was the right one. The hum of thousands of conversations bouncing around the hall made it sound like an angry beehive—a big, angry beehive. As far as I could see, there was still thick gray fog outside. I hoped Air France had decent navigation instruments. Judging from the fact that the windows were periodically resonating from the roar of plane engines (and not explosions), I knew planes were still taking off.

Maybe they're falling into the ocean.

○)) ●

"… and they promised me a four-film movie deal until the end of January!" said the girl behind me in a raised voice, probably so that her friend felt especially inferior. I turned and pretended to look at the monitor on the column. The girl who was speaking was really cute. She was another perfect mixed-race specimen, shorter than Hanako, but really something.

"And you won't be embarrassed?" whispered the other girl, but not quietly enough for *these* curious vampire ears.

"For that kind of money? Some rich guy is for sure going to notice me. Why wouldn't he?!" She giggled quietly and wiggled her bosom. It was more significant than Hanako's, but suspiciously so, given how thin she was.

"And is it going to be like *pretend*, or like for *real*?"

"Like for real?! For sure for real." She gave a bashful look and a gesture that was anything but.

This time, both of the girls giggled, and the one who wasn't going to France to make porno movies looked at her friend with awe. Though she might only be good enough for Snow White and the Seven Dwarves—animated.

○ ○ ◑ ●

"Yes, sir?"

I got up to the counter in deep thought. I loved those smiling clerks who looked like they were ready to put their lives on the line for you.

"Yes, I have a reserved plane ticket under the name di Torro, miss. To Marseille." On purpose, I spoke like I thought an Italian might speak English and slid my passport across the counter.

"Mr. di—" She looked at the way the name was spelled, and her fingers quickened on the keyboard. "Unfortunately, we don't ..."

"Maybe I typed it in wrong, these computers, you know ..." I grinned and waved my hands around like an Italian might.

"Mr. Dit Oro? Is that possible?"

"When I get my hands on these awful keys, anything is possible."

Even though the girl continued to smile, I saw something strange in her face, this slight stiffness that didn't belong there. Anyway, the airport noise seemed to have dimmed a bit. Sometimes, it happens on its own, but this was too much. The young woman bowed (they do this very elegantly), but she glanced somewhere over my right shoulder.

"Ufff." I set the box with the apparatus on the counter. "This is heavy."

"Please, go ahead." The young woman elegantly bowed again. The process had already taken three times as long as for the people in front of me. It looked like some kind of printer problem. Meanwhile, I was fussing (very urgently) with the tape that appeared to be accidentally taped to the side of the box. It was clear now that we were moving on to plan B of my departure—the worst possible option. At least I would save on the ticket.

○ ◗ ◗ ●

Trying to get your guns out of a stereo through a hole in a box isn't easy—better said, I was barely able to grab the barrel of the AutoMag when someone tapped on my shoulder.

"Excuse me, sir."

"Yes?" I turned around.

"Are you Mr. di Torro, sir?" Another smiling Asian person was standing there in a black suit. Next to him stood another one, and a little farther back, four uniformed policemen happened to have something really important to do right there. There were even more by the exits—suddenly they were like flies.

Behind my back, I was still digging in the depths of the box. I had prepared it well except the hole wasn't exactly where it should have been. Then I finally felt the Glock's trigger.

"Di Torro, yes, that's my name," I said really loudly on purpose, but as I was pulling the gun out, the polystyrene squeaked way louder than I spoke.

"Mr. di Torro, can you please put your hands where I can see them?" He wasn't smiling anymore.

"May I ask why?"

"Singapore police, Detective Zhong." He showed me his badge in a black flip case.

"My hands ... huh ... but of course, Detective." I put them in front of me so that the Glock was aimed at his breastbone. "Anything else?"

He didn't hesitate, grabbed my wrist with both hands, and with a well-practiced move tried to twist the gun away.

He was probably a little surprised that instead, he performed a short, clumsy flight with a layover in the garbage can.

"That had to hurt," I said to the detective's colleague who was reaching for his revolver, and with a gentle tap on the chin, I knocked him out cold.

As he fell, he took with him a pair of newlyweds who this whole time had been discussing how much they'd enjoy the Riviera.

Their skulls thumped on the marble. The people around me realized I had a gun and started screaming. The future Miss Movie Star was especially good at it.

I knew what I had to do, but I didn't really want to do it.

"You gotta do what you gotta do," said My Other.

Suddenly, I glimpsed the derby hat and his buddy; they moved quickly against the flow of the crowd. Instantly, I realized that the difference between good and bad was much more flexible than I expected. I grabbed the actress around the neck with my arm, pressed her to my chest, and stuck the Glock up her nose. My choice wasn't random: The police hate to shoot pretty women.

I gotta do what I gotta do.

"What if we play hostage, miss?" I whispered and then screamed at the top of my lungs, "I will blast her head off, assholes! Get away from me! Now!!!"

"Easy, Mr. di Torro, take it easy. We don't want anyone getting hurt, do we?" said Detective Zhong, an orange ice cream wrapper stuck to his shirt, his tie crooked.

With his hands outstretched in a gesture of trust, he walked toward me. He probably watched too much TV.

High time I showed them I meant business.

"Allah akbar!" I screamed and began shooting, what looked like random shots into the air. Three of the cameras watching me exploded, and an honest-to-goodness panic broke out in the hall. The derby hat and his buddy stood in place for a bit, and then the crowd dragged them away. In the meantime, I flipped over the counter with the actress.

"Get outta here!" I hissed at the ticket lady, but she was in a fetal position, hands over her ears. "Fine, stay here, you dummy. You, don't you move a muscle!" I growled into the actress's ear, so she didn't get any brave ideas. I stuck the Glock behind my belt and frantically yanked the other parts of the AutoMag out of the box.

"It's no use, Mr. di Torro! Release your hostages and surrender! We won't hurt you, and you will receive a fair trial!" Over half the hall around us was empty—except for about thirty policemen and airport security. I saw how the others tried to evacuate the shop-lined corridors and tried to prevent people from crushing each other in a panic. Some people (especially the Japanese) didn't panic and instead feverishly photographed me—their flashes looked like a disco ball.

Within an instant, on the third floor, a little to the left, I saw the first salamander in a bulletproof vest. He had a sniper rifle. Apparently, the black masks slow the criminals' reaction time, but it makes the salamanders so obviously visible.

He wouldn't try anything as long as there were people around.

"Fuck off!!!" I answered the next request. "If you come any closer, I will blow her head off." I dramatically jostled the actress around and quietly added, "I don't mean it, but my life is more valuable to me than yours. Scream!"

"Aaaaaaaah!!!"

I wondered why the glass didn't break.

"You're too good to be in porn."

Finally, I got all the necessary things out of the box, held down my hostage with my knee, and put the AutoMag together.

There had to be a camera that I didn't notice, because the police took advantage of my lack of attention and attacked.

Two detectives crawled to the other side of the counter and jumped me like Bruce Lee. All the while, they yelled as if they had glowing-hot pokers up their butts.

They were amusingly slow.

I shoved a magazine into the AutoMag, pulled the slide, put on the safety, and stuck the weapon behind my belt. Then I smacked one of the screamers in the chin with the toe of my shoe, and the other one in the chest with the knee of the same leg. I tried to be as gentle as possible, but I heard a crunch here and there anyway.

All the cops were aiming my way, and those two were crawling away, their hands slipping on the marble. It was strange that they didn't cover themselves very much, probably because they didn't expect I would shoot at them.

The airport security even had to block off the hall with a red rope to keep the huge mass of gawkers at bay. The clicking of cameras and whirling of videos blurred together into one continuos buzzing sound.

I pulled the magazines and shells out of the box and put some of them in my pockets and some in the bag.

"Here, you carry this." I handed the bag to the actress. "What is your name?"

"Na … Nata … Natasha Blast."

"Nice name. I'm John … excuse my boldness, miss, but I will call you by your first name." I shook her hand. Politeness is so deeply engrained in Asian people that she smiled and bowed. Then, however, fear crept back into her eyes.

"No worries," I whispered. "Consider this like a part in a movie. Practice, get experience, and most importantly, don't let go of that bag."

I was loading the magazine for the Glock and watched Wries and Van Vren. They were discussing something with the cops and in their hands had some kind of badges. I noticed a golden glare. The uniforms saluted to them and let them go behind the red rope to see Detective Zhong.

"Mr. di Torro, give—!"

I shot the megaphone out of the cop's hands because I couldn't hear what those guys were talking about. In a moment of silence before people started screaming (again), I heard Wries's quiet voice. "… FBI …"

"Oh, shit," said My Other.

It was high time to move. If Wries and Van Vren had convinced the local cops that they really were FBI … or if they were FBI for *real* …

"Listen!" I screamed. "I want a clear path out and a plane! Now! *Allah Akbar!*"

"Calm down, Mr. di Torro, you will get what you want, but you have to release your hostage. She's a woman. You wouldn't hurt a woman, would you?"

"You bet I would hurt her, you pig!" I screamed and added some psychological imbalance to my voice. Up on the third floor, there were already six salamanders, and they all had me in their sights.

"Time to change positions," I whispered to Natasha. I picked her up so she shielded my chest and began to shimmy sideways to the turnstile and the glass doors behind it. Beyond the doors were escalators and corridors that led scores of passengers to their planes.

The problem was that the salamanders could get me while I was moving—they were barely fifty yards from me and had high-quality German rifles.

I switched guns. I couldn't do this trick with a Glock.

"Hey! Zhong! I'm holding the hammer, and I'm squeezing the trigger! If someone shoots me, then my muscles will relax and the miss won't be eating any more rice!" I pushed the AutoMag under Natasha's chin. There was no other way of getting rid of the sharpshooters without killing them.

"Mr. di Torro! Release the hostage and surrender!"

These cops were really a boring bunch.

I backed up through the turnstile. The detectives who were hiding there were smart enough to pull back. I backed up all the way to the glass doors.

They were blocked.

"Open up!"

"We can't; you damaged the security system when you shot out the cameras! Release the hostage and ...!"

They were really pissing me off with that. Apparently, that must be a new police tactic: repeating the same thing over and over until the criminal is bored to death. A damaged security system? That was bullshit. I was beginning to regret that I wasn't a bad guy. It would make my exit a lot easier, blowing away the hostage.

"That's the fate of us good guys." I sighed. Everything is more difficult.

The glass looked unbreakable and bulletproof.

The good news was that the coppers didn't let Wries and Van Vren any further. They were respectful, but they kept them away from me. Not even these guys would dare to massacre an entire airport— moreover, the first TV crews had just arrived. I lifted Natasha even higher and hid behind her hair.

The bulletproof glass was bulletproof, but not that much. They didn't count on an AutoMag.

I was beginning to really like this weapon.

○ ◯ ◑ ●

When Natasha's screaming and the canon fire stopped, I kicked out the remaining pieces of glass. As I turned, one of the salamanders drilled me.

I knew all about it. It was a standard procedure when they wanted to save lives. You aimed at someone's knee or the top of their foot. The pain was so crippling that even the toughest terrorist had trouble controlling his own sphincter—and was usually unsuccessful—and couldn't worry about controlling the world.

I was grateful to Captain di Torro for having such big feet. The bullet did get me, but in the tip with the paper towels.

As a reflex, I raised my hand and another roar traveled through the hall. To other people, the shots from the pistol and rifle must have sounded the same.

"Oh, crap!" I looked at my hand; the AutoMag was still in there.

Even though I aimed at his weapon, the salamander did not fare well. The huge bullet ripped off the scope, and by chance, as it sometimes happens, jammed it into his right eye socket—deep.

The eye, a window to your soul.

If the lens of the scope had had a red light in it, he would have looked like Arnold in *The Terminator.*

"Hasta la vista, *baby,*" Natasha whispered. She had seen it too.

"He shouldn't have started it, asshole," I said, and blood began dripping from the third story.

○ ○ ◑ ●

In a moment, we were racing through the empty corridors filled with electronic direction boards, but ... the cops not only cleared out the corridors, but those cowards also turned off the boards, so I couldn't get my bearings. So I got lost as usual. Natasha, however, was (luckily) cooperating; sometimes it even looked like she was overacting her hostage role a bit.

"This way!" she pointed when I had definitely lost my way. Of course, any kind of press is a good thing, and the longer she stayed with me, the more popular she'd be. I could see it already as they filmed something like *Fire in the Clouds.*

I wondered who was going to play me.

○ ◐ ◑ ●

The only plane ready for takeoff was ours headed for France. Unfortunately, they had already pulled back the accordion canopy and moved the jet bridge away a little. We heard the resonating footsteps of our pursuers in the hallways behind us. I suspected that since I'd killed their colleague, they probably wouldn't coddle me too much.

"We'll go a little faster now, so hold the bag tight." I picked up Natasha and backed up little. The jet bridge was still moving, and the gap to the plane was increasing.

I took a running start, and Natasha let out her beautiful scream again.

○ ◐ ◑ ●

I landed just barely inside the door. My center of gravity was completely different than normal. I even had to help myself with that damned levitation.

"Ufffff!" There was a thud on the floor. The shoe with the bullet hole in it, finally fell apart.

"Ouch!" complained Natasha; her back cracked. The flight attendant who was preparing to close the door just stood there and stared at me with a terrified look. Then she stared with an even more terrified look at the foggy distance I'd just covered. I gracefully motioned that she could close the door now and wondered just how good I would look in the light of the TV cameras.

Surprisingly, no one welcomed us on board.

"You may close the door, miss." I grinned at the flight attendant when she didn't get my graceful gesture. Then I ran over to visit the pilots.

"Can-you-set-me-down?" Natasha chattered to the rhythm of my leaps, and the passengers turned to look at us with curiosity.

Sweet ignorance.

"Walk in front of me." I slowed a little and let her down, and her high heels joined my one-shoed footsteps. I don't get how someone could run in something like that, but she managed just fine.

The door to the cockpit was already locked, but I had no problem kicking it down. By then, the passengers were already standing up and demanding an explanation. Luckily, the plane wasn't full. Many people didn't get a chance to board, and I don't believe they regretted it.

"Stay in your seats, all of you!" I turned around brandishing my weapon and wondered what airplane hijackers declared in similar situations.

"Allah akbar!"

Clearly, I shouldn't have repeated this particular thing considering the way everyone freaked out. What can I say? I was new at this airplane-hijacking thing.

I waved my hand and turned around into the cockpit where two pairs of determined eyes were looking at me.

"What do you want?" said the captain.

"How about we leave? We're late."

"Where should we fly?"

"One moment ..." I turned toward the copilot who was just preparing to jump me. "Heroism usually hurts a lot, my friend, but have it your way." I shrugged my shoulders and let him decide. He sat back down, and I had time to think about where I wanted to go.

"How about Marseille?" I said.

"What? That's where we're headed anyway! You don't have to hijack us!" The captain raised his eyebrows.

"Now you know how tricky I can be."

○ ◗ ◑ ●

In twenty minutes, we were in the air. It wasn't nearly as easy as that sounds, but I can handle anything.

When those smartasses in the tower tried their tricks by saying the tires were flat, that they couldn't fuel the plane, and god knows what else, I told them that for every ten minutes of delay I would execute one hostage.

I hate it when public transportation is late.

Within the first ten minutes, I destroyed the onboard phones and collected everyone's cell. Three people had informed the TV press; only one called the police. I made it clear that whoever said another word would die. After that, it was quiet.

"May I, little girl?" I smiled at the blonde daughter belonging to one of the European couples. The five-year-old child smiled at me and handed me her doll. It looked like a baby and a very realistic one at that. The girl's mother's teeth chattered, as she tried to shield the child with her body. I made a *brmmm* sound at the girl by running my fingers across my lips, and the little angel began cooing happily.

Kids can tell who the good guys are.

In the galley, I filled the doll's head with ketchup.

"Anyone who wants ketchup on their hot dog is out of luck," I told the pale flight attendant.

Then I used the intercom to tell the captain to call the police because ten minutes had passed, and I didn't notice that we were moving. This was probably because the pilot car just happened to be parked—unintentionally—in front of the plane. So they should look at the windows next to the door.

Within two seconds, virtually all floodlights were pointed there.

I was in a little hallway separated from the main cabin by some curtains. Fog or no fog, the light penetrating all three windows resembled glittering, horizontal columns. I wrapped up the plastic baby in a large napkin, plunged it into the light, and shook it to make it look alive.

The flash of the gunshot was visible even in the floodlights, and the ketchup splattered all over the windows.

It was very affective—and effective.

Instantly, the tires were inflated, the plane fueled, and in a minute, we were taxing toward the runway.

I handed the slaughtered baby doll to the pale attendant. "That's in case someone really insists on having ketchup with their hot dog."

○ ◐ ◑ ●

I had to be careful, because armed air marshals sometimes traveled on these large planes. They had weapons loaded with special buckshot, as to not make holes in the plane's body. I wouldn't want them to blind me with those. I couldn't shoot (during the execution of the doll, I made damn sure that bullet wound up in a seat cushion), but I waved my AutoMag around a lot on purpose, so they would think twice about attacking. All the passengers—who knew what a blast out of a cannon like this could do—were very pale.

"May we serve refreshments?" The head attendant came up to me. By then, we'd already flown out of the fog, reached cruising altitude and were heading to France. The sun was shining brightly, and the white clouds were far beneath us.

I stood next to the open cockpit door, and Natasha sat on the first bench across. If someone was to shoot at me, they would probably get her too. I didn't make her do it. She sat there on her own with my bag next to her.

"Go ahead, serve them." I waved the AutoMag patronizingly. When she brought me a cup of coffee, I politely refused and asked her to just put on a movie. "These long flights are so boring, aren't they?" I gave her a chummy look.

The window shades were drawn, the lights turned on and then slowly dimmed like those in a movie theater. Then Forest Gump began prancing around on the little built-in screens. The people put on their headphones and relaxed a little. From behind my dark glasses, I looked for the air marshals. There would be two of them, maybe even three, but most likely just two.

After about an hour, I was pretty certain. There really were two of them, and they were sitting in the aisle seats four rows apart. I took off my shoes—ehm, shoe.

"Can you take out my boots, Natasha?"

"Gladly." She smiled. Since the trick with the doll, she'd lost all fear of me. She must have forgotten the dead salamander. When I was tying my shoelaces, she sat next to me. It was a little too close for comfort considering how long it had been since I had spoken intimately to a girl.

"Back up," I said sternly. God only knows what one can expect from an up-and-coming porn star, in a dimmed plane, where everyone is staring at *Forest Gump*. It was important for me to be most vigilant.

"Pffffm!" She was offended, but did as I said.

○ ◔ ◑ ●

The flight took just about twelve hours and was very calm. Airbus could do it without a layover. After the movie, most of the passengers wrapped themselves in their blankets and fell asleep, hijacking or no hijacking. Because we were flying against time, we reached France just six hours after the departure from Singapore.

It was clear to me that I couldn't go to the airport. Airplane hijackers may be popular and interesting to the media, but not to anyone else. During the flight, I listened to the radio, and my mock execution of a baby became the number one story all over the world. Not even Osama could beat that. I was lucky that there really was a baby on board. They knew about it at the airport from the passenger manifest. Everyone on the plane knew about it because for the past hour, it had been crying nonstop. It was a little bit of a problem because it was starting to get on people's nerves and the parents were beginning to lose it.

Some passengers were probably saying to themselves that I shouldn't have taken the doll, but they are probably the ones that didn't like their hot dogs without ketchup.

So it was up to me again—like always.

○ ◑ ◑ ●

As I walked over to the screamer, I passed the blonde girl quickly. How do you explain to a child that you executed her dolly?

"Let me have him." I pointed at the screaming infant. His mother was so far gone that she was shaking him like she was trying to kill him rather than put him to sleep. She handed me the kid, maybe even gladly—the responsibility shifting away from her ... finally! The other passengers froze, but I knew how to go about this. Several times, I was in the hospital where Babe worked and I saw how she handled similar situations. The kid wasn't hungry and didn't need a diaper change, so I was going to try ... Surprisingly, I didn't have to try anything, no tricks. I just picked him up, and the screaming immediately stopped and was replaced by satisfied cooing, which was a thousand times quieter. He was looking at me with his big blue eyes, and his little thumb disappeared between his drooling lips.

"What a disgusting little fatty you are," I whispered to him in Czech, and the baby smiled. The passengers began clapping, at first timidly, but then wholeheartedly.

If all else failed, I could make a living hijacking airplanes—or as a babysitter.

"Sir!" the captain called to me.

"Coming." I walked over to the cockpit with the purring munchkin in my arms.

"We should begin our approach for a landing soon. Yes?"

"Yes, but first circle over the ocean."

"Why?"

"Because *I am* the hijacker around here." I pointed the baby at him.

○ ☽ ◗ ●

As I returned to give back the child (it was starting to fall asleep), the air marshals attacked. Finally, I thought. On one hand, I had my back to them so much it was ridiculous, but on the other hand, it was very reckless.

I got a round in the kidneys, and the air was knocked out of my lungs—the buckshot went deep under the skin. I couldn't turn around too fast because I didn't want to break the kid's neck.

The next round went into the middle of my back. That was when I dropped to my knees. These bastards were brutal.

"Catch!" I threw the pip-squeak to Natasha. With her, I was sure he would land on something soft.

By now, even the other undercover marshal had gotten into the mix—from the front. The shot made a hole in my jacket and ripped off half my tie. By then, I had my Glock already in hand. I felt like I was in slow motion, as I tried to move like a human.

I shot him in the arm, in which he held his weapon.

It's difficult to hit someone and take them out without killing them while at the same time make a hole in the plane exactly where you need it. I had to equalize the pressures so the door could be opened.

The bullet shattered his wrist, slipped along the bone, zoomed between the seats, and broke the window.

Fortunately, we had already descended under eleven thousand feet, but the glass still imploded and the cabin filled with a howling wind and fog.

There was a loud pop in my ears, and yellow oxygen masks dropped down from the overhead compartments.

Even though everyone began to choke and blood gushed out of some noses, the other cop didn't have a problem with it; he jumped me from the back.

I didn't want to make my superhuman abilities apparent, so I just broke his nose with the butt of my gun. Natasha couldn't catch her breath, but that didn't stop her from kicking the guy with the shattered hand. She must have been on my side; women always are when you act nice to a baby.

"Don't kick him. You should bandage that up instead." I stood up, but the buckshot was really weighing me down, a lot more than I expected—especially in my back.

I had to play this out to the end.

So I began to act like I was seriously wounded (exactly according to plan) and forced the pilots to make one more circle over the ocean. Then I performed a heart-wrenching scene where a mortally wounded hijacker chooses death over falling into the clutches of the police.

As the flight attendant opened the door for me at ten thousand feet, she cried. Even Natasha cried, and the baby cried too. Papers and plastic cups were whirling around.

"Farewell! I am dying for my truth! Only that way can I live forever!" I screamed into the howling wind, and my hair was whipping me in the face.

The girl, whose dolly I had killed, waved to me.

Then I jumped out.

○ ◑ ◐ ●

23

I missed the wing by a few feet and thought that maybe I should have said something not so stupid.

I was hoping that no one would think it strange that I jumped out not only with my truth but also with my bag.

It was pretty hard holding on to it because even though the plane had slowed down, it was still zooming along at almost four hundred miles per hour.

The seams of my clothes were coming apart. My coattails frayed. My puffed-up pants ripped and their remnants fluttered around my head. In the end, it wasn't all that bad because the bag acted as a pretty decent aerodynamic brake.

The sun shone brightly, and the beautiful azure ocean beneath me was ruffled up with little waves. Ships looked like toys, and Marseille was absolutely gorgeous from up there.

Was I ever afraid of heights?

When the air resistance slowed me down to like a hundred, I switched from a sightseeing freefall to a controlled descent. I was hoping that with my luck, I didn't land on some cliff.

Because the plane and I were under the scrutiny of just about every TV camera in France, I couldn't put on the brakes too soon.

Ten feet above the surface, however, wasn't enough.

Hitting the water at one hundred miles per hour is not a joke, even for me—especially after my buckshot massage.

There was an incredible blow to my ankles and knees, a percussion rattling of my vertebrae, a yank that almost took off my right arm, and everywhere around me, billions of silver bubbles and a rapidly increasing pressure.

Instinctively, I inhaled the ocean.

All that was left in my hand was a handle; the bag whirled high above me. That was the yank. I stopped my descent, swam to get it (with difficulty), grabbed it with my teeth, and began to descend again.

The ocean may have looked azure from above, but down there along the shipping lines of Marseille, it was dirty. So at thirty meters, I figured I should be invisible from the surface.

○ ◔ ◑ ●

At night, I moved over to clearer waters a little to the south and away from the shore. There I settled thirty-five meters below my problems in a small underwater cave. Well, it was more of a gap than a cave and there wasn't too much settling going on either; the current kept washing me out or little greenish-brown fish with big eyes wanted to come in. They weren't edible and really tickled me.

I needed to heal my wounds, but more importantly, I needed the hoopla to die down.

I decided to wait exactly five days.

○ ◔ ◑ ●

When it was light out, I watched (from below) the windsurfers, boats, and jet skis (they're damn noisy), but mainly the divers looking for my corpse. They gradually thinned out, and all that was left were tourists spear-fishing or looking for clams—which usually happened in the shallows closer to shore anyway.

At night, I came up to the surface for air.

Except for the time when I was changing my clothes (really an underwater *adventure*) and when I observed my body expelling the buckshot and except for one very brave woman diver, it was a damn boring five days.

351

○ ◑ ◐ ●

Changing clothes underwater is pretty much impossible, but I couldn't climb out in a shot-up and shredded suit. The good old T-shirt and shorts from the bag were a sure backup. I thrashed around in the cave so much while changing that even the most curious fish were scared off.

It was fun with that diver too.

Out of sheer boredom, I was trying to fix the handles on the bag when she swam into the cave. It was pitch dark in there for her, so she didn't see me. I wondered what she would say if she met a guy, thirty-five meters underwater without scuba gear, just fixing his bag. Instead, I assumed the defensive position à la bulgy-eyed corpse.

I felt sorry for her when she aimed her light right at my face. Whoever says that you can't scream underwater doesn't know what he's talking about.

She fainted, and her breather fell out of her mouth, so I put it back in and pressed her chest until the stream of bubbles became regular again. Then I swam out with her and hooked her to a nice piece of rock thinking she must have a diving buddy nearby who could help her out.

For me, this encounter meant one positive and one negative thing. It meant that someone could confirm they saw me dead, but it also meant I had to move, damn it.

○ ◑ ◐ ●

At around three in the morning on the fifth night, I landed on the beach, holding the bag handle with my teeth. I felt like some kind of an invasion vessel. *This is how the Allied forces must have felt when they opened up the second front,* I thought.

It was warm, there was a comfortable breeze, and the sand glistened in the moonlight. Every ten yards, there were tourists bundled up in sleeping bags or a pair—maybe even a couple of pairs—of people working on new, full-fledged members of the European Union. I almost stepped on two of them because they were lying behind some sand castle and I was watching the road for suspicious vehicles.

The girl screamed, and the guy cursed at me in French.

"Sorry, sorry." I turned away and with a quick step headed for Marseille.

My shoes were squishing, and my skin was a little loose after five days in the water. After about two miles, my T-shirt dried, but the salt, on the other hand, uncomfortably stretched my skin.

Because even my money was wet, I sat on the breakwater and dried my francs and shorts on the rocks that were still a little warm. With newspapers from the trash, I even dried my shoes—kind of.

At sunrise, I rang a little bell at the reception of a tiny hotel deep within the maze of Marseille streets.

The room wasn't exactly a presidential suite, but sometimes, all you need is a shower with fresh water and a hunk of soap.

○ ◑ ◐ ●

I didn't go outside until the late afternoon. I looked a little red in the face, but otherwise pretty good because I'd had my clothes laundered and even ironed.

As a first order of business, I visited the barbershop.

The problem was how to explain to the guy with a mustache that I wanted a crew cut. He refused to speak English and all I knew in French was *happy cow*. I honestly couldn't imagine how I would look with a *happy cow* haircut. Finally, I made it clear to him not only what a crew cut was, but that I also wanted a shave. So after several weeks, I saw my beautiful self again. My nose, cheeks, and the part around my eyes were tan, but the color under my beard had faded already. The last time I had tanned that part was on Madam Dao's ship.

So, I finally saw what I looked like—what a damn coward looked like.

I was glad to get out of the hall of mirrors and snipping scissors.

○ ◑ ◐ ●

Now I needed oil for my guns, some kind of cleaner and rags, and gunpowder so I could make rounds for the AutoMag. Salt water is not beneficial for the reliability of weapons or ammunition.

In the end, all that stuff was easier to get in Marseilles than a new haircut.

○ ◌ ◑ ●

"Here we are, sir." The clerk at the gun shop put what I asked for in front of me. "But for the gunpowder, I need your passport and gun permit."

"Fine, I will come back for that later," I said as if nothing had happened, but I cursed under my breath. Even if I was crazy enough to try and use the document with di Torro's name, it was illegible to the point of uselessness after five days in the ocean.

If you can't find something in a foreign land, go to the thrift shop, Dread used to tell me. In *Vampires*, I used a store with guns masquerading as a thrift shop; there, a rough but honest shopkeeper named Rat Rolls took care of arming the hero.

First, I had to go to the bookstore to find in the dictionary how to say *thrift shop* in French. As soon as I put the dictionary down, I forgot it, so I had to endure the procedure of asking for a piece of paper and a pencil. The French really don't like speaking English.

○ ◌ ◑ ●

I passed secondhand and antique shops for tourists on every corner. It started to get interesting deeper in the old districts, closer to the port, where I began seeing signs that warned tourists not to enter, especially at night.

The store fronts became more and more distressed, the houses clustered closer together, the usual smells intensified. Noise from the underground bars got rougher, and the hookers were more frequent and uglier. It was barely five, but here, it was already getting dark.

Several sailors staggered down the middle of the cobblestones and hollered a familiar song. After a moment, I recognized *Baby One More Time* in French. I moved out of the way, but then this huge black guy almost peed on me.

○ ◌ ◑ ●

After about an hour of wandering around and careful asking (it cost me a pretty penny), I reached a dead-end street so narrow it was almost covered by the roof overhangs above. If Marseille had an end anywhere, it was here.

The light was so scarce here that somewhere in the middle even a lamp was on—just one. I clutched the handles of my bag just a little tighter. The last hooker I asked said that if there was a thrift shop where you could buy anything, it would be right here.

Rodents rustled in the overflowing garbage cans, and a stinky little stream rolled around the middle of the well-trodden cobblestones. (It didn't flow, really, it just sort of rolled around.) I bet that if I had landed in Marseille five hundred years ago, this alley would have been exactly the same.

○ ○ ◑ ●

"Bon appetit, monsieurs … not appetit, I meant evening, but I don't know how to say that," I said, and a little bell rang above my head. I closed the door behind me.

The shop looked absolutely stylish: dust, cobwebs, ancient walls, cracked shelves filled with unbelievable crap. Two men sat on the left side by a small table in front of a wooden counter. One was an old man wearing a shabby suit, wrinkled tie, and a typical French hat. The other was a young man in an equally typical black leather jacket and black pointy shoes, his black hair greased back. He had a bulge under his right armpit, but he definitely didn't look a like a cop. They played dominos. The old man puffed away at a pipe, and the younger one smoked a fat, unfiltered cigarette. You could hardly see anything because of the smoke.

An unshaven forty-something stood up behind the counter, his pale face swollen and his hair so short it looked like his head was sprinkled with soot. A cracked sign hung right above his head on two chains. It had calligraphic lettering and a drawing of a mermaid. It looked very old and very authentic.

"Do you speak English, please?" I politely answered his question which was spoken in French with the heavy smoker's cough.

"We don't serve tourists. Get out," he answered less politely, lit a cigarette, and flicked the match on my shoulder. I knew I was in the right place. That Old World feel reminded me of the Night Club.

"I am not a tourist. I need some black gunpowder, about a pound, and some shells, nine millimeter, Parabellum."

"Didn't you hear the man?! Get out," said the younger fellow, and his hair gleamed dangerously.

Aha, apparently, I came at a bad time—that happens sometimes. Right away, I knew why.

The door opened, the bell rang, and three black guys entered. They looked like sailors. They were so black that their skin absorbed all the light, and the room darkened. They looked at me funny, and then the one with the curliest hair said something. His three extended fingers indicated that there we supposed to be three people in the store, not four. Yellow eyeballs studied me from within their black faces and presumed I was a tourist so they just ignored me. I guessed the situation to be a contraband handover, when I noticed that the shabby old man had a sawed-off shotgun across his knees under the table.

It was probably not very safe contraband.

Instantly, the situation changed.

○ ◑ ◐ ●

These kinds of things always happened unexpectedly.

I figured that the Africans were supposed to bring something and get money in exchange. Apparently, all they brought were guns, and I doubted that they wanted to leave them there.

One aimed at my stomach, the others aimed at the other people, and the curly one looked at the greasy one and was saying something quietly. From their behavior, I could tell they weren't amateurs, who always scream, jump around, and wave their guns. Professionals aim, speak, and when necessary, shoot. I was pissed that I couldn't understand them—language barriers can be so frustrating.

"What did he say?" I turned to the salesclerk, but he didn't answer me because with his arms in the air, he was reaching for something above the mermaid.

The curly one raised his voice and repeated what he had said before. He was probably demanding money. When no one reacted, without any warning, he just shot the old man in the knee. *These African types.*

○ ◑ ◐ ●

The one who was alternately aiming at me and at swollen face shook his head, and the clerk dropped his hands down to his shoulders.

Curly pulled back the gun's hammer very overtly and didn't say anything more.

Marseille is one of a few remaining cities where on your morning baguette trip, you can meet a corpse with a knife in its back. It is one of the few cities where criminal gangs resolve their differences the old-fashioned way: with Uzis, bombs in restaurants, bodies in the water, bodies in cement ... The movies make us all believe that crime only happens in cities like Chicago or New York, but try to shoot a gangster film in Marseille and you might get shot doing it.

So I knew that the black guy would squeeze the trigger a second time. He was aiming at the old man's forehead.

I liked these types. His knee must have hurt like hell, and the blood running down his pant leg made a puddle around his shoe, but he just bit down on his pipe.

Now he was looking down the barrel of a six-round thirty-eight. He spat out a piece of the shaft with a sneer, and said something of which I could only understand the word *Negro*.

The black guys' expressions turned very ugly, and the one with the revolver changed his target to the man's crotch under the table. Only I could see how his knobby fingers cocked the shotgun—very slowly, so it didn't make a sound—and aimed the short barrels in the appropriate direction.

The black guy's finger caressed the trigger.

The greasy one in the black jacket was pale, and his chin quivered.

They could give me my gunpowder and shells for free, out of gratitude. When you think about it, sometimes I am damn lucky.

"Hey, nappy-head, shouldn't you be picking cotton somewhere?" I was counting on the fact that they knew at least that much English, and I was right. I was even right about the fact that all three of them would turn toward me.

I couldn't remember the last time I saw so many *friendly* faces.

The old man didn't hesitate. The roar of the shotgun in the room was absolutely deafening; the shot went through the table—and missed.

○ ◐ ◑ ●

A bunch of splinters fell from the ceiling along with some dust and slaughtered spiders. The broken domino pieces were worse than shrapnel, and the bouncing buckshot sounded like steel rain.

"Merde!" The old man pulled the shotgun from beneath the table and decided to aim more carefully the second time around. All the while, he paid no heed to the black guys shooting at him like crazy.

During a firefight like that, it was no wonder the bullets hit everything else except the old guy.

The grease man lay on the floor, was covering his head and screamed like a girl. Swollen face grabbed the thing he was reaching for the first time—again, a revolver. I don't understand why people always use these six-shooters.

Even the first black guy was real sorry now, because his gun just clicked on empty, and the old man decided that his aim was finally right on target.

The shot from the other barrel was very loud too.

It was then that many of us found out that these black guys were just as red on the inside as everyone else.

I'll never be racist again.

The spray of shot hit him square in the chest and judging by what followed next, it wasn't just any old buckshot. The black dude sort of puffed up (only I saw that), then he burst (again only I saw that), and a hurricane of entrails, blood, and broken ribs blew through the room. Then everybody saw a dynamic and three-dimensional mural on the plain brick wall, which wasn't so plain anymore. It looked almost as good as Picasso's *Guernica*.

The old guy opened the shotgun's break action with such gusto that two green casings jumped high in the air.

Swollen face wasn't shooting; he just held the six-shooter in front of him, and his hand shook like a leaf.

Grease Man was still on the floor, still covering his head, and still screaming as if his balls had fallen off.

The guy who had held me in check earlier stopped artistically perforating the counter behind the old dude and decided to aim carefully too; he had a high-quality Beretta.

The old guy was trying to fish more shells out of his jacket pocket, but it was hard to do while sitting. He stared into the barrel aiming at him with the same cold expression, and I liked him more and more.

Nobody was paying attention to me.

Ignoring tourists can be fatal.

○ ◐ ◑ ●

I grabbed one of the black guys by his chin and turned his face toward me. The crack of his own spine probably surprised him because he looked stunned. Saliva spurted out of the corner of his mouth. I noticed that he probably should have gone to the bathroom before he came here. I grabbed the hand holding the Beretta and from close proximity solved the remaining Afro-Frenchman's dandruff problem. He wasn't the curliest one, but the burning gunpowder set his hair on fire pretty quickly. He must have had some sort of pomade on it because it burned like a torch. Suddenly, it was much brighter in the thrift shop, and the spiders that were now burned to a crisp for a change, fell from the ceiling.

Because the bullet had gone into the top of the guy's head and ripped off his lower jaw, he didn't look like the fire bothered him much.

He stood upright for a while longer until his muscles realized that he was dead, then he crumpled down. After his head whacked the floor, black, curly ashes flew everywhere.

"My god, someone open the window," said the old man. "It smells like a monkey's ass in here."

Despite his serious injury, the man's eyes were shining and the cold expression on his face was replaced with a smile.

"This was just like in my younger days, my boy!" His English, despite its heavy accent and many years of neglect, was still completely understandable. "François, an absinthe for me and for the boy here. Also bring some kind of bandage and call Doc Grivoise. Without a good dose of morphine, I won't be able to straighten this knee out. You, chicken shit, stop screaming and start cleaning." He poked grease man on the floor with his shotgun.

"Could you please put that away?" I asked swollen face, and he looked at the revolver in his outstretched hand with bewilderment. All embarrassed, he hung it back up behind the sign. I stomped on a spider that had lost all its legs to the fire.

"Did you see how his hair caught on fire? T'was great." The old man laughed, and as he moved, he winced with pain for the first time. "I bit my pipe in half cause of those assholes." He looked at the remains of his smoking apparatus with sadness.

Swollen face put a glass of green liquid as well as a pitcher of water in front of him. I refused by waving my hand. He cut open the man's pant leg without a word.

"How does it look, François?"

Swollen face tried to catch his breath and fainted in the same spot from which grease man had stood up a moment ago. I put my bag down on the counter and looked over the oozing red and blue wound.

"He missed the joint, but the bone got it." I gently moved the calf back and forth, and the old man winced again. "Broke completely through." I looked into his eyes. They were completely blue, clear, and full of pain, but still there was this wild exuberance in them. I knew that look; I knew it well. That was the look of those who never retreat.

Not like us cowards.

"Merde!"

The drink turned milky after he added water, and some of it gurgled in his wrinkled throat. He poured the rest of the water on the fainted swollen face.

Grease man was able to talk into a phone (and with decent authority) when he wasn't looking at the dead bodies. In barely fifteen minutes, a three-wheel rickshaw arrived with a huge freezer for delivering meat and fish. Two guys with empty eyes and bloody aprons carried out the bodies.

There was a smiling pig head with an apple in its snout on the side of the freezer.

Swollen face locked the door. Grease man, along with a revolting woman who arrived with the butchers, pulled on rubber gloves and poured some cleaning products, lye, and lots of hot water into a bucket.

I sat on the counter and watched how well they were doing, and no one complained in the least about my presence.

When Doctor Grivoise was taking away the old man, even though hopped up on morphine, he said, "You accommodate the tourist, François, in any way you can."

"Yes, sir," said swollen face and locked the door behind them.

○ ◐ ◑ ●

"Didn't you say something about shells, Mister, hm, Mister …?"

"Tourist will suffice, and yes, I did. And gunpowder too."

"Follow me, please." Without turning around, he disappeared through a small door behind the counter.

We walked through a storage space with unbelievable, dusty junk. François stopped by one of the cabinets and gave me this look, but after a healthy pause, he said nothing. Needless to say, our joint presence at a triple homicide made for a strong bond.

The cabinet had a false back, behind which was a steeply descending and dangerously worn-out staircase. The hallway was low and arched.

"This must have been here a long time," I said appreciatively.

"Maybe five hundred years, maybe even longer. Just the electricity is new." François flipped a switch that must have been from Edison's time. The wires strung loosely below with arches were wrapped in waxed thread. We had ones just like that in the Night Club, when I was little.

At the bottom of the stairs was another door, and behind it, it was obvious how François and many others made their living: dealing in stolen goods on a large scale. When I say large scale, I really mean large. A huge underground warehouse was stuffed with all kinds of things from boxes with TVs to spare parts for trucks. Several workers were romping around on forklifts loading pallets onto elevators.

"We have to go over there." He pointed to the left to a square bunker made of bricks. "It's all right!" He called to a guy with an M16, but who still looked at me with suspicion.

"We have weapons here." François closed the door behind me and switched on the lights. The fluorescent tubes buzzed and flickered. What didn't look so big from the outside stretched deep inside, and the combined smells of metal, oil, and wax paper were unmistakable.

"You could start a war with this stuff," I said. "Maybe even win." My eyes rested on some rocket launchers and crates with disassembled anti-aircraft canons.

"We don't make war … just sometimes."

"What were those black guys supposed to bring?"

"Diamonds. For a shipment …" He paused and began rubbing his ear. Aside from the murder pact, I didn't care about their business.

"So, what'll it be?" He stood behind a little table and turned on a desk lamp. A thick book looked as though they carefully noted who *Paid* and who *Owes*.

"A few boxes of shells for a Glock, nine millimeter, a pound of black gunpowder, that's it."

"What's the powder for? I have it, but it's not a usual request."

"I need to make some projectiles."

"That's pretty clear, but what for?"

"For this." I pulled the AutoMag out of the bag and handed it to him, butt first. "It's loaded."

"AutoMag." He handled the weapon expertly and read the inscriptions on the barrel. "First series, quite the rarity." He looked at me carefully and again began rubbing his ear. "Maybe I'd have something else here for you. Could you use some magazines to go with that?"

"I could. I didn't even want to ask. Must be a custom item."

"Not here. In the old days, they used these puppies to blast open bulletproof jewelry shop windows and such. Then they started making them thicker, so a few things are left over."

"How many do you have?"

"How many do you want?"

"Fifteen?"

"Why not?"

For almost ten minutes, he disappeared in the aisles between the deadly steel.

"The nine millimeters are pretty weak for a guy with an AutoMag." He laid several boxes of unmarked projectiles next to a dark green tin can which held the gunpowder.

"That's for this." I pulled out the Glock. Five days under the azure shores were obvious on this gun: unlike the stainless-steel AutoMag.

"Man, it's all rusty."

"It will clean off."

"Treating a handgun like that." He shook his head with disgust, so much that his swollen cheeks bobbled around.

"There was no other way." I was a little embarrassed anyway.

François thought about it, and I could almost see a movie running behind his eyes. The main roles were played by three dead black guys and an old man with a bullet wound in his leg, who said something about accommodating. In the end, his innate penny-pinching was beat out by the film. It was either that or my gaze through the black glasses.

"We also have *Glocks*—a special custom delivery—ten caliber, elongated barrel, twenty-five round magazine. You can shoot in bursts.

"They make those?"

"If you're an Arabian sheik and you want at least one hundred of them, then yes."

"Interesting." I put on the expression of an expert. François left again and returned with a black plastic case. He placed it in the light of the lamp, and with a typical magical gesture, he unfastened the locks and plucked a familiarly shaped (this one a bit more substantial) pistol out of the gray foam and handed it to me.

"Reeeally," I said, again with an expert expression, and tested the slide, squeezed the trigger on empty, and shoved in and released a magazine.

"You like?"

"A lot."

"So we're even?"

"Yup."

François went to grab me the right ammo, and I put everything in the bag. This is what two dead bastards are worth in France. Initially, I was going to ask for a room and a passport too, but I noticed the light come on in those cloudy eyes and that swollen face when he saw the rusty Glock. It wasn't just a movie about three dead black guys. Wries and Van Vren for sure had spread the news about what I looked like, what I might be carrying, and what I would be needing around the local underground. Madam Dao had enough money to pay even François.

○ ◑ ◐ ●

Outside, it was already pitch black. It had rained a little, and the sewers stank to high heaven. The lonely lamp buzzed, and the worn-out cobblestones coldly glistened. François said something like, "Bon voyage," and he didn't go back in until he saw which direction I took at the corner.

I walked through the port without any problems. I dodged the drunks. The guy that François sent after me I killed right away so his dead body wouldn't reveal my direction. As soon as the sewer rats smelled blood, they began swarming excitedly and slinking around my feet. There were some huge ones there that could easily take care of a big cat.

When I made it out of the crooked neighborhoods, there was the real world again with no sewer rats, no corpses with their faces chewed off to the bone. There were only Pepsi ads, movie theaters, crowds of people with umbrellas, and all-night supermarkets.

I stood out like a sore thumb in my T-shirt and shorts because the late Indian summer had ended that night, and the French, so used to warm weather, huddled in all but winter coats. I bought a popular black leather jacket, a pair of black pants made of thick canvas with many pockets, several leather belts, and a laptop in the electronics department.

○ ◑ ◐ ●

"That IBM over there, if it really has a modem in it."

"Of course, sir," said the salesclerk, all offended. He was just dozing off, so now he was blinking his eyes. Standing up too quickly made him waver a little.

I flipped open the display, and the hard disk began to spin with a quiet hum.

"Aha, you wouldn't have one with a normal keyboard, would you?"

"We also have an *English* model," said the clerk frigidly.

"I would like to see it." I grinned. I also checked to make sure the machine didn't have French Windows (it didn't). I paid and got out of there.

Because I had changed in the store already, people didn't stare at me, and the black made me blend in with the night. I pulled the jacket zipper all the way up to my neck and stopped by a newspaper stand to buy a map of Marseille. On a brightly colored English newspaper, I saw a photo of Natasha Blast, so I bought that too. It was the *Daily Mirror*.

"Merci."

"Merci."

On the map, I found a suburb where, according to the distances between homes and good amounts of green, stood the summer villas of the rich and famous. I couldn't go to a hotel or a bed-and-breakfast. Wries and Van Vren would have me within hours. I couldn't go anywhere official.

Even though it was far, I walked. Cabbies are chatty in an unhealthy way, and if derby hat and his buddy got the local police involved … I wondered if they were really with the FBI. It would be an awesome cover.

○ ◑ ◗ ●

At around nine forty-five, I was walking by high whitewashed fences made of rock. They were more like walls than fences. All they needed were gun ports and they would have been regular castle walls. With chunks of glass cemented into the top, cameras in the corners, and rows of barbed wire, it was worse than a documentary from Auschwitz.

I walked swiftly, but not too fast, and when the police patrol drove by, I blended into the shadows.

○ ◑ ◗ ●

"Am I there yet, damn it?" I whispered.

The city was far behind me, and there weren't too many buildings along the road anymore. I thought more of them would be empty for the winter, but the French apparently enjoy the nostalgia of falling leaves or maybe they even live there year-round. The house that I picked faced the ocean, and the two neighboring homes looked empty too. The owners cared about their privacy, so the usual palisades were encircled by a tall hedge on the inside—an evergreen, prickly, wet shrubbery. I looked around, pushed off, and landed behind the wall right in the thorns.

"God fucking damn it!" Thrashing loudly, I clawed my way out onto the lawn and froze for a good fifteen minutes.

Nothing moved anywhere; the only sounds were the rain quietly falling and the low rumble of the surf. The grass was tall, and the leaves weren't cleaned up; I got it right. "Home, sweet home."

○ ◑ ◐ ●

Cautiously, I crept up to the dark villa—vigilantly because pressure monitors could be in the yard too. In the Night Club, we were taught the art of breaking into secure properties from childhood.

I compensated for the lack of gadgets with my vampire senses and abilities. The bathroom window on the second floor didn't have an electronic sensor. Reaching it, however, was practically out of the question without a ladder, but a ladder would trigger the motion detector that was inconspicuously hiding under the rim of the roof.

With the handle of the bag between my teeth, I was up on the cornice in a flash. My fingernails slid under the window frame, the screws ripped out, and I was inside.

As I tried to close the widow behind me as quickly as I could while being as quiet as possible, I stepped into the toilet—but that's all part of the job.

Carefully, I opened the door into the hallway. There would be thermal sensors, motion detectors, and pressure sensors under the carpet.

Very quickly, I realized that I didn't have to worry about the thermal sensors, because one of them just happened to be—very unexpectedly—right above my head just as I was climbing carefully out of the toilet.

"Shit!" I whispered with surprise and spent the next half hour in front of the window ready to jump out and escape. But the police patrol drove by without showing any interest in the house. Then I realized that the sensor probably wasn't calibrated for someone with a body temperature of seventy-three degrees Fahrenheit.

○ ◑ ◐ ●

The house was very big, very luxurious, and well locked up for the season. I left the detailed exploration till morning, pulled the covers off an enormous bed, and relaxed until sunrise.

Because I was relaxing in damp clothes, I got rather clammy, but a little bit of discomfort never killed anyone.

Misty light came in through the gaps in the window blinds, and if I were human, vapor would be coming from my mouth (and I would be damn cold).

During my exploration, I discovered that I couldn't take out the security system because it would send a signal to the police station, and they would certainly come by to check to see if it was the owner or someone else. So I blocked the motion sensors (one was even in the eye of a stuffed moose head in the hallway), and I put pieces of yellow toilet paper (so I wouldn't forget), on the carpet where the pressure sensors were hiding. You had to get them wet, so they would stick; otherwise, the draft would take them away. I couldn't go into the giant living room on the ground level unless I wanted to star in a short film about a *clever* thief in action. Two other cameras were watching over the entrances, but otherwise, the rest of the house was mine. Judging by the custom-sewn covers on all the furniture and the fact that there was not a houseplant in sight, I could expect quiet until at least Christmas.

In the basement, I found the breaker box and main water valve, so I flipped on the boilers and could even take a hot shower. Luckily, you couldn't turn on or monitor electricity use over the Internet; all they had was a plain old hard rubber lever.

○ ◑ ◐ ●

Already in a long terry bathrobe, I hung up all my wet clothes. Though it was chilly in the house (and turning on the heat wasn't a good idea), I discovered an electric space heater in the basement. I dusted it off and made myself comfortable in a cozy den with a fireplace.

I pulled off the covers and folded them carefully. To make doubly certain, I added two blackout blankets to the window shades, so not even a little ray of light could escape.

I put my bag on a dark wood desk, turned on a lamp with a green shade, and pulled out the things I was going to need. The space heater quietly crackled and smelled of hot metal and burning dust. To be on the safe side, I put it on a stone hearth in front of the fireplace. Then until nightfall, I cleaned guns, filled magazines, and made cartridges for the AutoMag.

There is something calming about that.

An engraving on the small press used for handloading cartridges, stated how much gunpowder to use. But I knew that they test fired guns at pressures many times higher than are produced by a standard charge. So I poured in as much as would fit—which was a lot because the AutoMag took modified rifle shells.

I didn't stop until I ran out of bullets. I filled all the magazines and still had almost thirty shells left over. Then I filled the magazines for the new Glock and from the belts and suspenders made places to stash them all so they didn't rattle. Lastly, I modified the breast pockets on the jacket to fit the AutoMag and the ten millimeter too. When you know how to go about it, it's better than a holster. You just have to make sure there isn't any leftover lining on which a quick draw could get caught. Then I went to the cellar and buried the Glock from Thailand. True, it was expensive, but it had been compromised.

Then I had nothing to do.

So I read the paper. Natasha talked about her first film that was about to start shooting. It seemed that she had become a media star after the hijacking, but now—only about a week later—she had to take her bra off to make the front page.

I folded up the paper and carefully laid it on the edge of the table.

Again, I had nothing to do.

I returned to the basement and buried di Torro's passport.

Still, I had nothing to do.

It was around nine in the evening. The surf was rumbling outside, and rain driven by wind gusts was making a racket on the roof. I stared blankly at the shiny AutoMag shells all standing in a row under the lamp.

"You should go and kick Wries' and Van Vren's asses … not just them, everyone's ass," said My Other.

"Yeah, like I really missed you here. You and your big ideas."

"You should do it. You really should."

○ ◗ ◑ ●

I should. I knew that too, of course I did, but it was much easier to cover up all the mirrors so I didn't have to look at myself.

For a while, I told myself it was some kind of a vampire instinct, but the explanation was much simpler and still the same: *I was afraid. I am afraid. I will be afraid—of Wries, Van Vren, Mr. Ho, Madam Dao, the silver chain ... and I don't wanna have to look at the eyes of a coward.*

"That's the mirrors, now what? Will you hide under a blanket? Or in the closet? Maybe under the bed will be the best ... You can't stay here forever anyway; the owner is going to return one day."

"Don't tell me what to do, okay?! Just don't!"

○ ◗ ◑ ●

Minutes dragged along slowly and turned into hours. I watched the red-hot orange spirals of the space heater where bright little sparks flared up once in a while.

The minutes dragged more and more slowly.

It was barely one thirty, and the surf and rain still sounded the same.

I knew this state. I knew it well. When nothing is going your way, there is only one solution. I unplugged the cable from the phone and stuck it into the IBM. I plugged the computer into the outlet (fortunately a French adapter was included), found the address of a free provider, and sailed out onto the Internet.

For a while, I tried to remember my log-in and password (for a pretty *long* while), and then I downloaded my unfinished book from the X drive.

I stared at the little letters, and my eyes became misty—again these memories.

The last normal evening of my life ... At the end of the paragraph was an incomplete comment that I didn't finish because someone had knocked on the door of my room. First Carolina, then ... I had thought about Hanako many times since then, and the initial hatred had dissipated. Even though the Night Club was destroyed because

369

of her, I understood that vampires must protect themselves. In my *Vampires*, there was an unbelievable number of unbelievably accurate facts and details.

"The Night Club wasn't destroyed, not really. You are the Night Club, not some building or room. Night Club is a state of spirit, state of mind, not anything material ... That's what you always said to yourself—when you were winning. Didn't you?"

I was beginning to really hate My Other.

"Coward, a coward," I whispered, but this time, My Other didn't say a thing.

Doesn't silence mean agreement?

○ ☽ ☽ ●

I realized that I couldn't continue on with this book. It was the same as when the parents, whose child dies, leave the child's room in exactly the same state as on the last morning that he or she left it. It's that *something*: if you don't accept change, then everything will certainly return to better times.

So I began writing another book.

○ ☽ ☽ ●

It was the one that came to me on Madam Dao's boat, the one about the tough guy who was left in a world from which most of the people had disappeared and those who remained turned into the walking dead. The writing went along pretty well, but only until I wrote in My Other simply out of sheer lack of characters. From that moment on, the real Other wouldn't shut up—he would never say that, he would say this differently, and that another way ...

Well, that was My Other.

○ ☽ ☽ ●

Vampire speed translated into writing too, so I finished three quarters of the book in only ten days. That was when the tough guy fell under the power of a silver headband that turned him into a mindless and completely obedient robot. He had it easy compared to reality. I remembered the harness with the charge on it. Not having to think is always better—especially not having to think that I could end up in it again.

○ ◐ ◑ ●

"What are you going to do after we finish *writing*?" said My Other in the morning. "Will you start writing another one? Then another? And another?"

I was looking over the last paragraph I wrote the night before, and I knew that he was right. I couldn't keep hiding. I would have to go out eventually—at least to get something to eat. I was doing okay in that regard. I was not getting any exercise, and in the ocean, I had my fill of fish. Their blood tasted like gasoline, but I stuffed myself till I almost burst.

"So I don't have to go anywhere yet." I put my fingers on the keyboard and sent the hero off to face more dangers.

Around noontime, My Other and I waged a bitter battle over the final name of the super-vehicle that the hero drove, right when he was trying to resurrect it from a wreck back into a super-machine while in the middle of the desert. I won the name game, but until the evening, My Other kept bugging me that it was just crap.

○ ◐ ◑ ●

When around eleven I tore myself away from the book, nothing had changed. I was still scared, I still couldn't decide, and I still knew that My Other was right. A few pages ago, the hero in the book had amputated his own leg, carved out a crutch and a prosthetic, and walked across half of Africa on them. Boy, I'd like to be that tough and determined too.

I stared at the screen saver, and then I did something that I had wanted to do for a long time, but something that was painful even before I started; browsing through my once-favorite pages on the Czech Internet.

Some had disappeared. Some had changed so that they were unrecognizable. Some ... then I connected to the live streaming of Radio One.

Listen to Radio One, they have everything, I heard Dread's voice from the past. Babe frowned in disagreement from the same far-off place, and Kamile wound her golden locks around her finger. Father Kolachek was cleaning his glasses and smiling ... I stopped because I couldn't remember Thomas's daughter's name. The way she looked the last time I saw her appeared to me in nightmares, but her name ...

"Janie, of course," said My Other.

"Of course! Janie. How could I have ...?"

Nothing had changed on Radio One, fortunately. The music was still good. Only the musicians had stopped whacking sticks over sheet metal and got themselves a tiny little drum and a billion drumsticks and went at it.

"... That was for Elephant and Brick, and now we have a special request for Helmut ... and what would Helmut like to hear?" The DJ laughed, and I realized how long it had been since I'd heard anyone speak Czech.

The song for Helmut sounded exactly the same as the one for Elephant and Brick—a drum and sticks. I put my feet up on the table, closed my eyes, and returned to the Night Club. Good thing My Other was quiet.

"Hello? Radio One."

"Hi. Hey, can you play Die Krupps?"

"Sure. Any requests? Wanna dedicate it to someone?"

"Request ... dedication ... Yup, it's for me, and everyone can just kiss my ass."

"You can't say things like that on the radio." The DJ laughed quietly.

"Whatever, see ya."

"So a special Die Krupps, and none of you other guys listen!" A heavy electronica sound came from the laptop speakers. I imagined myself sitting in the bar after work. I am comfortably warm. Janie is bringing me another glass of wine, and Kamile and Ripper are discussing the virtues of Tatyana Mikova, and the smell of dinner wafts in from the kitchen ...

Die Krupps ended.

"Hello? Radio One."

"Hi, could I make a request?" said a sad male voice distorted by a bad phone connection and computer compression.

"Hey there, Night Owl! I thought you might not call in today."

"I never forget," said the sad voice.

"What's it gonna be?"

"Yup. So today, like always, anything ... for everyone, for me, and most importantly, for the Happy Willies!"

The part "... most importantly for the Happy Willies!" the DJ said along with the sad caller.

Apparently, it was a frequent request, maybe even a daily one, maybe even for more than a year.

○ ◐ ◑ ●

The last breakfast in the Night Club flashed before my eyes—how Ripper and Babe fought over the radio.

I didn't recognize that sad voice.

Suddenly, I realized that I wasn't afraid anymore.

○ ◐ ◑ ●

24

"I'll take that KTM. That green six hundred," I said. The salesman folded the newspaper and looked at me with surprise. During the fall, especially a rainy one like this one, he probably didn't sell too many motorcycles, let alone to foreigners.

"Of course." He stood up once he realized I was serious. We were in the glass hall alone—if I didn't include the hundreds of motorcycles and the hum of the pouring rain outside.

The salesman began praising the dark green touring machine to high heaven, but I wasn't listening because I had looked it over already.

"Can I test drive it?" I said when he paused to take a breath.

"Of course ... do you have a helmet?"

"I should buy one."

I suffered through another flood of chatter and head measuring, and I picked out a full-faced one with a dark visor.

"Good choice, sir. It has an anti-fog modification, and ..." The salesman went on and on. I tried to move my head inside the helmet and asked for a size smaller.

The salesman checked the oil level and the tires, and we pushed the Austrian machine out to the parking lot in front of the store. The starter almost didn't turn over, but I got a new battery right away—for free. The rear brake pads I would have to pay for myself.

"Good," I said when the big single cylinder coughed and began spewing clouds of smoke into the moist air.

A khaki KTM is a military model with a more resilient construction than their regular bikes, even though those could also handle just about anything. This one had a five-gallon gas tank and a practical plastic suitcase on the back. I jumped into the high seat, and the shocks groaned. Clutch, first gear … I made sure it drove straight even without holding the handlebars. I checked the brakes and made several circles around the parking lot then came back.

"I'll take it."

"Yes? Should we take care of it right away?"

"Yes."

○ ○ ◑ ●

With a helmet, rain suit, gloves, and full service, it cost over twenty-one thousand francs. Because I had changed all my money for francs (and sold the laptop), I knew immediately that I had just enough left for about three tanks of gas.

I waited a half hour for them to change the plates. I signed some papers (illegibly), got my registration and keys, stashed the bag in the trunk, and in the next ten minutes, I was on my way.

○ ○ ◑ ●

I didn't take the freeways so I didn't have to pay any tolls, but the local highways were pretty fast too.

Gray clouds raced in the shallow puddles. Water from the wheels rattled against the fender, and I anxiously tried not to commit any traffic violations. I didn't forget for even a second that besides the registration card, I had no other form of ID.

In order to avoid needless border crossings, I drove around Switzerland and zoomed into Germany in the lane for European citizens. With a French license plate, I had every right to.

○ ○ ◑ ●

It had been dark for a long time already when the foggy peaks of the Sumava Mountains rose before me. After nearly eight hundred miles, I felt virtually no discomfort. The moisture didn't leak into my rain suit (it leaked into my boots though), but having less and less gas made me nervous. If I drove efficiently, I could make it to Prague—maybe.

Because the Eurolane didn't extend into the Czech Republic I turned into the woods about a mile before the border and turned off the lights and the engine. I had to wait for the machine to cool off, so I sat under a tree and thought about stuff. You could smell snow in the air. It was barely forty-one degrees Fahrenheit, and the rain hissed in the tops of the spruce trees. Around eleven o'clock, the engine was cooler than my hand, so I tied the handlebars to the side, the helmet went into the trunk, and with the KTM on my back, I headed across the border with a brisk step.

I realized that I didn't need to worry about cooling off the engine because I barely saw one border patrol. With thermal binoculars hanging around their necks, they hurried to get the patrol over with. They didn't even think about looking through the sleet.

Soggy moss squished under my feet, and I was sinking a little—the motorcycle weighed over three hundred pounds—but I felt like I was carrying a backpack and I even jogged once in a while.

○ ◐ ◑ ●

I listened for the road, and when I was half a mile into the Czech Republic, I turned toward it.

I climbed out of the forest at a small rest stop. Except for two overflowing trash cans, it was empty. If each country has its own characteristic smell, then the Czech Republic stinks like old garbage.

The KTM started on the first try, and a beam of light bit into the fog. The road dropped down with sharp turns, and I realized that this was how *Vampires* started: a likeable hero vampire goes to the Czech Republic to catch a deer or something. I imagined myself staggering through a ruined forest and shook my helmet in disbelief at the things that a reader would fall for. The tires slipped dangerously in the turns, so I slowed down to a crawl. My imagination forced me to see myself in the same light as the fictional hero, who was followed by the slippery Slimer Salazar, on a scary, modified eight-cylinder.

Ha-ha-ha.

My imagination did have one advantage: I didn't have to think about what was in store for me.

○ ◌ ◗ ●

In Plzen, I got lost, as usual.

From Marseille all the way to the Czech border, I didn't lose my way even once. In Germany, there were signs on every corner, but driving through Plzen on to Prague was simply impossible.

I asked maybe three times, but because I was keeping my cover, my English question was usually followed by a lot of pointing, punctuated by German words like *Dort, dort!*

Finally, I found the beginning of the highway, and in barely an hour, I was greeted by an alley of orange streetlamps illuminating the entrance to the capital city of all Czechs.

○ ◌ ◗ ●

I ran out of gas just before Kosire.

I pushed the KTM between some garages, screwed off the license plate, and ripped off the oil change sticker, so identifying this bike as French won't be so easy. The rest would be taken care of by predictable Czech hands. Within two hours, the machine would be gone.

I pulled the bag out of the trunk, stuffed the rain suit and helmet in there, and locked it. I left the keys in the ignition to make it easier for the would-be thieves. It wasn't easy saying good-bye to this high-quality machine, but it was evidence. Anyway, large bikes were still pretty noticeable in the Czech Republic—especially in early winter.

○ ◌ ◗ ●

I walked over to a tram stop. My shoes were squishy with water. The night tram came within ten minutes, and the usual bunch of people coming from bars and restaurants didn't pay any attention to me. There was a strong smell of alcoholic vapors in the car, someone was snoring in the front, and three guys by the middle door were singing something by Landa[2].

---

[2] **Translator's note:** Daniel Landa is a popular Czech singer and actor.

I made myself comfortable on the red plastic seat and stuck my left foot behind the heater. Everything was so familiar, so simple. These were things I had experienced a thousand times over. I watched the reflections in the glass. The tram chimed and jostled, and it seemed that Madam Dao's ship with Wries and Van Vren never existed.

○ ◐ ◑ ●

I knew I was making a mistake, but I couldn't help myself. At Narodni station, I changed trams, and within a half hour, I was getting off near my official apartment. Where else was I going to go?

On my way through the familiar streets, I was again overwhelmed by a surreal feeling: I hijacked a plane? Immortal killers? Vampires? Phew.

My old car was still rusting in front of the apartment building, and the layer of black dirt and bird droppings hadn't even gotten that much thicker after a year. I had an extra set of keys hidden under the bumper by the front wheel.

Because it was late in the night, my arrival wasn't noticed by even my neighbor, who otherwise kept careful track of my comings and goings. She even complained about me to the cops several times for making drugs, smuggling gold, selling nuclear weapons, and such things. Each time, I had a nice chat with the detective at the police station, who called me Mr. Novelist. Instead of investigating, he always apologized for bothering me with such nonsense.

If only he knew!

○ ◐ ◑ ●

The apartment welcomed me back with the stale smell that comes with a lack of ventilation, a layer of dust, and several large cobwebs. Otherwise, nothing else had changed. I didn't turn on the lights and quickly looked through both rooms for any kind of electronic sensors. Surprisingly, there weren't any.

"Is it possible that Wries and Van Vren didn't know about this place?"

My Other didn't answer.

○ ◐ ◑ ●

I sat there with the gun in my lap, listened to car alarms going off, and stared at the wall till morning.

When people in the building began getting up, I washed off the remains of my long trip, shaved, and around nine o'clock, I took off. The critical things I was taking with me were my real ID and my fake ID, but most importantly, my visa card, which fortunately wasn't expired yet.

"Mr. Jones, it's been a while since I've seen you last!" My favorite neighbor lady skulked out of her apartment like a tarantula out of her lair.

"Greetings, ma'am."

"Where in the world were you? Some men have been asking about you."

"Really?" I stopped. "What kind of men?"

"But I don't know what kind." She withdrew, and I realized that her incessant chatter had betrayed her. Apparently, the gentleman had a lucrative offer for her, a phone number, and a persuasive suggestion not to ever mention them to me.

"What men?" I said sternly.

Again nothing.

At least now it was clear that I couldn't ever return here again—ever. *That would be something, shooting her between the eyes, that old hag! Finally, after all these years! With the AutoMag.*

She must have suspected something because she disappeared without a word, and her door locks rattled good-bye to me.

How rude.

For a brief moment, I daydreamed about how those awful thick glasses would rip through her brain.

"I can't have everything." I sighed and quickly walked away.

Within five minutes, the *gentlemen* would know that I had been there. The question is what kind of *gentlemen* were they. The moment I lost the cover of the Night Club, just about anyone could have found out about me.

○ ◑ ◐ ●

... to be continued

Made in the USA
Middletown, DE
21 July 2023